The Million Dollar Girl

The Million Dollar Girl

A Novel

Robert A. Harris

.:Virtual**Salt**
Publishing
Tustin

The Million Dollar Girl
A Novel

Copyright © 2005 Robert A. Harris

ISBN 978-1-941233-07-8

VirtualSalt Publishing
Tustin, California
www.virtualsalt.com

cv1

Chapter 1

The sun was low in the sky as the jetliner angled itself steeply on its climb-out from the airport. In the cabin, some of the passengers were adjusting their seats, while others reached for the reading light or the air nozzle to make themselves more comfortable. A few were already absorbed in the in-flight magazine or a newspaper. One continued to work a crossword puzzle that had been started in the terminal. Only fifty or sixty passengers were aboard the wide-body on this early evening in June, so several began to contemplate putting up the armrests and stretching out across the seats. One or two people checked their watches and wondered whether a meal or a snack would be served. On the flight deck the crew was finishing the post-take-off checklist and making a few adjustments. The cabin darkened as the plane entered the clouds.

"Passing one one thousand," the copilot noted. "Speed two six zero." In a few moments, the warm, golden light of the sun flooded back into the cabin as the airliner passed through the top of the clouds. Both passengers and crew took a few moments to look out over the cloud cover.

"As often as I see this, I never get tired of it," said the flight engineer, looking forward between the captain and the copilot.

"Me too," agreed the copilot, looking up momentarily. "A gold Christmas ball over a blanket of cotton." Then he added, in a somewhat more formal tone, "Autopilot engaged." Now he took a longer moment to lean forward and look around outside.

The captain finished putting away the departure chart and settled back into his seat. He pointed out a distant plane above and to the right, on a path to cross behind them. The copilot nodded as he saw it also. "The sky is still pretty big," he said.

"Yes," said the captain.

Suddenly, there was a loud thump. One of the rudder pedals shot back, throwing the captain's leg against the seat. The huge airplane veered to the right. All three engines went to idle, causing everyone on board to swing forward a bit as the plane slowed faster than their bodies. In the rear of the cabin, two flight attendants were hurled to the floor as it partly gave way under them. The sudden decompression of the airplane caused the galley elevator door and the door to the cockpit to blow open. Hearing the door slam open, the flight engineer looked over, surprised that he could see into the cabin area. He watched as a floor hatch in the fourth row blew off and hit a passenger. Several ceiling panels fell. The air turned white as a condensation fog formed. He swung his head back quickly, to search his instruments for an under-standing of what was going on. But before he could focus, the decompression sent a blast of air spraying dust and debris all around the flight deck and into the eyes of the crew mem-bers.

"What happened?" shouted the captain over the rushing sound. "Something hit the windshield?" But as he reached out, the windshield was still intact. An alarm bell began to ring, just as a horn sounded.

"Fire in number two," yelled the flight engineer. "And cabin pressure warning."

"I've got it," said the captain, grabbing the controls and disconnecting the autopilot. "Autopilot disconnected."

"Air speed indicator has failed," yelled the copilot.

"I've only got minimal elevator control," said the captain. "It's heavy. Help me, Pete."

"We've hit something," said the flight engineer, still shouting above the noise.

"We've lost, uh, lost an engine," said the copilot, loudly.

"Which one?" demanded the captain.

"Number two engine must have blown," answered the copilot. "We're losing altitude too fast."

"Yes, two," said the flight engineer.

"I've got no rudder! It's jammed!" yelled the captain.

"Master warning. Engine fire," the flight engineer announced.

"Do we have hydraulics?" the copilot asked.

"No," the captain yelled with frustration.

"I read hydraulic pressure is okay," said the flight engineer, staring blinkingly at his gauges between wipes of his gritty eyes.

A disheveled flight attendant stumbled halfway into the cockpit. Hanging on to the doorframe with one hand and wiping her eyes with the other, she said, "The aft lounge area has collapsed. There are no oxygen masks deployed."

The image of a desperate crew froze on the screen. In a few moments, the lights came up in the room. Fifty-four students blinked, stretched, and rubbed their eyes as they accommodated mentally and physically to their return to a lit classroom.

"Okay, class," said the professor, who had now made his way to the front. "You are the captain of this airplane. What do you do? Quickly, you must act. What are you going to do?

Your plane is in major trouble and you're losing altitude fast." Professor Miller hoped the sense of urgency created by the film would not be lost by a long wait time for an answer, but he was not necessarily hopeful. A hand went up in the second row. The girl was smiling brightly at him. "Yes?" he said. "And you are?"

"Julie Carmichael."

"Yes, Julie. What would you do?"

"Radio for help?" Professor Miller wondered whether Julie was one of those girls whose statements always have question marks attached to them.

"Well, of course you would at some point want to contact the ground and alert them to your emergency, but no one on the ground can help you right now. What would you do *right now*?" He was looking at the class in general when he spoke the question, indicating that Julie's opportunity to answer was over. Professor Miller always tried to put a favorable spin on even the most tangential—or inane—answers, in order not to discourage students. But once he decided the student was not near enough to a fruitful avenue, he cut his losses and changed students. Seeing another hand, he pointed toward the middle of the room. "You in the green coat. Your name?"

"David Simmons," the student said. Then, without waiting for another cue, he continued, "I don't think this is a very realistic scenario. The loss of all those controls is virtually impossible with the amount of redundancy now on airplanes."

"Thank you David. That's an interesting comment, but this little scene is not a Hollywood fantasy. It is a reenactment of an actual incident in 1972. This situation is historical, very real." David looked unconvinced, but said nothing.

He made a short note in his notebook computer, then returned to working on some programming code, unseen by Professor Miller.

A girl in the back row stopped chewing her gum just long enough to say softly to no one in particular, but with unmistakable derision, "Like I'm going to be a pilot and need to know this stuff." The two or three people who heard her smiled wryly. The girl resumed chewing and continued to write a letter she had just begun.

"Anyone else?" asked Professor Miller. This time he had to wait longer. Seconds ticked by. There was a bit of squirming. "Sophomores," he thought to himself. "I've got to talk Chuck into giving me more grad classes." Finally, another hand went up. "Yes?" he said, acknowledging the hand with a lift of his head rather than taking the trouble to raise his hand and point.

"Um, this may sound dumb," the student began. Professor Miller felt like wincing, but he showed no response at all. "But, how can we do anything when we don't even know what's wrong? I mean, even the crew doesn't seem to know what is wrong or what to do."

"Exactly!" shouted Miller, with possibly too much drama and a slightly fake gesture.

The drama and the affectations of gesture were recent additions to the professor's manner. Just over a year ago, he had published a critical thinking textbook that had so far enjoyed a meteoric success, selling just short of a hundred thousand copies in its first full year of adoptions. As a result, Miller had begun to view himself in a new light. He had begun to ask students to refer to him as Dr. Miller rather than as Professor Miller, even though his level of education had not changed—he had been a PhD for ten years. But now he had begun to feel like a suave, dynamic, even elegant intellectual, a success at writing, at teaching, at life itself. In fact, not only did he view himself this way, he had begun to watch himself while he was teaching, examining his words, attending to his gestures, practicing his facial expressions. Unknown to him, however, the result was not altogether happy. Miller had little acting talent and no fixed idea of how a great professor should act, other than to be arrogant. The result was that he had begun to play himself. His mannerisms often seemed forced and his words too carefully chosen for their effect as words rather than for their power to convey meaning. He was not as irritating as Professor Gordon in the English Department, who recalled every word at least twice in order to replace it with another, thereby requiring nearly a minute to produce every sentence. Nor was he as pompously pedantic as Professor Shaumwicz in the Philosophy Department, who had carefully selected from the English language the most obscure polysyllabic Greek-root abstractions he could find and struggled mightily to squeeze them densely into his conversations and lectures. But, in spite of Professor Miller's freedom from these failings, the general response of his students was not one of profound awe, as perhaps he had expected.

"Even in a dire emergency," Miller heard himself say in a slow, carefully paced way, "the first activity that must be performed is conceptualization." He paused to allow the students time to write down his words. Hardly anyone seemed to be taking notes. Nearly everyone was looking at him, their faces reflecting varying degrees of puzzlement. Miller wondered whether the problem was an inability to spell *conceptualization*. He turned and wrote the word on the board and then underlined it for emphasis. "Before you can act in any important way, before you can even make a decision, you must answer the question, 'What's going on?' Until that question is answered, you cannot proceed even if you want to. Cognitive stabilization is the first step in analysis, in thinking, in decision making, in thinking critically." He paused to write *cognitive stabilization* on the board. Seeing the words he had written so far pleased him, as he thought how impressive they would look to a stranger who might come in after the class was over. He decided not to erase the board when he was finished.

"The better you can think," he continued, "the faster you can analyze a situation. That means that learning how to think critically could save your life."

The students listened politely, and several more began jotting down a sentence or two. For students whose note-taking habits frequently convert an hour of lecture into four or five brief sentences, a sentence or two in this instance is a compliment to Professor Miller. He was secretly dissatisfied, of course. Here he was sharing the benefit of his great learning and profound insights with students who seemed incapable of grasping how fortunate they were to sit under his tutelage. How could any sane person *not* be writing furiously, to capture all the ideas he was sharing? What exactly would they use to study with on the night before an exam? A couple of sentences?

"Do you see the importance of this?" he asked, with a slight edge in his voice. "You may be facing an emergency, such as a fire, an earthquake, or as in our example here, an impending systems disaster. Or you may have a decision-making problem on your hands that allows you plenty of time to think. In either case, the question, 'What is the situation?' must precede the question, 'What should be done?'" A hand went up. Professor Miller raised a hopeful eyebrow. "Yes?" he asked.

"What does *precede* mean?" the student asked. Two or three other students tittered quietly.

"It means *to come before*," replied Miller, not wanting to lose his rhythm. He decided instantly not to write the word on the board because that might reduce the impressiveness of the concepts already there. If a stranger thought he was teaching the word *precede*, the perceived level of the class would be reduced.

"You can see, then," he continued, handing them their conclusion, "that a poor conceptualization, a poor under-standing of what the situation is about, will result in a poor decision. Then, no matter how much effort you put in, your outcome will be poor." He wondered if he had used *poor* too many times in a row.

The presentation went on for the period, with Professor Miller commenting about how many people had died in sink-ing ships and even automobile crashes because they failed to appreciate the gravity of the situation rapidly approaching them. "They died, wondering if they should do something," he told the class. Conceptualization was often difficult, he noted, because the available information is frequently am-biguous or even contradictory. The solution he promised for a later meeting was to "disambiguate the situation through a series of hypotheses and tests." On the board he wrote *situa-tional disambiguation* because it looked more sophisticated than *disambiguate the situation*. He also jotted down *hy-pothesis evaluation*. No hands went up to query the meaning of these terms because the lectures were promised for a later time. Many students were thinking that it was pointless to learn something until it was required. Another promised lecture was on the value of "the pursuit of disconfirming evidence." The board welcomed this term, too. Finally, the rustle of papers and the gentle slapping and banging of backpacks, books, and other materials alerted Professor Miller to the end of the hour.

"This course not only will show you the value of quick thinking, but it will help you learn how to discover your options and grab the best one in each case," he concluded. "We'll also cover the standard material about fallacies, syllogisms, and the like. For next time, please read in your text pages 17 through 54, and be prepared to answer the questions at the end." A few moans and groans could be heard. "And remember, if you don't know how to think, you don't know how to live. Reason is the golden key to life."

Two students stayed after class. One was David Simmons, the young man who had called into question the credibility of the scenario in the film. The other was a young woman from the front row who had been quiet all period.

"After you," David said, deferring.

"Thanks. Hi, Dr. Miller. I'm Gina. Your class is going to be really interesting." Her voice was soft and rather girlish. Now taking a good look at her for the first time, Miller noticed how attractive she was. Fresh-faced and well endowed, Gina had a winning smile, her even teeth showing readily through her full lips.

"Do you think I will be able to do well?" Gina asked. "I mean, you use words like *disambiguate* and *conceptualization* and stuff."

"I'm sure you will do all right," he said. "Since you have remembered the words, you can look them up if you don't know them."

"Can I come to you for help if I get stuck?" she asked.

This is a real cutie, he thought, noticing her unusually long eyelashes as they batted beckoningly at him. "Uh, yes, yes, I have my office hours posted," he said after a delay just a fraction of a second longer than it should have been.

"Thanks. See you next time," she said sweetly, and sauntered out of the room. Miller watched her long, curly, honey-blonde hair bounce back and forth as she left. He felt like shaking his head to clear it. Had she been wearing perfume?

"Yes, David, isn't it?"

"Yeah. I just wondered. You said that the scene you showed was based on a real incident. What really happened?"

"The cargo door blew off and the decompression caused the cabin floor to collapse, and damage the controls."

"Cool," said David. The boy walked out of the room nodding his head with satisfaction. Professor Miller wondered why David had not asked about the outcome—what happened to the passengers and crew. Perhaps he had forgotten to ask.

The girl from Audio Visual arrived to retrieve the video equipment.

"Did it go okay?" She smiled warmly at Professor Miller. After all, he was good looking and friendly, and—for a professor—reasonably well dressed. She liked his sweater.

"Yes, fine," Miller said. He tried to remember her name for a few moments so he could use it, but nothing came to him, so he simply collected his notes and stuffed them into his new leather briefcase. "Thanks," he said as he left.

"Sure," the girl said, wrapping up an extension cord. "Anytime." She tried to load the last word with meaning.

❖ ❖ ❖

On many campuses, after an 8 A.M. class like Critical Thinking, a handful of students drag themselves over to the student union to get some coffee or espresso, so that they can finally wake up and face the day. Thus it was on this day that just a few minutes after nine, several members of Professor Miller's class sat in comfortable lounge chairs around a long coffee table just inside the double doors of the student union, known as the Cave. The fireplace area was already filled by early risers who had not yet gone to a class. They were waking themselves up first with coffee and chocolate and a discussion of some horror film most had seen the night before.

Miller's students were busy pouring little packets of sugar and chemicals into their paper coffee cups. The student union had ceased to serve coffee in ceramic cups a year or two earlier because the cups had gotten into the habit of taking indefinite vacations from the building and the cost of buying new ones every term was prohibitive. The student customers of the Cave had always been rather vague and casual about the difference between "for here" and "to go," with the result that most of the ceramic cups had found employment in dorm rooms or campus apartments. The new rule was, Everything in paper cups. Drink it here or take it with you; we don't care anymore. And who knows? Through their frequent patronage at brand-name coffee houses, perhaps students have gotten so used to the taste of coffee in paper cups that anything served in ceramic or china would seem to have an odd flavor.

"Why can't we have real, liquid, half and half?" one of them asked, scowling at the package of artificial creamer. "This stuff is made with coconut oil. That's artery cement."

"Well, they figure you'll live long enough to pay off your school debt and then they don't care," another said.

"The question is not why they do not serve cream," said a girl with a distinctly British accent, "but why they do not serve coffee." She made a face while looking at the cup. "This is the last cup of this liquid I will ever purchase."

"I'm Jennica," said a blonde with friendly eyes, turning to the girl who had just spoken.

"My name is Markayla," said the girl.

"I'm Markayla's roommate, Amy," said another of the students.

"You're the one who was taking all the notes," said David Simmons, who was part of the group. He was speaking past Amy and looking at Markayla.

"How can you remember what was said if you do not take notes?" Markayla asked rhetorically.

"What do you think of Miller?" David asked of no one in particular.

"He's okay," Amy said.

"He's good looking," Jennica added.

"Yeah, but a guy with a perm is sort of over the top," Julie Carmichael said, raising her eyebrows.

"Plus, he seems like he's acting. He seems to be listening to himself."

"That was a cool movie. Too bad it ended so soon and he started talking. I was beginning to enjoy the critical thinking class."

"How can you enjoy anything that comes at 8:00 A.M. three times a week?"

"He said he will teach us how to think."

"Yeah, but what if you already know how to think?"

"I think he's perfect," someone said. But it was not someone in the group. It was Gina, sitting in the next booth, stirring a coffee and talking on her cell phone a little too loudly, as many cell phone users do. "Yes, just right," she went on. "He knows everything. Just the type." At this point, Gina, who had been looking around the room as she spoke, noticed that the students in the booth next to her had begun paying attention to her conversation. "Okay, Judy," she said. "Good luck with the repair. I'm sure the guy will work out for you. Bye." Then she hung up.

"Want to join us?" said someone in the group.

"I'd be glad to," said Gina, looking at her watch, "but I've really gotta run. Thanks anyway. See you in class." Somehow her warm smile made the refusal seem kindly.

"Who was she talking about?"

"I saw her give Jeremy a look over when she came in," said Jennica, nodding her head in the direction of a booth where Jeremy sat. "If he hadn't been with Jodi, Gina would have gone over, I'll bet."

"Well, he's certainly one of the best looking guys on campus."

"If they're that good looking, they have to be evil. I'll bet he goes through girls like popcorn."

"Oh, and those big, juicy grapes you can't have are just so sour, aren't they?"

"Shut up."

"Miller thinks Gina's pretty hot, too," said David. "He raised his eyebrows after class and had one of those smiles. I was there."

"I'm glad we have a good-looking prof," Jennica said. "It will help make a long, boring class a little more bearable."

"I hope we get more films," David said.

"I hope someday to have a decent cup of coffee," Markayla said, putting the cup down for the last time and giving it a little shove of rejection. The cup scooted back a little.

Two or three of the others gave Markayla an odd look.

"Don't ask," Amy said. "She's just like that."

Chapter 2

It was a quiet night on the campus of the university, though not so quiet that the crickets could be heard easily. The distant sounds of pounding rhythm from suffering boomboxes and component stereos blended with an occasional laugh or playful scream. The trees in the courtyard of Pelletier hall wondered whether they would make it through another year of climbing, hanging lights, stapled signs, toilet papering, and miscellaneous twig theft. Already on this first Friday night of the new school year, someone had attempted to hang a swing from a too-slender branch with predictable, agonizing results. That sickening, cracking sound, the pain, the oozing of fluids. It was awful. The perpetrator was not hurt at all. He simply took his swing to another tree and left the injured one to bleed until it could be treated by the landscapers.

The night grew later and later, until the numbers on the clock stopped getting larger and started over again. The background rumble gradually diminished, but somewhere there was the determination to enjoy a night of total abandonment with music and dance and eating and drinking all night long to celebrate the completion of a week of classes. Had the partiers been listening, at some point they might have noticed that the occasional shout from a room on the second floor had became frequent enough to define an altercation, punctuated by the sound of a slamming door.

A few minutes later, a young woman could be seen walking around the landing, carrying a set of bed sheets and a blanket. She looked tired and exasperated (*torqued*, she would have said), and her eye makeup made it appear that she had been punched in both eyes. Her hair had once been long and dark brown and hung toward the ground, but now it was short and largely blonde, with tips of purple and orange, and largely pointed toward the sky. Her ears, eyebrow, lip, and navel all bore silver studs, matched with a leather collar and wristband containing stainless steel. On her cheek and tummy were tattoos. She wore a fairy-tale orange shirt (that is, Once upon a time it had been orange), and her jeans were ripped open at the knees. On her usually bare feet were house slippers, a concession to the cool of the very early morning.

The young woman stopped outside of Room 204 and knocked with one of her ring-covered hands. When the door did not open as quickly as she wished, the young woman grew impatient and used her fist to knock more enthusiastically. The thought crossed her mind just to use her master key to let herself in.

"Amy! Markayla! It's Melanie. Open up, please." Melanie was beginning to feel cold.

The hardware clicked as the deadbolt slid back and then the door opened, revealing a very sleepy girl, still holding the doorknob in one hand. Her hair had been put up before bedtime, but by now several strands had escaped their bondage and hung down miscellaneously.

"What's going on?" Amy asked, squinting from the outside light shining through the doorway.

"Can I come in?" said Melanie, who then walked inside.

"Sure," said Amy. She put her arms around herself from the cold and padded back toward her bed to grab her robe. Her usual sleepwear was just an extra-large T-shirt, which on her frame was long enough to be a very short dress. Tonight she had been sleeping in a freebie from a conference her father had attended. There was a logo and the words "Digital Imaging" written in large letters on the front. Amy covered the logo as she wrapped the robe around her and then returned to where Melanie stood near the door.

Melanie closed the door, robbing the room of the light that had allowed her to see, so she flipped on the lights. They were much brighter than the light from the doorway.

"Ooh! You are blinding me," said a voice from a nearby bed, in a distinctly British accent. "What is happening here? What time is it?"

"It's Melanie, the RA," Amy said. "And it's 2:34."

Markayla wondered what the resident assistant would want with them at that hour.

"Is the building on fire?" she asked abruptly, suddenly thinking of what she considered a likely reason. Markayla swung her feet out of bed and was about to stand up. Unlike Amy, she believed in formal sleepwear, and was wearing deep purple satin pajamas.

"No, no, everything's fine," said Melanie, in a calming tone. "But I have a problem and you can help."

Markayla was putting on her silver-rimmed glasses, but still keeping her eyes mostly closed as they gradually adjusted to the light. "A problem?" she asked skeptically. "What kind of problem gets brought into our room at 2:30 in the morning?"

"We have a personality conflict, and I was hoping you two would be willing to take another roommate, at least temporarily, to solve the problem," Melanie said, looking over at the third bed and desk in the room and then glancing meaningfully at the sheets and blanket in her arms. With the growing preference for single rooms on many campuses, the older dorms with rooms built for two or three were less popular. As a result, the campus housing authorities made an effort to limit the rooms in Pelletier to two persons each, even though most of them had been built for three. Some rooms were tripled by choice of the residents, and a few by necessity because of an unexpected housing crunch. But many triples still had only two residents, and this was the case for Amy and Markayla.

"I guess we could take her," said Amy, still not very awake.

"Tell me first," said Markayla, in a much more alert and commanding tone, "whether your solution is to give this 'problem' to us, and whether there are other available beds in the dormitory, and why you have chosen us." Markayla's ambition was to become a lawyer, and Amy thought she already acted like one. No, Amy thought Markayla already acted like a judge. It fit Markayla's calm, circumspect personality. Maybe the culture shock of coming to the United States had made her cautious.

"Well," said Melanie, "the girl is a little weird, but she's okay."

Amy was now awake enough for this statement to cause an automobile accident of logic in her head. In Amy's personal mental dictionary, there was a photograph of Melanie next to the entry for *weird*. If, therefore, Melanie called the girl in question "a little weird," what could that mean?

Markayla's thought, on the other hand, had taken the train and avoided that nasty accident. She reasoned that

Melanie thought Markayla and Amy were among the weirdest people on the planet, so that Melanie's description of someone as "a little weird" was non-information. The truth was that, while Melanie thought the two roommates were a bit too tightly wound, she actually admired them to some extent and occasionally wondered what it would be like to resemble them. The wheels of her life were already rather deep into the ruts of her chosen street, so she did not foresee a personal change, but she was still curious about the choices these girls had made.

"You guys are nice," Melanie said, appealing to the girls' feelings. "You talk about compassion and stuff, and I thought you would be the best for her." Both girls realized that it is sometimes impossible at the outset to distinguish between a sincere compliment and a con. They hoped Melanie was serious.

"Is there something wrong with her?" Amy asked. Amy was beginning to wonder if taking the girl in would be a mistake.

"Well, she's just kind of different," said Melanie, not looking at either of the roommates, but putting the sheets and blanket down on Amy's desk.

"Different in what way?" asked Markayla.

"You'll see. She's actually quiet and nice. I think you might even like her and can help her somehow. She's not dangerous and doesn't do drugs or guys."

"What's her name?" asked Amy, chewing over Melanie's comments about the girl not being dangerous.

One of those odd quirks of human nature is that when we are uncertain about making a decision involving someone we do not know, we always ask the person's name, as if that will help us make a decision.

"This guy is a hard worker, but he keeps burning down the office buildings he works in. Do you want to hire him?"

"I don't know. What's his name?"

"I just met a girl whose eleven previous husbands died under mysterious circumstances. Think I should marry her?"

"I don't know. What's her name?"

It is as if we can discern something about people by their names. It is no wonder so many actors adopt improvements over their given names. Percy Skimpleblatt leaves home and becomes Biff Winners in Hollywood. Henrietta Pflugg stars in her first film as Lacey DeLovely. Perhaps the reason is that we have been upgrading the names of locations all along, realizing that many people confuse the name and the thing. Coyote Wash is renamed Timid Creek so that a housing development next to a gravel drainage ditch can be called Creekside.

"Her name's Tina. Tina Davidson."

Amy thought of the ballerina on her desk, whom she had also named Tina, and to whom she often talked during times of reflection. Some people talk to their teddy bears or dolls; Amy talked to the figurine.

Amy and Markayla, not having the luxury of a private conversation while Melanie was standing there, searched each other's faces for signs of preference in the decision. Both seemed to be somewhat uncertain. Amy was wondering if they were inviting trouble—by which she meant interference with her studying—by allowing the girl in. This would be a heavy semester, and it would require extended quiet time to concentrate. Markayla was less worried about noise because she had a better ability to concentrate in a busy room. But she was generally more cautious about sudden, new arrangements, especially those proposed in the middle of the night.

However, not seeing any definitive signs of refusal in each other's faces, the two roommates soon nodded to each other slightly, both feeling mostly agreeable to taking the girl in. It was worth some risk where there was a possibility of helping someone who might need them.

"Well," said Markayla, at last, "let us see this girl, then. We will take her in for a time."

Tina appeared in a T-shirt, faded jeans-shorts, and experienced athletic shoes with no socks. In one hand she had her cosmetics bag. Cradled against herself in the other arm were some clothes for a change in the morning and a silver lockbox. Her short brown hair was a little ruffled, and her eyes had a somewhat watery look, but overall she looked normal enough. Amy would have said that Tina was tall, since the girl had an inch or two on Amy, while Markayla would have said she was short, at a few inches less than Markayla. Amy thought their new roommate was irritatingly slender, while Markayla thought her of average build. And this, dear reader, is only one example of the confusion caused by using ourselves as a standard of reference for the rest of the world.

When she walked through the doorway past Amy, Tina paused and looked into Amy's face. "Hello," she said simply. There was neither warmth nor coldness in her voice.

"Hi. I'm Amy," Amy said, wondering if she should offer to shake her hand. "And this is Markayla."

"I am glad to meet you, Tina," Markayla said.

"Is this okay?" Tina asked.

There was a slight pause while the two roommates wondered what the object of *this* was. But instead of asking, "Is
what okay?" Amy and Markayla said almost in unison, "Yes."

"Welcome," said Markayla. "Here is your bed and desk.
You must need some sleep. I know I do. Let me first help you
make your bed."

Melanie had been standing just inside the door to see
how things went. As Tina walked over with Markayla to look
at her bed, Melanie whispered to Amy, "I'll bring her things
over tomorrow. Night night. Oh, and don't let her burn candles. It's against the rules, you know." She closed the door as
she left. As she walked back to her own room, she crossed
her fingers on both hands.

Under normal circumstances, the introduction of a new
female roommate into the room of two other females would
require the pronunciation of thousands of words, perhaps
tens of thousands. Life histories, personal tastes, future
dreams, every kind of subject imaginable, from food to nail
polish, from music to romance, would be covered. In this situation, however, the late hour and the odd circumstances
conspired to prevent such exchanges. Tina announced that
she was tired and threw herself on top of the bed. Amy went
over to see what Tina might need.

"You can have one of my T-shirts to sleep in if you want,"
she offered.

Tina looked at her, again with an expression of doubt on
her face. "Is it a four?" she asked.

"It's an extra large," Amy said.

"Never mind," Tina said. She lay back and closed her eyes. "I'm sorry," she said to the ceiling.

None of the girls slept much the rest of the night. When the light was turned out, Tina stayed quiet for about ten minutes and then sat up in bed. The room was dark again except for the dim light from a nightlight in the bathroom (whose door was partly closed), so Amy could not see anything other than Tina's figure sitting up. In a few more minutes, Tina got out of bed and walked to the door.

"Are you okay, Tina?" Amy asked quietly, in case Markayla was asleep.

"Yes, yes," Tina said.

"What is it?"

"Nothing. I thought I heard something."

Tina was soon back in bed. A few minutes later, she was up again, this time standing near the window on the other side of the room.

"Tina?" Amy said again.

"Do you hear a baby crying?" Tina asked.

Amy listened intently for a few moments. The night was now quiet. Even the hold-out music had ceased, allowing a few crickets to be heard. The sound of a car could be heard in the distance, but that was about all. "No," she said. "I don't hear any baby crying."

"There is no baby crying that I can hear," Markayla said, to Amy's surprise.

"Oh, okay, never mind," Tina said. She got back into bed.

As worried about this behavior as the roommates were, they must have dozed off eventually, because when their alarm went off seemingly a few minutes later, they both awoke. Tina was asleep on top of the bed, still dressed.

"Should we wake her?" Amy asked Markayla. "Or let her have a Saturday morning sleep?"

"Let us see if the noise of the morning wakes her," Markayla answered.

The whooshing rush of shower water, the whiney whirr of hair dryers, and the screechy skrunk of coat hangers sliding along the rod all apparently failed to awaken Tina, who lay on her back, legs spread out and arms over her head. She looked either like an extremely relaxed person in the world's most comfortable bed or like a prisoner stretched out on a torture rack, ready to be pulled apart.

Amy finished pulling on her jeans and looked over at Tina. "We don't want her to miss breakfast." A girl that skinny could scarcely afford to miss a meal, Amy thought.

Markayla walked over to where Tina lay, and said softly, "Tina?"

Tina opened her eyes but nothing else moved. Her roommates were both surprised to see her awake. A moment later she retracted her limbs like a pill bug rolling up.

"What time is it?" she asked, facing the wall.

"Quarter to eight," Amy said from across the room.

"Okay, thanks," Tina said. She lay motionless a few moments longer. Then she got up off the bed and went into the bathroom. Amy wondered whether to make some conversation. "Did you sleep okay?" or "Want to go to breakfast with us?" were two possibilities. But she thought better of it and said nothing. Tina seemed to be something of a loner, or at least she was not in a talking mood. Amy remembered going to summer camp with a girl who in the morning would sit on the edge of her bunk and stare silently for twenty minutes before she could utter a single word. Her body awoke long before her brain did, so she waited patiently until the mental and verbal functions booted up. Once awake, she was as normal as a doughnut. "I've got to stop using food metaphors," Amy thought.

Markayla sat down at her desk for her next morning ritual. After getting dressed, her first requirement was a pot of good coffee and a few minutes reading. Some people, when they find a situation less than to their liking, spend as much effort as possible complaining about it. Markayla was not one of these. Not by nature a negative or critical person, she instead believed in taking charge of a situation and applying whatever remedy was possible. While in the United States, she had developed a definite taste for really good coffee. The coffee in the dining commons she found virtually undrinkable. But instead of criticizing it every day with every sip, she had almost given up drinking it at all, and instead had obtained the necessary items for making her own coffee in the room before going to breakfast. She had fresh beans, a grinder, a drip coffee pot, coffee filters, and on special occasions, bottled water to use in the brewing. A tiny refrigerator housed the half and half. On special occasions, when the tension between taste and healthy eating yielded in the direction of taste, the fridge might even feature whipping cream.

When her parents had questioned all this paraphernalia as she packed it up to bring with her, she said, "Just because we are going away to the university, we do not have to be uncivilized."

Her almost daily habit was to make a small pot of "real" coffee and sit down with it to read. She always began with some chapters in the Bible. Then, without the smallest feeling of self-irony, Markayla closed the Book and opened the

Wall Street Journal. This was not a turning from God to Mammon, but a practical shift from the Big Picture to the Small. Markayla was majoring in international business, even though she planned to work as an American lawyer, so she thought that the business newspaper offered her the practical knowledge she needed to accompany the more general knowledge her classes provided. She believed that, if she laid a solid foundation in righteousness, she could build a worthy and level structure of any kind in business or law, even, in spite of their tendencies for corruption.

Markayla and Amy had met when Markayla's first year in the U. S. placed her as a high school freshman in classes with Amy. The girls soon became friends. Amy invited Markayla to church and they soon became inseparable, eventually deciding to go to the same university. Having each other as long-time friends and then roommates (beginning last year as freshmen) did a lot to remedy the separation anxiety the sociologists are always talking about when young people leave home for the first time. And their friendship provided the moral support essential for facing the grind of the university.

When Tina emerged from the bathroom, she had on a clean T-shirt, and the same cut-off jeans and worn shoes as the night before.

The three went to breakfast, where Amy and Markayla talked about the expectations of the day. Tina said very little. The two girls' Saturday was not planned for recreation or socializing (though Amy hoped to see Matt at some point) but for work, to get ahead of the game by reading upcoming chapters and thinking about paper topics. "More work, more reading, gotta do some research on the Web, write out some notes." Their assignments were still very light, but both girls made notes about their day's projected activities to help them get into the habit once again. Amy's notes were mental, while Markayla's were written.

As Amy watched Markayla write out a lengthy to-do list, she remembered a night near the beginning of last year. Amy and Markayla were sitting at their desks, deep into the books. Both were taking notes. Amy remembered feeling tired and glancing at the clock, to learn that it was 11:20, almost time to quit for the night. Suddenly Markayla had tossed her pen onto her desk.

"American television has deceived me," Markayla had said, with a straight and serious face.

Amy had asked her what she was reading, wondering what subject had provoked that conclusion. But Markayla was referring to her own experience.

"When students are shown on television and in films," she had said, "none of them ever do this much work. Everyone is always at play."

"And you believed television?"

"I think television is not real," Markayla had said, thus comprehending one of the most fundamental truths of modern life. "I have seen through these false appearances."

Now, in their sophomore year, neither harbored any illusions about the work load at the university. Some institutions have diluted their curricula and lessened workloads to cater to a new, lazier, less able student population, but this university was not one of them. The word on campus was that describing a class as *impossible* meant that it was relatively easy. The truly challenging classes were called *preposterous, insane,* or *suicidal.* Amy and Markayla talked about the syllabi in their classes and argued whether Critical Thinking was going to be insane or merely impossible.

During the work-planning conversation, Tina paid attention mostly to her food, but she occasionally looked around the room, and once stared in one direction. Amy noticed this lengthy look and looked to see what interested Tina, but could find nothing out of the ordinary.

After breakfast, Amy and Markayla decided to head to the library to work in the silent, nearly abandoned building, surrounded by the wisdom and folly of the ages. They invited Tina, but she said she would study in the dorm.

Chapter 3

On the Monday beginning the second week of classes, the bees and grasshoppers really hit the windshield.

Class enrollments begin to stabilize as the course shoppers have made their choices and dropped the courses they deemed too hard or too boring. Most students have bought their textbooks by this time, and, if the professor's first meetings of the class have gone well, most of the students have made some commitment to the class. Even those professors who were too lazy to have a syllabus on opening day usually have one ready for this second week, laying out the reading for the term. Thus, those members of the professoriate who had held back during the first week now know that this second week is an opportune time to begin requiring actual work from students, whether in the form of reading or writing or some other mental effort.

Amy slogged back to her room after her third class on that Monday, feeling as if she had just driven through a locust plague. The windshield was totally gross. She thought how the semester was beginning and how a new journey was underway. The entire term lay before her. Even with her Saturday effort, she now felt substantially behind. Nearly every chapter was still to be read, every page to be written, every test to be taken. Probably a lot of sleep to be lost. She took a deep breath and let it out with a quiet sigh. She remembered the saying she had read on a card in a gift shop several years ago. "The sea is so wide and my boat is so small." It seemed impossible, or rather, insane.

But she knew from the experience of last year that once things really got underway, the boat would just bob along and, with an enormous rowing effort, eventually find landfall at the end of the term. Or, to change metaphors, the train ride would be wild, fast, and sometimes rough, but the cars would eventually pull into the station—if she could keep the steam up.

Now she remembered that the saying on the card had actually been a prayer, something like, "Lord, go with me, because the sea is so wide and my boat is so small." She nodded in agreement and said the prayer over again, just as she reached her door and unlocked it.

As she swung her laden backpack around from behind her, carefully arced so that it would land squarely in the middle of her bed, she noticed something on her pillow. It was a little clear bag of potpourri. As she picked it up, the cellophane made a happy crinkly sound and the faintest of sweet aromas greeted her nose. A small card was attached.

"Thank you," was all it said. And then the signature, "Tina." Amy felt a wave of emotion, though she was not quite sure why. Scarcely a hundred words had passed between them in the last few days. Tina might be a little odd, but she seemed like a nice enough person. Amy struggled to make her feelings mean something rational. "Why am I feeling this way?" she asked herself. "There must be a reason."

Her father, after many years of being a police detective, had told her that sometimes our feelings run in advance of our thinking. That's what women call intuition and men (not wanting to admit having intuition, too) call a hunch.

No clarification coming to hand, Amy dropped the thought. She put the potpourri on the table next to her bed and opened her book bag. She carried the books over to her desk, pushed her notebook computer aside (which she noted had been turned around backwards), and put them along the back of the desk.

The textbooks were joyfully welcomed back to their new home by the other books that had lived on her desk all the way through the last year and which had now settled in comfortably for another stay. The dictionary was a bit too wordy (or should I say oververbalized?), and the thesaurus repeated itself in so many words, but the Bible was circumspect and said that prodigals were always welcome to return. The new spiral notebooks, filled mostly with blank paper, now each had several pages of lecture notes in them, and they strutted with their newfound knowledge. They stood upright, taller than most of the books, as if lording it over everyone else. Little did they realize the threat posed them by the notebook computer sitting nearby, for Amy had often thought of taking it to class for note taking and abandoning the spiral notebooks. Only the concern about the weight of her backpack kept the spiral notebooks safe from the wolf of shiftless unemployment, victims of the technology freight train. It was a tenuous arrogance, but they lived it without fear. As the saying is, they were content to whistle in the dark, until someone pushed the *on* switch.

People faced with an enormous workload respond differently. Some sit as if stupefied, not doing anything, not knowing where to start or not able to muster the energy to begin. Others try to multitask and do everything at once. Amy was an organizer and a bit of a plodder. Her friend Matt, who had been raised on a family-run farm of a few hundred acres, had a saying that she liked. "You don't clear a field by lifting all the stones at once with your mind. You clear it by lifting one stone at a time with your hands." Then he added, "And if you're really clever, you use the stones to build a wall around your field." His homely wisdom had helped gain Amy's interest in him. He was not pretentious, but there was something thoughtful about him that she admired.

Matt's announcement that large tasks are accomplished in increments did not stun the world. The idea is not unique or amazingly new. It is the lesson of Aesop with the tortoise and the hare ("The race is won by the steady"). All of us know, once you remind us, that persistence built the pyramids and etched the great canyons. Amy did not need to be reminded because her father had first taught her, with his version: "No case was ever solved by giving up on it." Markayla had reinforced the same idea with her version: "Haba na haba hujaza kibaba," a Swahili proverb meaning literally, "Little and little fills the cup." Markayla quoted it often at the university, as she, too, faced quite a workload in her major. But there is value in redundancy, especially when the redundancy is that of encouragement. To be reminded that the difficult is nevertheless possible seems always to be a source of renewed strength.

This is a creaking way of getting Amy to open a book, but you now know her attitude as she did so, preparing to read a chapter to start digging on the mountain.

Just as she pulled the cap off her highlighter, there was a rapid knock on the door. Amy tossed the highlighter into the handy valley of the book and got up to open the door.

Standing there in neat, corduroy overalls was a red-headed girl about Amy's height. She was holding a notepad and pen, as if preparing to make notes. There was an expectant look on her face, similar to what might be expected from a reporter. "Excuse me," she said brightly, "but can you spell the sound of a toilet flushing?"

The suddenness and oddity of the question made Amy's brain stall momentarily. She nearly uttered a "Huh?" but she caught herself and said, with the politeness one uses for questions from strangers, "Uh, I don't think so." She wanted to ask what this was all about, but before she could speak again, the girl continued.

"I can't either," the girl said, now wrinkling her brow a bit and looking both thoughtful and dissatisfied. "But there must be a word for it. Otherwise, how can we be blamed for writing poorly when our language is that deficient?" Then, putting the pen and pad in her pocket and holding up her hands to suggest a picture frame around her face, she smiled and said, "Hello. I'm Shelley."

"Hi, I'm Amy. I'm—."

"Amy! Oh, good. Normally, I wouldn't just introduce myself to a stranger, being rather shy and all, but they say crazy people live here and since we're practically sisters, I thought I'd better find out what's going on."

Amy just stood there, mouth partly open, one hand still on the door. The combination of the little drama, the comment that *crazy people live here*, and the words *we're practically sisters* left her mind fumbling for an entry point into the conversation. She was too surprised to think about Professor Miller's comments on cognitive stabilization. His lecture was not at all useful here.

Noticing Amy's confusion, the girl introduced herself again. "Hi," she said, extending her hand. "My name's Shelley. Mind if I come in?" She was already looking past Amy and around the room.

"Uh, no. Come in. My roommates aren't here right now."

Shelley was looking across the room. On the wall over Amy's bed was a large poster, about two by three feet, showing the tread designs of two dozen or so athletic shoes. There was a large variety of patterns, with many shapes of bumps and grooves, molded in various colors: black, blue, red, pink, white, brown, gray. At the bottom of the poster was the caption, "What will a man give in exchange for his sole?" Shelley turned her head sideways for a moment, contemplating the poster, but said nothing. Then she turned back to Amy, who had retreated to her desk, but turned the chair around to face Shelley.

"I'm a theater major," said Shelley. "What's yours?" As she spoke, she glanced over Amy's desk. "Oh, a ballerina." Shelley had noticed the tall figurine on Amy's desk. "Are you a dance major?"

"I'm still undeclared," said Amy, almost apologetically. She felt guilty that at the beginning of her sophomore year she had still not chosen a major. "I was thinking about English," she said, to show that she had at least given the subject some consideration.

"I used to be an English major," Shelley said. "But it was too weird."

"Weird?"

"Yeah. I like Dickens and Shakespeare and Ibsen and Jane Austen—"

"I love Jane Austen," Amy injected.

"—But the stuff we read for class was all bizarre stuff, weird, crazy stuff about people eating each other, and really boring book-length monologues, and characters complaining about how evil men are. I like men. What about you?" Amy was not sure what the question meant or what an appropriate answer was, since she had just met her questioner minutes earlier.

"Guys are okay, I guess," she said. "I—." The pause had been too long.

"Anyway," Shelley went on, speaking rapidly, "we had all these books that were sort of like political statements instead of novels or stories, and get this, even the books I liked got interpreted to mean that everybody was oppressing everybody else. I mean, no matter what we read, all the books meant the same thing: men are oppressing women and the evil capitalists are oppressing the workers. Everyone in the world is a victim of white males, many of whom have been dead for a long time. You know that fountain outside of Kemble Hall?"

"The round one in the courtyard? With the bench-like thing around it?"

"Yeah. Professor Linkrodt says it's a rape symbol. She calls it 'a tool of oppressive patriarchal hegemony,' and says we are all being raped by it when we walk by. That's what I mean by weird. And I've always thought of myself as an ordinary, conservative girl. So I changed to theater."

"Is the ballerina why you said we are practically sisters?" Amy asked, not wanting to touch the claim about crazy people living in her room.

"Oh, no. It's because my boyfriend Ron and your boyfriend Matt are buds."

"He's not my boyfriend," Amy said. "He's just a friend."

"Whatever," Shelley said, as if she thought Amy was splitting hairs. "Anyway, isn't that cool? I'm just over in Hurlock. We're neighbors. Ooh, your roommate looks interesting." Shelley was looking over at Markayla's desk. Amy's desk was, to be blunt, somewhat pedestrian compared to Markayla's.

Amy had books, her notebook computer, her ballerina, and a few ordinary items like tissues and pens.

Markayla's desk was a work of art. On one end was a bowl of fresh fruit. Not the kind that lasts forever because it is made of plastic, but the kind you can pick up and sink your teeth into, while the juicy ripeness caresses your taste buds and drips down your chin. Apples (two different kinds), oranges, bananas, and sometimes pears and often grapes, sat tantalizingly in a brass bowl. The bowl had a raised base, giving the impression that the fruit was being lifted up toward the observer. Markayla kept the inventory carefully and fully stocked. In the few days since Tina had moved in, there was evidence that the bowl would have no trouble featuring the freshest of fruits because the supply runs would now have to be more frequent.

At the opposite end of the desk stood a heavy lead crystal vase, occupied as often as financial reality would permit with fresh flowers. Give Amy an unexpected ten dollars and she would likely buy a mystery novel or some nail polishes. Give Markayla an unexpected ten dollars and she would buy some fresh flowers or coffee beans. Shelley was fortunate on this Monday because the vase had been supplied only the previous Saturday, and the bright yellow, red, pink, blue, and purple flowers still looked perfect.

Covering Markayla's desk was a woven cloth with tassels on each end. On the cloth was a design done in a primitive-art style.

"Does she ever study at this desk?" asked Shelley doubtfully.

"Oh, yes. She studies more that I do, and you can see by my pale skin that I hardly ever see daylight."

"Uh huh."

On the continuum from very insecure to very self confident, Amy's self image was just a little toward the insecure side. Shelley's agreement with the pale-skin comment thus caused a little twinge of dissatisfaction. A comment such as, "Oh, your skin looks fine," would have been more welcome. And it had not gone unnoticed that Shelley had quickly abandoned an examination of Amy's desk for a much longer look at Markayla's. People inadvertently had a way of not noticing Amy. She sometimes felt like a pedestrian by the side of the road as an eighteen-wheel truck blasts by at seventy-five miles an hour. The accompanying wind leaves the pedestrian sprayed with dust and sand, disheveled and windblown, and feeling used and abandoned. Amy's long but so far unfulfilled dream was to be fussed over.

Behind Markayla's desk sat a coffee grinder, a coffee pot, several jars of coffee beans, and a gallon jug of spring water, about half full. The beans and the flowers and the fruit joined to play an aromatic symphony in the surrounding area.

"Your roommate seems really interesting," Shelley said. "Is this one the, um, new girl that just joined you?"

"No, this is my high school friend. The new girl, Tina, sleeps over there. And that's her desk."

Shelley looked over to Tina's bed and desk. A radio, a CD player, a few books, a silver box, a couple of jar candles, some other clutter, nothing as interesting as Markayla's. It could wait.

So tell me about this roommate. What's her name?"

"Markayla."

"What's she like?"

"Well, she's smart, serious, a business major, wants to be an attorney—." Shelley had begun to make a face, which showed that she was not impressed.

"No, really," Amy continued. "She's a great person. She can be funny. She's understanding. Even though she thinks she has to put up with a lot from Americans."

"She's not an American?"

"Not yet. She's from Kenya. Her family moved here when her father had to come over because of his job. He works for an oil company. They asked him to stay, so now Markayla is planning to become a citizen and get a law degree."

"Do we really need any more lawyers?"

"She already talks like a judge."

"What about your other roommate?" Shelley asked, suddenly turning toward Tina's area of the room.

"Tina just moved in Friday night or actually early Saturday morning. She's pretty quiet."

"Oh, really?" Shelley's tone teetered along the edge of a wall between belief and skepticism.

Amy remembered herself in junior high school as a quiet, awkward, loner, not unlike Tina now, so she wanted all the more to avoid criticizing the girl. She remembered the gift of potpourri sitting on her bedside table and felt that any negative comments about Tina would be a violation of gratitude. And besides, so far Tina had been fine.

"She's undeclared, like me," Amy said at last.

In Shelley's continued scan of the room, she had now returned to Amy's desk, where she once again noticed the ballerina. The figurine stood a little over a foot high and was made of imitation bronze. The ballerina's costume had been painted to imitate the green oxidation often seen on copper rooftops. The girl stood on one leg while the other swept out with the toe pointing at the floor. Her arms were crossed in front of her away from her chest, fingers straight.

"What a cute ballerina," Shelley said, walking over to it.

"Her name's Tina the Ballerina," Amy said.

"Tina the Ballerina? That's cute. Not just Tina."

"Um hm. She used to be just Tina until last week when Tina Davidson became my other roommate. So we have to distinguish. We call the new Tina 'Tina Nicole.'"

"Where'd you get her? The ballerina, I mean."

"My father gave her to me when I was in junior high."

"Birthday present?"

"No, he just brought her home one day. He said, 'Amy, I saw this and thought of you.'"

"Oh, how sweet," Shelley said, in that precious tone of voice that some people use to talk to their pets. Seeing Amy's face, she added, more seriously—as seriously as Shelley could get when in a playful mood—"No, really. I think that's neat. Were you taking ballet at the time?"

"Yeah, but that's not why he gave it to me."

"No?"

"He said it was a symbol to remind me how to live."

Shelley looked from Amy to the ballerina and back and forth and back a few times, eyebrows knitted in a concentrated, doubtful look. Then she suddenly brightened. "Oh, I get it," she said, striking a pose, holding one arm across her chest and the other with the back of her hand against her forehead. "No, no, I couldn't possibly do what you're asking," she said in a high-pitched, melodramatic voice. "Father warned me about boys like you."

"No," said Amy.

"Are you sure?" asked Shelly. "Those crossed arms are pretty hostile. It's like, 'Keep away from me, you bucket of sludge.'"

"No, that's a ballet pose. It's beautiful."

"So, did your father say just how Tina the Ballerina is supposed to remind you to be good?"

"It's not a reminder to be good."

"I am so relieved," Shelley said with dramatic emphasis. "Now we can go to that wild party after all."

"Shelley, what will you do if you ever get into a serious conversation?"

"You mean like, 'Darling, come away with me to my mansion in the south of France and be my princess'?"

"Never mind."

"But you have to tell me," Shelley pleaded. "Your clever scheme has drawn me in. 'I cannot choose but hear.' That's from *Rime of the Ancient Mariner*. Didn't know I was cultured, did you?" Shelley fell silent and smiled brightly with expectation. After a few moments of silence, she said, "Well?"

"When he gave her to me, he said, 'Amy, I'm giving you this ballerina to remind you of something I hope you will always remember.'"

"Which was?"

"He said, 'The ballerina lives not for herself but for her dance.'"

Shelley thought for a minute, a somewhat doubtful expression on her face. She was turning over this saying in her mind, attempting to translate it into a more literal expression. In a moment she said, "Okay. That's very interesting. Did he explain what that means?"

"No. He said I should think about it."

Shelley already thought the saying was open to more than one interpretation, and had an idea in mind. But when she was an English major, her professors had strongly insisted that all interpretations are personal, so she decided to with-

hold her own comments and see what Amy had concluded.
"And did you?"

"Yes. In fact, I still think about it."

"So what does it mean?"

"Well, at first I took it literally, and thought he meant that
I should work harder at my ballet lessons. I was never the
graceful nymph I thought he wanted me to be." Shelley nodded as if she agreed that Amy was not very graceful. Amy
frowned slightly as she seemed to understand what Shelley
was thinking. "But ballet didn't exactly thrill me, either. So I
told him, 'Daddy, I'm not going to be a professional ballerina. There are other things in life besides ballet.' And then I
growled a growl as only teeny boppers can growl, right
through my arrogant little braces."

"You wore braces? How long?"

"Just got them off two years ago. I was so glad to have my
senior picture taken without them."

"But growling arrogantly at your father? Oh, Amy, that is
so shocking."

"I was in the middle of my junior high rebellion. I thought
my father was a clueless drone."

"So what do you think the saying means now?"

"Well, I keep finding different meanings. Right now I
think it means that I should try to live the best life I can, to
make my 'dance' so to speak, the best it can be." Amy had always wanted to be admired for something, to be really good,
or even outstanding. She had not yet chosen a major or career to excel at, so right now she wanted her whole life to be
as good as she could make it.

"I like that." Shelley's expression indicated that she was
about to ask another question when her cell phone rang. She
glanced at the display on the phone, then answered. "Rent a

Date. Shelley speaking. How may I help you?" Amy glanced over at the clock and noticed that it was time for her to get ready to go to work. The Math Department was at some distance from the dorm, so she had a few minutes' walk ahead of her. While Shelley was occupied with the phone call, Amy stood up and walked to the mirror to check her hair.

"Ron? Ron who? Oh, yes, sir. We can arrange that. You want a red head? Those are extra," Shelley continued. "How much? How much have you got? Okay, then. No, I'm not there. I'll meet you in front of Pelletier. 'Kay. Bye." Shelley closed the phone and put it into her pocket. "Well, my guy wants to take me for a ride, so I've gotta go. The way he rides, he'll be here pretty fast."

"And I've got to get to work. It was great meeting you, though."

"Oh, I know. No, really, I like you, too. I'll be back."

Chapter 4

"The world is awash in false, misleading, and manipulative information," Professor Miller was saying. "Be cautious. Think first. Examine claims. Ask yourself not whether there is any reason to reject some story but why you should accept it in the first place. There is too much gullibility among you. You must begin to demand qualitative criteria for belief." Miller liked the last phrase, so he wrote *qualitative criteria* on the board.

The theme of the week was information quality. The class that day covered urban legends. Miller had begun the class with a few short film clips showing reenactments of some of the better known ones, and then he talked about the general nature, sources, and persistence of such stories. The class discussed quite a number of legends, focusing on those commonly spread by email and by word of mouth. Professor Miller betrayed a tone of amused superiority as he mentioned $250 cookie recipes, free vacations for forwarding email, and lover's lane killers with hooks for hands. He observed several students fidgeting uncomfortably as they heard him explode as fabrications or distortions many of these stories they had believed to be true. Some appeared still unconvinced by his explanations.

"So the prevalence of urban legends is a warning to all of you not to accept uncritically every piece of exciting information that comes your way," he continued. Even before the success of his critical thinking book, Miller had developed the habit of using *you* when discussing deficiencies of reasoning rather than what many faculty consider a more engaging *we*. Instead of saying, "We all need to think more carefully," he would say, "You all need to think more carefully," because he, possibly unconsciously, excluded himself from the deficiency.

"As we have seen, there are no rings of kidney thieves, no mutant organisms masquerading as chickens, no flesh eating bacteria on bananas." There was a note of frustrated insistence in Miller's voice. He could sense the resistance. "And yet these idiotic tales persist. They cannot be killed. I mean, get a clue, people. Wanting a story to be true because you like it does not make it true."

"But don't most people believe what they want to believe?" David asked.

"Yes, and that's just the problem. Too many people want to believe some pleasing delusion and reject the conclusions of reason. Of course, most people don't even know what the conclusions of reason are because they don't think well enough to reach any rational conclusions. Most people, I would say, do not think much at all." Miller stopped the train before it ran off the bridge. He did not want to alienate his students by implying that they were all idiots. "I hope that this class will help you all to learn a little about thinking," he added in a calmer tone. "Once you begin to examine claims and evidence and begin to challenge the information that's thrown at you, you will begin to develop discernment, judgment." Miller wrote *discernment* on the board and circled it twice.

During the course of the lecture, Miller had also jotted on the board the Web addresses of several sites that analyze and expose urban legends. He motioned to these jottings once more and encouraged the students to "check these out."

"Look up your favorite legend and see what has been said about it. What does the actual research, the facts, the investigation reveal?"

"Is this a homework assignment?" someone asked.

"Do we need to turn something in?" asked another.

"No," said Miller, now aware that virtually no one would look at any of the sites he had written down. "Your homework, in addition to the reading in the next chapter, is to write a 500-to-750-word essay on the value of reason in your own life." Groans, expressions of surprise and dismay, and a "What?" or two bounced around the classroom. Even near the end of the hour, most of the students were suddenly paying attention.

"Say that again?"

"When is it due?"

"How many pages is 500 words?"

The questions arrived in a gang, muscling into each other.

"The essay is due a week from Monday," Miller said over the minor din. "Typewritten—or rather, printed out—double-spaced. And please, people, put your name and a title on it." Then he remembered that most in the class were sophomores. "And take your draft to the Writing Center and have them look at it. Don't give me a piece of trash. Fix the spelling and grammar, and spend more than twenty minutes writing it."

There were more questions, such as "What was the topic again?" and the like. The class broke up, and a dozen students began to make their way to the front for further clarification. The rest headed for the exits.

"Oh," Miller said. "Gina Roper, I need to see you." Gina included herself in the group heading toward the front.

Professor Miller answered the questions as clearly and patiently as he could, even though he felt some exasperation at times. A few students seemed to imply that such a paper would be impossible to write because they personally had no role for reason in their lives, viewing it as thought control. One, a budding postmodernist, said that reason was merely the political construct of an oppressive power structure, thus making the assignment an act of oppression. Besides, the student said, writing about the supposed role of reason would be merely a subjective exercise that could not be graded. The implication seemed to be that the student was fishing for a guaranteed A on whatever he turned in. Gina waited patiently though these discussions. Miller glanced over at her once or twice to be sure she was still there. She smiled when he did so.

At last the other students left, some feeling clearer about the assignment and some not. But at least they all left.

"Ah, yes, Gina," Miller said at last, relaxing. Gina was a friendly, warm, attractive, seemingly open hearted girl. His first impressions of her had been well reinforced. He liked her. He thought she might like him, too, but he knew he had to be cautious. He had known many women students who were warm and friendly during a course, sometimes even affectionate, and then after the term was over, they acted as if they could not even remember who he was. Those, he believed, must be hoping for a sympathy grade. He wondered if Gina were different.

"Gina," he said, "I've just checked the new roster and you are still not listed. You did enroll, didn't you?"

"Oh, yeah. I'm just having trouble with the business office. Financial aid and how much I owe and all that. They won't let me register officially until I come across with the cash or the right paperwork. Don't worry; it'll all work out."

"Is there anything I can do?" Miller asked. He thought doing her a little favor might help him get closer to her.

"Nope. No worries. I've got it all under control."

"Okay," Miller said, a little disappointed.

"But that was really nice of you to ask me. You're a very nice man. Handsome, too."

There is a saying that words too foolish to be spoken are turned into lyrics and sung. So too, compliments too saccharine or cheesy to be uttered by ordinary people are put into the mouths of beautiful young women, where the sentiments are accepted at face value. Miller was flattered. Worse, he was encouraged to water and fertilize a budding scheme that had even now been planted in his mind.

Gina and Professor Miller remained talking in the room for some time, even after the important and useful topics were exhausted.

"I like this topic," Markayla said to Amy as they left the building. "Reason is the cornerstone of the law. It is one of the principles of life, as well."

"Yeah. I can use examples from my dad and how he taught me to think as a little kid. Remember that saying of his, 'Our lives are told by our receipts'? Maybe I can work that in as an example of how reason helps us draw conclusions from evidence. If we think about it, that is, reason about it, everything we do tells a story. A story about us."

"So, then, reason can tell us about ourselves? Hence, the value of reason for us? Brilliant, Amy."

"Thanks. Or I might do something else. I don't know yet. What about you?"

"Perhaps I will bring in my desire to be a lawyer. The ability to reason is important there."

"Just as it is everywhere."

"Of course. 'Come, let us reason together, says the Lord.'"

"Better not quote that to Miller. I don't think he would appreciate it."

The two roommates, along with a few other students from the class, began their stroll down the concrete sidewalks, past the trees planted in the great lawns of the school, and toward the Cave, where they were getting into the habit of relaxing after each meeting of the critical thinking class. Today, however, Amy and Markayla did not go with the others to the coffee house. Markayla had decided that paying for the liquid advertised as coffee was an injustice. She would rather make her own coffee in her room or go off campus to a nearby coffee house that brewed something more to her liking.

The rest of the regulars went to the Cave not so much for the coffee as for the interaction. Especially today, they wanted to talk over the assignment for Miller's class, to get ideas they might use. Thus, for awhile, the subject around the table after class was the paper.

"Miller seems to think reason is the be-all and end-all of existence."

"I'll bet he's really into horror films."

"Or slasher films."

"Yeah. He likes showing those film clips of people panicking."

"I wonder how reasonable he'd be during a tornado or an earthquake."

"Well, I think he's right that reason is important."

"Personally, I think reason is overrated. Most people decide what they want to do first and then cook up some reasons to make it look respectable."

"You're supposed to reason from evidence to conclusion."

"Yeah, but who does that? Don't most people decide on something first and then prop the decision up with a few *ex post facto* reasons?"

"But that would be thinking backwards."

"I didn't say it was right. I'm just saying that most of us can make anything seem reasonable if we want to."

"That's rationalization, not reasoning."

"There's no difference anymore."

"Professor Fulks says that the whole idea of reason is a leftover of the Eurocentric power structure which has been rejected by the postmodern world. Reason denies power and value to those cultures that don't use it."

"And Professor Linkrodt says that reason oppresses women."

"Oh, come on."

"What do you mean, 'Oh, come on'? You can't just dismiss important ideas."

"No, we should reason about them, and then dismiss them."

"Oh, ha ha."

After awhile, the discussion turned to miscellaneous subjects. A popular subject for discussion among the students was whoever was not there at the time. Because only a few of the students in class were at the coffee shop, there were many possible topics.

"Did you see Gina today? Where did she get that outfit?"

"I thought she looked great." David Simmons was on the edge of the group of girls who dominated most of the conversation. He had to jump in quickly.

"Well, a guy would. She was dressed totally tacky."

"I don't know. David has a point. I thought she was kind of stylish. She's got great assets and doesn't mind showing them off. What's wrong with that?"

"She sits on the front row. I'll bet Miller gets an eye full."

"She advertises too much."

"Yeah, well advertising works. I saw her talking to Jeremy Schneider the other day. He can have any girl on campus, but she got his attention."

"No wonder Miller noticed."

"You don't have to guess where she's going to hide her crib notes."

"She does show off a lot of hardware," David said.

"Hey, it's her life. You guys are just jealous."

"She's just practicing some rational grade enhancement techniques. Everybody knows Miller likes the cute, flirty ones. Maybe he'll give her a good grade."

"Are you saying he grades on the curves?"

"Oh, that was bad. I thought puns that bad were illegal now."

"Going back to the reason thing. How can we say Gina isn't being reasonable if what she does helps her grade? I mean, that seems totally logical."

"But that kind of thinking would justify anything. Why doesn't she sleep with him for an A? Why don't you?"

"From what I hear, you wouldn't be the first."

"Yeah, like, 'Hey, Dr. Miller, let's go back to your place and be reasonable about my grade.'"

"Shut up, you guys."

As the only child of a Houston police detective, Amy had been taken under her father's wing at a young age and shown how to think about the world. For her, it seemed to be a given that to open your eyes on the world is to look for meaning. Her father taught her that everything speaks not only of itself but of something else, something larger, more important, often more beautiful. The world, he had said, is filled with clues, signifiers of events, purposes, truths.

When she was still a little girl, he would point to something and ask her about it. He would pick up some grass clippings from the driveway and ask, "What do you think this is? Where could it have come from? The sky? How often do you see it? Do you see it before or after daddy mows the lawn? Where did daddy put the grass after he mowed the lawn?" At first, the little girl said she did not know; then she made something up. At last, she had seen her father empty the lawnmower, spilling a little grass on the driveway as he removed the mower bag, so she discovered the answer. Later, when he asked other questions she began trying to guess. But there were always more clues and more questions.

Eventually she began to analyze and infer fairly well. About this time, her father began asking for at least two possible explanations for the things he pointed out. "Why do you think that field caught on fire? What is the most reasonable explanation? Can you think of another? We need at least two different explanations so we can choose the better one." He continued this informal training until Amy rebelled in junior high school. Detective Herbert had just gotten to the point where Amy was asked to generate questions ("What do we need to know in order to answer this question?") when the adolescent rebellion set in and she no longer cared about her father's lessons.

"No teenybopper cares where a trail of slime on the sidewalk came from," she had told Markayla last year while remembering these events.

By her second year in high school, Amy had recovered her sanity to a sufficient degree to become interested once again in her father's instruction and even more, in his work. He took her down to his office to show her his work habitat. On the wall was a framed photograph of the *Titanic*. Underneath the ship was the caption, "RMS *Titanic*, photographed April 16, 1912." He asked Amy what she thought of the photograph.

"Grainy," she said. "And it looks old."

"Okay. Now suppose we add some background information to your observational knowledge. The *Titanic* sank on April 15, 1912. Now what do you think?"

"There's something wrong. The caption says April 16. Is that a typo?"

"Suppose it isn't."

"Well, that can't be. You said the ship sank the day before."

"That's right. And do you know that very few people have ever remarked that this photograph is impossible?"

"Maybe they don't know when it sank."

"That's probably right. The more you know, the better you can see. A little knowledge and a little thought are all it takes to see through many deceits. But you have to want to get the knowledge. More people ask whether the photograph is a valuable antique than ask if it is a fake."

"It looks real."

"That's just the point. The statement is a lie. And yet the photograph makes it seem true and real. You quite literally cannot always believe your eyes, at least not until your eyes are educated. And just trying to reason about it won't be enough."

Amy knew her father was trying to make the point, as subtly as he knew how, that she needed to get more education. She had wavered for awhile about going to college, and he was on a campaign to persuade her to go. He had never said that he wanted her to follow in his footsteps in detective work, but she sometimes thought that the idea lurked somewhere in the back of his comments.

During this time also, Amy began to ask her father about cases he had worked on. This curiosity fit in well when she and Markayla went away to the university, because it provided a topic of conversation for her and her father. Detective Herbert was generally a man of few words when the subject was chit chat. Even in a world of email and live chat, he preferred regular telephone conversations with his daughter. He wanted to hear her voice, hear her laugh, and discern her feelings. At first, the conversations had been somewhat awkward. After the hello and how are you, the discussion would stall unless Amy did the talking. She discovered that if she wanted to hear her father talk, she had to ask him questions. But questions about himself were always answered briefly.

"Hi, daddy."

"Hi, Seepy." Seepy was Amy's nickname from her toddlerhood, when she commonly told her father, "Daddy, I'm seepy," meaning *sleepy*.

"How are you?"

"Fine."

"Um, how's mom?"

"Oh, she's fine, too."

As a result, Amy developed a routine for their weekly telephone conversations. She always asked the "How are you?" questions, of course, and if she had news of her own to deliver, would do that also. Then, to hear her father talk, she always asked, "Catch any crooks today?" This was his cue to tell her about an arrest, or more commonly, an ongoing investigation. Get a man to talk about his work or what he knows well, and you can have a real conversation. Ask him how he feels, and he will say, "Fine," even if he has to wince through the pain to do so.

This evening, when Amy asked her father if he had caught any crooks that day, he said, "Actually, yes."

"Tell me all about it. And don't leave out the details."

"Well, we've got a case downtown where a guy has stolen the identity of another guy and is using the guy's credit cards. Most of the fraudulent purchases have been made by mail order or over the phone, so our trail is pretty thin."

"Didn't the guy cancel his cards?"

"Well, sure, but the charges were made in a short period. But, as you say, the guy canceled his cards, and it turned out to be just before the crook charged a suit at Goldfarb's. So the cashier got a confiscate message for the card and took it from the guy."

"And so she arrested him?"

"No. In fact, she just let him leave. Store employees are not supposed to play cops and robbers. They don't want to wake up dead the next morning."

"What about store security?"

"Security arrived after the guy had flown. Mall security was called, but he was gone."

"Did the cashier give a description?"

"No. She said she couldn't remember what the guy looked like, other than to say that he was average height, average build, average looks, average everything. It's the average folks that can get away with anything."

"Oh, really?" Amy had always felt of herself as pretty average, sometimes more depressingly than others, so this comment interested her.

"And the real piece of bad luck was that there was no security video of the checkout process. We're still looking into that, but either the camera was broken, not aimed right, or the video got lost or erased. We heard several excuses."

"So do you think someone in the store is in on the crime? An inside job?"

"No. In fact, the security people have been more than helpful. They said, 'Gosh, we've got sixteen other tapes that worked. Why not look at those and see if you can find anything?" A pause.

"Daddy."

"What?"

"Did you find anything?"

"Okay, so we watched a lot of hours of boring security video. You wouldn't believe how many couples kiss in stores.

We also found a couple of shoplifters doing that, by the way. So, we eliminated everyone of the wrong gender and age and race and focused on average guys who had been in the store within an hour of the attempted fraud. There were only three who came close to fitting the description. We chose one and traced him from camera to camera. Are you on the edge of your seat yet?"

"Daddy, unless you caught the guy, your job sounds really boring."

"Thanks, Seepy. Well, the security video showed Mr. Likely walking through the store, browsing, looking at the merchandise. He examined some coats, then some art prints, then some housewares. Then Folio stopped the tape and said, 'He picked up the vase.'"

"Who's Folio?"

"John Folio. He just left Homicide like me and has now joined me in Fraud."

"Go on."

"So anyway, he said, 'He picked up the vase,' and we looked at him and he said, 'Barehanded.'"

"Which means?"

"His fingerprints would be on the vase."

"Ooh, cool."

"So we printed off the screen image to help us locate the merchandise, went onto the retail floor and did a little comparison. We found the vase section. There were only five that looked like the one he picked up. We dusted them all and got a whole lotta prints." He stopped talking.

"And. Daddy. And." Amy knew he was tweaking her.

"Oh. Well, we matched a thumb and index from the vase to the thumb and index on the credit card."

"So you caught him?"

"Not quite. But now we know what he looks like. We have a photograph of his face and we can estimate height and weight from the video. We'll get him."

"That's neat. And the moral of the story is?" Amy knew her father would give her an application, either in the form of a proverb or a general comment. She was betting on a proverb, perhaps one of his own, because she knew how much he loved them. But tonight she got both proverb and commentary.

"Well, the point is that everything we do leaves evidence. Without our knowing it, we leave a trail of artifacts behind us, generated by our activities. That's what forensic evidence really is. As the Chinese say, 'The only way to keep something secret is not to do it.'"

Chapter 5

During her freshman year at the university, Amy had gotten a job at a furniture store, where she quickly moved from sales ("I'm just not a salesman") to customer service ("All these angry people with returns just stress me out") to furniture assembly. The store included a large warehouse stocked with assemble-it-yourself tables, bookshelves, desks, and the like. Many customers liked the look of the furniture, but they also wanted it put together for them, so the store offered to assemble their purchase for an additional fee. Amy possessed some mechanical knowledge, courtesy of helping her father work on his lawnmower and build a patio deck, so when the opportunity arose because of a Christmas backlog, she begged to be put on assembly. The other person working on assembly was Matt Prager, the fellow student whom, even after a year, Amy still refused to call her boyfriend, but who nevertheless had become, over the course of that time, her principal interest among those of the other gender.

Their usual work during their hours at the store was to sit on a cold concrete floor and put together the furniture designed for assembly at home: the kind that is completely precut and predrilled. All that is needed is to drive in the screws or tighten the bolts. The pair quickly got into the routine of trading off tasks. First, one would hold the parts while the other used the drill driver or wrench, and then they would switch. Even though they put together many of the very same units ("Not another 407? Who likes this stuff?"), the hours passed quickly because each made the task fun for the other.

Matt liked Amy because she was a good, cheerful helper who seldom complained and who did not blame him for any mishaps, such as a misdriven screw or a pinched finger. How pleasantly surprised he was the first time he accidentally pushed two pieces together before her fingers could quite let go of the end. As she shook her hand in pain, she had responded to his apology by saying, "Hey, no problem. It was an accident. I'll live. Relax."

Not only was she not fussy about getting dirty, working in a dusty warehouse-like environment with sometimes oily fasteners, but she once showed her creativity by offering her hand as scratch paper for Matt to write a phone number on when he had called directory assistance. Cupping her yielded hand in his like a pad of paper, writing on it, smudging out a couple of erroneous digits, and rewriting the correct ones made quite an impression on him. Matt also liked the fact that Amy laughed at his jokes. Shy people are often forced into some kind of performance to get beyond their own enclosed personalities, and Matt's method was humor. Finding someone who laughed at his attempts was a treasure. And I will not even mention how Matt felt those times when, after he had figured out how to fit a particularly troublesome piece or showed her a shortcut to lining up some parts, Amy told him, "You're so smart."

Amy liked Matt because he was a funny guy. As their relationship developed and they began to tease each other (said to be the test or proof of a growing relationship), Matt's teasing was always gentle and kind. Amy also appreciated Matt's allowing her to her help with all of the assembly tasks. Even though her main motivation for moving to assembly was to flee customer service and the hysterically angry people who demanded refunds *and* apologies for the furniture they themselves had clumsily broken, she still wanted to participate meaningfully. Her initial fear when she first started was that she would be little more than a ten-fingered vise, holding the parts while Matt drove in the fasteners. She found instead a full partner, who let her do at least half of the fitting, driving and tightening, and even the occasional drilling. When the instructions for a new item were too terrible to figure out easily, they both puzzled through the assembly steps and agreed on the best method. And, although Matt was shy, he was not insecure as a man, so he never needed to make deprecating or qualifying comments related to Amy's gender: "You do a good job, for a girl," or "You hold a wrench just like a girl." It was a small thing for Amy, but she liked it.

Their relationship would have developed a lot more rapidly had they not both been introverted and cautious people. Nevertheless, by the end of their freshman year, they were relaxed and talkative enough and had been dating (though Amy would probably not have used the term) for quite some time. Amy enjoyed getting off campus and eating dinner at an inexpensive coffee shop with Matt. Just getting away from campus was a psychological relief. Getting away from the dining commons was a digestive relief, and an aid in combating the "freshman ten"—the tendency for women freshmen to gain ten pounds during the year because of the starchy, fatty cuisine. And, of course, the companionship was the principal joy in the outings. For a girl who had never thought of herself as being special in any way, and whose four years before college might be summed up as "not popular in high school," being treated special by Matt was highly flattering.

No doubt there were thoughts trying to get into her mind that she would not allow herself to think.

They had summered apart, but between email, the phone, and snail mail, they had kept in good communication and maintained their relationship. When they saw each other again for the first time at the beginning of the new year, they immediately felt like old hands in familiar gloves.

By this point in the term, it was as if they had never been apart.

Those who do not believe in serendipity have never been students on an enormous university campus, where probability seems to be regularly defied by the frequent chance meeting of friends. Thus it was that Matt and Amy crossed paths one afternoon in the middle of campus, along a pathway through the grass and eucalyptus trees.

"Hey, Aim-o."

"Hi, Matt. What's happening?"

"I was just thinking about you."

"Oh, right. Are you sure you weren't thinking about a new wrench set or a floor jack?"

"No. I think about you all the time."

"Uh huh." Matt knew that her tone of dismissive skepticism was fake.

"Hey, nice shoes," he said, changing the subject and trying to sound sincere.

"Oh, that's great. Well delivered, too. Now tell me I have nice hair and ask me if I've lost weight."

"Huh?"

"Aren't those the next lines in the book?" She was smiling at him archly.

"What book? Amy, sometimes I just don't understand you." Matt wrinkled his brow.

"It's because women are mysterious and complicated." Amy closed her eyes and tilted her head upwards, as if revealing an aura of sophistication.

"Yeah, and some of them are sane, too."

"Be careful, buster," she said, pointing a finger at him and making a face. "You're treading on very thin ice."

"So where you off to?"

"Back to my room. What about you?" In an instant, they had fallen into their familiar tones.

"Got to go to town to get a part for my car."

"Need any help?" Amy brightened suddenly. Matt knew from the action of her eyebrows that she wanted to go, too.

"No, no, I think I can do it by myself."

"Well, do you know anybody who might want to go with you, just for the companionship?"

"Hmm. Well, maybe, but she's not here right now."

Amy growled and tried to look angry. "Might there be just a speck of kindness and politeness in your otherwise evil heart that would make you look around and see that there might be someone who needs to go into town to get some popcorn of the type she always shares with you and who you could offer a ride to?"

"That's what I like about you, Amy. You're so subtle. So, then, would you like to go to town with me to buy a vacuum booster for my car?"

"Oh." Amy acted as if she had been caught off guard. "Um, well, I'm pretty busy right now. But I guess I could go, if you really insist."

"Don't change your major to theater," Matt said. He was paid for his generous advice by a punch in the arm. He let his arm hang limp and swung it back and forth as if Amy had broken the bone.

"Ooh," he moaned. "At least I still have one good arm."

"You're supposed to be encouraging the hesitant lady," Amy said.

"Well," Matt said, "I might encourage you, but every journey has an uncertain ending. Traveling to a strange city is always risky. And, since, as you say, you're so busy, I really don't want to put you out. I can just go by myself."

"Maybe I'm the type of person who secretly likes to take risks and go on dangerous journeys. I've always thought riding in your car involved both of those."

Now Amy was cutting close to home. Matt's tone became half serious. "If you insult Bertha, she may not run."

"If I breathe too hard, she may not run. On the other hand, if I blow on the windshield, we may get there faster."

"For a nice girl, you sure have a big streak of wickedness and cruelty in you."

"Thanks," Amy said, as if he had complimented her.

"You ready?"

"I want to change shoes first. And do you mind if I ask Markayla if she wants to go?"

"Naw. Beautiful women are always welcome in the Bertmobile. And do change those shoes," he added, holding his hand to his cheek as if making a fashion comment.

"But you just told me they were nice. Hypocrite. Where's your car?"

"Southeast corner of R6."

"Matt, you know I don't know directions."

"Near the big, crooked tree near the monument sign at the entrance of Campbell Way. I'm in about the third row. Just walk into R6 and head toward the monument sign at the end of the street."

"Okay." It was a warm and happy "okay" with a warmer look. The bounce in her walk told Matt that she was happy.

When Amy returned to her room, Shelley was there talking to Markayla. Tina was reading at her desk.

"Matt and I are going into town to get some stuff. Anybody want to go?" Amy plopped herself on the bed and began to change her "school shoes" for a pair of athletic shoes.

"I'll chaperone you two," Shelley said.

"I'd like to go," Tina said, standing up and walking toward them. "If it's safe."

"Well, good," said Amy. "And it is safe. Matt won't lead us astray."

"Good," said Shelley. "I've been to Astray and it wasn't all that great. Oh, sure, big town, bright lights, lots of noise, but the food wasn't what I expected and it was way too expensive." She seemed almost serious.

"You children go," said Markayla. "And I shall take advantage of some peace and quiet to do some work. Forget that you are at the university to learn something, in hopes of passing your courses and gaining a degree. Go, indulge yourselves in conspicuous consumption and forget the burdens of scholarship. I realize that the true purpose of America is to convert finite natural resources into disposable items of passing indulgence. Landfills must not remain empty." Amy wondered if Markayla was being serious. It was difficult to tell. Perhaps she had just been around Shelley too much, or maybe she was echoing something she had read for one of her business courses.

"Goodbye, mother," said Shelley, picking up on the reference to children. "If the snow isn't too deep, we'll make it through the pass. We promise to write, if we don't end up eating each other." As they walked down the landing, Shelley turned and yelled back at Markayla, "Or if there's an Internet connection in the New Country, we'll email!"

Matt was surprised but secretly glad to have the three girls join him. Those who might be hesitant to seek the company of others are often glad when it is brought to them.

"I hope you don't mind driving all of us to the store," Amy said.

"Well," Matt said, "I did have to cancel the babes to make room for you guys."

"You wish," Amy said.

"We're your reality," said Shelley. "And you can't escape it. However, an automobile filled with attractive women can't be all bad for a guy like you."

"What do you mean, a guy *like me*?" Matt asked.

"Don't ask her," said Amy.

"I need a radio," Tina said, to no one in particular.

"Where's Markayla?"

"She thinks she's come to school to study. We left her with her nose in a book." Amy said.

"What is she thinking?" Shelley asked rhetorically.

"Why would she put her nose in a book?" Matt asked. "It seemed okay where it was on her face." One of Matt's methods of humor was to pretend to misunderstand English, whether a metaphor or a literal expression. He especially liked to do this with road signs. A sign reading, "Speed

Checked by Radar," would be commented on with "Boy, Officer Radar seems to be everywhere. And why do they have to tell you that he's the one checking your speed?" Or he might say, "Slow Children Ahead? Do they have to advertise the fact that their kids aren't very bright? That seems cruel." It was a simple kind of humor, which often received groans. Shelley was a little more direct.

"Wow," she said. "With some butter and salt, we could have corn on the cob."

"Just drive," Amy told him.

The fifteen-year-old car was in reasonable shape from the now almost constant attention of Matt, who had become quite adept at problem solving the car's geriatric issues. However, as with most things so old, there remained a considerable amount of deferred maintenance, as it is sometimes called, including the suspension, which is expensive to repair. As a result, the car wiggled and bounded over the speed bumps in the parking lot, leaving its passengers rather unconfident that this squishy vehicle would continue to hold together. A few visible rust spots showing through the paint lent support to any negative conclusions the girls wanted to form.

When the car came to a stop at the edge of the parking lot, a hissing sound followed by a klunk came from under the hood when Matt applied the brakes. He had to press hard on the pedal to stop the car.

"What's wrong? Don't the brakes work?" Shelley asked.

"They sort of work. That's why I need to get to town, to get a part for the brakes. The power booster has gone out. I told you that."

"We're not going to get stalled on a railroad track and be hit by a train, are we?"

"Don't be paranoid. When the booster fails, you don't usually lose the brakes."

"Don't use the word *usually.*"

At the next stop sign, Shelley, who was sitting in the back seat directly behind Matt, grabbed his shoulders. "We're going over the cliff! Drop the oxygen masks. Inflate the boats, get the parachutes ready, not to mention a pillow."

"Shelley," said Matt, "has anyone ever told you you're crazy?"

"Matthew," said Amy, "don't." She was thinking of Tina and of Shelley's comment earlier about crazy people living in her room. Tina did not seem to be crazy, but Amy was afraid that such comments might be offensive. Matt knew that whenever Amy called him Matthew, she was being serious and he should restrain himself, even if he did not know why. So he let the subject drop.

Soon they stopped at the store. Matt announced that he was going to the hardware department to look at tools, so Amy said she would look at munchies and meet back at the checkout. Shelley headed for cosmetics. Tina attached herself to Amy and they went over to the snack department and looked at potato chips, peanuts, double-fudge cookies, marshmallow center oatmeal cookies, and candy bars. Amy looked at the nutrition label on a few of the items, sighed, and put them back.

"Look at this," she said. "Forty-three grams of fat per serving. And this tiny box has six servings."

She finally chose a package of microwave popcorn, the one with the label, "Half the fat. All the taste." Amy picked up a few other necessary items like cotton balls and a bottle of nail polish remover. Tina wanted to go to the electronics department, so they went on over.

"What do you need here?" Amy asked.

"I need a new radio."

"Doesn't your clock radio still work?" Amy asked.

"It doesn't get the right frequencies," Tina said.

Tina glanced over the display of radios and then began to pick up each of the boxes, turning each one over. She appeared to be looking at the barcode of each item.

"The price isn't on the barcode," Amy said. "It's on the shelf."

"How much is this one?"

"Nineteen ninety five."

Tina continued to pick up the boxes and look at the barcode of each radio. Finally she selected one to her liking. "This is a good one," she said.

After just a few minutes Shelley found Matt in the automotive department next to hardware. She had a bottle of shampoo and some pain pills and was finished with her shopping. Rather than browse the clothing, she decided to see what Matt was up to. He was looking at the spray lubricants.

Matt had a can of something in his hand.

"Hi there, Matt. Whatcha doing?" Shelley had lively eyes and an engaging smile that made her instantly likeable. She seemed to like others the minute she met them, which encouraged them to liker her, too.

Matt turned and nodded a greeting to Shelley and then said, motioning with the can, "Now this is serious stuff. 'Ultra Tech, Super Penetrant, Xtreme Duty Spray Lubricant.' Now we're talking heavy hitting. No more kiddie lube for us. We're bringing out the big guns now. I mean, this is probably the stuff used by sweaty men with veins popping out of their arms. This baby will make fly paper slide across a bed of nails." Then he turned to Shelley, who was reading him, checking her boloney gauge to determine how serious he was. "Think I should get it?" he asked. All he needed was permission.

"Definitely," Shelley said.

"Amy would say I have enough oil."

"But do you have a can of this fabulous product?"

"No. And it does sound so good."

"It does sound so good." Shelley wanted to grab Matt's arms and make a comment about his strength, but her hands were full, so she just leaned her head up against his shoulder, looked up at him and batted her eyelashes playfully. "And you know how women like big, strong men who use macho tools," she said in a soft, alluring voice. Then, with a bit of a frown and a tone of mild displeasure, she added, "Though we can do without the sweaty part."

"So, then, you think I should get this?" Matt asked, staying focused. "After all, it's only a couple of dollars."

"Well, then you absolutely must get it." Shelley now realized that she could pile her purchases into her arm and hold them against her chest, freeing the other hand. She did this and took the can of lubricant from Matt, examining the label as if she were critically evaluating the product. "Yes," she said, handing the can back to him, "that looks like great stuff."

"Done," Matt said, putting his arm around Shelley and giving her a little sideways hug with the arm whose hand still held the can. "Thanks." She smiled up at him, then winked.

In the store's security booth, a man in a khaki uniform with the sewn nametag *Morty* on the pocket sat behind a bank of video monitors. He was watching Section C, Aisle 6, where he had just seen a smiling young woman come up to a young man and, after a few moments, lean her head against him and then receive a hug. "I wish I knew girls like that," he said aloud, though he was alone in the room. "I wonder what that is he's buying."

Shelley liked Matt because he seemed to be a lot like Ron, her boyfriend. Friendly, respectful, someone you could trust and be friends with. And with only minor flaws. While with some guys the tendency to overindulge a weakness can be either self-destructive or harmful to others, Matt and Ron's self-indulgence tended to be in the areas of too many tools, too many books, and too many music CD's. Ron's (and, she would discover, Matt's) lack of housekeeping skills she did not consider a flaw because, first, she had low expectations of the ability of males to keep rooms clean, and second, she herself was no neat freak.

Matt did have one weakness he did not have in common with Ron. Matt was a snacker. On the way back to the check-out, Matt and Shelley stopped by the snack food aisle, where Matt picked up an almost shocking number of bags of potato chips, corn chips, tortilla chips, and popcorn, together with a few cans of peanuts and almonds and shelled sunflower seeds. Shelley shook her head, thinking, "Why can guys eat like horses, and eat all the worst food, and not gain an ounce, and girls can eat one tasteless cracker and gain five pounds?" She quietly gritted her teeth and scowled in a direction seen only by the security cameras. Fortunately for the endurance of his fantasies, Morty was not watching that particular monitor at the time.

The four students joined up at the checkout line. The line was not long, only half a dozen people, but every transaction seemed to take forever. First a price check on an item with no price tag, then some sort of confusion over a maxed-out credit card. Another customer waited to pull out her checkbook until the checker was completely finished. Everyone waited while she filled in all the information, asking for the date and the name of the store. The customer just in front of them objected to the scanned price of an item, claiming that the posted price was much less. Another wait for a price check. Then an argument when the price came back as scanned. Finally a huffy, "Then I don't want it," and an end to the transaction.

While Tina was paying for her radio, Shelley looked over the items on the impulse rack. She chose a pack of gum and then picked up a box of bandages.

"You know," she said, holding up the box, "I do need a new bathing suit."

"Just pretend you don't hear her," Amy said to Matt.

While Shelley watched Matt's many bags of chips and cans of nuts go across the scanner, Amy thought that Matt was paying a little too much attention to the checker, an attractive enough college-age girl with a ponytail. When they all got outside, Amy stopped him. Pulling out a tissue, she said, "Just a minute, Matt. Let me wipe the drool off your collar."

"What?"

"I saw how you eyed that girl," Amy said, wiping his collar with the tissue, just as if there really had been drool on it.

"What girl?"

"Oh, and here's some on your mouth. It's making your tongue slip," she said, wiping his mouth lovingly. "There we go, all better."

Matt just shook his head.

"Did you see all the security cameras in there?" Matt asked, to change the subject.

"Where?" Shelley asked.

"The dark brown domes. I counted thirty-six of them from the checkout line. The whole store must have fifty or a hundred."

"Wow," Shelley said. "They really are watching us."

"Yeah, there are cameras everywhere now," Matt added. "They say that eventually we'll all end up being shown naked on the Internet."

"Oh, Matt," Amy protested. "Don't say that."

"What's that?" Tina asked, not very clearly. She looked troubled, worried.

"Matt is just kidding," Amy said to Tina. Then she looked at Matt before he could reply.

"That settles it," Shelley said. "I'm never taking my makeup off."

As they approached the car, Shelley eyed it with mock derision and then said, "Do you really expect me to enter this rolling death trap, risking life and limb in a creaking junk heap driven by a careless and immature college student?" The reference to the immature college student bounced off

Matt without a crease, but he was almost hurt by the insult to his car.

"It's not a junk heap," he said, just a little defensively. "These are my wheels. They work fine." A particularly astute interpreter might have detected a tone of affection in his voice. Then he added, in a lower tone, perhaps so that his car could not hear, "Someday I'll have a much cooler car." He would never say, "Someday I'll have a cool car," because that would imply that his current car was not cool. How we are too often blinded by love, even for our possessions, even for our modest and creaking possessions. They are familiar, and they are ours, and we love them.

"So it's either ride in this thing or hitch a ride with a parolee on a motorcycle," Shelley said, acting as if she were weighing the decision.

"No," Matt said, knowing that Ron rode a motorcycle, "your boyfriend is nowhere near here."

"Well, then, I guess you've forced my hand."

Amy and Tina thought the drama was over, so they began to move toward the car, when Shelley threw herself against the side, stretching out her arms as far as possible toward the front and rear and shouted, "It's too late for me, but you can still save yourselves."

"You know, Shelley," Amy said, "there are lots of sugar-free soft drinks on the market."

"So you don't think it's the quadruple espresso mocha, after all?" Shelley asked. Then, turning to Tina, she said, "What do you think, Tina?"

"I like juice," Tina said.

The girls climbed into the car while Matt put his four plastic T-shirt bags full of chips and nuts into the trunk. Then he got in and started the engine.

"By the way, Matt," Amy said, "don't think I didn't see that can of spray oil you bought."

"Shelley made me buy it."

"It's true," Shelley said, chivalrously taking the blame.

"Do you know how many cans of spray oil Matt owns?"

"I'm sure he needs them all." Shelley's tone was not sarcastic.

"He must have ten cans," Amy said with emphasis. Matt smiled to himself because she had guessed low.

"Must be farmer DNA," Shelley said.

"Give me a can of oil, a roll of duct tape, a few feet of bailing wire, and a pair of water pump pliers and I can fix anything," Matt said, almost seriously.

"Don't forget the chewing gum," Amy said.

Amy remembered the day Matt first came over to her room, not long after they had met at the furniture store and warehouse. He had scarcely said hello before he commented on the poor condition of her door lock and the hinges. He had asked if she had any oil in her room. She did not. Next time he came, he had a can of spray lubricant with him. He disassembled the door lock, cleaned out some dirt and grease, oiled it and put it back together. He mumbled something about ideally removing the hinge pins as he sprayed the hinges and wiped off the excess before it could drip onto the carpet.

Amy was amazed at how easily the door swung and the lock opened and closed. Not just the ease of turning the deadbolt, but the latch itself now closed so easily that the door could be pushed gently and it would close completely on its own. Before, it had always been necessary to turn the door knob to retract the latch and then hold the door while closing it. Otherwise, the latch would bang against the striker plate and the door would just sit there, still cracked open.

Matt oiled the bathroom door latch and hinges also, and now the door swung halfway closed on its own, being just a little off level. It was no longer stiff enough to stay all the way open when it was pushed. That was a mixed blessing, but at least it no longer creaked at night when someone entered the bathroom.

When Matt offered to let Amy keep the can of lubricant, she had refused at first, not wanting to deprive him of his own. However, she soon learned that he owned several—no, many—other cans, of every brand and kind. Machine oil, penetrating lubricant, moisture repellant, aerosol grease, liquid graphite, spray Teflon. Many cans used words like *miracle, super, ultra, tech*, and, of course, *multi-purpose*. He already had a lifetime supply of these cans, but whenever he visited an auto parts, hardware, or discount department store, he always checked to see if there was a type or brand he did not yet own. If so, it was almost imperative to obtain, possess, and use it.

The next stop was the auto parts store, where Matt assured the girls he would not spend a lot of time browsing. Had he been alone, the visit to the store would have taken perhaps an hour. However, with his cargo of young women waiting for him, he knew he should be brief. He did take the time to walk down the aisle with the specialty wheels—some chrome, some aluminum, some magnesium—where, if the truth were known, he was even more likely to drool. He even asked the price of a new radiator, knowing that it was only a matter of time (and possibly not very much time) before his was called to the great radiator home in the sky. Or, rather, the dump. He was soon back with the new vacuum booster in a box, together with a piece of connecting hose.

Shelley looked at the box as Matt carried it past the car on his way to put it in the trunk. She put her head out the window, both hands on the door, as if she might be ready to climb out. "This car needs a part that big?" she asked, with a wild look. The box was about a foot square. "Tina, do you think we'll make it home alive?"

Tina appeared to be lost in thought. After a few seconds she said, "What? Oh, oh, yes, let's go home now."

"So, when are you going to fix your car?" Amy asked, as they headed toward the university.

"Ron and I are going to get together Friday afternoon, I think."

Amy gave a little pout, but kept it hidden by turning her face toward the window.

"Ah, Ron, that dreamy man," Shelley said. "But it seems like I hardly ever see him. There's always something keeping us apart. You and Matt, on the other hand, are lucky that you are always able to get together. Nothing ever seems to keep you and Matt apart."

"Actually, there are several things," Amy said.

"Like what?"

"Oh, a buffet, a bag of potato chips, a car show, a basketball or football game on TV, any lock, hinge, or motor that hasn't been oiled—or a car that needs to be repaired. Need more?"

"You're cutting pretty deep into a guy driving you and your nutty friends around," Matt said, without taking his eyes off the road. Amy reached over and gave Matt's arm a caress. They looked at each other. She was smiling.

After the quartet returned to campus and got out of the car, Matt held Amy back for a moment.

"Amy, you know, all that talk in the car about potato chips and buffets makes me real hungry. Want to get a bite to eat?"

"You going to take me to a fancy restaurant?"

"Anywhere you like."

"In your pre-repaired car?"

"I'll drive carefully. You've already survived one trip."

"Sounds great," Amy said, dropping her teasing tone. "I'd like that."

"Just tell me where you'd like to go."

Chapter 6

The restaurant was the dark, elegant, and cozy type, where couples rather than families come to enjoy some food and private conversation. The patrons in the booths tended to sit much closer to each other than they would in an ordinary coffee shop because they had little feeling of being observed. There was good reason for the feeling. High-back booths kept would-be peeking anybodies from turning around to see their fellow diners. Elaborate decorations made of artificial plants and flowers obscured views in most directions. Papier-mâché fish hung from the ceiling in rather large numbers. The lighting in the restaurant was so low that virtually all the practical illumination came from a lonely candle on each table and from the weakest of flames under the alcohol-fired warming pans in one corner, nearly hidden by an accordion wall dividing off the main restaurant area from an expansion area now used to store party chairs.

The effect of the low lighting was that waiters seemed to appear suddenly with items of food or drink and then disappear into the darkness. Instead of the normal mingle of voices one hears in a typical restaurant, there was only a quiet murmur, accompanied by a limited clinking of dishes.

The quiet expression of joy as a ring box was opened at one table, the little smooching sounds of newly affectionate lovers at another, even the somewhat angered, "Oh, that's it, is it?" were all unheard or unattended by the others.

What those at two or three tables did share unexpectedly was the view of some flames leaping up from about table height near the warming pans. Among the scraps of mingled conversation, an attentive listener might have made out the words *flambé* and *cherries jubilee* and *fajitas.*

The flames, however, were more persistent than the flare-up of a cook's creation. They continued to burn, producing smoke that now began to darken the restaurant even more as the air conditioning system circulated the smoke from the room behind the accordion wall into the main restaurant area. The smoke and flame were not products of cooking food or even of burning food. Several people began hesitantly to use the word *fire.* A couple wondered if they should get up and leave. Their waiter reassured them that everything was under control and told them they would have to pay their bill first. He left to get help, while the couple believed he was going to prepare their bill.

Less than a minute had passed before people began to talk in louder tones of alarm and even stir themselves as if readying to leave. Someone on the kitchen staff used the words *fire extinguisher.* A waiter was overheard telling another table, "Don't worry. I'm sure they'll take care of it."

Two other waiters were talking about wet towels. Another could be heard to say, "It's really burning."

By the time several couples had given up on enjoying a quiet and romantic dinner and had stood up beside their booths to leave, a cook appeared with a fire extinguisher and readied it for use. He held it up while a waiter grabbed the end of the accordion wall with a wet towel and pulled it open.

Just as the cook released the stream of powder from the extinguisher, the flames responded to the rush of oxygen from the opened wall. The hot gasses that had been trapped along the low ceiling reached the flashover point. Fire exploded along the ceiling and out of the room, shooting into the dining area and instantly lighting the hanging paper animals and the artificial flowers. The fire ate ferociously into this eager new fuel, producing even more acrid, black smoke and streams of burning plastic.

The moment of flashover had triggered an instant riot. Screaming, choking, coughing, crashing dishes, clattering furniture, stumbling, shouting, all mingled together as everyone tried to find a way out. Some people passed out from the smoke, some tripped over the fallen chairs and upturned tables, some crashed into each other in their hysteria.

"I can't see!" someone yelled.

"Where are the lights? It's too dark," another said. More bumping and crashing.

"Where's the exit?" someone demanded, in a hysterical voice. A panicked face froze on the screen.

"Okay, review buffs," Professor Miller said, as the lights came up in the classroom. "What's an obvious reason these people didn't react fast enough?"

Three hands in the room of 50 students went up.

"Yes?" Miller said, pointing.

"It was too dark to see what was going on?"

"Well, yes, that was a factor, all right. Markayla?"

"They did not have time to conceive, I mean, to conceptualize, the situation."

"That's right. Conceptualization time is often a hindering factor when something develops so quickly." Miller wrote *delayed conceptualization* on the board. It was not a truly sophisticated term, but he wanted to get something up there. "In these situations, people just don't know what's going on. They are clueless. In fact, surprise is a compliance technique used by criminals. When you're taken off guard, you are more likely to agree to something you'd otherwise reject if you had time to think—to reason—about it." He debated with himself about adding *compliance technique* to the board, but decided against it. "However, we have already thoroughly explored the concept of conceptualization as a requisite precursor to decision making. The issue here is the observation of detail. My first question, then, is—." Miller paused for effect, making eye contact with several in the classroom. "—What color was the fire when it started?"

Amy's hand went up amid a few spoken offers of "yellow" and "orange" and one of "white."

"Amy?"

"Blue."

"Blue?" someone said in a tone of critical disbelief.

"Fire isn't blue," someone else said.

"Was that a blonde that said that?" David asked. He was sitting next to Jennica, who, he knew, disliked blonde stereotypes. He smirked at her. She punished him with a look of death from her eyes and a punch of pain from her fist. David considered her reaction a proof of his wit.

Miller was secretly disappointed that someone had given the correct answer without the need to review the film. He thought the point was much better made when everyone felt silly and incompetent for having such poor observational skills. He recalled semesters when he had to show the film clip several times before someone could overcome the expectation of seeing a yellow flame and see it as it actually was.

In this case, Miller believed that someone from a previous class had passed the answer along to Amy: "If he shows the clip about the restaurant fire, the answer is 'blue.'"

But this was not the case. Amy's upbringing had taught her to be observant. Her father would often ask her an unexpected question about her environment ("Did you notice the footprints near the drive through?") and she had accustomed herself to look around and be ready to answer. Reading Sherlock Holmes had helped, too, as she attempted to imitate Holmes' keen skills. She almost ran a red light one day while too keenly observing the sidewalk near an intersection. And her father had brought home a few crime-scene investigation training videos which she watched with him profitably. Therefore, it was little challenge to ask her what color the flame was in a short film of a dark restaurant catching on fire.

Professor Miller decided he would test the girl's answer. It is one thing to have the right answer (possibly from guessing or being told) and quite another thing to know why the answer is right. He was well aware of the luck of the "superficially competent" in the younger generation and knew that often on the slightest test, the apparent expert would collapse. "Blue?" he asked, noncommittally. "Why do you say blue?"

"Because the flames were blue," Amy said.

Titters of laughter here and there echoed through the class as many students remained skeptical and waited only for Professor Miller's signal or critical word before they burst out with loud and derisive laughter.

"And where do blue flames come from?" Miller asked.

"The stork brings them," someone said quietly in back. A private laughter emerged in that corner of the room.

"When alcohol burns, the flame is blue," Amy said. "It's easy to see in the dark."

"What else can you see in the dark?" the back row said.

"Are you in the dark a lot?" someone else back there asked.

Miller could not understand what was being said in the back, but he could hear the talking. "You morons in the back shut up," he said. Then returning to Amy, he continued. "Well, Amy, you are right." A few surprised outbursts of "Huh?" sprinkled the room. "The flames were blue at first," he conceded. "In fact, it was an alcohol flame."

Markayla leaned over to Amy and whispered, "You are shining."

"Now the next question," Miller went on, "is, Where did the fire start?"

"Under the warming pans?" someone volunteered.

"Close, but no cigar," said Miller.

"I know," said another. "The fire started behind the flexible wall."

"Well, that's true, but that's a little too broad," said Miller. "More specifically, where did the fire start?" Amy's hand was still up, from the moment he had asked the second question. He finally acknowledged her.

"Next to the warming table."

Miller was still not convinced that Amy had gotten these answers on her own. Nevertheless, her answer was correct, so he said so. Markayla gave Amy a little shove of congratulation.

"Okay, last question," Miller said. "Where were the exits?"

Amy did not raise her hand right away. She scoured her brain for a memory that would answer the question, cranking her head to one side and rolling her eyes up. Before she could come up with anything, people began guessing. Eventually, someone got lucky with the few left over possibilities. The exit had been to the right, near the kitchen. There had been no lit exit sign.

Professor Miller went on with the lecture for the day, discussing the necessity of close observation and analysis. "Merely looking at something, merely seeing something, is not enough," he explained. "You must recognize what you are looking at, without allowing perceptual prejudices to interfere with your understanding." He wrote *perceptual prejudices* on the board. "Too often," he said, "you see what you expect to see, or what you want to see. That's why when 13-year-old boys are asked to describe a crashing plane's last moments, they always say they saw flames coming out of the engines, even though later investigation shows there were no flames. They have conditioned themselves to expect flames, so they see flames. You must learn not to see only what you expect." The words, *conditioned expectations*, went up on the board, and were then a little too dramatically crossed out.

"Careful observation, coupled with rational analysis, is the only guide to truth." *Rational analysis* went on the board in large letters and was circled and underlined. If you are to learn how to think, you must be able to take things apart, find the components, the causes, the actual small facts. Pull the wings off the flies and look at them under a microscope."

A hand went up. "Yes, Jennica?"

"But isn't it true that reason is only one way of looking at things? That there are other ways just as valid?"

"That's a bunch of postmodernist bunk," Miller said, with some edge. "Whatever cannot be reasoned about is unintelligible glop from the fuzzy edges of sanity. That's for people who talk to the dead and hang crystals over their beds." He wrote *intelligibility* on the board almost violently. His chalk broke.

"But how do you reason about stuff like love and beauty?" Jennica persisted.

"Vague abstractions with subjective and personal meanings are not the arena of reason. Those are more in the area of private feelings, not subject to analysis. Everybody defines those terms differently, so there is some question about whether they actually have any real meaning."

Professor Miller's tone indicated to the class that this was not a subject to be explored further, so no other questions were asked. Jennica looked down at her notes in order to hide the expression on her face.

"Blondes," David whispered, trying to get another rise out of her.

"Jerks," Jennica said, in the same whisper.

Miller continued his lecture by discussing the importance of analyzing the surrounding world. "Your own experience, your friends, and the media, especially advertising, condition you to pay attention only to certain things and to ignore others. When you are shown a scene, you have been pre-programmed to see either just the mud or just the just the marble. Unless you develop your own ability to think, you will pass through life as a slave. A slave to every phony snake oil salesman on the planet." Miller was a little disappointed in himself at not finding a more dramatic expression. He had wanted this last point to wham down on the table hard, so that it might sink into the thick heads staring almost blankly in front of him.

It was, however, his final, mildly spoken comment at the end of the hour that jerked attention away from the daydreams and focused it on him. "And remember that your essay is due next Monday. This is your last reminder." He had almost added the word *children* to the end of the sentence, but caught himself. "You're all adults here. I expect that you will remember this."

Miller gritted his teeth as he listened to the "What?" and "Huh?" and "How long is it, again?" and "What was the topic?" that indicated how many students had not even begun to think about the paper yet.

At the Cave the talk began with an animated discussion of the coming paper.

"Has anybody started yet?" asked David.

"I've started, a little," said Jennica, "but now I'm not sure what to do, since Dr. Miller trashed some of the ideas I was working with, about love and stuff."

"He really dissed love and beauty, didn't he?"

"What's love?" Gina asked, with a look of amusement.

"Started your paper yet?" Jennica asked Gina.

"Not yet. I'm working on another project first."

"What about you Amy? Have you started?" David asked.

"Well, yes," Amy began. She was hesitant to say how much she had done because she was almost finished. She knew that procrastinators never liked to hear about someone who was far ahead of them on an assignment.

"What are you writing about?"

"I'm trying to say that reason helps me understand the world. I'm using examples from my dad's teaching me to think as a little girl, when he pointed out butterflies and co-coons and stuff."

"Oh, good idea," said Jennica. Personal examples. I'll have to think up a couple of those."

"Just make them up," David said. "He'll never know."

"What are you going to write about?"

"I'm going to look at my lecture notes," David answered, "and just parrot whatever Miller has said. I'll put in a bunch of stuff about not wanting my mind to be controlled by the media. That kind of junk."

"You're just going to write a total kiss-up instead of what you really think?"

"Sure. Tell him what he wants to hear. That's the real secret to success in the university. Most of the professors just want you to agree with them. That's what they reward."

"But don't you think they want you to learn to think for yourself?"

"Naw. That's a bunch of crap. Public relations. Otherwise they wouldn't punish you when you disagree with their pet theories."

"What you are saying cannot be right," Markayla said. "Professors must have more integrity than that. They, especially Dr. Miller, must be more reasonable than that. He holds reason up very high."

"Believe what you want," David said. "You kind of live in your own little world anyway, don't you?"

"I am trying to live in a world of reason *and* truth *and* love," said Markayla.

"Good luck," Gina said.

"Does anybody get the feeling that Dr. Miller doesn't like our class?" Jennica asked.

"I think he likes Gina," said Julie Carmichael, breaking a long silence by talking to the table top rather than looking up.

"Oh, I hope so," said Gina. Then after a few moments pause, she continued, "But now that you mention it, I really have to go and do something with that paper. I've got a bit of other homework and a few phone calls to make before dinner."

"I saw tonight's menu. It's nothing to get worked up about."

"I don't live in the dorm. And besides, tonight I'm going out to the Shooting Star."

"Who with?"

Gina just smiled.

"Isn't that the place where they have $29 steaks and $12 appetizers?"

"I don't care. The guy's paying."

"That is so cold."

"Well, he asked me to go. I didn't force him."

"Do you care about this guy or are you just going for the food?" Everyone at the table knew that "this guy" meant Jeremy.

"I'm going for fun. It's just a date."

"The Shooting Star is not 'just a date.'" said Jennica.

"Think you could ever get serious about this guy? I mean really interested?" Julie asked.

"Depends."

"On?"

"Whether he has what I need to make me happy."

"And what is the key to making you happy?" David asked, hoping for some sort of risqué response.

"Money sounds about right."

"But they say money can't buy happiness."

"Yes, people without money are always saying that."

"I don't think wealth is enough for real happiness," Amy said.

"Then maybe I'll just buy imitation happiness and not look too close," Gina concluded as she turned and walked off toward the parking lot.

Julie breathed deeply and shook her head. "That girl has everything. Looks, figure, smarts, charm, you name it."

"Yeah," said Jennica, "but what does it get her?"

"Yeah," Julie continued, "only dinner with Jeremy at the Shooting Star and Dr. Miller wrapped around her little finger. Even David is drooling." Julie mussed his hair as punishment.

"Hey," is all he said.

"No guy has ever taken me to the Shooting Star. I heard that everything's a la carte. A side of asparagus is $17."

"It's more like Hamburger Cottage or Stan's Grill for me on a date," Jennica said. "Seventeen dollars is food for three."

Amy was nodding. She and Matt had gone to Half a Loaf the night before, an unpretentious and informal sandwich shop, just a slight cut above fast food. She recalled their conversation. She asked Matt whether he preferred to take her out for steak and lobster or for prime rib and truffles, only to have him mention Half a Loaf. ("I know it's only a cheap date," he had said, half apologetically. "But they have great sandwiches. Foot-long French rolls with four kinds of meat and two kinds of cheese and all the extras." Amy's response had been, "Well, let's go indulge you, then. I'll be your cheap date.")

"Why does dating have to be such a con game?" Julie asked.

"The whole world is a con game," David said. "Why should dating be any different?"

"Just like your con for Miller?"

"Sure. I mean, stop being so uptight about all this. Playing it straight gets you nowhere. You do what you have to. That's what I call being reasonable."

"So you'd lie to a girl to get a date?"

"Hey, I do what needs to be done. I'm not hurting anybody."

Jennica shook her head openly. Markayla rolled her eyes. Amy thought how much she appreciated Matt.

"But if everybody lies to everybody else, how can you trust anybody?" Amy asked.

"If everybody lies to everybody else, it's called the real world. Look around you. Corporations, politicians, lawyers, even professors are all lying and cheating all the time. Welcome to planet earth." David knocked his knuckles on Amy's head. "Hello. Is anyone in there?"

"Ow. David, stop it."

"Bad examples should not be examples for us," Markayla said. "Just because others do wrong makes no excuse for us to do wrong. That is folly."

"You're going to go really far," David said.

"So then you believe in the 'cheat to compete' thing?" asked Julie.

"It's not like the university is the real world," David said.

"But in the real world, too?"

"Survival of the fittest."

"Do you know what they call a guy who cheats his way through medical school?" Jennica asked the group.

"What?" Markayla said.

"Doctor."

"That is so scary," Julie said.

Chapter 7

The Shooting Star restaurant was known more by reputation than experience among the university students. It was simply too expensive for all but the most important dates. Even at graduation, not many parents, however proud they were of their sons and daughters, took them to this restaurant to celebrate. A few students with sufficient means or overriding commitment took their dates here to impress them. Some faculty liked to brag, discretely and nonchalantly, about visiting the restaurant because they thought it lent a cachet of sophistication to their lives. The more satiric among them even had a saying about the restaurant. "The price for being sophisticated is long years of study. The price for *feeling* sophisticated is about a hundred dollars a person at the Shooting Star." The satiric, of course, never ate at the Shooting Star, or they would have realized that a hundred dollars a person was just about the price of the wine by itself. Food was extra.

The restaurant was every bit as dark and cozy as the one that so famously burned each term in Professor Miller's film. However, there were no plastic plants or hanging paper fish. Every decoration at the Shooting Star was real. The plants were live, the flowers freshly cut, the paintings on the wall genuine oils, the sculpture produced by well known artists. Every feature spoke of elegance. The thick, starched table cloths, the dim lighting, the tuxedoed waiters with little moustaches, the crystal glasses and fancy silverware. Each table was attended by a personal waiter, who stood attentively but not officiously, holding a napkin over his arm until beckoned for service. The waiters were beckoned often, as the customers quickly became drunk with the power of having someone on ready call. More butter, more rolls, refill the water or the wine, another napkin, another spoon. Even these obvious requests were almost endless. If the diners were fully satisfied with the essentials of their table, then new needs must be imagined. The candle is smoking too much, we would like some capers, and could we have more lemon for the ice water?

Although the restaurant had won only one or two Silver Award dining plaques in the past few years (Platinum being the best, or an A, and Gold next best, or a B), the food was reported by those who paid to eat there as superb.

Sitting at table 8, as she had predicted, was Gina Roper, adjusting the many eating utensils surrounding a large silver plate. She had just ordered a filet mignon, extra rare, with truffles and baby asparagus. Caesar salad and lobster bisque soup. No wine or champagne, thank you, just cranberry juice.

Her companion, sitting across from her, ordered a rib eye steak, medium well, baked potato, and broccolini. House salad with Roquefort, cream of mushroom soup, and the house Cabernet. He did not need to show his identification to the waiter to prove that he was old enough to drink wine because Gina's companion was not Jeremy Schneider. In fact, her companion was twice Jeremy's age, and his newly permed hair had already begun to recede in the front.

"This is really nice, Dr. Miller," Gina said. "I've never been here before." Her cranberry juice arrived in a crystal wine glass. As she took a sip, a casual observer would have thought she was skillfully taking a sip of fine red wine. Professor Miller was taken by her full lips as they seemed to caress the glass. He tried not to stare.

"So tell me. Why'd you ask me to dinner?" Gina said, putting down the glass and looking into his eyes.

"You're a beautiful young woman, Gina." Miller paused for a few moments to construct and test his next sentence before delivering it. "I find you very attractive. I wanted to get to know you better." Thinking he was sounding either like a high school student on his first date or a bad movie plot, he tried to rescue his own dialog. "I thought you would be interesting to talk to. Your voice is charming. Beautiful words from a beautiful woman are like, oh, I don't know, apricots in summer."

Gina smiled. Miller wondered whether she thought he was an idiot. He now remembered, too late, that in the past the students had all pursued him more openly, so that he had not felt the need to be charming or to produce explanations about his motives.

"Thank you," she said. "And you're a good-looking man, so I'll return the compliment. I really like your class. You're very educated and smart."

"Well, thank you," he said, relaxing a little. "I enjoy thinking. And I enjoy relaxing and socializing in good company. Hence, here we are." Gina took another sip of her cranberry juice, but said nothing. "Tell me," Miller continued after a bit, "what's your major?"

"I don't know yet. I want to take a bunch of different classes and see what I like. I've really come here to learn all about life and have lots of experiences. I can choose a major later on."

"This is a good place to have experiences." They looked into each other's eyes, as if trying to see what the other thought this sentence meant. How much reading between the lines, how much translating, how much symbolism, how much innuendo, would accurately discover the meaning? After a few moments, both looked away. Miller went on. "Got any career plans?"

"Well, I've thought about modeling for awhile. It's pretty good money."

"Well, you certainly have what it takes to be a successful model. And money is important to you?"

"Money is necessary for living," Gina said. "I'm not after money for its own sake. I just like the things that money can buy. Things like this restaurant. I hope that doesn't make me sound materialistic or greedy. I'm really not."

The soup arrived and they began to eat. Miller fought with himself over the next question and rephrased it several times. Finally, he forced it out.

"Are you seeing anyone right now?"

Gina looked up at Miller, barely lifting her head, as if looking at him through her eyelashes. Her eyes sparkled. Miller was captivated. His mouth dropped open a little to let out a short, involuntary breath.

"Just you," she said, winningly. Then she added, in an ordinary but still soft tone, "No, right now I'm kind of stuck at the university and I'm not much interested in college boys. They're so immature, and they're mostly cheap. No college guy would bring me here, that's for sure."

"And you like being here?"

"Oh yes."

"So then, you're looking for someone who is well heeled and willing to share the bounty with you."

"Yeah. I hope that doesn't sound bad."

"And how well heeled a guy are you looking for?"

"I've always thought I'd like to have a million dollars."

I am sure that by now you have seen a dozen times the setup where someone says something surprising just as the other person is taking a drink. The other person spews the liquid out, often onto the speaker. It is a dusty old bit. Unfortunately for this scene, Miller was not drinking anything when Gina mentioned the million dollars. He did begin to think, "This girl is a little gold digger, who's going to use her assets to go for the mother lode." However, such a goal did not deter Miller in the least because he was not interested in a long-term relationship. He already had one of those. He was thinking more in terms of weeks than of years.

Gina noticed the pause her comment had caused, so she restarted the conversation. "So, what should I major in to make that kind of money?"

Miller thought to himself that the right answer for Gina was "princes from oil-rich countries," but he suppressed the urge to say it and instead chose something more mundane. "Business, I guess."

"Business is yucky. Try again."

Miller thought about suggesting history or political science as a pre-law path, but then an idea occurred to him that might help further his own plans.

"I'll tell you what. As luck would have it, I'm giving a paper at a philosophy conference this weekend in California. Why don't you come along and sit in on a few sessions and see if philosophy appeals to you? A degree in philosophy would make a perfect pre-law major, thus putting you on the path to a good income. At least the training in thinking and logic would enable you to make a smart choice of rich husbands. And I'm sure you would enjoy the experience."

Miller thought he was being clever by the way he framed the question. He thought Gina might read between the lines and understand his intention, but if she got upset at the suggestion, he could say, quite plausibly, that he obviously meant they would have separate rooms. After all, professors with strictly honorable intentions often invite students to attend conferences with them. Students and professors attend conferences together hundreds of times a year, under the most innocent circumstances, he could tell her.

Miller waited to hear what Gina would say. Would she take the bait? Would she get upset? Would she bring up the issue of sleeping accommodations?

The expression on Gina's face changed completely. What Miller saw was not anger, but a look of worldly-wise understanding. Gina gave a wry smile. She was obviously thinking, "Now I know why you invited me here and what you have in mind." Had Miller been half the critical thinking professor he thought he was, he could have spoken up and said, "Now your sudden reconceptualization has disambiguated the agenda behind our entire interaction." Gina suppressed a smirk and was silent for a moment. Miller searched her face to try to understand what she was thinking. She rolled her tongue around her lips thoughtfully, gazing out into the room. She saw their waiter, just arriving with their dinner.

The waiter seemed to take too long to deliver the food. "That's fine, that's fine, yes, just leave it," Miller heard himself say testily. He was waiting for important news.

At last everything had been delivered and arranged and the waiter dismissed. Gina picked up her fork and then looked at Professor Miller. "Actually," she said, "you know, the conference doesn't sound all that interesting to me. Thanks anyway." At least she was rejecting his proposal without getting upset.

"Oh, this steak is perfect," Gina said, enthusiastically, as she cut into it and watched the bloody juice run out onto her plate. "Mmmm."

They ate for awhile in silence. Miller often looked up from his food at Gina. She had a way of eating provocatively, he thought. The way she pushed the food into her mouth. Her chewing. The way she looked at him with those glistening eyes. Maybe he was being stupid, or even delusional, but he thought he saw something there. Anyway, he did not want to give up his idea completely, so he sounded the water again.

"Does anything else appeal to you? I mean, is there anything else I could do to, uh, help you, uh, choose a major?"

Gina's eyes had a curious, unreadable expression.

"I don't know," she said, with a pause that indicated she was thinking. Miller felt encouraged by Gina's lack of hostility. He decided to climb the next step.

"I've got a few bucks to have fun with," Miller said. "We could go somewhere. Anywhere."

Gina now looked at him with a trace of amusement.

She was taking her time chewing a bite of steak. Then she had to take a sip of cranberry juice. "Why doesn't she just say something?" Miller asked himself.

After a few more moments, Gina looked at Miller, her eyes still sparkling, and said, "You know, why don't we go to Las Vegas? Maybe tomorrow. We could squeeze it in before your conference." This time I really wish Professor Miller had been drinking something when Gina spoke, because this would have been an excellent opportunity for the spew gag. He did at least clear his throat to bounce back a bite of steak that was too large to swallow at that moment. But the effect is just not the same. Miller wondered if he had heard right.

"We could stay at a nice hotel, see a couple of shows. I could get a massage at a spa." Gina paused. She was picturing these things in her mind. "And we could see if we could win some money, using those 'few bucks' you have so handy." Miller looked at her. It was as if he had just been told he had won the lottery, but he was afraid that he was dreaming.

"What do you think?" she asked brightly.

Clearing his throat again, he said, "Tomorrow? Uh, okay. Sure." He could scarcely believe how fast this had happened. Gina was not one to put things off, it seemed. "Yes. I'll get the tickets on the Net tonight. We can leave right after class, so we'll only miss Friday." He could tell his wife that the conference was four days instead of two and that he had made a mistake about it earlier. He would have to fly in Wednesday to get ready for the next day. Yes, it would all work out well. Surprisingly well. He looked over at Gina.

"Uh, what kind of accommodations would you like?"

Chapter 8

Moths must be insecure creatures, for they never seem to fly with much confidence. So it was that on a cool evening (meaning about 11:00 P.M., which is evening by university student standards), a little moth fluttered over toward the Woodland Apartments. It lost and gained altitude and veered and swerved, but for the most part maintained its direction. After all, it was navigating by the pure moonlight. At least, that is what the moth thought. Now, the moth might have been taking what it believed was a harmless shortcut through life, but we will assume that it believed itself to be flying in a straight line across the land by keeping a constant angle between its heading and the moonlight far above. In fact, the light in the moth's eye came from a porch light at the apartment building, deviously leading the poor creature astray.

More deviously, or perhaps merely opportunistically, a spider had spun a web near the light. It had probably noticed the large number of flying insects attracted to the bright light and set up its own self-serve restaurant close by. Had this moth, or any insect, been less dazzled by the light, it could have seen, on the ground under the spider web, the dried and shrunken carcasses of numerous fellow insects that the spider had cut loose and dropped after sucking out the last bit of tasty juice. Many bugs had "seen the light," but it was not the true light. They had been welcomed with silk and attention at first and their little bug egos were flattered. But they had neglected to ask or think or look around, and only too late learned the real meaning of the spider's declaration that he wanted to *serve* them.

Just as the moth began to suspect the failure of its navigational equipment and to make some panicked last-second steep turns to keep straight, it crashed into the light and bounced into the web. Just at that moment, voices could be heard inside the apartment.

"We're dead," said one of them. "There are three major tests and a final in Elderberry's class and we are gonna die. The first major one comes up in a couple of weeks."

"You worry too much," said the other voice.

"What can we do?" asked the first voice, which belonged to David Simmons. "Elderberry changes his tests every semester, so getting the old ones from the guys in Delta would be useless."

"Well," said the other voice, which belonged to Jeremy Schneider, "he must have finished writing the first one by now. Why don't we see if we can get it off his office PC? He leaves his machine on all the time. That would give us two weeks to memorize it."

"I don't know."

"How hard can it be?"

The two juniors were sitting around a computer at a messy desk. Jeremy sat in an old secretary's chair in front of the screen while David sat on an empty aluminum beer keg with a pillow on top. The room itself was a litter pile. Books, papers, magazines, dirty clothes, carelessly abandoned computer parts (monitor, keyboard, printer, CPU, disk drive, expansion boards), empty food containers, bedding, toys (mostly broken), sports equipment—all were strewn seemingly randomly around the room. A burglar entering any window would create a loud and prolonged clatter by kicking and stepping on the ocean of empty soda and beer cans covering the floor. The only apparently organized items were a few stereo components under the window. Even the computer set up seemed to have been arranged in haste. The CPU was turned half sideways under the desk, the monitor was diagonal against a corner, the keyboard on Jeremy's lap. A printer sat on the floor.

"You haven't been wandering around much, have you?" asked David. "Faculty have their own network, carefully segregated from the student backbone. It's pretty secure."

"Oh, that should be hard. I'm so worried."

"You don't get it. Nobody can get in."

"Which means that you tried and you couldn't get in."

"You want to try?"

"There is no try. There is only do."

"Yeah, well you put your mystical powers from the Force on this and I'll watch."

Jeremy's first attempt was to hack in through the student network, to see if he could find a weakness in a bridge somewhere. He attached a packet sniffer to capture the passwords and other interesting tidbits of network traffic, and collected data about many of the student computers on the local network covering the dorms. Many students were online at this hour, and the traffic was heavy. He tried getting in through the faculty mail server, then through the main campus Web server, and then through the physics department server. Many keystrokes later, he was still out in the cold.

"Let's try coming in through the outside," Jeremy said.

"I'll bet Gunther could get in," David said, referring to a student in Germany with the reputation for getting into virtually any system.

"Yeah, well, Gunther isn't here."

Jeremy next went out to a network at a research lab in another state. He had compromised this system nearly a year ago and could get control of all the resources at the lab. From there he mounted an attack on the research network at his university, hoping to get access through it to the math department's computers. The only result was that the IS department at the university became the object of a number of obscenities for the quality of its security.

Jeremy and David traded ideas and argued strategies, working long into the night. David even took over the grungy, food-sticky keyboard for awhile. They tried port sniffers, hacking scripts, known weaknesses in server software, and brute force attacks, bombarding the network with huge loads of traffic in an attempt to bring it into submission.

"I can't believe they've already installed that buffer overflow patch," Jeremy said.

Nothing worked. The ports were either locked or had been made invisible by good firewalls.

Jeremy finally stood up, his eyes still glued on the screen, as if he could not look away, as if one more moment of looking would show him what he needed to know to get in.

"I've got to get back to my room and take a shower," David said. "It's almost 5:30. I gotta get ready for class and go get some breakfast."

Jeremy exhaled. "You can eat something here."

"All the food around here looks like upchuck for roaches. I think I'll get something that's been made within the last three years."

"Suit yourself. But I've got some good hacking books that have chapters on school networks. I just got a book on server exploits. Maybe we can find some useful information there. A little help from the experts might get us in."

"Maybe we can try again tonight," David said as he headed for the door.

"Hey, I know," said Jeremy, with a new-idea look on his face. "What we need is to change directions. Let's do a little creative thinking here. Maybe we don't need to break into the network ourselves. Maybe we can get someone else to break in for us."

"Oh, yeah, sure," David scoffed. "Why don't we just get someone to grab the test from his office?"

"That's right. Why don't we? You've got keys to most of the doors on campus, right?"

"Yeah," David said, warming to the new concept. "Including the math department."

"What kind of security do they have?"

"Usual campus patrol, I think. We'd have to pick the lock on the filing cabinet or desk if there's a hard copy locked up or else hack the password on the PC if he keeps it there."

"Hey, why should we do all the work? Why not try a little social engineering? Who is Elderberry's student worker? Some girl, isn't it?"

"Yeah. Amy Herbert, I think. Why?"

"I sort of know her. Kinda dorky, but not all that bad looking. Think one of us could make a play for her? Ask her out this weekend, make her happy, get a copy of the test? A little attention and some champagne should make her reasonable."

"I don't know. She's in my critical thinking class. She comes across as pretty straight laced. And she already has a boyfriend, I think."

"Who?"

"Matt Prager."

"He's nothing." Jeremy showed a look of contempt. "I think we could turn her over with no problem."

"Maybe you, Jer. After all, what girl has ever turned you down? Me? I get shot down so much my pants are always on fire."

Jeremy's opinion of himself made David's attempt to put the task back onto him seem highly sensible. He thought it over for a few moments. "Well, she's not really my type." He was thinking that Amy would be something of a step down for him.

"It's not like you'd have to take her to a popular spot where you'd be seen," David said, guessing the reason for Jeremy's hesitancy.

"Yeah, I suppose." After another brief pause to think, Jeremy said, "I guess I could take her to Don Pepe's down the freeway."

"What if she doesn't like Tex-Mex?"

"She's from Houston. Houston girls are weaned on Tex-Mex."

"How do you know she's from Houston?"

"Vee haff vays," Jeremy said with a staged German accent. "I even know that her favorite food is cookie dough."

"So give her some cookie dough and get the test."

"I was thinking more along the lines of champagne. I've got a bottle waiting in the fridge right now."

"Think that will do it?"

"I've always found that alcohol is an excellent meat tenderizer."

Two wide grins darkened the room.

By this time, the moth that had by accident been caught in the spider web just outside the door had been long ago subdued, neatly wrapped up, and hung in the spider's larder to wait until it was chosen for a meal. Even the faint vibrations that had indicated the moth's futile struggle in the end game had ceased hours earlier. The little cocoon now hung motionless, tightly wrapped, and unnoticed by a busy world.

Chapter 9

"Does the word *love* really have any specific, definable meaning?" Professor Miller asked, as he glanced at Gina and then quickly away. He almost looked at Amy, but settled on Markayla instead. Markayla raised one eyebrow.

Miller was hoping that he was not looking at Gina too often or too long as he presented his discussion about words. The class was somewhat small this morning, so there were fewer students to alternate eye contact with. A few students had decided to begin their papers about reason in their lives, and by their logic, working on a paper *and* going to the class requiring the paper, all on the same day, would have counted as double work, or at least overtime. So they chose to work on the paper and skip the class, thus keeping in balance the amount of time dedicated to each course and each part of their lives. A few other students decided to head off just a few days early for the weekend.

But even with the small attendance, Miller did not want to appear too obviously attentive to his front-row student. Usually, he enjoyed talking about semantics, but this morning he was distracted by the thought of flying to Las Vegas right after class. In fact, it would be a rush to get to the airport on time.

"After all," he continued, "You might tell your significant other, 'I love you,' and he or she might reply, 'I love you, too,' but you two may not mean anywhere near the same thing. Besides, don't you also say, 'I love ice cream,' and 'I love music,' and perhaps, 'I love my parents'? Do you love your sister the same way you love your girlfriend?"

"What if your sister is your girlfriend?" some wag mumbled for the benefit of those nearby.

"Oh, yuck," said the wag's actual girlfriend.

"I hate my sister," someone else said quietly.

A cell phone rang. The student tried to answer it discreetly, perhaps not realizing the impossibility of such an event in a classroom.

"Brandy, hang up or get out," Miller said. He was being unusually tolerant this morning, allowing the choice of hanging up. Brandy hung up and apologized.

"The point is," Miller said, driving onward, "that a single word can mean many different things. When people begin to talk about justice or truth or democracy, they get themselves into trouble because they all have different definitions."

A hand went up.

"David?"

"So, then, everything is just relative, and people who talk about justice or something are just playing semantic games?"

"The point is that you need to define your terms. Reason needs specific and clear language to operate properly. Vague and unintelligible concepts only get you into trouble."

"In Poli Sci they said that justice is just what those in power say it is. Is that what you're saying?"

Miller was about to answer when he noticed, in his wandering glances, that Gina looked mildly bored. Whether he took her expression as a token for the entire class or whether he was afraid of appearing less than exciting to her, he decided to move on.

"Well, we mustn't allow ourselves to get off onto philosophical tangents here." He looked at the clock deliberately, in order to show his concern with the time. "The next concept is that words represent connotative characterizations, sometimes arbitrary and sometimes non-arbitrary, applied to concrete things to shape your perceptions of them, and to abstractions often to produce a specious reification." Miller smiled at himself as he turned to the blackboard. He found space next to *verbal token* on the crowded board to write *connotative characterizations* and *specious reification*. He therefore did not notice that three students threw their pens on the desk in disgust. *Specious reification* was just too over the top for them. Even Markayla was shaking her head, carefully marking the words for later lookup in her desk dictionary.

As Miller turned back to the class, Julie had her hand up.

"Yes, Julie."

"Could you give us an example of a suspicious reification?"

"Specious reification?" asked Miller, using a question to correct her. "Certainly." He thought for a few moments. "Well, for example, on those documentaries on TV, they often say things like, 'Unless this plant gets adequate light and nutrients, its leaves cannot grow to the size that nature intended.' Do you see that? Nature is an idea, not a person. It has no intentions. Nature is purposeless and without direction. There are no intentions in the world good or bad except the intentions of individuals."

"What about governments?"

"Well, let's not get back off into political science. Anyway, I see that our time is getting close." It was actually ten minutes before the hour. A couple of students blinked. This was the first meeting where Miller had ever called the time himself rather than wait until the slapping of books told him to quit. And he was ending early.

"I have an appointment after class today, so I won't be able to stay and answer questions. And do remember, people, there's a paper due Monday."

The mumblings and groans were mostly drowned out by the sounds of books slamming shut, backpacks being jostled and zipped, and the happy conversation of students unexpectedly receiving the gift of ten minutes.

The moment was now just right. "Oh, I almost forgot," Miller said, as if in afterthought. "I'll be out of town on Friday, at a conference." He forced himself not to look at Gina. "Therefore," he continued, "there will be no class." Better spell it out to them, he thought, or they'll expect a substitute.

To say that the class cheered might be somewhat of an exaggeration, but not much. Nearly all of the students were delighted to have a class cancelled, and during the time just before a paper was due, too. What good luck. A few were thinking they could use the class time Friday to start the paper, even though most were more likely just to sleep in.

Coffee at the Cave possessed less than its usual interest this morning. Hardly anyone was there. Markayla had gone back to the dorm to make herself a cup of "real coffee, not that dark, bitter, hot water from the Cave." The few students who did join the group this day once again polled each other about the status of the paper for Miller's class, with much the same results as before.

The only event of interest at this meeting came at the end, as everyone was leaving.

"Amy," David said. "Can I talk to you a minute?"

"Sure."

"Has Jeremy called you yet?"

"Jeremy? Jeremy Schneider?"

"Yeah."

"No. Is he supposed to?"

"Yeah, he wants to talk to you."

"About what?"

"I don't know. Do you know if he has your extension?"

"I doubt it. I hardly know him." Amy was truly confused. Jeremy was not in any of her classes, and David was the only acquaintance they had in common. She was not exactly part of Jeremy's social circle.

"I can give it to him."

"It's 7204. Seven is the number for Pelletier, and 204 is the room."

"Gotcha. Thanks."

"No problem," Amy said, as she slung her backpack over her shoulders. "See you Monday."

"Have a weekend."

"You, too."

Some philosophers claim that there are truths too complex to be analyzed by the powers of reason, but that they are truths nonetheless. Similarly, we sometimes become aware of conclusions we have never thought about or turned over in our conscious minds. Such was the case as Amy walked back to her room. She began to feel a little sad, thinking of herself as hopelessly ordinary. She had not consciously noticed Miller's extra attention to Gina this morning, and she had only briefly remarked on how nice Jennica looked in her cable knit, turtleneck sweater, and she had no idea what to make of David's comments about Jeremy. But somehow all these factors, possibly combined with the fact that a carload of boys had nearly run her over in the parking lot on the way back from class, had made her think of herself with regret. "Sorry, I didn't see you," the driver had said.

"Sorry for being invisible," she had thought.

This mood explains the scene that followed when she walked into her room. Markayla noticed that Amy had a glum expression.

"What is it, Amy?"

"What's what?"

"You look sad. Did something happen at the Cave that has made you sad?"

"No. I'm not sad. I'm not happy. I'm just—average."

"Things are not going as well as you wish them?"

"Oh, things are okay. It's just me. I'm just average."

"What do you mean by just average?"

"Oh, you know. Average height, average build, average brown hair, average brown eyes, average looks, just average. Depressingly average." Amy was pulling at her hair and clothes as she spoke, as if a prospective buyer were critically assessing a definitively ordinary product.

"What is wrong with you?" asked Markayla in a tone more gentle than her words might imply. "Here you have every benefit of being a young, attractive woman in the richest nation on earth, with dependable drinking water and telephones, and yet you decide to be unhappy. Over what?"

"I'm just so average. Look at me. Just boringly average."

"Have you been staring at your nose in the mirror again?"

"No." Amy was embarrassed that Markayla knew enough to ask this question.

"I've seen you pushing your face around. Your eyes are too far apart or too close together. Your lips are too thin or too thick. Your eyebrows are too thin or too thick. Your nose is too big and it is sideways, and your ears are too big and they stick out too far and one eye is lower than the other, and your mouth is too big or too small and your teeth stick out."

"Stop! Markayla, no," said Amy insistently.

"Well, let me tell you. God loves average people. That is why he made so many of us."

"He made lots of bugs, too, and we use bug spray on them."

"Amy, this is not like you. What is getting into your head?"

"So many other girls seem to have all the advantages. Look at Jennica, the cutest blonde you'll ever see. And funny. And Shelley. I wish I could be that outgoing." Amy pouted.

"You want to be like Shelley?" demanded Markayla. "Shelley is crazy. That girl knows no boundaries. She frightens me."

"Oh, Shelley's okay. I think she's a good person. She's just an extravert. She's so comfortable around everyone. And then there's Gina Roper, that girl in our critical thinking class. She's just perfect. Her hair, her eyes, the way she walks, everything about her is cute. I mean, when *I* smile, I look happy. When Jennica smiles, her face lights up. When Gina smiles, the room lights up."

"Is this envy I see making you as green as a frog? Shame on that."

"But people just think, 'Wow, Jennica is a really cute girl. And Shelley is a really funny, playful girl. And Gina is a gorgeous girl. And oh, then there's Amy. Yes, Amy is a girl, too.'"

"What?"

"It's just that I'm a girl of no adjectives."

"I am thinking of some adjectives right now," Markayla said. "You are like the man who complained about the lifeboat because the seats were not padded." Amy was unsure of the application of this saying to her situation, so she let it pass.

"It's just that no one even notices me. I almost got run over in the parking lot—again—just now. I'm so ordinary that it's like I'm invisible. I'd just like to be attractive enough to keep guys from running me down."

"Well, you are quite attractive enough. The boys in the parking lot would run down a model from a fashion magazine. You are a nice looking young woman. Healthy and young and well enough shaped. I do not know what you want."

Amy would not permit herself to say or think that she wanted to be like Gina.

"I'd like to be more confident, to be liked more easily. To feel natural, normal, and relaxed around everyone. I'm just too shy and too plain to be noticed."

"When you spoke up in class, everyone noticed you. You were a star. You were not shy then. And besides, Matt is a kind and smart and honorable young man. Not many girls have such a nice boyfriend."

"He's not my boyfriend. He's just a guy I hang out with."

Now that Markayla had been in the United States for four years, she had already begun to try to think of herself as an American. Therefore, she had promised herself never to say,

"You Americans," in a critical tone, a comment she had made more than once when she had first come into the country. Amy's denying that Matt was her boyfriend, however, sorely tempted her. Instead, she judiciously decided to blame Amy's attitude on her environment.

"Oh, that is a term for our age, 'a guy I hang out with.' Instead of, 'Would you like to go out with me on a date?' we must say, 'Wanna hang with me this weekend?'" Markayla's British-accented mimic of American speech made Amy smile against her will. "Hello, Mr. Jones, I am Markayla, and this is Amy, and this is Matthew, the guy she *hangs out with*. We are so glad to meet you."

"Markayla, stop it."

"Poor Matthew. He probably thinks you are his girlfriend, but, alas, you are only *the girl who hangs out with him*. Little does he know his lowly status in your mind."

"Markayla," said Amy, a little more emphatically.

"And not *the* guy she hangs out with, merely *a* guy. Oh, my. Tell me, Miss Herbert," said Markayla, adopting the deep tone of a judge, "how many other male companions do you at this time 'hang out with' as the expression is?"

"He's not a male companion," Amy said, repulsed by the term that sounded like a euphemism. "He's my—" and here she had to stop herself from using the term "boyfriend" and instead said "—friend."

"Ah! So he is your admitted friend," said Markayla, archly and with stress. "He is not merely a guy to be hung out with but an actual friend." Markayla's future as a lawyer was evident in her tone and body language. She was born for the role. Had she the knowledge now, she would already be a competent trial lawyer.

"Don't you have homework to do?" Amy asked. "Besides, *boyfriend* is such a loaded term, with all kinds of scary implications."

"But you do like Matt, in a special way."

Just a little red appeared in Amy's cheeks. "I guess so. I somehow feel relaxed with him. I'm usually afraid of guys. But Matt is nice." Amy wanted to change the subject. "Where's Tina Nicole?"

"She has gone to the bookstore to get a radio."

"Another radio? She has three already."

"She said she needed a radio."

"Why? Did she say?"

"No. And I did not ask. I think Tina is maybe not all right."

"I'm beginning to think so, too. But maybe she just likes radios. After all look at how many cans of spray oil Matt has. And I think he's okay. Even though he likes me."

"That is not funny, Amy. You do not deserve to be pitied, so you might as well not try to get any from me."

Amy's fake pout showed that she was beginning to rally out of her blue mood. Just as she frowned so winningly, the phone rang.

Since Tina never got a phone call, and Markayla's were rare, Amy answered, hoping it might be Matt.

"Hi, Amy. Remember me? Jeremy. We met last year."

David had evidently wasted no time in giving her number to Jeremy. Amy knew who Jeremy was and saw him around campus occasionally, but did not remember actually meeting him. She knew that he was intensely good looking and had the reputation of being something of a lady killer. He was seldom seen with the same girl.

"Hello," she said.

"The guys all say that you're really smart in the critical thinking class."

"Thanks."

"And I've noticed that you're a really classy chick."

Amy thought Jeremy sounded fake, insincere. "Oh, come on," she thought. "'Classy chick'? Who talks like that?" She thought of Shelley's friend Brandy, who in her desperate desire to be thought cool called girls *chicks*, as if that were the term approved by the *in* crowd. It seemed just as phony in Jeremy's mouth. What kind of person would think of her as a *chick*?

"Um, thank you, I guess," Amy said, feeling awkward. Jeremy was usually seen talking to or walking with a beautiful girl. Amy wondered what in the world he could want from her. His clumsy flattery was alarming.

"Say, Amy," Jeremy continued, plowing through the stiffness of the situation with remarkable smoothness, "I've never gotten to know a really thoughtful, nice girl before. Everyone says you're so sharp and kind and fun."

"They do?"

"Well, yeah, so I was wondering if you'd like to get together. I was thinking about dinner tomorrow night. We could go to someplace nice and quiet, have some good food, relaxed conversation, and get to know each other better."

Jeremy's sweet talking her reminded Amy of one of Matt's homey sayings from his farmer upbringing. "They put the butter on just before they eat you," he would say. After repeating this to Amy the first time, he had added, "I know it's corny," and then laughed pretty hard at his own pun.

"I'm very flattered by your offer," Amy said, ever trying to be polite. "But I'm sort of already in a relationship. And tomorrow looks pretty full. But thank you anyway." The truth was that Amy was not at all interested in Jeremy, handsome and suave though he was, and that she was afraid that his intentions were merely to make her another comment in his little black book. She was glad she had her friendship with Matt to use as an excuse. She was even willing to exaggerate her idea of it if need be.

For his part, Jeremy was surprised. He had very seldom been turned down for a date. His charm and good looks were almost always a winning combination. But just in case, he had been careful to circulate stories about his future. Everyone knew that after graduation he would become an automatic partner in a financially highly successful family business. Yet here he had been turned down. He wondered for a moment if Amy remembered what he looked like, who he was, what his future was. Should he have asked her in person to be sure that she would say, "Yes"? Had he the slightest doubt of being accepted over the phone, no doubt he would have made the attempt face to face. But to think that a girl of average appearance would reject his overtures was something he really had not considered.

"Wouldn't you prefer a steak or some lobster at the Argentine to the junk at the commons?"

"Oh, I don't mind the commons food."

"You're always going out with Matt Prager, aren't you?"

"Well, yes, but he's a special friend." Amy wondered just how Jeremy knew this fact.

"And you'd rather go with him than with me?" Jeremy was beginning to lose his temper.

"Well, I've known him a long time. And I don't really know you."

"We could get to know each other really well. I could teach you a few things. Things Matt doesn't even know."

Amy was feeling deeply uncomfortable now.

"Thank you again, but I don't think I'm interested. Sorry."

"You'll only be sorry if you don't reconsider." There was a cold, not quite threatening tone in his voice.

"No, thanks. I've got to go now. Thanks for calling. Good bye." She hung up. She had not meant to be impolite, but the conversation had become too much to take.

"Who was that?" asked Markayla.

"Jeremy Schneider."

"Who is he?"

"Just some guy. He asked me out."

"You see? You are not the unwanted, unattractive girl you have been moaning about all morning."

"But he's a creep," Amy said. Then, thinking better of her unguarded comment, she added, "I mean, I don't really know him, and I'm sort of seeing Matt pretty regularly. So I told him no."

"But he likes you."

"That's one interpretation."

Chapter 10

Miller had left the classroom as quickly as possible after his early dismissal of the students. He nearly succeeded in keeping his eyes off Gina before he left, and she cleverly walked the opposite way down the hall. She had suggested that Miller pick her up outside a local coffee shop near the campus, in order to reduce the chance of their being seen together. When Miller drove up just a few minutes after leaving class, Gina was already there, waiting with a single suitcase. She smiled at him briefly but brightly.

"I'm ready," she said.

Miller took a quick look around. He saw no students or faculty he recognized. Soon Gina's suitcase was safely hidden in the trunk and Gina was sitting next to him as they hurried toward the airport.

As the plane took off, the sky was overcast, but in a short time they climbed through the fog and mist and broke out on top of the clouds. The morning sun was bright when not filtered through a layer of heavy moisture. Sitting next to the window, Gina pulled down the shade halfway.

Miller checked over the rental car and hotel reservations, to be sure he had handy all the paperwork he needed. He put away the airline information. Gina pulled out of her purse a somewhat wrinkled paperback novel, *Betrayal: A Love Sto-*

ry, and began to read. Miller changed to the in-flight magazine and both sat seemingly engrossed, not talking, until the peanuts and sodas began to make their rounds. Both passengers looked up to attend to the coming snacks.

Gina glanced out the window and noticed that the cloud cover was gone and that she could see the ground.

"Oh, look. You can see mountains. And little roads."

Miller leaned over toward Gina to look out the window. A subtle but not unaffecting charge of perfume rising from Gina distracted him momentarily. This was the first time he noticed that she was wearing a short cotton blouse with frilly ruffles and low-cut jeans. Her hair was up for the convenience of travel, although a carefully liberated ringlet hung down in front of each ear. He looked out. "Yeah," was all he said. His only thought about the scenery was, "Little roads, little people."

"And the mountains?"

"Uh huh," he said, casually putting his hand on her leg as if to support himself as he leaned over a little farther. Gina turned her head from the window to look at him. She gave him a wry smile.

Miller sat back in his seat and began to read the same article again. Gina watched the engine pod on the wing bounce when the airplane hit a patch of turbulence. She turned to Miller. "The world is a very hazy place, isn't it?"

"What?"

"Look at how hazy all the mountains are in the distance. Up close, it looks like clear day, like we can see clearly, but it's really hazy if you think about it."

When the aircraft began to descend, the roads came into more prominence. Most were still unpaved. Except for an occasional structure, no houses or other buildings were visible.

"Look at all the roads in the middle of nowhere," Gina said.

"And they go nowhere," Miller said. He was feeling like a man who was going somewhere.

"Who drives on them, I wonder?"

"Nobodies."

The background roar in the cabin of the airliner was loud enough to muffle the words somewhat, so that Gina thought Miller had said, "Nobody." The roads did appear to be deserted, so Gina let the conversation drop. She returned to her book.

It was not long before a house appeared here and there among the scrub brush and the brown hills and valleys. Then a small tract of houses, then dozens of houses seemed to pop up, connected by wider roads. Soon the land was divided into squares by roads crossing each other, many paved, some not. The ground began shyly to show a little green here and there. Eventually, a golf course was visible, then tracts of nice houses, turning into larger neighborhoods with lawns and more established trees. The houses had won and the vacant land receded. It was as if civilization had suddenly sprung into being, as if the desert had bloomed with people and houses and cars.

The aircraft made a turn. A whining motor sounded as the flaps were set. Next, there was the thump, bump of the landing gear lowering. Soon the plane was on the ground, the engines screaming as the thrust reversers helped slow it to taxi speed.

❖ ❖ ❖

And so, telling himself that he was being guided by reason, the professor who taught the need for a careful discernment of reality entered a city where appearance is more important than reality—no, where appearance *is* reality. His companion, on the other hand, also thought of herself as having a reasonable view in mind. She had come along, she had said, to have fun. To relax in the sun, to eat some good food, and to see a show.

Las Vegas is, indeed, an icon, a testament to the power of appearance. The hotels of the strip are filled with synthetic marble, phony façades, imitation bronze statues, fake jewels, artificial flowers. Visitors know that the walls of the hotel are not really made from ancient, weathered stone, but even knowing that, the effect is the same. The sense of amazement and the enjoyment of beauty one would gain from walking up to an ancient European building is perfectly reproduced by walking up to the artificial façade of the hotel. The false stonework evokes genuine feelings.

There is an old debate about art. Those who like to tweak art collectors are fond of asking, "What's the difference between a $50 million original Van Gough and a $50 print of the same painting, if you cannot tell the difference from six feet away?" Is the aesthetic response different? If not, why not create museums filled with inexpensive copies so that people everywhere can enjoy them? Would people visit a museum filled with copies?

If there is somehow a difference between the original and the copy, how does that difference change if the original is discovered to be a fake? Is it no longer beautiful? No longer valuable? Is the value of art only in an expensive name? Or is the enjoyment painted there on the surface of the canvass, only millimeters thick, and capable of being copied at will both by those who print reproductions of originals and those who counterfeit the artist's style?

Which brings us back to Las Vegas. Aesthetic appreciation and enjoyment are derived from appearance, not reality. American commerce would collapse if the appearance businesses were stopped. Cosmetics, plastic surgery, fancy clothing, even decorative trim and paint are all part of the business of making us look good. We are an aesthetic society. Some fashion models have described themselves as optical illusions because they are transformed from plain Janes without makeup into gorgeous supermodels with makeup—and with computer graphics to trim their thighs, remove their blemishes, and bronze their skin. Is their apparent beauty any less if we know their bodies and their photographs have been doctored? Is our enjoyment of the hotel diminished by knowing that the façade is not ancient stone, or even actual stone, but textured plaster or concrete?

Many people subscribe to that great maxim of self delusion, "Seeing is believing," making them easy marks for a world of surfaces. Substance may need to be sold at a discount and still have only a few takers, because most people are busy bidding up the price of appearance.

And yet, the enjoyment of a painting or a hotel or a supermodel on a magazine cover is a passing enjoyment. The minute we begin to think about permanence—owning the painting, buying the hotel, marrying the supermodel—suddenly the issue of reality comes in. Fool me for a minute and I will enjoy it. But when I get serious, and think long term, I want something genuine. The longer the time frame, the more important an accurate knowledge of reality becomes, the more crucial it is to find the truth. A lifetime is a pretty long time frame. And eternity is even longer.

It was just after noon when Professor Miller and Gina drove from the airport to the hotel. Even this late in the fall, today the air was warm and the sun shone brightly in a cloudless sky. Gina rolled the window down to enjoy the rush of the breeze. She relaxed with the seat back while Miller struggled somewhat with the idiosyncrasies of an unfamiliar car. The controls, the unfamiliar braking and acceleration, the odd mirrors, all made him feel awkward. The hostile and unforgiving Las Vegas taxi drivers rattled him even more. But the drive was short and they arrived successfully at the valet parking of the hotel.

Their room was not yet ready, so they had some time to kill. Gina said she felt hungry, so they decided on lunch in one of the hotel's restaurants. They asked for a recommendation. "Through the casino, follow the signs, turn left," they were told. Indeed, virtually every set of directions in a Las Vegas hotel begins with "Go through the casino," because the hotels have been cleverly designed in just that way. Restrooms? Go through the casino and turn right. Guest elevators? Through the casino, angle right, then left. Coffee shop? Through the casino to your left. And so on.

It is a planned seduction.

The use of flashing lights to get attention is an old technique. The downtown section of Las Vegas where the old hotels were built still feature the million-light-bulb exteriors that were originally the signs of beckoning to tourists. But now we have become inured to flashing lights, simply because we see them everywhere. The new casinos still make use of thousands of lights, flashing bulbs, vibrant strips of neon, rotating beacons, and so on. But now another old method of charming the traveler has been raised to the next level of power and effectiveness. It is the siren song of sound.

The casino is a cacophony of noises. Each of the new video slot and poker machines provides at frequent intervals a few bars of musical invitation to play when it is sitting unused. When used, each machine produces a musical accompaniment as each card is dealt or each wheel is spun to a stop. Each machine notifies the player (and everyone else within thirty or forty feet) with a happy *ding* when a coin has been won. Because most payoffs include several coins and because many machines are normally being played and giving frequent payoffs, the result is a constant, multi-channel surround-sound experience of a rapid ding, ding, ding, ding, ding! Even more, when a player elects to have actual coins paid out of the machine, they drop quickly but one at a time into a stainless steel bin, resulting in another constant, multi-channel surround-sound experience of chink, chink, chink, chink, chink!

The effect is almost one of giddiness. Everyone appears to be winning piles of money at jet speed. Those who would pass through casually wonder whether they should forget their destination, rush to a machine and begin to scoop up the riches before someone else wins everything.

Added to the mechanical music and percussion of seeming wealth, soft rock or pop music plays in the background, often featuring love songs of varying quality, but seldom only instrumentals. The sound of singing adds a living, human element to the ambience. Laid over the top of all these sounds is the conversational chatter of the players and observers themselves. Where a dozen people are observing a roulette or craps table in operation, an occasional roar of approval or disappointment adds a note of theatricality to the room. To be heard, talkers must raise their voices over the background noise, so that all across the giant rooms conversations, undecipherable, mingle. What is being said, the observer cannot tell, but it seems to be a lively and animated talk.

Thus has the modern casino created an atmosphere—a semblance—of a festive, happy, wealth-granting life to be had by all who play.

It is a generalization drawn from cursory appearances. A close look at many of the slot players reveals an almost hypnotic trance on their faces as they play one round after another, scarcely seeming to check whether they have won or lost. "Zombies pushing coins," someone has called them. An occasional overheard snippet of conversation reveals that not everyone is winning. "I've just lost two hundred dollars," one woman tells her friends. Whether these people leave town happy or sad depends on why they came. Some people travel here to win something, and some come to lose something. Some come to find a more intense reality, and some come to escape reality. For those whose daily reality is dissatisfying, the world of imagination and appearance has particular charm.

As Miller and Gina passed through the casino toward the restaurant, the distinctions between reason and rationalization, between reality and appearance, seemed, well, academic. This state of mind was perfectly agreeable to both of them.

Chapter 11

Tina still had not returned from her trip to the bookstore by lunch time, so Amy and Markayla left by themselves for the dining commons. When they returned to the room, there was a message on the answering machine.

"I wonder if it's from Tina," said Amy.

"I've seen her walking around the campus, but not going anywhere particular. Maybe she got lost."

Markayla pushed the *Play Messages* button.

"Hey, it's Ron. I'm looking for Matt, but he's not in his room, either. I'm supposed to help him fix his car at one today. But I'm here in the health center with Shelley. She's barfing and feeling bad. Maybe bad food or the flu. We don't know. Anyway, I can't make it to help Matt and wanted to tell him. If you see him, can you let him know for me? Thanks. Talk to you later."

Amy looked at her desk clock. It was 1:33.

Women of leisure and prom-night high school girls may indeed require two or three hours to get dressed, but your typical college girl does not have the time to dilly dally over a few curls or just the right level of blush. These young women, when victimized by broken alarm clocks, have been known to arrive in class unshowered and wearing hooded sweatshirts to hide their dysfunctional hair. Even with the benefit of a working clock, the late hours and the pressure to sleep often restrict get-ready time to a minimal amount. Therefore, you should not be surprised to learn that Amy, upon realizing that Matt was working on his car alone, was skilled enough to change clothes in an instant. She threw off her sweater and black jeans, leaving them on the bed, and then jumped into some old jeans and a T-shirt. With a rubber band in one hand and a fistful of hair in the other, she put her hair up with magical dexterity. Somehow in the process her shoes got changed also, but this all took place so fast that it is hard to say exactly when it happened. If this scene is ever filmed, it will certainly require special effects and slow motion photography to make it comprehensible.

Somewhere during the flurry of change, there was a brief dialog.

"Why are you changing the clothes that you have just put on?" asked Markayla.

"I'm going to help Matt with his car."

"Oh, Amy, be reasonable. You do not know anything about cars."

"Maybe I can learn. It'll be a good experience."

By this time Amy's feet were bouncing down the landing toward the stairwell. "Back later," she called to Markayla, who once again sighed, shook her head just a little, and went back to her newspaper. "Advertisers find universality in emotional appeals," she read.

Amy went to the area of the lot where Matt had parked after their outing to Half a Loaf a few days earlier. The car was still there. As she walked toward it, she heard music from a radio and some muffled talking. Her first thought was that either Ron had made it after all or that Matt had found another helper. Her heart sank a bit. Even though it might be great that another, more skilled person had volunteered to help, she had wanted to be the helper. She wondered if that was being selfish.

When she reached the car, she saw Matt alone. He was lying on his back in an odd contortion, his head under the dash near the pedals, his legs sticking out the door and his feet touching the parking lot. He was holding onto the steering wheel with one hand and working with the other hand where Amy could not see. The talking was the result of a conversation he was having with himself.

"How are you going to do that?" he asked.

"Boy, I don't know," he answered.

A hand reached out from under the dash and hunted around on the seat until it found a half-empty bag of cheese puffs. The hand fingered a couple and returned under the dash, where a munching sound was soon heard. After another few moments, the conversation continued.

"Can we push that in while we hold this?" There was a quiet grunt, then a soft, metallic klink.

"Ow, ow. Well, that was dumb."

"Want to try it again?"

"Oh, sure, now that you've shredded my finger. Lousy pliers."

Amy was not comfortable with the idea of people holding conversations with themselves, even though her experience with Matt had proven him to be a pretty normal guy.

"Hey, Matt," she said.

"Hey, Aim-o," Matt said, recognizing her voice. Soon he cranked his head so he could see her with one eye. "You haven't seen Ron, have you? That guy seems to have left me to bale the hay by myself."

"Ron can't make it. He called and said Shelley got sick. They're at the health center."

"Bummer. Hope she's okay. What's she got?"

"Flu maybe. She's throwing up."

By this time, Amy had walked around the car, climbed into the passenger seat, and flipped herself over. Her head suddenly appeared near Matt's under the dash. Her foot pushed against the car to move her a little closer. "Can I help?" she asked.

Even after a year of dating, or rather, hanging out together, Matt was still surprised by Amy. He had never known a girl willing quite literally to throw herself into a task the way Amy would. He knew she was not afraid of tools or getting dirty, because they had built many pieces of furniture together last year in a dusty warehouse. But diving upside down under an automobile's dashboard was unexpected. Of course, he acted as if it were the most ordinary thing in the world.

"I need to detach this linkage from the pedal to the power steering unit under the hood. The linkage goes through the firewall here." Then, perhaps not noticing, he changed from the singular to the plural: "We need to remove this retaining ring." Amy caught the *we* and smiled inside. "Can you hold the pedal for me?"

"Sure. Got it," she said with confidence. That seemed easy enough. She had been planning merely to offer to hold a flashlight while Matt worked, but now she was in on the repair itself. The time spent helping her father when she was too young to do more than hold a tool or bring the tape had taught her that moral support, simple companionship, was appreciated enough to make it worthwhile. But being able to help in a more direct way made Amy feel even more useful. She was part of the action. And it was fun to be up close and personal in such an awkward place.

While Amy held the pedal, Matt struggled with the retaining ring. He tried various angles, but his hands were in the way of his work. The small retaining ring was difficult to grab and rotate with one hand while his other hand held the linkage. He could not do it.

"Can you grab the ring?" Matt asked at last, giving her the pliers.

"I think so." Amy's hands were smaller and fit better. She wriggled in closer and grasped the ring with the pliers. Matt put his hand over hers to add strength and together they rotated the ring until it slipped out of the linkage.

"Yay," Amy said.

They slid out. Amy felt something in her eye, so she wiped it, pulled the lid down, and cleared it. Matt smiled, noting a little mascara smear. He handed her a rag to wipe her fingers. Then he walked around to the front of the car and Amy followed.

Under the hood, Matt showed Amy the bolts that held the brake cylinder and the booster to the firewall. He began to detach the components and handed her the bolts as each one came out.

"I wanna do one," Amy said.

"Okay," said Matt, handing her the socket wrench.

"Which one? This one?"

"Sure."

Amy unscrewed the bolt, at first tentatively, then with nonchalance.

"This is like building furniture," she said. "Only greasier." She grimaced briefly.

Matt pulled out the old booster drum, asked Amy to clean the mounting area, and then slid in the new drum. He started the first two bolts and then let Amy put in and tighten the others. While she worked, Matt stood back and watched, finishing off the bag of cheese puffs.

"Now this is living," he said.

Amy turned her head and looked at him. "What, having someone do your work for you?"

"You got it. And by the cutest repairman I've ever seen." Amy returned her attention to the task at hand. "I just wish I had me an 80-gallon air compressor and an air wrench. We'd tighten those puppies up in a second."

A song on the radio ended, and Amy heard Matt say, "Well, that's about the worst song you've every put on your show. Wonder how much they paid you to play that. Don't do it again."

"Matt," Amy said. "The guy can't hear you. You're talking to plastic."

"Of course they can. Don't you know the CIA has microphones everywhere, to give sound to the satellite pictures. Even now, they're probably focusing on you bent over under the hood."

Amy stood up too fast and hit her head on the hood. Holding the back of her head, she looked at Matt, who was grinning, but trying to suppress it. His weakness was that he could not hold a blank expression very long, thus too quickly giving away his deadpan comedy. Seeing her expression of mild pain, he stopped smiling and became sympathetic.

"Are you okay?"

"I'll live. And if I don't, my blood is on your car." Amy looked at her hand to see if there was blood on it. There was none.

"It wouldn't be the blood on my car that would be the problem. It would be getting rid of your dead body that would be a lot of trouble."

"Ooh, you!" Amy said, with an expression and tone of fake hatred.

"Here, let me see." Matt hunted around in her hair, look-ing for a wound. "You're not hurt. No blood. No bump. Oh, I get it. The old sympathy ploy. You're just acting." Then, look-ing up to the sky, as if looking into a satellite camera, "Good show, huh, boys?"

Amy held the socket wrench like a gun and made a girly imitation of a gunshot, as if shooting Matt. Then she went back under the hood. "You'd better just hope I don't 'fix' your brakes," she said without looking around.

"Don't worry, Babe. You're going on the test drive with me."

"And don't call me 'Babe' either."

Under the dash again, Amy proved all the more helpful by holding the linkage while Matt pushed the pedal to it. Amy replaced the retaining ring. Matt grabbed a can of spray lube and oiled the linkage. He oiled the driver's door hinges while he was at it.

"Every time I smell oil, I will always think of you," Amy said.

"Like an exotic, alluring perfume, huh?"

"Something like that."

Amy felt happy that she had been able to help out with a task she had never tried before. She liked the new experi-ence. She had learned from the evidence games with her fa-ther that solving a challenging problem successfully gave her a feeling of self worth. Now as a late adolescent troubled by a common degree of self-doubt she continued to find that completing a difficult task was a source of emotional reward. She felt like doing a little dance. But, of course, we often dis-guise the way we feel. Embarrassment is the great evil of teenagers, and revealing the way they really feel would often embarrass them.

"Well," said Matt, "that really turned out to be a two man job."

"Anytime you have another two man job," said Amy, in as deep a voice as she could manage, "remember, I'm your man." She held up one hand as if volunteering. Matt noticed her hand was dirty. Grasping the hand, he looked down at her palm, which was a little greasy. Taking a rag not much cleaner than the hand, he rubbed her palm. Since his hands were greasy also, holding hers transferred the dirt from him to the back of her hand. The effect was like a magic trick. He rubbed her dirty palm. Most of the dirt magically left the palm and appeared on the back of her hand. Noting this, Amy gave Matt a look.

"Thanks," she said.

"I was trying to help."

"Don't worry," she said. "I clean up well." Then, just as he smiled at her accommodating attitude, she added, "And being around you, it's a good thing, too."

"I've got some waterless hand cleaner in the trunk. It eats grease for lunch."

Amy was skeptical, but was willing to give it a try. Matt got the can and told her to scoop out "a bunch" and rub it all over her hands. It felt like grease. Seeing Amy's expression, Matt said, "Pretend it's hand lotion. After all, it's got lanolin in it." Then he used his hands to rub it into each one of hers. "Mmm. Ahh. Ooh," he said. "Doesn't that feel great?" Amy was embarrassed by the sounds of pleasure Matt was making, phony though they were. She pulled her hands away.

"Has anyone ever told you you're twisted?" she asked.

Amy looked at her hands. At least the cleaner did take off the grease. And she had not even broken a nail, largely because she kept her nails short for ease of typing. But her hands had a distinctive aroma.

"Now I smell like an auto mechanic." She made a face.

"There are worse things to smell like. Besides, you'd make a cute auto mechanic." Matt was the only guy who had ever used that word in reference to Amy. And now he had used it twice in an hour. Amy wondered whether he really thought she was cute.

"We need a test drive to be sure the new booster works," Matt said. "And to make sure no one sabotaged the brakes," he added looking darkly at Amy. "How about going to dinner tomorrow night and combine the test with some food?"

"Skip the cafeteria? I'm on that!"

"No, the correct answer is, 'Why, Matt, I would so enjoy your company. What a pleasure. Yes, yes, I'd love to go.'"

"That must be another girl you're thinking of."

"Oh, you're right," Matt said, rolling his head up to one side as if in contemplation about whom exactly he was re-membering.

"Come by my room at six."

"Yes dear."

"And bring lots of money. I plan to be very hungry for the most exotic food in town."

"Chili again? Doesn't Markayla complain about the mid-night symphony?"

"You monster! You wicked, wicked man!" Amy gave Matt a shove.

❖ ❖ ❖

When she bounced back into the room, Amy did a little dance, with her own brief "doo-dee-doo-dee-doo" song. Markayla looked up from a complex graph in her textbook.

"Correction," Amy said. "You said I don't know anything about cars. I know how to put in a power steering thingie. Bolts, retaining rings, linkage alignment, the entire mechanical procedure. And I have the grease to prove it. You, my dear Markayla, are looking at Miss Handywrench!"

Markayla shook her head. "I seem to be smelling Miss Handywrench, too."

"Oh, that's just the aromatic hand cleaner." Amy headed for the bathroom and began to wash her hands with the scented pump soap.

"You know," Amy added, "I think I like Matt."

Markayla gave a blowing tsk. "And have you also noticed that there is more light during the day than at night?" she asked.

Amy knitted her brows at the comment. However, she was washing her nose and cheek to clean off some smudges she had just noticed in the mirror, so Markayla did not know that the expression was for her. "You know, Markayla, sometimes you're weird."

"And thus does the murderer call the thief a bad man."

"Huh?"

Amy gave Ron a call to see how Shelley was doing. He was not in, so she called Shelley's room. Shelley answered.

"You're back?" Amy asked.

"I'm doing really good. I'm supposed to stay in bed for awhile until I feel perfect, so I'll probably rest for a few hours. Ron thinks I'm doing well enough that he doesn't have to keep me company. He's off somewhere watching a game, I think. Wanna come over for awhile?"

"Sure."

Amy made the trek over to Hurlock Hall and up to Shelley's room in just a few minutes. Shelley was alone in the room, the beneficiary of a new dorm with many single rooms. Her room reminded Amy of Matt's apartment. Chaos. She was propped up in bed.

"How are you feeling?" Amy asked.

"Fair to middling. I think it was a bad piece of fish, not the flu. The nurse said I was probably pregnant. That's what they always tell me. Same thing last year. Good old, dependable health center. Nausea? That's morning sickness. You're probably pregnant."

Amy could discern that Shelley was not operating at a hundred percent, but the patient seemed to be doing very well, nevertheless.

"Can I get you anything?"

"Naw. Food is not on the horizon, and I've got some anti-barf stuff already. So how are you?"

"I helped Matt fix his car."

"Miss Handywrench, huh?"

"Hey, that's just the name I thought of."

"And how's Matt?"

"He's taking me to dinner tomorrow night."

"Some place fancy? Hot date?"

"Probably fast food."

"Fast food and slow kisses. Mmm."

"Shelley."

Shelley's mention of hot dates and slow kisses reminded Amy of Jeremy.

"By the way, do you know Jeremy Schneider by any chance?"

"Jeremy? Yeah, but only indirectly," said Shelley. "Why?"

"He asked me out. I have no idea why."

Shelley looked at Amy for a few moments, her face expressionless. "Well, I'd be really careful, if I were you," she said at last, in a tone more serious than Amy had ever heard from her. "Jeremy is not known for being a nice guy. I'd call him pond scum, but then again, what has pond scum ever done to me?"

"So he's one of those notch the bedpost types?"

"That's not the half of it. Last year the girls next door noticed something strange going on and they thought Jeremy might have something to do with it."

"What happened?"

"Well, Kristen has a Web cam on her PC so she and her buds can see each other when they do a live chat. Last year they began to notice that the camera kept getting angled over a little bit. Instead of pointing straight toward the person using the computer, it was angled over across the room. At first they thought someone had bumped it inadvertently or used it for something and not put it back right. But then they sort of connected the movement with visits by Jeremy. That made them a little suspicious."

"Did they find out what was going on?"

"Sort of. Becky, that's Kristen's roommate, called David Simmons, the total computer nerd, and he came in and took a look. This is a secret, by the way, because David is a friend of Jeremy's, since they're both techno types, so you didn't hear this anywhere. But after a little cutesying from Becky—that woman is shameless—David took a look and admitted that there was some kind of program sending the camera pictures to another computer, um 'somewhere.' We all think he knows where, namely to Jeremy, but he wouldn't say. He said he took the program off, but now Kristen keeps her computer turned off when she's not using it and puts a baseball cap over the camera when she's not chatting to friends. You never can be too careful. They are watching you."

"That sounds paranoid."

"Maybe so, but as David says, 'On the Internet only the paranoid are sane.'"

"So this is one of those cases where nothing can really be proved, but you think Jeremy may have been involved."

"Jeremy is the kind of guy who makes me glad I have Ron. Matt seems like a nice guy, too."

"Yeah. I like him. I might even keep him for awhile."

When Amy told Markayla about the suspected camera incident, Markayla said, "I am sure that is not legal, even in America."

Chapter 12

After only a little misdirection Professor Miller and Gina found their way to the restaurant they had been seeking. It had a Southwestern décor, with pottery and a few weathered wagon parts on shelves and in cutouts in the wall, together with some imitation cactus plants in pots on the floor and in planters next to the tables. The paint scheme included those colors associated with the Southwestern look: oranges, browns, reds, and a little turquoise.

"Ever been to Vegas before?" Miller asked, as they sat down at a comfortable booth with high backs, just right for some cozy conversation.

"No," said Gina. "This is such an amazing place. Listen to all the money being made." The restaurant was open on the casino side so that the noise and bustle could be seen and heard. "Hear those coins plunking into the bins? People seem to be doing pretty well. After lunch we should try to win something."

"If you want to," said Miller, without much enthusiasm. Miller prided himself on being an educated man who believed in acting on the basis of reason. He knew the odds of many of the games played in casinos, and he understood the laws of probability. "Casinos are not built by philanthropists," he had once heard a colleague remark. "Casinos are built by people hoping to get lucky." Still, he thought, he would not constrain Gina from a little irrational, wishful thinking. She was entitled to lose a few dollars indulging a foolish pursuit. After all, her thinking ability was weak and he could not expect her to be reasonable or to listen to a lecture on probability when all she had in mind was fun. And, who knows? Perhaps she would win something.

Soon the waitress was with them. Miller ordered a steak sandwich and Gina ordered a Chinese chicken salad.

"Want some champagne?" Miller asked.

"No, thanks," answered Gina. Then looking at the waitress, she said, "Just water, please."

Miller thought to himself, "This isn't even going to be as expensive as I thought."

While they waited for their food, the pair talked about what kind of shows they might want to see during their brief stay. There were circuses, singers, magic acts, floor shows, comedians—seemingly an endless number of choices. Instead of deciding right then, they agreed to find more information and get tickets later.

Soon their food was delivered and the conversation dropped off to an occasional "This is good," or "How's your food?" as they began to eat.

A few minutes later, Gina gulped and said, half covering her full mouth, what sounded like, "Oopth. Thorry." She smiled at Professor Miller girlishly.

"Sorry for what?" asked Miller.

Swallowing, Gina said, "For stepping on your shoe."

"You didn't step on my shoe."

"Oh? Isn't that—" moving her leg under the table, "—your shoe?"

"No. You must be hitting the center post of the table." He reached under and tried to touch the post, but there was none. The table was cantilevered out from the wall. "Is there something down there? Someone left their shoes?"

Gina looked under the table, then reached down and came back up holding a fat leather wallet. It was almost too fat to stay closed and easily fell open on the table. The way it had been found, its fatness, and the fact that it flopped open to reveal the inside, made the wallet an object of instant curiosity. Miller and Gina saw a driver's license, several credit cards, a hotel receipt, some business cards, and a lot of cash.

"Whose is it?" asked Miller.

"The driver's license has the name Trimmer on it," Gina said. "And so do the business cards. Look, 'Larson E. Trimmer, Field Representative, Confidential Brokerage Services, Inc.'" She showed Miller one of the cards. In the bottom corner was the logo of the New York Stock Exchange.

"Some kind of stock broker, evidently," said Miller. "And pretty successful," he added, looking at the thick stack of bills. Gina glanced around the room to see that no one was either walking up to reclaim the wallet or looking at what she was doing. Satisfied, she slipped the pile of currency from the wallet. She gave a girlish laugh and a shrug the way she might have if she had been breaking into the principal's office in high school.

As she began to count by placing the bills on top of each other, she said with surprise, "Look at this." She counted the money quickly. There were twenty bills, each a hundred-dollar denomination.

"That's two thousand dollars," Gina said with awe in her voice. "I've never seen that much cash all in one place. In fact I don't think I've ever even seen a hundred dollar bill before. Are they real?" She handed them to Miller.

Miller looked them over briefly. "Yes, they're real, all right."

"Oh, look," Gina said enthusiastically, "here's his room number." She had the hotel slip in her hands. "Room 13-208. We can take it back to him."

"What's that on the back?" asked Miller. As she had held the slip up to read it, he had seen some writing on the back.

Gina turned the slip over. "Just a lot of letters and numbers. Doodling, probably." She handed it to Miller.

"This isn't doodling. It's some kind of code."

"Do you think he's a spy?" Gina asked, her eyes widening.

Professor Miller suppressed the urge to tell Gina how naïve he thought she was. "Cute but clueless is just about right," he thought to himself. Then he said, "This isn't a spy code. It's a set of notes, of abbreviations. Look, these numbers are dates, today and tomorrow. And these initials are probably the ticker symbols for certain companies. And these notes, 'buy,' 'sell,' are the actions he plans to take. And these figures look like times of day. So this one seems to mean, 'Buy FRGP today at 12:45 Pacific Time.'"

"I guess that's why you're a critical thinking professor," said Gina. "It's almost 12:20 right now. Maybe we should go call him."

"You're right," said Miller, pulling out his cellular phone. "Finish up and I'll give him a call." Miller took another bite from his sandwich and chewed rapidly. He took out his own room reservation and got the hotel's number. "Room 13-208, please." Miller barely had time to grab another bite before they were connected. "Hello, Mr. Trimmer? My name's Miller. You don't know me, but I think I have found your wallet. What? Yes, did you lose one?" Gina could not hear the other end of the conversation, but she could discern that the man on the other end was highly animated and seemed to be speaking rapidly and excitedly. "Okay, then," said Miller to the man, "we will be right up." Miller pushed the disconnect button on the phone and took another bite of his sandwich. "As you might imagine," he began, "Mr. Trimmer is quite anxious to get his wallet back. Let's go do a good deed, shall we?"

Trimmer opened the door with enthusiasm and even hugged Miller and Gina. Then he shook their hands. He was smiling broadly. "Larson Trimmer," he said. "Call me Lars." The man had an instantly likeable personality, friendly and effusive. Miller and Gina introduced themselves. When Gina gave her name, Mr. Trimmer looked back at Miller with just a slightly quizzical expression.

"My niece," Miller said.

"Glad to meet such honest folks," Trimmer continued. "I thought I'd never see my wallet again. I was about to call the credit card companies and cancel them. But, of course, I don't have their phone numbers handy, so I was going to have to call home."

"We're glad to be of help," said Miller. "I know how I'd feel if I lost my wallet."

"Here, here," Trimmer said, pulling the bills out of the wallet, "take this cash as your reward. You've really saved my bacon today." Gina was bug eyed. She was about to reach out for the cash reward when Miller grabbed her arm and pushed it back down.

"Thank you for the offer," he said, "but we don't want your money."

"The money's not important to me," said Trimmer, to the surprise of his new friends. "It's this information here that's of enormous, time-sensitive value." Trimmer was holding the little slip with the code numbers on it. "Please take the cash.

I can't thank you enough. The money is a pittance, a token of thanks for returning this."

"Thank you anyway," Gina said, trying to regain the high ground after Miller had been forced to stop her arm after the first offer. "We're just being good Samaritans."

Trimmer thought for a moment. "Well, then," he said, "let me take this money, which I declare is now yours, and invest it for you. You see, I work for a syndicate that makes a nationwide play in day trading, and if you know about day trading, things move very fast." He looked at his watch, gave a look of surprise, and began move toward the door, effectively pushing Gina and Miller out into the hallway. "In fact, I must be going right now or I'll miss an opportunity." He began to move down the hallway. "Tell you what. Please be my guests for dinner at the Del Oro Steak House here in the hotel. Will you meet me there at eight?"

"Ooh, I love steak," said Gina.

"That'd be fine. Sure, steak is good," said Miller. By this time, Trimmer had backed down the hall quickly and was almost halfway to the elevator.

"All right," he said. "Eight o'clock. And once again, my deepest gratitude."

Gina and Professor Miller rode the elevator down to the casino, where the pair wandered around for a few minutes looking over the many possible games. Miller stopped at a change booth and turned some bills into coins. He gave Gina two rolls of quarters for playing the slot machines. She chose one at random and sat down to feed the machine. For a few plays, the machine returned music but no money. Then, to the accompaniment of flashing lights, music, and beeping, sixteen quarters plunked into the stainless steel bin. "I won. I'm rich," she said.

"You're cute," Miller said. "I'll grant that. Rich, however, is another question. I think that once you count your coins, you'll see that appearances can be deceiving."

"I'm going to keep this machine. It's lucky," Gina said, undaunted by Miller's negativism. She continued to feed the slot machine, one quarter at a time. She tried three at a time, but her supply of coins was reduced too quickly that way, so she returned to one-at-a-time play. A few small wins here and there kept the play going longer than Miller expected. Out of boredom, he, too, began to feed one of the machines. He was almost entirely inattentive to his task. Before lunch, his mind had been preoccupied with Gina. Now it was consumed with the strange, friendly man they had just met, a man who had tried to give away $2,000 as if it were an extra napkin at a fast-food store. Such a casual view of so much money was very interesting.

Gradually, Gina's supply of quarters diminished, and eventually the money ran out.

"I'm broke," she said, simply.

"Well, as long as you had fun, that's all that matters."

"I had more fun when I was winning. I like to win."

"Well, of course, who doesn't? That's how they hook you. You come here thinking you are going to win and instead you get fleeced."

"But I'll bet some people win. The clever ones."

"Luck has little to do with cleverness or skill."

"Unless you make your own."

"We can probably get our room now," Miller said, no longer interested in this particular conversation. After all, he told himself, his interest in Gina was not for her philosophical insights about the operations of chance.

Their room was ready, and soon they were on the seventeenth floor looking out a window with a view out over the city toward the back of the hotel. Miller put his hand on Gina's back as they stood there.

"Oh, look at the huge pool area," said Gina. "Let's go down there and get some sun. I brought lotion and everything."

Gina spread out the large pool towel on a chaise lounge and Miller took one next to her. He watched her as she began to put suntan lotion over her arms and legs, but became conscious that he might be too obviously staring at her, so he turned to the magazine he had brought. He glanced over occasionally to observe her progress. At the last glance, Gina looked at him and reached the bottle toward him. Miller was about to decline, thinking that he would cover up before long and therefore not need lotion, when Gina spoke.

"Want to put some lotion on my back?" she asked. Miller put down his magazine, took the bottle and began to squirt some lotion into his palm. Gina turned onto her stomach and unhooked the top of her bikini so that Miller could spread the lotion over her back without bumping into the strap.

As he spread the lotion over her warm, soft skin, he felt amazed at his good fortune.

"I really ought to be a gambler," he thought. "With this kind of luck, I'd break the house and own one of these hotels in a day or two." Then he told himself that it really was not luck but the result of a carefully reasoned calculation on his part. He preferred to think that he deserved the successes of his life because of his intellectual prowess, his own ability. Attributing success to luck or good fortune diminished the credit due him. His book, for example, was, frankly, one of the best books in the area. It was no fluke. He was a good writer, a good thinker, and he had written a book that deserved to sell well. And the girl? Why should she not find him interesting—and yes, even suave—enough for an outing to Las Vegas? Perhaps a small amount of her interest was based on his good looks, but he largely discounted that, thinking himself modest for doing so.

"Thanks," Gina said. "That's perfect." She snuggled down into the chaise lounge, finding a comfortable position for a long tanning session. "Maybe you can give me a back rub later."

Miller smiled. "This is all part of your plan, isn't it?"

Gina lifted her head, opened her eyes and looked at him, smiling. She gave him a curious little wink and put her head back down.

Miller watched her for a minute. Her breathing was relaxed and regular. She might even be falling asleep. He remembered the comment of one of his woman colleagues who had caught on to his habit of romancing his students. "She's wrong," he thought. "I haven't stuffed a sock into the mouth of my conscience. I'm not taking advantage of anyone. This girl knows what she's doing."

He picked up his magazine again. It was a tourist magazine, listing all the shows in town, together with advertisements for hotels, buffets, and various amusements. He began to look for a show that interested him. He turned the pages slowly, pausing long over each advertisement. After a look at an ad, he would look up to gaze out over another part of the pool area.

Around the pool were dozens of chaise lounges, most of them filled on this warm day with sunbathers like himself and Gina. Only a few people lay unoccupied, doing nothing but soaking up the sunshine that shines on everyone alike. Most people seemed to have something to do while their tans increased. Several people talked on cell phones, a few taking notes as they did so, as if conducting serious business. It was still a workday for most people, and so it seemed that many here by the pool were at work. But they were fortunate enough to work in surroundings like no office could provide. One man was reading a small blueprint. Another, poor drone, sat with a notebook computer at a table in the shade. Those who did not need to work today read novels or, like himself, magazines. Many sipped on creatively made tropical drinks. A few even had food.

Miller paid special attention to the young women. Some in the pool and several sunbathing were quite attractive. He began to play a mental game, asking himself which of them he might be willing to trade Gina for and why. After a few minutes, he smiled at himself and went back more seriously to the magazine. He found a show that looked interesting. "The Amazing Khan," the ad said. A photograph showed a man in a highly theatrical costume, designed perhaps to remind the viewer of Genghis Khan, the medieval Mongolian ruler. With him in the photograph were several circus animals, lovely assistants, and an enormous amount of cash, strewn all over the stage. Miller's curiosity was engaged. "In the world of magic," the ad said, "nothing is as it appears—or disappears! You will not believe your eyes!"

Miller read the latter claim and thought, "No, it's the cliché I won't believe. I think I'll believe my eyes. We'll see if my eyes are better than your tricks." He loved the idea of a challenging intellectual game, where he could pit his analytic mind against the trick of the magician. How many tricks could he figure out simply by thinking about how they must be done?

"Rated the number one show in Las Vegas!" the ad concluded.

"I imagine that pretty much every show is rated number one by someone," thought Miller, using his critical thinking. "You see, oh Khan, I have already figured out one of your tricks. Besides that, a number one rating is something of an *ad populum* fallacy. Popularity is no guarantee of quality. Still, a magic show would be interesting. An interesting thought problem." He looked over at Gina, who was still lying on her stomach, eyes closed as if asleep.

"Gina?"

"Mmm."

"How about a magic show tonight?"

"Mm hm."

"Okay. It's at the casino across the street. We can even walk."

"Mmm."

"Are you going to turn over and cook the other side or just broil your back?"

"Minute."

"I don't want you to get sunburned."

Chapter 13

"Hey, Markayla," Amy said as she came in and plopped her backpack on her bed.

"Hello, Amy," Markayla said, barely looking up from her textbook. Amy looked over to say hi to Tina, but the girl was lying on the bed with her headphones on. Amy pulled a couple of books from her backpack and was about to carry them over to her desk, when she suddenly became aware of a bouquet of flowers sitting there in a vase. Markayla's vase, with some very wilted flowers in it, was still on her desk. Markayla was still deep in her book.

"What's this?" Amy asked.

Markayla put her finger on the page and looked up at Amy, then turned her head to where Amy was looking. "The guy you hang out with left those for no apparent reason," she said. She then tilted her head back down to her book and removed her finger. Amy could not see the smile.

Amy danced over to the flowers and pulled off the note, almost knocking over the vase. The note said, "To a charming and cute repairman. Thanks. Matt."

"Ah, how sweet."

"Would you like to use my vase?" Markayla said, looking up again. "It is much heavier and my flowers are ready to retire." Amy nodded. Markayla emptied the past-due remains of a previous bouquet into the trash and handed her the heavy vase. Amy soon had it rinsed and the new flowers brightly installed. Amy thought about her nap, but, seeing

Markayla so dedicated, she decided to do something useful, too. So she sat down at her desk ("where I can be near my flowers," she thought) and opened her notebook computer. It occurred to her that she had left it open earlier. She wondered how it had gotten closed.

She had just begun to check her email when the giver of the flowers himself made an appearance.

"Hey, Aim-o," Matt said. "What's happening?"

"Nothing, really."

"Nothing at all?"

"No, why?"

"Are those Markayla's flowers on your desk?"

"No, they're mine. Some guy gave me flowers. Isn't that sweet?"

"Some guy?"

"Yeah, some guy left a really nice bouquet of flowers and a mash note. Probably wants to date me."

"And do you have any idea who this guy was?"

"No idea."

"No idea? Didn't he sign the note?"

"Well yeah, but he hid his true identity by forging your name, so I have no clue about who it really was. Isn't that a scream—he signed your name so I'd think they were from you." Amy realized she was losing control of her straight face, so she pretended to sneeze.

"Tell me, Matt," Markayla said. "What made you want a crazy person for a girlfriend?"

Just then Amy screamed. "Matt, there's a huge spider!" she said excitedly, pointing at the wall. On the wall a few feet from her desk a tiny spider sat in the light of Amy's reading lamp, possibly getting a tan under the 60-watt sun. When Markayla saw it, she screamed, too, and backed up half way across the room. Matt looked over at it, leaning toward it just a bit.

"Hey, Chuck, my boy. How's it going?" he said to the spider. Then, turning to Amy, "Oh, that's just Chuck. He's okay. He's been living with you guys for quite awhile now. Don't worry, he doesn't crawl into bed with you unless it's really cold."

Sounds of "Eww!" The girls were not amused. They definitely had the creeps and were acting trembly. The screams had gotten Tina's attention, too, and now she looked on the scene as well, though from several feet away, still on her bed.

"Matt, kill it!" Amy pleaded.

Matt got closer and peered at the tiny insect. His mouth opened with shock and he exhaled heavily. "You're right," he said almost breathlessly. "That's not Chuck. It's a *Fangextensis girliphage*, the long-toothed girl eater. Oh, those are bad."

Perhaps the little bug detected the hostility of the monsters glaring at it—those thousand-foot monsters, with teeth so huge that the smallest one was larger than the spider's entire body. Or perhaps the spider's suntan lotion was a low SPF and he thought it was time to get into the shade. Whatever the reason, the bug took a couple of steps toward the far wall. Stereo shrieks immediately shattered the tense silence.

"Matthew! It's moving!" Amy was doing that little running in place dance that girls sometimes do when they are freaked out by bugs.

The spider had stopped to contemplate his next move, when suddenly and unexpectedly his decision making career ended as a meteor landed on him, spreading him out flatly along the wall.

Matt grabbed a tissue from Amy's desk and wiped off his finger.

"Whoo! That was close," he said. "Good thing I got him. One of these babies can eat a girl, of, say, five foot three, in under two minutes."

"Matt," Amy said.

"They've been *timed*."

"A little spider can't eat a whole girl."

"Well, sometimes instead of eating the girl right up, they just tie her up with a few strands of silk and then snack on her at their leisure. It's pretty gruesome."

"You're being silly."

"Oh, like *irrational*?" His smile showed that he meant the irony gently.

Just then Ron stopped in. "I'm just on my way to see my pukey girlfriend," he said, "and thought I'd say hello."

Matt was breathless again.

"Oh, Ron, you just missed it. I just killed a *Fangextensis girliphage*." He pointed at the smudge on the wall. "It almost got me."

"A *Fangextensis girliphage*?" Ron echoed with amazement. He gave a low whistle. "You're a braver man than I am, Matt," he said, slapping Matt on the back and then shaking his hand with congratulation. "That is one mean dude." Then he turned to Amy and Markayla, with a nodding glance at Tina to include her, too. "Lucky for you girls Matt was here."

"Not you, too," Amy said.

"Hey, I told them," said Matt. "The long-toothed girl eater is ruthless and voracious."

"You guys would have been lunch on the hoof if Matt hadn't been here with his trusty finger weapon," Ron said.

Matt held his hand like a gun and blew the imaginary smoke off his finger tip.

"You heard about that girl in Iowa just last week?" Ron asked Matt.

Matt nodded. "Under two minutes." They both laughed.

"This is something you two have made up," Markayla said. The tone in her voice indicated that she was largely but not completely sure.

"Men!" was all Amy said.

"I don't like spiders," Tina said softly from across the room.

"So now that you're all alive and safe," Ron said, "what's the news on Shelley? Anybody checked on her recently?"

"I was over this morning," Amy said. "She's doing okay. No doubt she needs your tender care, though."

"Yeah," said Matt. "She seems to be hung up on some no good physics major who has made her crazy through drugs or hypnosis or something. She thinks he's some deal. I've told her to get a cooler boyfriend. I think that's what she's planning to do as soon as she can get out of bed. Ha ha! In fact, realizing what a lame-o boyfriend she has may explain why she's barfing!"

"By that reasoning, Amy would be dead now," Ron said.

"You guys," Amy began. Both ignored her.

"It's just lucky for you that the women here have such low standards," Matt told Ron.

"You know, you're right," Ron agreed. "It's no wonder they say women always choose men who don't deserve them. Look at Amy here. Kind of cute, smart, fun, nice figure—."

"Ron, that's enough," Amy interrupted.

"Shelley always tells me to keep going and add details. Anyway, what I meant to say was, who could ask for a better cuddle bunny at a cold football game—."

"Ron! That's more than enough," Amy said more forcefully.

"And yet she keeps going out with some hayseed farmer's kid who has conned her into believing he owns a car. It's a good thing he grew up on a farm where he learned how to use baling wire to hold junk together. Let's just hope she isn't with him when some kid in a red wagon challenges him to a race. She'd never survive the humiliation."

Matt nodded his head as if he agreed with what Ron was saying. "And you know, that's not the worst of it. The worst of it is that his best friend is an outlaw biker who mistakes his bike's noise for speed."

"It'll blow the doors off your rolling coffin any day."

"My rolling coffin? Shelley says you're the only guy who can make her think about death. It happens every time she gets on your bike. And besides," he continued, turning to the insult against his car, "Bertha may not be fast, but she's reliable."

"Bertha? Don't you mean Eek and Creak?"

"Boys, stop," Amy said. Markayla had ceased paying attention to them and had sat down to read, or to pretend to read.

"So, I'm off. Doctor Ron needs to make his rounds."

"I hope she survives your treatment," Matt said.

Ron turned to go. "Just remember, Matt. If they ever find a use for rust, you'll be a rich man."

After Ron had left, Amy turned to Matt. "In spite of the way you tortured us, thank you for killing the spider," she said, stroking his arm.

"So now you're really grateful, huh?"

"Mildly grateful."

"So your gratitude and indebtedness to me are great, wide, and deep."

"You want something." Amy looked at him narrowly.

"Well, there is this concept called reciprocation, you know. And I have just saved your life."

"Oh, so now it all comes out. It's all clear now. My mistake. Excuse my blindness. Here I thought we were friends, but no, what we have here is a transactional relationship. Every good deed must be repaid in kind, and with interest. You do something for me only because you want something in return. Now I see it. Okay, fine. No love lost here. I'm ready. Just what is it you want?"

"Well, I have to take back the old vacuum booster to get a refund for the core charge, and I thought that if you wanted to go, we could do dinner tonight instead of tomorrow night, thus accomplishing both tasks on one tank of gas."

"So dinner with me is a task now, is it?"

"Did I say *task*? I meant *pleasure*."

"And I guess there's a game on tomorrow night that you just found out about."

"No, Amy. I didn't just find out about any game."

"You knew about it before, but you had forgotten." Amy had learned a lot from her father about interrogation and the techniques of evasion. She knew that people often construct statements that are literally true but that create a false implication. To her surprise, she had hit the truth. Matt reddened a bit but said nothing.

"Aha!" she said with triumph. "Well, we'll let that one pass until a time when I can get more mileage out of it."

Matt relaxed. "Thanks."

"But dinner with you as payment for killing the spider? Man, your price for a good deed is way steep."

"I do not understand American romance," Markayla mumbled to herself. Tina looked genuinely concerned, as if the two were in conflict.

"The price may be high," Matt said, "but, as the commercial says, I'm worth it."

"You wish. Looks like in the future, I'll have to ask first what I'm going to have to do to repay you for a good deed."

"But the future is so far away. Live for the moment."

"Well, I guess I'm trapped now. What time?"

"Well, the auto parts store closes at 5:30, and it's almost 5:00 now."

"Do you realize that many girls will not go out with a guy unless he asks them at least three days in advance? And here you are asking three minutes in advance."

"Yeah, but I don't date those girls."

"Oh, so this is interesting. That means you do date other girls. Which ones?" Amy gave Matt a look of intense scrutiny. "Confess." She tapped her foot rapidly.

Markayla could take this silly banter no longer. "Go on. Get out of here. Go to the store. Go to dinner. Come back late. Some people would like to graduate from this university."

As Matt and Amy got ready to head out the door, Tina walked over to Amy. "You're both going away?" she said, with evident anxiety.

"Just out for awhile," Amy told her.

Amy looked at Matt. She dared not invite Tina on a date Matt had set up.

"Would you like to go, too, Tina?" Matt asked, not realizing how many points he was gaining.

"Yeah."

"Thank you, Matt," Amy said as Tina ran over to her bed to put on her shoes and add a sweatshirt.

"What about you Markayla? Want some dinner?"

"Oh, the dining commons is fine. I am not picky. I eat anything."

"Oh, right," Matt said. "Like with coffee." Then he tried to imitate Markayla: "Why was my father not a coffee importer rather than an oil man? This coffee is beneath every standard of acceptability. I cannot drink it. It should be outlawed." The imitation was ridiculous. Matt's imitation of a girl was to use a very high pitched, screechy voice. Putting his version of a British accent on the screech only made it worse.

"The food I can stand. The coffee is another matter completely," said Markayla.

"Come on. We'll go to the Klatch after dinner and get you some real coffee."

"But I'm only on page 145."

"You can study tomorrow. The whole day. We won't bother you. It's time for a break now. Time for food, fun, and fellowship. And besides, if you're totally obsessive, you can study again when we get back. Amy's parents won't let me keep her out late."

"That's right," Amy agreed.

"Yeah, three, maybe four A.M. is the max."

Matt's offer was persuasive. Markayla went to the closet for a sweater.

"You like Mexican, Tina?" Matt asked.

"If it's the good kind."

"How about you, Aim-o. Is Don Pepe's okay?"

"How can I refuse? It's part of my required payment for your chivalrous deed. I'm just a slave to your wishes." Then she took hold of his arm and added quietly, "Don Pepe's sounds great."

As they pulled into the parking lot of the auto parts store, Matt heard Amy say, "Remember that you have to pay for dinner. Don't spend all the refund on cans of spray oil or tools."

"I've been cut," Matt said, feeling of his chest where he thought his heart was. "I don't know where these ridiculous attacks come from."

"Experience, knowledge, observation," Amy said.

"Ow. She not only puts salt on the rusty blade, but she twists the handle, too." Matt coughed for effect.

Don Pepe's was down the freeway a trace, so it was forty-five minutes later by the time the old booster had been returned and they had driven to the restaurant. Four hungry students therefore exited the car, which was grateful to feel the weight being taken off its sagging suspension.

As they walked up to the door, Tina stopped.

"What's wrong?" Amy asked.

"They don't want me to eat here."

"Who doesn't want you to eat here?" Matt asked.

"The Abierto group," Tina said.

"Who's that?" Matt asked again.

"It's been taken over by the Abiertos," Tina said, pointing to the sign in the window that said, "Open. Abierto."

"That means they're open," Amy said.

"I'm not an Abierto," Tina said.

"Don't worry, Tina," Amy told her. "You're with us. It's okay. Come on."

"Are you sure?"

"Yes. Come on. They have good food here."

"We are with you," Markayla added.

Tina was persuaded, and they went in.

They were soon seated in a padded red booth and brought a large tray of chips and salsa.

"My three girlfriends and I would all like water to start with," Matt said as he took the last menu from the waiter.

"Yes, sir," the waiter said. Back in the service area, they could hear an exclamation that sounded like, "Ay, Chihuahua!"

"Matt, you've totally scandalized that waiter," Amy said, in a scolding tone.

"What? I don't know what you're talking about."

The food arrived and the four held hands as Matt gave a brief blessing. He gave Amy's hand a little extra squeeze before letting it go.

The food was quite good, but Amy was now worrying about Tina more than ever and wondering what was really wrong with her. What could be done to help her? Did her parents know? Could the school counselors or health service help? Amy also felt grateful to Matt. Here he had wanted to be alone on a date with Amy, only to end up with her two roommates as well, one of whom clearly was not quite well. What a nice guy he was. She looked over at Matt, a look of sadness on her face and her eyes glistening with emotion. Just then, he happened to look over at Amy. Not knowing the complexity of her thoughts, he read her face to be an expression of her deep feeling for him and felt fully repaid for any loss of intimacy the presence of the other girls had caused.

Matt was his usual happy self during the meal. He ate heartily. Once, when the waiter returned to fill the water glasses, he said, "My women and I really like your food." The waiter merely nodded. Markayla put her hand up in an effort to hide the look of embarrassment on her face. Tina did not appear to be paying attention. Amy stepped on his foot. "Ow," Matt said, looking at Amy with a pained expression. "You stepped on my foot."

"And I'm not apologizing, either," Amy said.

Markayla praised the flavor of what she called "the ethnic food." Tina looked over her food almost with suspicion and picked out several little pieces that looked just like all the other pieces, but she ate nearly all the rest of it. Amy's stomach was not communicating with her brain at all, and she could not have said with accuracy whether she was still hungry or not. However, she remembered having been hungry as they drove to the restaurant, so she made herself eat.

"Well," said Amy after they were almost finished eating, "I guess I should forgive you for preferring some sports thing over me and bouncing me from tomorrow night to tonight. This food was really good."

"Yeah," said Matt. "All in all, it was worth a little extra to get the flowers with the spider. The result has been quite gratifying. Good food, beautiful women—"

"Do you mean that you brought that spider in on purpose?" Markayla asked, her eyes wide.

"It's okay, Markayla. He's just teasing. In his twisted sort of way."

"You started it."

"What makes you think I was teasing?"

"Don't argue, please," Tina said, looking at Amy. Her face wore a pleading, troubled look.

"It's okay, Tina. We're just having fun. Matt and I are friends."

"Of a very odd nature," said Markayla.

Matt picked up the bill. "Ow, ow, ow, ow," he said, as if in pain.

"Do you need some help, Matt?" Amy asked. "You don't have to pay for all of us."

"No, I've got it. I'll just use pretend money." He took a credit card from his wallet and took the bill over to the cash register. Amy stayed with him while Tina and Markayla went on outside.

"These things are great," Matt said, waving his card. "Have all the fun you want, live with wild abandon, and don't have to pay for it until later."

"Matt, I'm really worried about Tina," Amy said softly. "She needs some kind of help."

"Why don't you talk to the RA?" Matt said. "Or the health center?"

"That's a good idea. I'll do that tomorrow, or tonight if Melanie is around. Thanks."

"Hey, no prob."

"And thank you so much for the dinner and for just being you."

"Well, thank you for helping me with the car."

"Any time. It was fun."

"You're the only girl I know who thinks getting greasy is fun."

"I didn't say that part was fun."

"But you like tools, don't you? Admit it."

"Tools are tools. You use them."

"Tools are my friends."

By this time they were out at the car. Matt opened the doors for everyone and soon they were gently swaying and bounding down the road, bottoming out at every bump or dip.

"Gotta get that suspension fixed," thought Matt.

Chapter 14

Professor Miller and Gina had not been seated long at the Del Oro Steak House before Mr. Trimmer arrived. He was smiling the smile of self satisfaction. As he sat down, the waiter came over to him with a table setting and a menu. "No menu," said Trimmer. Just bring me your best sixteen-ounce filet mignon, rare. Baked potato with too much butter. Something from the vegetable kingdom, but nothing disgusting. And a bottle of Cabernet, you choose, and make it a good one."

Miller thought the clues were obvious, but asked politely, "Success?"

"Oh, yes, my good sir," said Trimmer jovially. "In fact," he went on, reaching into his coat pocket, "here are the results of your investments today." He handed each of them a certified cashier's check for $6,240.

Gina was struck with amazement. "I can't believe this," she said. "Yesterday I was a poor, simple college student eating burgers and fries. Now I'm in a fancy steak house with a check for six thousand dollars in my hands. I must be dreaming."

Miller was impressed by the check, but his mind was already far beyond it. He was calculating the possibility of further investments and how larger sums might return even larger rewards. He was a shrewd one, all right.

"This is wonderful," he said, to fill in an expected response.

"Wait until my friends hear about this. New outfits, tuition and everything."

"Your friends mustn't hear about this," Trimmer said quickly and a bit sternly. "This is a confidential business we are involved in. A business which requires the utmost trust and secrecy. I thought that by your returning my wallet you were people who could be trusted."

"You can trust me," Gina said, now feeling chastised. "I promise not to tell. Why is it so secret?"

Miller had an expression on his face that was the equivalent of saying, "Any idiot knows this must be kept secret."

The three were silent while a waiter brought ice water and a setup for Mr. Trimmer. Trimmer waited until the man was several steps away before speaking again. He kept a low tone.

"My company gathers inside information of the most confidential sort about various companies, and that information allows us to know which stocks are going to rise suddenly and which are going to fall suddenly. That information allows us to make informed purchases and thereby make guaranteed profits."

"I don't understand," said Gina.

"That's not important," said Trimmer. "The important thing is that the information must be kept secret until the time we share it with the world."

"But if you share it, then why keep it secret at first?" Gina asked.

"Well," said Trimmer, "if we know the information about a company is good, we can buy a stock at a low price before others find out about it and buy the stock, causing it to go up in value."

"Buying a stock makes it go up?" Gina asked. Trimmer and Miller looked at each other, as if to agree that the girl was hopelessly clueless.

"That's right," Miller said, only a little patronizingly.

"So we buy a stock, it goes up, and we're rich?"

"Something like that," said Trimmer.

Miller was beginning to catch on to the plan. "You buy a stock, then put out the news about how great it is, and when it goes up suddenly and dramatically, you then sell it at a big profit, right?" he asked.

"That's one method. Or if the news is going to be bad, we sell the stock short and then buy it after it falls. Are you familiar with short sales?"

"Only a little," said Miller, hating to have to admit ignorance in any area.

"A short sale involves selling a stock that you don't yet own. Perfectly legal and ethical. Then, when the stock falls, you buy the stock at the low price and use those shares to cover the ones you sold but did not have. It is simplicity itself."

"And if the stock goes up rather than down?" asked Miller.

"Ah, but we are sure it won't. When we share the news about the stock, we know that it will go up on good news and down on bad news. There is no risk involved. As I said, I work for a large company with field representatives like me and operations like this one all over the country. None of us believe in gambling."

"How do you share the news?" asked Gina.

"If you'd like to open a trading account, perhaps with your current profits, I would be happy to show you," said Trimmer. "After all, you will never believe how you helped me by returning that time-sensitive information this morning. It made a substantial difference. Substantial."

"You mean you'd let us trade with our $6,000 and make some more money?" gasped Gina. Then turning to Miller, "Let's do it!" she said. "I promise not to tell."

"Yeah, why not?" said Miller. "Seems like a reasonable deal. And I could always use a little extra money. And Gina wants to take the night helicopter flight over the city, see a show, and upgrade our room to a suite." The possibility of making a large amount of easy money was very appealing, even though it seemed to involve some kind of trading that was not strictly legitimate.

Gina excused herself to go to the restroom.

"A lovely girl," Trimmer observed, his eyes following Gina as she walked away. "I believe you said she was your niece?"

"That's the public information," Miller said. "And as we both know, public information is for those who don't know what is really going on. The girl's actually just a diversion." Miller liked pretending that this trip was merely one of many others, one of so many that he was almost bored with it. "She's here for the same reason that psychic hotlines exist."

Trimmer looked at him expectantly.

"For entertainment purposes only."

They both laughed.

"I've been chewing on a huge workload at the university and thought it was high time for an after dinner mint," said Miller. Trimmer smiled again.

"Quite right," he said. "However," he added, changing his tone, "I hope you can count on her to be discreet."

"I'm sure I can."

"After all, if you want to make a few dollars in the market, you don't want her to call her mother and blab it all over."

"Oh I plan to take good care of her," said Miller. "She won't have a chance to talk to her mother, or anyone else for that matter."

"You'll keep an eye on her, then."

"Both eyes."

"Good."

Miller took advantage of a pause to ask a question. "How is it that your company has all this exclusive information about certain stocks?"

"Research," said Trimmer, winking. "We find out the most amazing information and share it with the world and the stocks cannot help but move in the predicted direction."

"And the authorities take a dim view of your public spirit-edness, no doubt," said Miller, catching on to the disinformation game Trimmer's company was playing.

"Alas, that is so," said Trimmer with affectation. Then, continuing matter-of-factly, "Our position is that day traders know what they are doing and are responsible for their own actions. If they act before checking out the information, then too bad for them. We are sincere when we say a stock will rise or fall, and, as I said, we are always right. You might say we are fortune tellers. We're just sorry that the authorities can't be reasonable about all this. So, we just operate quietly."

The conversation changed to Miller's good luck in "reeling in" Gina, as Trimmer called it. When Miller attributed it more to skill than luck, Trimmer became very interested in Miller's technique. He was clearly envious.

Professor Miller spoke complacently about his happy position in the world as a professor constantly surrounded by attractive young women, many (he said) of whom he found it easy to attract for romantic adventures (as he called them).

Gina, of course, was proof and example. Mr. Trimmer admitted that he would not mind having a romantic adventure with Gina and congratulated Miller again and again over the course of the conversation.

"Something about her smile," Trimmer said, "and those eyes. Powerful, aren't they?"

"Yes," Miller agreed.

Trimmer listened with great attentiveness to Miller's opinions and ideas and echoed many of them. The man seemed almost like an uncle to Miller. He was one of the most affable people Miller had ever met. Just as Gina returned, Miller had concluded, "This man thinks just the way I do."

"You're a very accommodating and generous person," said Miller. "I imagine that you don't even get upset when you see people take an unreasonable amount of crab legs at the buffet."

"Ah, no," said Trimmer. "I'm one of those who likes his crab. I like to pile those crab legs up as high as anyone does. And I consider my behavior to be quite sensible. After all, what's reasonable to you may not be the same as what's reasonable to me. Who's to set a standard for crab legs? We live in a world that has found standards inconvenient. They interfere with our desires." He gave just the slightest tilt of his head in the direction of Gina, who was conveniently looking at her food and did not notice.

The meal that night seemed exceptionally good to Professor Miller, his taste buds being enlivened by the general gusto he was feeling. He relished every bite as it seemed to symbolize his prospects for eating large at the table of life. Trimmer ate his steak happily; Gina ate hers with expressed satisfaction. Her eyes sparkled and she smiled at the two men. "This is all so great!" she said, more than once. Miller thought she chewed in a provocative way, almost as if she were pursing her lips, moistened by the eating, but perhaps it was just her smile or his imagination. Trimmer gave her an admiring look and plunged into his baked potato. The butter spilled over the top and onto his plate.

While the full plates and empty stomachs were in the process of trading adjectives, Professor Miller and Gina were entertained by the jovial and knowledgeable Mr. Trimmer. He seemed to know about every show, every attraction, every restaurant, and every behind-the-scenes tidbit in the city.

"This man is a walking encyclopedia," Miller thought, "only funny."

"This is an excellent Cabernet," Trimmer noted, as he began his third glass.

During the intervals between stories, it was decided that Miller and Gina would join Mr. Trimmer the next day and go to his trading office to invest their current earnings.

"There's a nice trade coming up tomorrow morning that should be good for us all," he said. "We don't even have to get up very early. I don't have final word yet, but my estimate is that the trading window will be around noon, which is three o'clock market time."

"What's market time?" Gina asked.

"The stock market is on the East coast," Miller said. He was actually amused that Gina was so uninformed. Smart women can be dangerous, he thought. They might put two and two together.

Though the time seemed to pass quickly, everyone eventually became aware of being tired of sitting. When the dessert tray came around, Miller declined any, saying that he and Gina might indulge in a midnight snack after the show they were going to see.

"We've got tickets to the Amazing Khan, the 10:00 show," he said, looking at his watch.

"Well," said Trimmer, "you two go have some fun, then. Stroll down the strip and enjoy the evening. There is much here to see, much to enjoy. I'll meet you, oh, say outside the buffet at, oh, half past nine. That will give us plenty of time to eat, get down to the office, and get things ready. Yes?"

"Nine thirty it is," said Miller.

"This is so cool," Gina said, as they walked toward the front doors of the hotel on their way to the strip. "We need to do this more often!" She laughed. Miller smiled to himself. He had been thinking the same thing.

The Amazing Khan exploded on stage in a shower of fireworks and a cloud of smoke. A loud orchestra underscored the drama of his entrance, and of his every move throughout the performance. In fact, there was never a moment of rest for the audience. An announcer gave what amounted to a play-by-play of the Khan's tricks; huge video displays showed the tricks from varying angles and in replay; the orchestra kept up an almost incessant accompaniment; and even an occasional horn or bell could be heard.

Noticing this constant busyness, Miller leaned over to Gina and said, "They don't want us to get bored or fall asleep." Regular visits by cocktail waitresses provided further stimulus for staying awake. Miller ordered a glass of wine and Gina asked for iced tea.

The Khan began with simple tricks, including materializing a dove from under a handkerchief, pulling an extensive ribbon from his mouth, and doing a few card tricks with extra-large cards.

"Look at his left hand," Miller whispered to Gina while Khan held a dove in his right hand. "While we're supposed to be looking at the dove, he's reaching under the edge of his coat behind him with his other hand."

"Wow."

"It's called misdirection. They get your attention focused on one thing and then do something else while you're not looking. It's the basis of magic."

"You really know a lot."

A lovely assistant joined Khan on stage. Stage hands dressed in black wheeled a large cage into the center of the stage and left. Khan put the girl into the cage and then threw a black sheet over it. Loud music, reaching a crescendo, cymbals, a firework blast, smoke, and then the sheet was ripped off, to reveal a live tiger in the cage in place of the girl.

"So that's how you turn a woman into a tiger," Miller joked.

"Maybe there's a tiger inside every woman, waiting for a magician to let her out."

The tiger was no sooner wheeled out than four men dressed as bank guards rolled out a strong box, covered with chains and locks and elaborate closures, which they laboriously proceeded to undo, until the lid of the box swung open. While Khan tilted the box toward the audience to show that it was empty, the guards left the stage briefly. Soon they returned carrying large money bags. Each guard opened his bags and poured bound stacks of bills out onto the floor, forming one large pile.

"There is a million dollars in cash here," Khan said. "Do we have an honest volunteer from the audience to come up and check it?" Hands all over the room. "You, ma'am," said Khan, pointing to an elderly but eager woman. The woman made her way up on the stage and over to the cash, picking up four or five bundles and looking them over.

"It's the real thing!" she said, and then pretended to secrete some of it in her blouse. The audience laughed.

The guards now put all the money into the large chest and once again laboriously closed each latch, connected each chain, and fastened each padlock. Then the guards left. Khan acted as if he were going into a trance to get extra magical power for the trick he was about to perform. The orchestra grew louder. Khan waved his arms over the chest, this time not using a black cover, but uttering some magical incantation. At the last word, there was another firework, more smoke, more cymbals. The chest looked the same. Guards rushed out and rapidly removed the locks and chains. The lid flew open and out jumped Khan's lovely assistant, dressed in a costume that appeared to have been made of the currency that had been placed in the chest.

"A babe dressed in money," Miller thought. "What more could a guy want?"

"Ooh, wow," said Gina, in awe. "How did they do that one?"

"Well, it's really hard to see up there. Notice the black stage, the black curtains, and the dark room. The darkness makes it hard to see what's going on. It's almost blinding."

"Hah! Blinded by darkness. Now that's funny."

Miller was somewhat annoyed by Gina's flippancy. Her laughter made him feel less respected as an analyzer of magic. But he said nothing.

For the last trick of the performance, Khan and his assistant rode an elephant on stage. The elephant turned from side to side and bowed, as the performers thanked the audience for their appreciation. Then, just as the elephant gave another bow, there was a final firework and puff of smoke and all the lights in the room went out. Two spotlights came on and hunted the room for the performers briefly. Then the lights came back up, only to reveal an empty stage. This final trick almost stunned the audience, for no one believed that a slow-moving elephant could either walk or be moved off stage during the short time the lights were off. It was truly amazing.

It was midnight before Professor Miller and Gina rode the elevator back to their room.

Chapter 15

Melanie had not answered the knock on her door when Amy got back from dinner with her roommates and Matt. Amy did not want to knock with too much persistence, since she knew that sometimes Melanie took a little personal time off and simply did not answer her door, even though she was in her room. Often, too, she was out with friends in the evening. Getting no answer, Amy had decided to wait until the next day to try again.

Melanie was not known to be an early riser, so Amy went to breakfast and then on to her morning class without checking to see if her RA was available. She was encouraged to be a little relaxed because this morning Tina had seemed to be fine, almost cheerful. When Amy had left for class, Tina had been humming a little bit as she put on her shoes, even though she was not wearing her headphones or playing one of her radios.

When Amy returned from class, Tina was gone. Markayla sat at her desk, sipping what, by the aroma, must have been a really good cup of coffee. She was reading the paper.

"Where's Tina Nicole?"

"She went to see if breakfast is still on, and if not, I think she was going to the student union to get something to eat."

Amy looked over at her own desk, to determine how inviting it looked for doing some studying. She noticed that her computer had been turned around again and that there was a small unlit candle on her desk. She examined it. Then she noticed several others placed around the room.

"What are all these candles doing here?" she asked.

"Tina brought them in. When she put one on my desk, I said thank you and asked her why she was giving me a candle. She said it was for security. I told her that the rules of the dormitory will not let us light them, and she said we did not have to light them. Then she said we should light them anyway to disinfect the room. She lit two or three in the bathroom and then left. I put them out."

"Do you think she will light the ones on her desk when we're not here?"

"I do not know. We must keep an eye on her. We do not want to be to told to leave the dormitory."

"Or fined. What do you think she meant by *security*?"

"I do not know."

"I've got to talk to Melanie or someone about her."

"Why not call her and see if she is in? Oh, that reminds me. Before you call Melanie, you should call Shelley."

"Oh?"

"Yes. She called while you were in class."

Amy returned the call and found herself invited to visit Shelley "to witness my remarkable recovery" from her food poisoning.

Amy was soon again in Shelley's room, sitting in a somewhat wobbly office chair. Shelley was trying to be up and about, but had to sit down most of the time.

"I'm just about back to normal," she said.

"When I got food poisoning in high school, I was out for a whole week. So you really are making a remarkable recovery."

"Thanks. Can't keep a good woman down. Or even me." Shelley smiled, but there was no happiness behind it. Amy could see that her friend was still not completely herself or up to speed. Shelley was more quiet than usual, almost thoughtful. In fact, the conversation dropped for a few moments. Amy looked at Shelley, trying to think of something interesting. In a random glance around the room, she noticed the adjusting cord on the blinds of the window behind Shelley had been pulled in half and hung fuzzy-ended and short.

"What happened to the string on your window blinds?" Amy asked, just to say something.

"Oh, it got into an argument with the vacuum cleaner. Ron is supposed to fix it soon."

"It broke in half? I could tie it for you. Where's the other half?"

"In the vacuum cleaner's tummy. That's why I need Ron to fix it." Then Shelley suddenly changed expressions. "Uh oh," she said, getting out of bed and heading for the bathroom. "Time for a word from our sponsor. Be right back."

When she returned, Shelley got back into bed and pulled the sheet up. "Thanks for coming," she said. "Sorry about the emergency."

"I've walked that road," Amy said.

"At least I'm no longer going at both ends. I hate barfing. I'm so glad that's over."

"I know what you mean."

The conversation lulled for another moment. Then Shelley said, "Tell me something, Amy. Do you think I'm shallow?"

"Shallow? What do you mean?"

"You know, shallow. Like all froth and no beer. Lacking substance."

"Why would you think that?"

"Sometimes I think people think of me as just a bunch of noise and smoke. I mean, everybody laughs when I act up, but is it me or just the appearance of me that's funny? Now that I'm sick and not funny, is there anything there?" She looked at Amy for a moment and then added, "Oh, I don't know what I'm saying. Must be the drugs I'm on."

"What are they giving you?"

"The pink medicine."

"I don't think the pink medicine will affect your thinking."

"But, no, really. I mean, even Ron. Will he think, a year from now, 'Well, I had a lot of laughs with Shelley, but then it was time to get serious, so I married Hortense, here'?"

"Hortense? Oh, Shelley."

"You know what I mean. I mean, don't get me wrong. I'm all for showing the usual shallow phoniness to be thought cool. It's like, what else is really important? But sometimes it seems like such an empty conformity. I mean, when someone says, 'Take Shelley, for example,' I just hope they won't reply, 'No thanks, I don't like bubble gum.' You know what I'm saying?"

"Shelley, you're probably the most creative person I know."

"Really?" The comment obviously pleased Shelley.

"And I wish I could be like you in your warm, outgoing way. I feel trapped by my own shyness sometimes."

Shelley wrinkled her brow in sympathy. "But you seem to have depth. Some kind of anchor that holds you together."

"Depth?" Amy had never thought of herself as deep.

"Yeah, like, you believe in God and stuff, don't you?"

Amy smiled. "Yeah, God and stuff."

"Can you hear my tummy rumbling from there?" Shelley, said, holding her stomach.

"No. I don't hear anything."

"From here it sounds loud enough to break a window." Shelley reached over to her bedside table and grabbed the bottle of bismuth. "I think I'll take just a smidge more of this pink stuff." After swallowing a small amount of the medicine, Shelley made a face of disgust and said, "Oh, that stuff is so great. I'm just glad the health center takes care to buy the cheapest, most disgusting form of this stuff. Uck. Vintage year. Not content to leave it as tasteless chalk, they have to add some nasty flavoring so you'll know it's really medicine. Mm, mm, good for you."

"You sound like you're feeling better already."

"Oh, I know," Shelley said, holding up a finger to signal the arrival of a new idea. "They add the flavoring so you won't drink it unless you really, really need it. Saves money that way, you see. We can't have these thirsty students swigging down our chalky sludge like it was a strawberry malt."

"I'm sure you're right."

There was another pause. Shelley burped as quietly as she could. Then she continued. "Anyway, so that spiritual stuff is important to you and you think about it, huh?"

"That's where I find truth and meaning." Amy felt a little awkward talking about her deepest self. But Shelley seemed interested.

"See? I want truth and meaning, too. I want to be more than a label that describes what I do. Student, girlfriend, maybe wife, high school teacher, business employee, film star, whatever. But I really don't know who I am yet. I'm still trying to find out. I haven't gotten around to finding out who God is."

"Well, maybe you could find out who God is first and then you'll find out who you are."

"Yeah." Shelley did not seem convinced. "Too bad I'm not dying." Amy stopped looking at the mess on the floor and looked at Shelley. "I mean, then you're supposed to see everything clearly and know what really matters and all that stuff."

"You don't have to be dying to think about those things."

"I know, but it'd be easier to find time to focus. Right now, life is so busy. Ooh, tell me again how creative I am."

Amy smiled. "You're always saying something funny, and doing funny stuff, pretending to be other people."

"That embarrasses Ron. He wants a normal girlfriend. Sometimes I pretend to be one. But then I feel bad."

"Bad?"

"For being deceitful."

"How?"

"By pretending to be an ordinary girlfriend, the kind Ron wants. I pretend to be interested in sports and motorcycles and the stuff he's interested in. Basketball bores me, but I could never tell him that."

"So how did you ever start dating Ron?"

"His roommate asked me out first. So I started going with him. He was almost cute and had this kind of shy personality that attracted me. Oh, once he took me fishing and I thought I'd drop dead from sheer boredom. I was bored out of my skull. I think he caught one or two little fish in five hours. I didn't even catch a cold. I did get sunburned.

"So he was boring?"

"Not exactly. He was okay, just a little weird. Like, his recreational reading was either true crime or disaster investigations. He would have loved Dr. Miller's critical thinking class."

"I'm in that class right now."

"Then you know what I mean. Lots of disaster films. I had that class last year. Anyway, Jon and I would be snuggled together in front of the TV and he'd be like, 'Did you know that if management had listened to the engineers about operating the high pressure pumps, the nuclear plant wouldn't have melted down?' and I was like, 'Chocolate or vanilla?'"

"Not your area of interest, huh?"

"No, but what is? That's the thing. I mean, I liked him because he cared about something. He wanted to know what made planes crash and how the cops caught the killers or whatever."

"Sounds a lot like my dad."

"Really? See, I respect that. Anyway, one night at dinner I watched him spend at least an hour trying to balance a chocolate chip cookie on two hard boiled eggs. He kept saying, 'This means something.'"

"Was he going crazy?"

"Nah. Mechanical engineering major. He thought he was onto some new idea. Anyway, I suddenly realized that we were not meant to be. Different planets and all. Ron noticed and made me an offer, so I rushed into his arms."

"How did the other guy take it?"

"Oh, Jon was cool. By then he thought *I* was crazy. I think it was 'good riddance' for him. We're still friends. I still ask him if he's got the cookie balanced." Shelley put her hand on her stomach. "Speaking of cookies, I hope I don't have to toss mine any more."

"Do you feel upset?"

"No, just my tummy is still rumbling. I don't feel pukey at all." After a sip of water, Shelley continued. "So Ron kind of caught me as I bounced off the wall."

"And you're not sure you are compatible with him?"

"See, that's what I mean, Amy. You think in terms of compatible and stuff. I mean, most people are like, 'Wow, he's good looking, so he's for me,' or 'Check out that babe. What a hottie. I'm all over her.' But you're thinking about what makes people compatible." Shelley paused and looked at Amy for a few moments, thinking. "You're not really into this live-for-the-moment stuff, are you?"

"Not really."

"You're already thinking about getting married and everything, huh?"

"Oh, no," Amy said, shaking her head and raising her hand to reinforce her words. "I want to get married someday, but right now the thought totally scares me."

"But you're thinking about what you want and what will last for a long time. That's what I want to do. I mean, I know I won't always be fresh and tasty, so I want to make myself valuable to someone for other reasons, too, to have some substance and find a guy who values that. Somebody who will want to keep me after the 'Best if used by' date."

"Shelley, I think that's very wise."

"Wise? Really? Me? Be my friend forever." Then, almost apologetically, Shelley added, "I get like this whenever I get sick. It makes me thoughtful."

"I think being thoughtful is good. My dad says one of the problems today is that nobody takes the time to think."

"It's nice to be able to talk like this. To have you here. I don't think guys particularly like thoughtful girls."

"I hope at least some do."

"Anyway, I get sick, I get thoughtful. Never fails." Then, more dramatically, "When I face death, I see my life passing before my eyes. Only it's not my past life I see, but my future. It's depressing."

"My dad is always telling me how lucky I am to be young because my whole life is before me, all the choices still available, all the opportunities to come. Or as Matt says, 'The banquet of life is still to be eaten largely.'"

"Don't you hate guys? They're always talking about food."

"And eating large quantities of it."

"Yeah. They'll eat a couple of racks of ribs and not gain an ounce, but if we just kiss the barbecue sauce off their lips, we gain five pounds."

Amy had never kissed the barbecue sauce off anyone's lips, but she nodded anyway.

"And then burping."

"Or worse."

Both girls showed expressions of disgust.

"Why do we put up with guys, anyway?" Shelley asked at last.

"Because they need us."

"Oh, that's a really progressive view. How selfless, how generous of you. 'My guy's a slug, but, gosh, he needs me.' Amy, that is so retro."

"Well, what's yours?"

"I think it's because we need them."

"That's worse. Not only retro but really politically incorrect."

"Yeah, I've probably been brainwashed by the dominant cultural paradigm."

"Where did that come from? A sociology class?"

"Nah, English."

"So then, you think you need Ron right now?"

"He makes me laugh. I like to laugh. And he's fun. I like fun, too."

"And is Ron someone who could be interested in this *substance* you want?"

"I don't know. I hope so. But sometimes I wonder if I've just paddled to the shallow end to feel my feet on the bottom. Jon acted like he didn't have time for fun, but I wonder if Ron has time for anything else. I mean, I wonder if he thinks I'm just a nice crunchy peanut, and once I get stale. . . ."

"Do you ever talk to Ron about your relationship?"

"Oh, that's real likely. Do you ever talk to Matt about your relationship?"

"Well, no."

"Talk to a guy about relationships? Come on, Amy. We're on planet Earth, remember?"

"What is it with guys and relationship talk anyway?"

"Yeah, what's wrong with guys? Hey, we ought to become feminists. Down with guys." Shelley made a fist and shook it weakly.

"I don't know. There are worse things in life than to be needed by a nice guy."

"Oh, Amy, I can't believe you said that." Then, changing tone, "But maybe there's some truth in it. I just wish I could figure out who to be. And don't tell me to be myself. That's the whole problem. I don't know who *myself* is."

"Is that why you're always playing different roles and pretending to be different kinds of people?"

"No, I'm just acting up. And you know I'm acting, right?"

"Well, usually. I think."

"I'm acting up to be funny. I like it when you raise your hand and start to cover your mouth to suppress a smile. Or a laugh."

"I had braces. I got into the habit of covering my mouth to hide them when I smiled. I haven't quite broken the habit yet."

"When did you get them off?"

"A little over a year ago."

"Did you feel dorky?"

"I still feel dorky. That's why I like Matt. He makes me feel human."

"Watch out, Matt."

"Shelley."

"There's nothing wrong with dorkiness. Look at Markayla. She's kind of dorky, but I'll bet she's going to go far. I'm sure she'll be the lawyer she wants to be."

"Judge, I think."

"And I'll probably end up teaching elementary school and acting in community theater. Or as a housewife. Scary, huh?"

"That's only scary because society makes fun of it. But we don't have to agree."

"Yeah, I guess. See, you're always thinking, and I'm just a cork on the river of life. A cork who pretends to be different people. Maybe I am trying to figure out who I am. The trouble is, acting is dangerous."

"How?"

"Well, in high school we did a play where I was the love interest of another character. Instead of acting badly, like most kids who are afraid to really get into a role, I just talked to the guy as if I really loved him. We were still in rehearsal when he fell in love with me and said he knew I loved him, too. I told him I was just playing a part, and he said, 'Shelley, that was not acting. That is real.'"

Amy made a face, sympathizing with the awkwardness.

"Even though the person knows the other is just pretending," Shelley continued, "having someone look into your eyes and say loving things is totally powerful. It's easy to believe because we all want to believe it. Even on a stage."

"No more plays for this girl, then," Amy said.

"That's why girls and guys are such dopes toward each other. We manipulate each other so easily because no one wants to believe they are being conned by a pretender.

"My dad says that the first rule of hoaxers and con artists is that they help us believe what we want to believe."

"Yeah, we're so gullible, it's ridiculous."

"No, what's sad is that people will lie about their feelings that way."

"It's hard to know who's genuine and who's just playing a role. In fact, maybe we're all just playing a role—or a bunch of roles. Maybe we're all impostors and it doesn't matter."

"Hey, I'm glad you said that," Amy said, becoming animated. "It reminded me of one of my dad's stories. It's all about role playing and stuff."

"Oh, I love stories. Tell me."

"Well," Amy began, settling into her chair, "this rock band traveled to India to find a guru named Swami Faquir they had heard about, who supposedly knew all about spiritual enlightenment. Ultimately, it turned out that his own spiritual enlightenment required large quantities of money and women."

"Your dad told you this story?" Shelley was surprised at the "large quantities of money and women" theme.

"Yeah, but it's true. He wouldn't make it up. Anyway, the women part is not the story. When the group got to India and began to inquire for the guru, they were intercepted by a man who said he knew the guru personally. He took them to another guy, who he said was the guru, but the guy was an impostor."

"'All the world's a stage.' That's Shakespeare."

"Anyway, the impostor quickly figured out how to tell the rock band members what they wanted to hear, and developed a number of supposedly wise sayings to flatter their own ideas about life and stuff. Some of them were really bad, like, 'In the shout of music, the soul sings,' and since the band members were pot heads, 'As the smoke rises, so does the mind.' Stuff like that."

"How do you remember all this?"

"I don't know. It's just interesting, I guess. So I remember it."

"And the group bought this stuff?"

"Yeah, and so, anyway, the band brings this faker back to the U.S. with them and he becomes part of their hangers on, partying with them and talking like a guru. Oh, I remember another. The impostor guru knew quite a bit about Swami Faquir's habits and was anxious to imitate them, so he had sayings like, 'A wise man knows the limits of pleasure, but how can we know the limits of pleasure unless we test them?'"

"Sounds like a guy I knew in high school."

"Well, the group and the phony Swami get pretty popular and people are always asking for interviews. At some point, the Swami says he's tired of talking to the unenlightened, especially the minor journalists and fans who want to drink deep of his wisdom. So the rock group says, 'No problem,' and they hire a guy to impersonate the guru and handle the interviews."

"You're kidding."

"No, seriously. They hire a guy to impersonate the guy who is pretending to be the real guru."

"So we have an impersonator of an impostor pretending to be a Swami who himself is a fraud?"

"Isn't that a scream?"

"So, how does all this relate to your dad?"

"Well, it turns out that the third guy, the impersonator, is caught on a surveillance camera buying drugs. The cops pick him up and find a fake ID on him, with the name Swami Faquir on it. That's when my dad heard about it, because it looked like there might be a fraud angle in there somewhere. The guy gets out on bail and disappears. The cops trace the name to India first, only to find out that the real guru—"

"You mean the fake guru."

"The real but fraudulent guru."

"The real fake."

"The genuine fraud."

"Okay. That's all clear now."

"Anyway, the first one, the actual Swami Faquir, is still in India and always has been. Perfect alibi. Hundreds of women will swear to it. So a little further investigation leads them to the impostor guy with the rock band in town, where they discover that the impersonator—the third guy—has disappeared."

"So what did the rock band say when they found out they had been duped by a phony?"

"They said the cops were lying and trying to fool them and that their guy was real. They wouldn't tell my dad how much money they had paid the guy, and they refused to have him prosecuted for fraud, so he's still their guru. To those guys, reality is what you want it to be. If it works, it's true."

"Does this mean I have to give up pretending?"

"You know you're pretending. That's the thing. It's when we want to believe one thing so much that truth no longer matters that we fall in love with a falsehood."

"So we're back to truth and meaning and stuff. That's what I like about you Amy. You still believe in that stuff. That's good."

Amy just smiled. "Well," she said, "I need to talk to Melanie, so I'd better get going and see if she's back in her room."

"Thanks for coming over. And for talking. My practically sister."

"You're funny, Shelley."

"Thanks. I try."

As Amy walked back toward her own dorm to see if Melanie was now available, she wondered if her talk with Shelley had helped her friend think about herself and her future in a good way. Amy recalled the saying her father had given her when he presented Tina the Ballerina. "The ballerina lives not for herself but for her dance." She thought now that perhaps the saying meant more than a call to be her personal best, but a charge to be a model for others. The dance of a candle flame. A light to the world. Show others a reasonable example that they might follow or at least get some ideas from. That was a good way to be useful to others. Feeling useful made Amy happy.

"Yeah, come," said the voice when Amy knocked on Melanie's door. Melanie was sitting on the bed, her knees pulled up to her chin, painting her toenails a shiny, deep black. She glanced up to identify her visitor, and then returned to her task. "Hey, Amy."

"Hi, Melanie. How are you?"

"Late." Amy noticed that Melanie's hair had recently been attended to. Maybe the girl was going out.

"Well, I won't keep you long. It's about Tina."

"I don't think I can move her. The floor's pretty tight."

"No, it's not that. It's just that I think she needs help."

"Is she hurt?" Melanie looked up and made eye contact.

"No," Amy said, drawing out the word a little. Melanie dipped into the polish and brushed the next nail. Amy continued, "There's something wrong with her."

"Like that's news."

"No, I mean, really wrong. I think she needs counseling or some kind of doctor. She thinks people are talking to her when they aren't. I don't know how to explain it. She has a bunch of radios, and she's trying to get messages."

"Has she threatened you?"

"No, actually, she seems to like me."

"I thought you might be able to help her. That's why I brought her over."

"Do her parents know about her problems?" Amy asked, changing tack.

"Don't know. We're not allowed to tell them anything, even if we knew something. Privacy laws. Tina's an adult."

"Isn't there anything we can do?" The tone made Melanie look up again.

"Look, Amy. I feel sorry for the girl. She's vulnerable and sensitive. And reality—whatever that is—has driven off and left her standing in the rain. But I don't know what to do." She returned to her toes to paint the last nail, then said,

"Maybe you could try the counseling center. But don't get your hopes up." Melanie released her feet from the edge of the bed and stretched out her legs to view her nails at a distance. She looked at Amy one last time, with an expression that seemed to reveal a caring heart somewhere inside. "Good luck, Amy," she said quietly.

Chapter 16

Mr. Trimmer was already waiting for Professor Miller and Gina the next morning when they arrived outside the casino buffet. In fact, he had already gotten in line and motioned them to join him. "Our work in the market is timed precisely and will not wait for us if we're late," Trimmer explained. "This is the next-to-the-last trading day of the week and we will do the trade near market close. There is no room for error, so we want to be sure we don't get held up here."

"Good idea," Professor Miller said.

"You probably frown if one of your students comes in late," Trimmer continued, "but here *late* means no trade and hence, no profit. My employers are considerably less understanding than you might be. I would get an F, if you get my drift."

"I understand," Miller said.

Professor Miller and Gina had an unremarkable eating experience, even at this luxurious hotel buffet, where every pleasure for the taste buds was carefully spread out before them. Following Mr. Trimmer's lead, they moved impatiently down the line, grabbing what would be a quick bite of this and that, all the time feeling a nervous urgency. None of them took the time to wait for a custom omelet or crepe, but instead they took everything ready to eat. Only Gina was willing to spend an extra few moments at the carvery to get a slice of ham. The trio seemed to think of eating merely as a means to an end, a required ritual to be performed at a prescribed pace before they went on to more important business.

Behavior like this would have broken Matt's heart. Had Matt and Amy been where Miller and Gina were, facing the half-dozen islands of food spread across the room, there would have been none of this bird-like nibbling. There would have been a symphony of pleasure, a whole season of episodes of consumption, a glorious, strolling indulgence of gustatory passion. Matt had always thought those menus that offer a "one-trip salad bar" put the restaurant on the edge of legality, making it guilty of cruelty to the customer. Any salad bar required a minimum of three trips. Buffets, on the other hand, usually required at least four or five, sometimes with two plates per trip. Amy had more than once accused Matt of having a hollow leg as he returned yet one more time, wanting to sample everything and then return for heavier layers of favored items. She would sit there with her modest selections as he came and went. One evening, at a particularly nice smorgasbord, she had surreptitiously observed his forays. First trip sampler, second trip main courses, third trip more main courses, fourth trip soup, fifth trip cheese and salad, sixth trip fruit and dessert, seventh trip favorite tidbits. There was ice tea to open, cola to add on, and coffee to close (decaf in this case). He was a gastronomical artist. Even at breakfast, he could eat an opening salvo of appetizers while his custom omelet was cooking, load the cereal with fruit, and alternate between bacon, sausage, and ham. "If he works as hard at any job," Amy thought, "he'll be a great success."

As the three ate, Trimmer checked his watch once or twice, as if concerned with the time, but he nevertheless maintained his jovial, talkative personality.

"This is a wonderful town, isn't it?" he asked. "Endless food, endless entertainment, endless opportunity."

"And endless money, too, it seems," said Miller.

"We did well yesterday, didn't we? And I hope we might do something today, too. I should caution you, however, that today there is only a relatively small play in hand. Tomorrow looks much better. But we should still be able to turn a good account. I'm still waiting for the final word on the company, but we are looking at a nice increase."

"How much, do you think?" asked Miller.

"Double your money, likely."

Gina almost dropped her mouth open. "Double? In one play?"

"A single transaction can have dramatic results. After all," he said matter-of-factly, "your two thousand dollars yesterday turned into six thousand dollars each in one transaction. Twelve for two is not bad."

"That was one transaction?" Gina was stunned. "No way." But she believed it. Miller said nothing, but his eyes showed he had heard.

"Well," said Trimmer, "even though today will not be as spectacular, we believe it beats letting our funds rot in a low-interest bank account. Why not let our money go dancing with kings and bring back a king's ransom?"

"What you've got is a gold mine," Miller said.

"Oh, no, my dear Dr. Miller. Gold mines are too much work. All that ore and dust and digging. We prefer to use our minds to make money. A keyboard and a good idea are infinitely less work and infinitely more rewarding than a mere gold mine." He smiled broadly.

After breakfast, they all walked toward the front of the hotel. Mr. Trimmer made a quick call on his cell phone.

"We're ready," he said. Turning to Miller, he noted, "My driver will pick us up."

"No taxi, then?"

"Oh, please."

They stepped out the front doors of the hotel just as a white stretch limo trimmed in gold pulled up. "Here we are," said Trimmer. They got in and the car drove off.

The office was a storefront in a strip mall. A sign on the door said, "Confidential Brokerage Services. Members Only." The windows were darkened with a very deep, reflective tint, preventing Gina and Professor Miller from seeing inside. Mr. Trimmer inserted a coded keycard into the electronic lock and the door opened. Inside, the entire store space was furnished as one large room. More than a dozen desks were occupied by men and women peering at computer screens, typing quickly, answering the phone, and printing off paper. The floor was littered with paperwork, much of it torn to shreds. Paper shredders by each desk looked full already. Miller checked his watch reflexively, just to be sure that the hour was still early. He was surprised at the level of activity.

Hanging along the walls all around the room were at least a dozen giant screen monitors, some with stock tickers running, some with background information about companies, some with rapidly refreshing Internet newsgroup postings, some with email messages, and some with active chat room conversations. Others showed bar graphs, line graphs, and grids of data, all in multicolors. Many of the men and women at the desks looked up at intervals to study one or more of the screens. Those talking on the phone wore wireless headsets that allowed them to pace around while looking from screen to screen. They spoke in urgent tones. Occasionally they would fly to a computer and begin typing furiously.

Professor Miller scrutinized the large displays, attempting to gain insight into the workings of the office. The earnings from his critical thinking textbook were still parked in a money market account, so he had not yet had the opportunity to visit a stock broker and learn about the details of investing, electronic or otherwise. He knew quite a lot from reading the business section of the paper, but had not yet taken the plunge into the capital markets himself. He was beginning to think that this might be a good way to do that.

Miller found it difficult to tell just what was going on because the display information changed so quickly. The tickers ran by so fast, and the symbols were so incomprehensible, that they meant nothing to him. The graphs seemed to indicate trends or historical activity of sales volumes or prices, but that, too, was difficult to make out.

In the midst of his puzzling, a somewhat older, gray haired man with an intelligent look came over to the three. "Hello, Lars," he said. "Are these people members?"

"No, they are friends of mine. I'll vouch for them. People of integrity. Remember my lost wallet? These are the ones who returned it."

"I see." Turning to Miller, he said, "Excuse me. I'm Roy Gandalf, the office manager. Non-members are really not supposed to be allowed in or permitted to trade."

"You remember how well we did yesterday with Synchro Transducer?" asked Trimmer. A fleeting, half smile passed across Gandalf's face.

"Well," Gandalf said, "perhaps you can make a play today."

Gina jumped and clapped her hands. Miller nodded and smiled.

"If you two don't mind joining together, we'll set up a single margin account in Dr. Miller's name," said Trimmer.

"I've heard of a margin account," Miller said, "but I'm not really familiar with it. What does that do?"

"A margin account allows you to leverage your money. You invest your $6,000 and borrow another $6,000 from the brokerage. When you make your profits, you repay the borrowed money and keep the profits it earned. It's leverage."

"Sounds like money on steroids."

"Exactly so."

"And if we lose money?"

"I thought I explained yesterday that my company is not set up to lose. We have factored that out of the equation."

Mr. Trimmer explained that, on his guarantee, Miller could set up a margin account with only a signature. When the account was set up, Miller and Gina deposited their checks into it, with an additional $20 cash to make a round $12,500, and borrowed an additional $12,500 against it. They thus stood ready to invest $25,000.

Gina sat down at one of the computers, where Mr. Gandalf helped her log on.

"If my information is correct," Trimmer said, checking his watch and confirming the time with two more clocks in the room, "and it always is, we should get final word in just a couple of minutes."

"Where do we get the word from?" Gina asked. As if on cue, Trimmer's beeper went off.

"Here's the play," he said. The tension rolled over into excitement. Looking at the message on the tiny screen, Trimmer spoke in Gina's direction. "Martrax Financial. Type it in, there, now." Gina typed. "It's four and a quarter," Trimmer said, pointing to a corner of the screen. "Let's see, you have 25." He grabbed a calculator from the desk. "Buy 5800 shares. Now. Do it, girl!" Gina typed in the information and clicked on *buy*.

The message, "Transaction completed," soon came on the screen.

"Now what?" asked Gina.

"We wait for the good news. Martrax seems to have a very bright future, according to some people." Trimmer glanced at some of the large screens to see if the news had begun to appear.

"Hey," someone across the room said, just loud enough to be heard, "Martrax is moving."

One of the displays overhead flipped over to a screen tracking just the price of Martrax shares. The stock was already at six and a half. Then eight.

Miller could almost taste the money. He knew how rapidly his free investment was growing, multiplying. This was better than grinding away writing textbooks, even successful textbooks. In fact, Trimmer was right. This was much better than a gold mine. This was even better than robbing banks.

"Wait until it gets over 17," Trimmer said. "There's much more good news to share with the world."

"The question is," noted Miller, "How credulous is the world? Will everyone really believe all this good news?" He looked at one of the message boards, claiming that Martrax would report lower than expected losses on bad debts in the last quarter. Another screen showed a newsgroup posting saying that Martrax executives were trying to keep quiet the repayment of a debt previously written off, until they could increase their own holdings.

"Not everyone will believe this news," Trimmer acknowledged. "But enough will. After all," nodding toward the board Miller was reading, "everyone knows that some insider trading goes on."

"So we get rich because some people are fools. They ought to use their minds."

"Mm hm."

"It's dropping from 16 and a half," Gina said, watching the tracking monitor. "Now it's at 16 and a quarter."

"I guess we aren't going to get the run to 17 after all," Trimmer said. "Okay. Sell it all."

"Sell it?"

"Yes, move on it, quickly. Sell 5800 shares. It's dropping." Trimmer's voice had an edge to it.

Soon the screen in front of Gina returned a "Transaction completed" message. The sale had gone through at 16.

"Well, your gross is about 92 grand," noted Trimmer, pointing at a total on the screen.

Miller did some quick figuring. "That's a $67,000 profit. In less than an hour." Miller sat down. He had just watched his investment increase five fold in the course of one quick transaction.

"This is unbelievable," said Gina. "I've never even seen this kind of money. And it was all so fast."

"It's even faster when we do a short, like the deal coming up tomorrow," said Trimmer.

"I want my money in," said Gina. "If that's okay with you," she added softly, and not without a bit of winsomeness.

Trimmer hesitated. "Well, all right," he said with some reluctance. "I guess one more outsider investment won't hurt.

After all," he added, brightening, "you two saved me several million dollars by returning that wallet yesterday."

"Million? Really?" Gina was awed. So was Professor Miller, though he hid it well.

"Mr. Trimmer," Miller began slowly. "Could I—." He hesitated. "Could I put in some additional money of my own on this one last play tomorrow?"

"How much?" asked Trimmer.

"Say, two hundred and seventy five thousand."

Trimmer did not react to the amount, as Miller had expected him to. No whistling or raised eyebrows. Instead, Trimmer said, matter-of-factly, stroking his face, "Well, I don't know. I wouldn't want to do anything that might affect my company's overall operation."

"Oh, please," pleaded Gina. She reached her arm around Mr. Trimmer's arm and looked into his eyes. He looked back for a moment. Miller thought he saw her wink at him. Trimmer and Miller looked at each other.

"Well, why not?" said Trimmer at last. "But that will be the final play. Then you will have to forget that all this ever happened. Where are the funds?"

Professor Miller exhaled before answering. "In my bank. How do I get them in time?" He was doing the mental calculations of a five-for-one profit on more than a quarter of a million dollars. He would be more than a millionaire by this time tomorrow.

"A wire transfer will work fine," said Trimmer, motioning for a runner to come to him. "This gentleman needs a wire transfer order." The runner dashed off to get one and was soon back. The form was already mostly filled in, with the name and account numbers of Confidential Brokerage on it.

"There is a phone you can use to call your bank and make arrangements."

Soon Miller was on the phone with his bank.

"I want to transfer $275,000 to Confidential Brokerage Services. I've got the account number right here." The reply on the other end was not what Miller wanted to hear. "But I need the money right away," he said with some temper. "What? Well, fax it right over then." The conversation went on, with Miller giving the fax number of the investment office and continuing to insist on speed. He hung up. "They won't wire transfer the money without an original signature. So they will fax the form to me and I'll overnight it back to them. The money won't transfer until tomorrow morning."

"That might not be enough time. The play could go forward before you got your funds. Maybe we should just forget this one." Miller was dismayed.

"Let me see," Trimmer continued. "I think this deal has to go at ten o'clock." He checked some notes. "Oh. No. It goes at noon. There may be enough time, but then maybe not."

"We can try," Miller said, trying not to allow a tone of desperation or pleading to enter his voice.

Within minutes the fax arrived, authorizing the transfer of Miller's funds to the brokerage. Miller filled out and signed the form, and then handed it to Mr. Trimmer, who put it in an express envelope. A runner then rushed it to the express office to overnight it to Miller's bank.

Miller was flying high with speculation. "We've got roughly eighty grand after paying back the margin loan." He could not suppress his smile. He liked saying the words *eighty grand*. He was talking like someone for whom large amounts of money were commonplace. "We can add the $275,000 to that for about $355,000. Might as well round it

204 ❖ THE MILLION DOLLAR GIRL

off to 350 grand," he said, nonchalantly. "Got to cover expenses of sale, you know."

Gina shrugged as if to say, "I have no idea what you're talking about, but it's okay by me."

"Then with a margin loan of another three fifty," Miller continued, "we've got seven hundred K to invest. If we can get a 5 to 1 return like today, we're looking at three and a half million dollars." He paused a moment. "Can that be right?" He rechecked his figures. They were correct. Then he turned to Trimmer. "Is it possible to make that much on tomorrow's investment?" Miller did not like the word *play*. He preferred *investment*.

"Well, five to one may be a bit optimistic, but I think it may be possible. Tomorrow's move is with a large metals corporation with quite a bit of market cap. There should be a goodly amount of cash in it for you. A couple of million, if not three point five. I'm hoping to do somewhat better than that for my syndicate." He smiled, as if he expected Miller to understand that "somewhat better" was a wild understatement. Hearing Trimmer say "three point five," made Miller wish he had used the expression, or at least "three and a half mil" instead of "three and a half million dollars." Nonetheless, the money was still real and virtually on the way, however it was described.

Miller was beginning to feel powerful, brilliant, almost godlike. Two, maybe three, million dollars for an hour's work. Just as a thank you from a friend. Just for being honest and returning a wallet and knowing how to be shrewd and clever about it all. True, he would have to share some of it with Gina. He wondered if there was a way to cut her out of the deal. Give Gina her half of the $67,000 now and not get her involved with the plan tomorrow. But Trimmer seemed to like her and was at least in part persuaded by her to let them in on the scheme one more day. He decided to drop it. She just had to be kept quiet about it all.

"Well, our work for today is done," Trimmer announced. As if on cue, the driver of the stretch limo came in the door.

"Your car is ready, sir."

The trio rode back to the hotel conversing much less than one might otherwise think. Each was busy with a full and active imagination. Mr. Trimmer's face showed a calm, businesslike expression. His head tilted toward the roof of the limo, but his eyes were closed as he seemed to be doing calculations or making plans in his head. Professor Miller and Gina both realized that they were facing a life-changing experience. The dream of financial independence stimulates many ideas. The staggering possibility that such a dream was on the verge of fulfillment made both of them quiet and contemplative. Professor Miller would remember this day for the rest of his life. What, a day before, was only an idle whim to be dismissed with laughter or scorn was now looming within reach, easy reach. Yesterday, he had thought himself successful and financially fortunate; today he looked at his book earnings as chump change, merely a tool to be used to make some real money. Never again would he labor for money. He had found an easier way. And there was no risk to it. It was guaranteed.

At the hotel, Trimmer excused himself from them, saying that he had a number of lengthy calls to make and that he would order room service for his lunch.

"Oh, I forgot to explain one of the details of tomorrow's transaction," he said, just as they were parting. "Got a few minutes? The young lady need not stay."

"Sure," said Miller. "Gina, you can go on up to the room. I'll meet you there and we can decide what to do with the rest of the day."

"Uh, we'll only be a couple of minutes," Trimmer said quickly. "Here. Why don't you play the slots for a bit and we will be finished soon." Trimmer gave Gina a bill to feed the slots.

Gina shrugged and headed for the 25-cent slots. Mr. Trimmer escorted Professor Miller to a coffee bistro just off the casino, where they could still see Gina.

"I wanted to talk to you away from the girl," he began. "But we must not allow her to be by herself. Had she gone up to the room alone, she might get on the phone to her friends or relatives and blab about the entire plan."

"That's true. Didn't think about that."

"And with the sensitive nature of the information, that must not be released until just the right moment, that could spell disaster for my organization. They would not be very happy." Trimmer drew his finger across his throat as he spoke.

For the first time, Miller wondered about the organization Trimmer worked for. Who were they? What exactly did he mean by *syndicate*? Was that like *mob*?

"So they might feel double-crossed."

"Not even that. They are nice enough when everything is running smoothly, but if you so much as step on their toes, they do not say, 'Quite all right.'"

"Well, I'll be sure to keep an even closer eye on Gina for the next 24 hours. After that, though, she will be on her own."

"After that, it won't matter. She can say what she likes. We will be in another city by then."

"I see. You move around a lot."

"Keeps one healthier to stir about."

"Okay. Got it. I'll take care of the girl, and we will see you here at the coffee shop about, when?"

"Let's say eleven o'clock tomorrow."

"Done."

Miller looked over at Gina, sitting on a stool in front of a slot machine. He thought her pose was particularly attractive. One leg hung down in a pleasant arc. Her profile revealed her perfect eyelashes, her rosy cheeks, her full lips. He permitted himself to gaze for a few moments, knowing that she was not looking back. He thought, "I can have a whole flock of girls like this now."

"Enjoy yourself," Trimmer said, getting up to leave.

"Of course."

The result of earning almost all of his $275,000 savings from the royalties on a successful critical thinking book was that Miller permed his hair and adopted the attitude of a brilliant professor. The result of the prospect of $3.5 million was even more dramatic. Miller's brain seemed to have gotten a perm. He grew expansive, almost swaggering. As he and Gina walked the strip for awhile, stopping in at a few stores here and there, he began to spend money freely, the way he believed the very rich do. Miller bought Gina some outrageously expensive perfume. For lunch, he took her to the most expensive restaurant in one of the fanciest hotels. He left a fifty-dollar tip.

"Let's get you a new outfit," he told her as they ate.

After lunch they went shopping. A couple of blouses, pants, shorts, shoes, a tennis outfit, some lingerie, even a hat, were all added to Gina's wardrobe, courtesy of Miller's credit cards. He enjoyed seeing her model the items under consideration. He pretended to be selective, often rejecting several outfits on minor objections just to see her try on and model more.

After settling on a new bikini, Gina wanted to stop shopping and try the suit out at the pool, to catch some late afternoon sunshine while there was still enough warmth in the air to make tanning bearable.

At the pool, Miller continued thinking about his wealth. "Twenty-four hours ago, I was just a professor, a drudge, grinding away trying to teach lazy and uninterested students who have no clue about how to do a bit of thinking." He could hardly wait to resign his appointment. He fantasized about going into his department chair's office and telling Chuck what he could do with the job. He replayed the scene several times because he liked the frightened and confused look on Chuck's face. No more years of combating new waves of ignorance and apathy every term. That life seemed so far away from him now. He hardly recognized the person he had been so recently. He wondered whether he should divorce his wife to free up his lifestyle. He wondered if he should ask Trimmer for a job with the syndicate. Who knows how much money could be made? Millions of dollars on one trade? What about trading every day? It was unreal. "Tonight," he thought, "we're going to the buffet, and I'm going to have too many crab legs. Who's to say it's unreasonable?"

Miller looked over at Gina. She was lying on her back, soaking up the sun as if she had not a care in the world. He thought she might be asleep, but he could not see her eyes through the sunglasses. He noticed that her toenails had red polish on them. He could not remember seeing that before. "Success has made me more observant," he thought.

"Gina?" he said. "You awake?"

"Mm hm."

"This is our last evening in Vegas. Too bad we can't stay the weekend, too. But I've got to put in an appearance at the conference." The conference, he thought, would be all the more useful for pretending that Las Vegas had never happened. And, as enjoyable as Gina was, he was anxious now to take care of his new life's fortune. There were many details to attend to. Maybe he would just say he was going to the conference, after all. He turned again to Gina.

"What do you want to do tonight? The city beckons once again."

Gina took off her sunglasses and rolled her head sideways to look at Miller. "The show was fun," she said, squinting at him.

"Another show? Okay. Any particular one?"

"You pick." She rolled her head back and put her sunglasses on again.

"Buffet for dinner?"

"Mmm."

Miller was not a suntanner, but, bored with his magazine and finished with his drink, he put the back of the chaise lounge down and stretched out. "I just hope I don't get burned," was all he thought.

For dinner, Gina put on one of her new outfits and her new perfume. Miller contented himself with adding a beret he had picked up during their shopping, telling himself that he looked "jaunty." Gina was polite enough not to contradict him.

They did indeed eat at the buffet, where Miller did indeed pile a plate with too many crab legs. He looked around to see if anyone was watching, especially with a disapproving look, but no one seemed to notice. Miller was not exactly disappointed, but he would have enjoyed knowing that his actions were being observed. He was important now. People should be watching him.

As Miller overstuffed himself, with Gina smiling cheerfully at him, he felt happy and powerful. Only once or twice did he give himself a rush of adrenaline as he momentarily feared that his money might not arrive in time for the big play, or rather, investment. He wondered if he could make a phone call or do something else to help assure its timely arrival. But then the worry passed and he was again happy and open.

The pair went to an early show this night, a popular circus performance. Miller was so late in asking for tickets that he had to pay $500 each for two specially reserved seats right in front. But it was a pittance. Only those in the working classes had to worry about trifles like the cost of theater tickets.

Gina loved the show. She turned frequently to Professor Miller to comment, smile, or whisper breathily in his ear. She laughed and was amazed. Miller, to his own surprise, thought the show was almost trivial. He had expected to enjoy entertainment all the more now that he was a wealthy man, a man of real status and power, but instead, he felt that the entertainment was somehow beneath him, unimportant and banal. He attributed these feelings to his preoccupation with the morning's work, and once again he felt a pang of concern about the arrival of his funds.

Gina excused herself and stood up.

"Where are you going?" Miller heard himself say in almost an accusatory tone.

"Powder room. I'll be right back."

"Oh, okay. Hurry. You don't want to miss this."

Soon after Gina left, Miller began looking at his watch, pushing the light button so he could see the time in the darkened arena. Each time he looked, it seemed to be nearly the same time as before. Gina seemed to be taking an eternity, but his watch said only a few minutes had passed. Was she calling her friends? Her family? He could almost hear her bragging to her mother about her coming wealth. But then again, would her mother ask questions that Gina might not want to answer? He could imagine the conversation: "Hi, mom. I'm staying in a Las Vegas hotel with one of my professors and we met a guy who manipulates the stock market. He let us make a lot of money and it's okay as long as we don't tell anyone or get caught." Miller wondered for a moment whether Gina might actually say something like that. He laughed. Just then, Gina returned.

"How are the folks?" Miller asked, thinking himself clever.

"I went to the bathroom," Gina said, in that college-student *get-a-clue* tone.

Professor Miller's only indulgence to be frustrated this night was his plan to get an enormous, glutton-stuffing ice cream dessert after the show. He had wanted to continue his newly liberal attitude toward culinary excess, but there simply was not enough Professor Miller. He was still very full from dinner, and the thought of even a small dish of ice cream was altogether unappealing. Gina pronounced herself content without a late dessert, so they walked from the arena through the casino and toward the elevators. Miller debated making a large bet or playing the $100 minimum blackjack table, but he still could not overcome his view of the folly of gambling. He took a cue from Mr. Trimmer and scorned those who take a chance on getting rich. It is far better to get rich without any risk.

As they rode the elevator up to their room, Miller thought, "I've managed to keep an eye on her pretty well."

Chapter 17

Amy had been enjoying Professor Miller's critical think-ing class because growing up with her father had taught her the value of reasoning and thinking well, and Professor Mil-ler had enabled her to stretch her thought processes. Though he was clearly affected and pompous in his lectures, he was still knowledgeable and informative. And though his films usually centered around violence or disaster, they made use-ful points. Even his textbook, which he bragged about a little too much, was really pretty good.

So it was that although most of the class had rejoiced when Professor Miller announced there would be no class on Friday, Amy did not rejoice with them. Even though she did not like getting up for an 8:00 AM class, she enjoyed it once she was awake. Today, though, since there was no class, Amy had planned to sleep in. She had deliberately not set her alarm clock. "I'll just sleep until I wake up," she thought. She had awakened at ten minutes after six. "Wow, a whole extra ten minutes of sleep," she said aloud to herself. "I must have been exhausted." Rather than try to go back to sleep, or just lie in bed resting, Amy got up and went through her usual routine. She was ready to walk out the door by seven. But why go through the usual routine? Why rush over to the din-ing commons when there is no class to go to until 11:00? "Maybe Matt would like to go to breakfast," she thought.

It was clear by the sound of the voice on the other end that Matt had been asleep when Amy called. "I'm sorry to wake you," Amy said.

"No, no, I'm awake. Fine. Hi, Amy. What time is it?"

"It's five after seven."

"Oh, great. That's a good time to get up. You going to class?"

"No, class is canceled for today, and the DC sounds lame. How about if I treat you to breakfast at Quinlan's?"

"Uh, oh, uh sure. That sounds great. Where are you?"

"I'm in New York City, but I can be at your room in ten minutes."

"New—. Amy, it's cruel to joke to sleepy people."

"I'll walk slowly." Amy happened to turn around as she talked and saw Tina standing there in her pajamas with the teddy bears on them. Amy had forgotten that Tina was a much lighter sleeper than Markayla, who was still asleep be- cause Amy had not set the alarm they both relied on. Amy had decided to let her sleep.

"Can I go, too?" Tina asked. "I'll pay."

Amy thought for a few moments. It was nice to be with just Matt, but poor Tina needed someone, especially when she was in an anxious mood. Many times Tina seemed to prefer being off alone and would disappear for hours by her- self, sometimes to return with another radio or a magazine. But other times she grew nervous or even upset when Amy planned to go somewhere without her. When Amy asked her to go along, Tina seemed almost happy. So, Amy tried to ac- commodate the anxious moods.

"Tina wants to come, too. Is that okay? She says she'll pay."

Matt may have rolled his eyes, but he agreed anyway. He did not understand Tina, either, but sensed that she needed "to be cut some slack."

"We're coming," Amy said.

"Okay. I'll try to be ready when you get here."

"Goodbye, you," Amy said affectionately.

Tina pulled on some sweat pants and the large, hooded sweatshirt she had begun to wear more and more often. The sleeves were so long that her fingers barely stuck out. When she wrote at her desk, only her fingertips touched the pen or pencil in her hand. When she pulled the hood up over her head, she seemed almost to disappear in her clothes. Amy had asked her early on if she was cold, but she said she was fine. When Amy turned the heat up anyway one day, Tina soon complained that the room was too warm.

"It's open," said Matt when Amy knocked.

When Amy and Tina stepped inside, they noticed the tell-tale signs of male housekeeping. Dynamite and wind machines were obviously the tools of choice for decorating the living room. Piles of laundry were one thing, but the magazines, bicycles, books, and tools seemed to be arranged randomly.

"Be right with you," Matt said from the bathroom. "Just doing my hair."

"Have you changed your major to art?" Amy asked.

Matt walked into his bedroom from the bathroom just as Amy stood at the door from the living room.

"Art?" Matt asked, stepping out of the bathroom for a moment, comb in hand.

"The way you have so tastefully arranged the materials in the living room. And I see your bedroom is even better."

"I wasn't expecting company. I was going to clean up this weekend. I've been busy. I did do the kitchen."

"I couldn't tell."

"Well, it's guy clean." *Guy clean* to a guy means *clean enough.* One brush of the mop, scrape the dried food off the countertop, swish the sponge over it. Vacuum the carpet every two or three weeks whether it needs it or not. *Guy clean* to a girl means *not clean.*

From her position in the doorway to the bedroom, Amy saw a photograph sitting on Matt's bedside table. It was angled so that she could not quite see who it was, but from what she could see, it was a picture of a beautiful, smiling girl. Getting a little closer she could see the brilliant color, the wonderful hair. Amy's heart sank. It is true that she had as yet no official claims on Matt, but she had felt that they were both becoming attached to each other. She liked him a lot. She had thought he felt the same way about her. Now she wondered if she was just a fill-in entertainment. Perhaps Matt had another girl, a real girlfriend.

By this time she had stepped into the bedroom far enough to approach the photo to see her hated rival. She turned the picture to look the girl full in the face. There looking back at her from the frame, radiant, eyes sparkling, cheeks aglow, was Amy herself.

"Is this me?" she asked, incredulously.

Matt was now in the room, buttoning his shirt.

"Of course it's you. Girl of my dreams. Who else would it be?"

"Do I really look like this?" Amy asked.

"No," said Tina, looking at the picture and then turning to look at Amy.

"Why does everybody have to be so honest all the time?" Amy thought.

"Remember when you and Emily and Karl and I went to that miniature golf course? That's when Karl took this. I nabbed a copy."

"But I didn't look all this, this nice." She was afraid to say *gorgeous*.

"Well, I just scanned it and used a little software to bring out your best. After all, if fashion magazines can take plain girls with chunky legs and make them slim and beautiful for their covers, I can take a cute girl and give her a little extra sparkle."

"Thank you, you fibber. At least it's nice to know that's how you imagine me. But where's Emily?"

"I'm afraid I had to edit Emily out of the picture."

"That sounds so cruel."

"But it's not Emily who interests me. What do you think I dream about at night, anyway?"

"Sixteen-speed drill presses and eighty-gallon air compressors, why?" Amy's tone implied that her answer was an obvious fact. "And don't deny it. I've seen the catalogs."

"Well, yes, of course," Matt said, taking her joke and turning it back on her. "But I mean in addition to that, what do I dream about after I get bored with tools?"

Amy gave a little cry of mock indignation and gave Matt a shove. Then she said, aloofly, "I don't really care, and I'm afraid to imagine. Besides, I doubt you ever get bored with tools. In fact, I see you're still sleeping with Baby Blue Eyes." Amy motioned toward the little air compressor in the corner, just feet from Matt's bed.

Amy had been with him in the discount store when Matt's eyes first fell on the little air compressor, for sale for $99. According to her later reports, his eyes glazed over, his tongue hung out, drool ran down his shirt, his knees wobbled, and he staggered toward the tool with arms outstretched, mumbling, "I need this so bad. I've got to have this. I can't wait any longer. Come to me!"

"You should have seen the lust in his eyes when he first saw that thing," Amy said to Tina. "It was thick enough to cut with a knife. No, that's not true. You'd need a chain saw."

"Hey, I don't have a chain saw yet. Great gift idea."

"Won't your air compressor be jealous?"

"Hey, I'm just keeping her here to be safe. Don't want her to get kidnapped," Matt said. "The bad guys are everywhere, you know."

"They're watching us," Tina said, flatly and seriously. Matt and Amy looked at each other.

"Tina, Matt was only speaking figuratively," Amy said. She could not keep herself from glancing about the room looking for any obvious camera lenses. Matt's computer was on screen saver, with his father's favorite saying scrolling slowly by: "Pray hard and pull with all your strength." Amy looked over the computer table to see if Matt had a Web cam. She saw none.

"Well, I'm ready," Matt said. "You want to go to Quinlan's?"

"That was just an idea."

"How about the Blue Ribbon Buffet? They have breakfast. And I think I have a coupon here somewhere. Matt walked out and into the kitchen. Amy and Tina followed. The kitchen table was deep in litter. Mail, old food containers, newspapers, homework, parts of something Matt was taking apart. Matt was rummaging around in the mess.

"By the time you find the ad, we'll need a dinner coupon," Amy said.

"Got it," Matt said, pulling the flyer out of the pile.

"How do they always do that?" Amy wondered. "Sure," she said, "Blue Ribbon is great."

"No," Tina said. "Blue is the enemy of Green."

"What do you mean?" Matt asked.

"Nothing. Can we go to Quinlan's? I like it."

"You've been to Quinlan's?"

"Oh yeah, yeah."

"Okay," Matt said, with a little resignation. "Quinlan's it is."

Tina had eaten about a third of her ham and cheese omelet when she stopped eating and looked at the plate of food suspiciously. She threw a partly eaten piece of toast down on the plate.

"What's wrong?" Amy asked.

"They switched it."

"Switched what?"

"They switched the food I ordered and put this icky stuff in its place." Tina would eat no more of her breakfast.

"Are you sure?" Matt asked. "It looks the same to me. I didn't see anybody switch it."

"I don't want it. It's got bugs in it."

"Bugs?" Amy asked.

"Why are they always doing that?" Tina demanded.

Matt and Amy finished their breakfast, while Tina drank a few sips of water. She had a look of quiet disgust on her face. She had been wronged.

"Tina," Amy said as they drove from the restaurant, "we'd like to help you."

"I don't need any help. Go away."

"But your thinking seems strange. Like this Blue and Green stuff. You seem confused."

"Have you been hypnotized by the Abiertos? Please leave me alone."

"And someone switching your food."

"They put bugs in it."

Amy decided to drop the conversation until she could learn more about how to help Tina. She did not want to alienate the girl by insisting on her seeing a counselor. Instead, she decided to call Counseling Services after getting back from breakfast.

"Not having your right mind is probably the most tragic thing that can happen to you," she thought. "If you lose an arm or a leg, you can still function and think and live and create and love. But if you lose your mind, you can't even decide you need help. Imagine not even being able to understand that something is wrong with your mind." Amy felt sad, but she tried to hide it from Matt. After all, she was happy to be with him, she told herself. And maybe taking Tina Nicole with them was good for her, too.

"When we get back," Matt said unexpectedly, interrupting Amy's thoughts, "I gotta write me a new chapter in my book, *The Man with Two Girlfriends*, by Matt Prager."

"I think you've miscounted by two," Amy said, not looking at him. Matt glanced over to look for a suppressed smile. Amy remained deadpan.

Amy got an appointment with a counselor for Monday afternoon. The receptionist told her to send an email in the meantime describing the problem, so she wrote out a short description of her concerns and sent it off. Someone had to be able to help Tina. The girl seemed to be getting further and further away from reality in her comments.

Chapter 18

The hotel's stores were already open by the time Professor Miller and Gina rode the elevator down to the lobby, so they did a little window shopping as they thought about where to go for breakfast. Miller took a fancy to a scarf in one display, and after a short deliberation, added the item to his own dress. Looking in the mirror, wearing his scarf and beret, he began to feel French. He suggested to Gina that they eat a French breakfast. Ever the accommodating girl, she agreed and they walked down the strip to a casino that featured a French restaurant. Apple and berry crepes, quiche, and some French sausage were soon laid out before them.

"Bon appetit," he said.

"You're not going to start talking with a French accent from now on, are you?" Gina asked.

"I don't know. It's an idea." Then he added, "Of course not."

Soon the conversation turned to the day's great event.

"It sure is nice of Mr. Trimmer to let us in on this dealing," Gina said.

"Well, as he says, he made boatloads of money with the information he thought he'd lost, so he's just showing gratitude to us. It's not so unusual. But it's great, isn't it?"

"Great is scarcely the word."

"Besides, Trimmer likes you, Gina. You seem to have influenced him toward us."

"You think so?"

"He seems to be pretty well off. Maybe there's the million-dollar sugar daddy you're looking for."

"I was just thinking that myself." Gina's tone was even, but Miller read irony into it. He smiled at her.

"Stranger things have happened," Miller observed.

After a pause, Gina said, "I wonder what kind of girl would go for a late middle aged, balding beer belly like that?"

"Still, he's nice and friendly, very enthusiastic, happy."

"So is a puppy," Gina said, with a trace of emphasis. Then, changing the subject, she continued, "You said we're going to make $3.5 million. Some of that is my share, isn't it?"

"Well, we don't know for sure that we'll make that much. It all depends on how far the stock moves. But yes, some of it is yours. You're putting in, I think it is, well let's just say forty thousand that you have from yesterday and I'm putting in that plus another 275." He paused for a moment as a wave of anxiety about the money arriving on time swept over him briefly. "That's 315. So you're doing forty and I'm doing 315. Can you calculate your share of three point five mil from that?

"No clue."

"Okay," he continued, feeling amused at Gina's admitted cluelessness. She would be an easy one to swindle, he thought. "We add yours and mine for a total of 355. No, wait, we said yesterday we'd round that to 350. So take 40, your share, over 350, the total and set it equal to X over 3500 and—" a little figuring on a napkin took place. "Looks like about four hundred grand, minus a few expenses, like your part of the loan payback and fees."

"Four hundred thousand dollars?" Gina could not find the words to comment on it. Eventually, she settled on an awe-struck, "Oh, my."

"Now you remember that this entire business, the money, the trip here with me, must be kept permanently secret, don't you?"

"Yes, I think I understand. And of course you don't want your wife to find out."

"How did you know I was married?"

"Oh, I don't know. Your wedding ring may have given me a little hint."

Miller looked at his hand. He felt stupid. He hadn't even taken off his ring. Maybe casual onlookers would figure he was with his daughter or a younger wife or maybe they wouldn't care. Why should he care, anyway? He felt angry with himself for feeling stupid. Who cared? He was living his life. He had only himself to answer to. He was fine with that.

"Your bank won't question the money, since the check will be from a brokerage house. They will just think you sold some stock or something, young as you are. Just don't tell others how much you've got. You wouldn't want guys chasing you for your money, now would you?

"Sort of like gold diggers in reverse?"

"Exactly."

"Don't you just hate it when people are just after your money?"

"You're the only one who knows how much I've made on my book."

"And now I'll have more money than that."

"Yeah. And I won't need to write any more books."

"Going to live a life of leisure, huh? What about teaching?"

"No more teaching. I think I'll spend some time traveling around and relaxing. Maybe we can hook up again some time and do this again. And maybe then we can stay the whole weekend—or a whole week."

"You never know what's going to happen."

Professor Miller and Gina were to meet Mr. Trimmer at eleven o'clock, which was check-out time at the hotel. Needing to check out a little early, then, Miller and Gina returned to their room to pack their suitcases after their leisurely breakfast. Gina showed Miller each of her new outfits one last time as she rolled them up and put them into her suitcase.

"Rolling clothes gets more in," she said. Still, it was a mighty challenge for her to put not only her new clothes but the ones she brought with her into the bag. This morning she had put on the same jeans and the ruffled, short top she had worn on the trip over. "My traveling clothes," she had explained. No reason to risk getting a new outfit dirty at the airport or on the plane.

At the check out, they arranged for their luggage to be held until they picked it up later on the way to the airport. Miller had scheduled both their flights—hers back to the university and his to the conference—for the late afternoon to maximize the time in the city. That allowed plenty of time to return to the hotel after their visit to the brokerage. And the rental car would not be charged a late fee until the next morning, since it was rented on a 24-hour contract. Miller stopped himself. Why should he care about something as insignificant as rental car fees? Let the car be late, a few weeks late, for all he cared. He was above those thoughts now. He ordered them out of his mind.

Mr. Trimmer walked into the coffee bistro soon after Miller and Gina sat down with a cup of coffee. He had a sprightly step and was all smiles.

"The game's afoot!" he said happily. He sat down with them.

"We're ready to go," Miller said.

"This is so exciting!" Gina added.

Trimmer's beeper went off. He looked down at it. "Ah. Great news. Your money has been received by the brokerage. You can go for the big score. Let me congratulate you." Trimmer shook Miller's hand. "Let's go on over and sign you up for the margin loan so that everything will be ready. My driver is waiting just outside."

A few minutes and a stretch limo ride later, they were all inside the offices of Confidential Brokerage Services. Miller signed the necessary documents, borrowing $352,000 against his and Gina's pool of $352,000. The brokerage fees had been a little higher than he had expected, but who cared? He now had $704,000 to work with.

"The company we are watching today is Continental Metallic," Mr. Trimmer announced, "a large metals firm. Their stock is quite healthy. It will be amazing to see what our news will do."

Trimmer's beeper went off. He looked at the message and scowled slightly. "Things are developing a little early," he said. "In fact, time's already running out on this play. News must be leaking." He appeared slightly agitated. "This will have to be a short one. Quickly, let's go."

"I'll do it," Gina said. She bounced into the chair. "Just remind me how to do it." Trimmer showed her how to bring up the trading screen. She began typing. "Got Continental on the screen," she announced. Others in the room began watching the displays more alertly. Several of the displays changed to monitor different newsgroups. The name Continental Metallic appeared in one or two messages. The screen that monitored the movement of Martrax Financial the day before was now showing Continental. Trimmer began to supervise another worker as she entered the numbers for his company's trade.

"Tell me what to do," Gina said.

Mr. Trimmer punched a few keys on his pocket calculator. "Since we're short, you want to do about 87,000 shares. That should pull you about two million, if all goes as planned." He looked up at one of the large displays, then uttered a cry of dismay. "Quick, do it short, hurry." He turned back to the computer operator to hurry her. "I wish they wouldn't allow these leaks," he muttered.

Soon the overhead displays began to show many more comments related to Continental Metallic on the Internet message boards, chat rooms, newsgroups, and listserves. "Continental Metallic has just admitted to three previous years of accounting irregularities that have misrepresented their earnings and debt," said one message.

Participants in the Metals Futures listserve began arguing about a coming "major restatement of income" for Continental Metallic in the current year.

Another message board began to solicit members for a class action lawsuit against the company for misleading investors.

Several participants in an online chat said they had heard that the CEO of Continental Metallic could not be contacted.

"The SEC may soon halt trading in Continental Metallic!" screamed one message. "Get out while you can."

"Transaction completed!" said Gina, as she got up to go the printer to get the confirmation.

Gina returned from the printer with her transaction slip and handed it to Miller, while announcing its contents to Trimmer.

"Continental Metallic. We bought 87,000 shares, " she said brightly.

"Bought? No!" shouted Trimmer, looking suddenly very alarmed. "Not buy! Sell! I told you this had to be a short! A short sale! *Sell* at 22, not buy!"

They all turned quickly to the information board. The stock of Continental Metallic was dropping like a load of refuse from a garbage truck. The plunge from 22 to 8 took only a minute or so.

"Metallic is tanking," someone across the room said.

"Gold into lead," another joked.

"Oh, no!" said Trimmer, looking at a computer display with Miller's account information. "A margin call. They're selling your shares to cover the loan! It looks like you've been zeroed. You may end up owing."

"You stupid slut!" shouted Miller at Gina, grabbing onto her ruffles. "You've ruined me!" He gave her a shove and she fell back roughly into her chair.

"I didn't know," Gina protested, looking very hurt. "I thought he meant buy."

"You idiot," Trimmer said hotly. "Why have we been talking about a *short* sale all this time? Are you too stupid to pay attention? To understand English?"

"I don't know," Gina said again, almost crying. "I'm only seventeen. I don't know all this money stuff." Miller, who had been looking at Trimmer when he spoke, jerked his head violently to look at Gina.

"Seventeen?" he demanded.

"Yeah," Gina said. "I'm only a freshman. No one told me to sell."

Miller closed his eyes just for a moment, trying to think how he could have been so careless and stupid as to sleep with an underage girl he had brought across a state line. Now he had a federal offense to worry about.

His thought was broken by the sound of Trimmer's beeper. Trimmer looked briefly at the message and then said, almost to himself, "We've been ratted out." Then, to the whole room, he shouted, "The police are coming! Everybody out!"

The room exploded in flying papers, falling chairs, and rushing bodies. Trimmer ran to the front and locked the door. By the time he returned to the panicked pair, someone began knocking insistently on the front door. Trimmer, Gina, and Miller looked reflexively at the door and saw a man peering in, trying to see through the heavy tint. He was holding a badge with one hand and knocking with the other. Soon he put down the badge and grabbed a radio handset.

"He's calling for backup. Let's get out."

Just as they turned and began to make their way toward the back, Mr. Gandalf, the office manager, strode across the room, jerked open a panel, and flipped all the circuit breakers off. Every overhead display, every computer display, and every light went immediately dark. The noise pattern in the room changed as all the machines fell silent. Only rushing and banging and running and a little yelling were left.

"Go in different directions," Trimmer said as they reached the back door. "Meet up later." They ran outside and took different directions. Someone behind them shouted, "You there, stop!" but no one turned to find out who exactly "you there" was.

Miller made his way between several buildings in the middle of the block and out to another street, barely aware of what he was doing or where he was going. His brain was reeling from the shock of the loss and Gina's revelation and the panic of being pursued. He knew there was paperwork in the brokerage with his name on it. He wondered how long it would be before he was arrested. Arrested at two in the morning by a knock on the door. What could he offer in his defense? He could hear his own unbelievable story. "I came to Las Vegas to have a simple tryst, but accidentally committed a felony, and then in the process I somehow got involved in a stock swindle designed to cheat investors out of their money, only I lost all my money when the girl made a mistake." Now, he thought, even if he could stay out of prison, he would not be divorcing his wife; it would be the other way around. And he would have to keep teaching—that is, unless he was fired, which now seemed likely.

Miller tried to shake off these thoughts, but they kept buzzing in his head. He felt faint, flushed, dizzy. His heart seemed to be pounding in his ears. He looked all around as he sat on a fire hydrant on the new street, waiting to hear approaching sirens. He picked out several directions he might run if necessary. Nothing on the street seemed to be unusual. A city police car drove down the street at one point, staggering him with fear, but it did not slow down or stop.

He must have waited for an hour, maybe two. When he felt it safe enough, he hailed a cab and rode back to the hotel.

Miller wondered what had happened to Gina. It occurred to him that he had not asked her for her cell phone number, or he could have simply given her a call. But there had been no need for her number. They were always together. And now, what if the police had caught her? Was she down at the police station telling the whole story? Would he be in prison soon? He wondered whether he should try to flee, perhaps flee the country, or whether he should return home and wait to see what happened.

At the concierge desk, Professor Miller picked up his luggage. There were only a few bags and the attendant allowed him to walk behind the counter and wheel his suitcase out himself. As he did so, he noticed that Gina's suitcase was no longer there next to his. She had tied a colorful little pom pom to the handle, making it easily recognizable. There was no bag behind the counter that was even close.

Miller felt relieved. Gina was not at the police department, singing her heart out about the professor and the stock swindle. And she was not there to see him panicked and flustered. He looked around the lobby to make sure. She could take care of herself, he thought.

"Did anyone leave a message for me?" he asked the attendant.

"Your name?"

"Miller. Mark Miller."

"No, Mr. Miller. No messages."

"Thanks."

Professor Miller wheeled his suitcase out to the rental car and drove to the airport. On the way, he wondered whether he would see Gina at the terminal, waiting to board her flight home. But this thought was pushed aside by his fear that every police car he saw might be after him. He was careful not to speed or make any illegal maneuvers. He had a throbbing headache. He wondered whether his wife would stick a kitchen knife into him when she found out that he had lost all that money, and in the process of having an affair. He wondered if he could make up a story that was credible, that did not involve Gina or the stock market manipulators. Would she believe gambling losses? He doubted it. Maybe he could try.

Gina was not at the airport. Miller looked for her. He thought about having her paged, but he really did not care to see her again. A wave of anger rushed over him. The stupid fool had cost him a fortune and ruined his life. A freshman, an idiot freshman.

Only when Professor Miller sat down in the airplane and adjusted his coat did he become aware that he was no longer wearing his beret or scarf.

Chapter 19

It is sometimes said that the past is the key to the future. For the modern mind, hating restraint and tradition, this saying's truth may hold only if we allow that the future may represent the rebellious opposite of the past. Of course, many who insist on being independent thinkers might bristle at the charge that their decisions are mere reactions to the past, but the urge to be different for the sake of difference is often strong. What have we learned from the media, if not that? "New!" "Been there, done that." "Let's do something else for a change." The pressure for novelty, so deeply rooted in human nature and amplified beyond hysteria by the advertising industry, twists many people in the winds of change.

All this philosophy is presented merely to explain that, because Amy wanted to sleep late the previous morning but did not, this morning she determined to stay in bed and snooze. Saturday morning is the perfect time to stay in bed a little longer than usual, to stretch and relax and feel the sheets and not get up yet. So it was that Amy stayed in bed, enjoying the feel of the pillow on her cheek and the softness of the bed—as dormitory beds go. Markayla also helped to prove the theory of rebellious opposites, because she was already up and out somewhere, having slept late the previous morning. Only Tina was her consistent self, still lying in bed, apparently asleep.

Of course, even our smallest actions have consequences; there are no isolated events. As a consequence of Amy's luxuriating in bed, the rest of her schedule was delayed. She was later to the shower, later getting dressed, and later to breakfast. Indeed, she entered the dining commons only ten minutes before it closed. The bacon was gone, the fresh cook-to-your-order eggs were gone, the wheat toast was gone, the oranges and pears were gone. Looking over the decimated area, Amy saw that her choices were watery, pre-manufactured, institutional scrambled eggs, grapefruit, white bread, and some kind of granular pudding (tapioca? yogurt? rice pudding?) with an iffy smell.

"How can the food be all gone?" Amy thought. "This is Saturday. No one even gets up for breakfast on Saturday."

She finally found a single remaining banana, a cup of what Markayla would deny was coffee (brewed long before and now strong and stale), and a glass of sweet, yellowish liquid that the commons had labeled *orange juice* in a whimsy of creativity.

An interesting insight into personality can be gained by studying how people respond to misadventures. Amy could have blamed the dining commons for failing to provide an adequate amount of food for the morning meal. Managerial incompetence, a deficient planning model, poor inventory control—any of these would have been reasonable charges. Or she could have blamed those students who did come to breakfast. Selfish overeaters, greedy eyes, inconsiderate of the needs of others. She could have named one or two people who might have taken most of the bacon just by themselves. But Amy's first thought was not to blame others or to hunt for the guilty. Her first thought was to blame herself. "I should have gotten up fifteen minutes earlier," she told herself. "I shouldn't be surprised if there's nothing left at ten minutes before close."

Back from breakfast, Amy noticed that she had the room to herself. Markayla had still not returned and Tina appeared to have left suddenly, judging by the mess in the bathroom and the clothes strewn on her bed. What urgent mission could have propelled that confused girl out the door? Even some papers had fallen or been brushed off Tina's desk and onto the floor. Tina's radio was still playing, squeaking weakly through the headphones. As Amy looked more closely, she noticed that Tina had left her silver lockbox open, and that, in fact, a book, something like a diary, was lying open outside it. Amy had never seen this book before. She had never seen Tina writing in any kind of diary. All of Tina's notebooks were the typical spiral bound kind common everywhere. No red-cloth hardcover books with gold edges.

Had it been closed, Amy would have insisted to herself that she not open it to look inside. But since the book was already open, her curiosity got the better of her sense of duty and she glanced over at the pages, still several feet away. From a distance, she could see that most of the two pages were covered not by handwriting but by lines that looked like barcodes. She stepped closer, compelled by the unexpected discovery.

They were barcodes. There on the two facing pages, several barcodes had been pasted, cut out from ordinary product packages. Interspersed among the pasted codes were written numbers, always ten digits long. Amy felt her heart begin to beat heavily as she looked around. She felt guilty. But she flipped a few pages. The book was filled with barcodes and handwritten ten-digit numbers, page after page. Each entry had a brief description of a product, such as

"Shampoo" or "Pen." For most of the entries, the number four had been circled in the barcode or number string, and a note written under it, "Authorized by Four." For other entries, the entries without a circled four in the code, there was a note, "Authorized by Green."

Amy ran to the bathroom and grabbed Tina's shampoo bottle. She quickly compared the ten digits written in the book to the barcode number on the shampoo bottle. They were the same. Back at Tina's desk, Amy noticed that the number four had been circled in green ink in the barcode on the back of one of Tina's CD's. Turning over the box of tissues on Tina's desk, Amy noticed that the bar code had been cut away, and a green checkmark, together with "A4" had been written. Amy reasoned that the barcode itself was probably pasted somewhere in the book.

She thought it odd that those bar codes that seem to be everywhere were so difficult to find when she looked around the room. Her desk calendar had come in a box, which had been thrown away. Her ballerina, still standing gracefully with her arms crossed and head slightly down, eyes averted, had come with a tag, no longer present. Clock. No, from a box. Dictionary? No. Shrink wrapped or on the dust jacket, which was gone. Box of floppy disks. There was a barcode on it. It had a four in the second set of digits.

Amy ran back into the bathroom. She looked at Tina's products first. The barcode of her hairspray had a four; her mousse had four fours; her mouthwash, none; her toothpaste, two fours. Amy's hairspray also had a four; her mouthwash (the same brand as Tina's) none; toothpaste, none; shampoo, two fours.

Everything of Tina's, except the mouthwash, had a four in the barcode. Why not the mouthwash? Otherwise, the consistency of fours seemed to have something to do with Tina's book. Amy had the feeling that she was learning something, gaining some kind of understanding, but she did not know what it was yet. She remembered one of her father's favorite sayings, "Our lives are told by our receipts." He had gotten insight into many cases by studying the paperwork and store receipts left lying around. Amy felt that she was looking into Tina's life by looking at the book. But she felt a little scared. She also felt uncomfortably that she was somehow spying on Tina, invading the girl's privacy. So she turned the book back as she had found it and went back to her own desk. Then she decided to take a walk, hoping that Tina would return and put her things back together soon.

Amy grabbed a little book of poems by her favorite poet and her father's namesake, George Herbert, and set out across campus. Matt was out somewhere playing basketball, so he was not available to talk to. "Who is Green?" she thought, quickly running over the names of every professor and student she could think of. There was a Michael Green in her critical thinking class, but no other Greens came to mind. She doubted that Michael was connected with Tina's barcodes. She sat by her favorite fountain on campus, the one with a fairly realistic small waterfall, and started to read. It was difficult to concentrate.

"Authorized by Four. Authorized by Green," she thought. She turned her book over to look at its barcode. It did not have a four in it. And the cover was blue. Then she remembered Tina's comment about Blue being the enemy of Green. "Must be the color green," she thought. But what did that mean? Then she also remembered how Tina had looked at the barcodes on the boxes of the radios she was considering. "She must be shopping by barcode number or something,"

Amy thought. The number four in the barcode is somehow significant. Everything she buys has to have a number four in it or be authorized by Green, whoever he is. Like the mouthwash."

Then it occurred to her. The mouthwash was green. Amy whispered, "Duh," to herself. Green was the color. Green things were authorized by their color. Things with a four in the barcode were authorized by the number, and if they did not have a four, they had to be green to be authorized. "That makes sense," Amy said to herself, and then felt startled to realize what she had just said. Still, she thought, given Tina's bizarre assumptions—that purchased items needed to be authorized in some way, and that the color and the number were the two methods—the girl was acting reasonably or at least logically. She owned nothing in violation of those self-imposed rules.

"Of course, the question is, what does it mean to say that something has been authorized? And why does it have to be authorized in the first place?" Amy wondered.

When Amy returned to the room, Tina was back and the signs of a hasty exit had been cleaned up. The silver box was once again closed and Tina's barcode book was not in sight. Tina sat at her desk, flipping through a well-worn magazine.

"Hi, Tina," Amy said.

"Oh, hello," Tina replied, without enthusiasm.

Amy did not know what to say, so she said nothing. She needed to talk to someone to find out what to do. She thought Shelley might be able to give her some ideas, so she called her. Shelley had just returned to her room, too, and invited Amy over.

"Hi, Amy," Shelley said. "Hey, you look worried. What happened? Did you decide you'd really try to do all the assigned reading in your classes?"

"No, it's not me, it's Tina."

"What did she do now?" The question seemed to imply that Shelley had heard something about Tina and her past behavior that Amy still knew nothing about.

"I'm really worried about her. She's totally losing touch with reality."

"What's she doing?"

"She's got a book with barcodes in it, for all the products she buys."

"What's so unreasonable about that?" Shelley relaxed a little.

"Well, it's not a question of being reasonable. It's a question of being sane."

"What's the difference?"

"Well, what's reasonable to us depends on our assumptions. Most people who act like idiots think they are being reasonable because their assumptions are dumb."

"Yeah. We're all good rationalizers. I've tried it myself. Works great. Except I sometimes feel guilty afterwards."

"That's just it. If our assumptions, our values, are wrong or foolish, our conclusions are, too. And if our assumptions are plainly bizarre, like Tina's, our reasonable conclusions will be bizarre, too."

"So if we try to reason without the right values, we're nuts?"

"No, most of us don't have Tina's excuse. We let ourselves get dragged all over the place by our passions and rationalizations."

"You have passions?" asked Shelley, with mock disbelief.

"You know what I mean."

"I sure do, and I can hardly wait to find out more."

"Shelley."

"I know. Be serious. Okay. So. The right values."

"Well, you have to get values from somewhere. Advertising, your friends, famous actors, whatever."

"And I take it you don't get yours from any of these places."

"Let's just say I try not to."

"So where do you get them?"

"Well, there's this Book."

"Okay, I get it. Your values come right from the Big Guy, huh?"

"Uh huh."

"Written on stone and all that."

"Well, some of them are written on stone, but the most important are written on the heart."

"Oh, Amy, you're sweet."

"Don't you mean quaint?"

"No, no. You're just so different. I mean, a lot of my friends would do just anything to be cool." Shelley paused to think of an example. "Which is why there's so much barfing going on every Saturday night. But for you, there's something more important than being cool. That's almost—almost mature."

"Oh, please."

"No, I'm serious. You're okay, Amy."

"Thanks."

"But, and I don't know how to ask this, but, you know, why?"

"Well, not only are those values worthy, but they don't change every five minutes."

"Yeah, but not just the values, but the whole God thing."

"God makes the world make sense."

"I don' get it."

"Well, without God, we would have a universe filled with beauty and kindness and cruelty and suffering and love and all of it meaningless and empty. That makes no sense to me. I think life has meaning. Love has meaning and suffering has meaning."

"But how do you know that what you believe is true?"

"I guess it's a combination of faith and reason."

"I thought faith and reason were opposites."

"No. My faith gives me my values and is the foundation for reason."

"Faith is a foundation for reason?" Shelley asked, this time genuinely confused, as if someone had said that high speed was the key to safe driving on icy roads.

"Yeah. In a sort of secular way, you have to have faith, or trust, to believe that your brain is capable of making rational decisions."

"Especially with so much evidence to the contrary."

"And my faith tells me that truth and justice and moral values and stuff like that are real and not just made up or personal, and so they can be included in making decisions."

"But if God is behind reason, we'll all have to do a lot better at thinking, and make better decisions."

"And some of those decisions will tell us we shouldn't do what we want to."

"Oh, I hate that. But Amy, haven't you ever lost your reason in the face of an overwhelming passion?" Shelley was gently baiting Amy.

To Shelley's surprise, Amy said, "Yeah. Remember I told you that Matt and I met at the store where we put together furniture? Well, we had been doing that for a couple of weeks and I was beginning to like him a little."

"A sort of 'love at first two weeks'?" Shelley asked. "Soon followed by overwhelming passion?" Shelley's eyebrows were going up and down.

"No, just liking. But anyway, he was still trying to get this other girl at the store interested in him. We'd be sitting on the floor, with me holding a couple of pieces of wood together while Matt tightened the screws on the other end and she would walk by and he'd just about lose control. Guys get so distracted over nothing, it's just irritating."

"So was she really hot?"

"Not to me. And that was all the more irritating. She was always ticked off about everything. She'd walk around and say, 'Where's the rag that belongs here?' or 'You pushed that sofa in crooked' and then make a tiny adjustment. She always had a sneering tone of voice. I called her Miss Angry. I couldn't believe Matt was interested in her."

"Sort of made you doubt his sanity, huh?" said Shelley.

"One time she came up to Matt and said, 'You forgot to turn the light off in the storeroom.' And he said, 'I did? I'm sorry.' So she says, 'I had to turn it off for you. You shouldn't leave the light on. I'm not here to turn off lights for you. Next time be sure you turn off the light.' And on and on. And all this in a tone like he'd burned her house down.

"She could've just turned off the light and not made herself a goddess over it."

"Yeah, I mean, he just forgot one time. Why give the guy this big verbal beating for it? But that's how she was about everything. What could he see in her?"

"Cute dimples?"

"I don't know. Well, anyway, one time I thought I'd use a little ploy—"

"Wait!" Shelley said. "You use ploys? Oh, Amy, I am learning so much about you. Please go on."

"No, I mean, I made him a sack lunch, hoping he would get a clue that I liked him."

"Ah," said Shelley, nodding largely, as if comprehending deeply. "The old food ploy. Yes, yes, though I should think that triple chocolate fudge decadence brownies might be a tad more effective than a sack lunch. Or maybe a home cooked dinner."

"Oh, right," said Amy. "A home cooked dinner here in the dorm. That's logical."

"But you see," said Shelley, pointing her finger, "I have no faith to base my reason on. You have to put up with my faithless logic. But do go on."

"So, I gave him the lunch. He even split the sandwich with me. I thought I was doing great, until Miss Angry walks by. I thought he'd twist his head off watching her."

"Ooh, major point loss."

"So, anyway, the next day I made him another sack lunch."

"You don't learn very fast, do you?"

"I gave it to him and said, 'Here's a sandwich, some chips, and an egg.' Only I didn't tell him what kind of egg."

"Ah, the old rotten egg ploy. Good girl."

"No, it wasn't rotten. It just wasn't hard boiled."

"So when he cracked it open and splashed it all over himself, you said, 'The yolk's on you, bucko!' Oh, Amy, you're so totally wicked. I love it."

"No," said Amy, a little defensively. "The second he broke it I repented—"

"Aw," said Shelley.

"—and apologized profusely, pretending that I made a mistake and it was supposed to be hard boiled."

"Tsk. Amy."

"So I even lied to cover up my original plan."

"Amy. Amy. Amy. I am so shocked. This is quite a confession. That is probably the worst, the wildest, the most dramatic example of passion wrenching control from reason that I've ever heard. And no doubt you thought you were being reasonable."

"I guess I didn't think about it in those terms at the time."

"Temporary insanity, I calls it," Shelley said, mimicking a classic Hollywood pirate.

The word *insanity* reminded both girls of their original topic, Tina. Amy briefly shared some of Tina's other strange behaviors and wondered aloud what to do for the girl.

"Worms in her food, huh?" Shelley mused. "Now in the DC, I'd believe it. But at a restaurant, that is strange."

"There were no worms. Matt and I both looked pretty close. She imagined them."

"Hmm. I don't know, Amy."

"And she can't or won't see that there is something wrong."

"So what are you going to do. Just leave her alone? Or ask Melanie to move her?"

"I'd like to help her. But how?"

"I don't know, girl."

"I've made an appointment with Counseling Services to see if they can help."

"You like helping other people, don't you, Amy?"

"I don't know. It's just that Tina really needs help. Needs someone."

The counselor was the best hope. But since Amy was going to call her parents tonight anyway, as she did every Saturday, she decided to tell her father about her plans. He listened without comment until she had finished.

"That sounds like about the best you can do," her father said. "Let's hope she realizes she needs help. That's the most difficult situation. When people need help, but they won't admit it or don't realize it. They may not be happy, but based on their view of reality, they don't see any solution. They won't listen to other people. They won't try your solution because it doesn't fit with what they believe is true. So they stay trapped by their own false beliefs."

"Which to them are reasonable."

"Yeah. And because for some reason they want to believe them. It's just like some of the shoplifters I've seen. They'll tell you they are honest people. And they rationalize their stealing. If they believed that stealing from the store was really wrong, that it makes them thieves, then they'd have to stop stealing."

"Or admit that they are crooks."

"Well, yeah."

"Speaking of that, Daddy, did you catch any crooks today?"

"Well, not today, but we did this week."

"So, tell me all about it."

Detective Herbert laughed. He knew he had received his cue.

"Just this last Thursday we broke up a boiler room operation where a bunch of guys were defrauding mostly older folks with a phony contest scheme."

"That's so sad when older people get cheated."

"It makes me angry. But we got these guys good. They should be doing a good bit of time."

"What did they do?"

"They called and said, 'Congratulations, you've won a week in Hawaii. All you have to do is send us the $149 processing fee and the $89 prize claim insurance fee and it's yours.'"

"Another case of too good to be true?"

"Yeah, another case of you can't believe your desires."

"Did a lot of people fall for that?"

"Evidently, yes. These guys had all the bases covered. If someone said, 'I didn't enter a contest,' they said, 'This was an automatic entry from your credit card company. During the last three months, every time you made a purchase, you were automatically entered in the contest.' Pretty much everybody had made a purchase in the last three months. And, of course, the opportunity to charge the so-called processing fees opened people up to giving out their credit card numbers. If they balked, the guys said that charging it would enter them into the contest again in a special prize category with increased odds. If they still balked, the guys said they needed the card number to supposedly confirm their entry numbers."

"Oh, Daddy. I can't believe people are that bad. And cheating older people, too?"

"We got copies of the script. They talk about the palm trees and the warm sand of the beaches, what a nice experience for the golden years. Things like that."

"So their imagination could carry them away."

"The crooks even claimed that the contest was guaranteed by some group called the NCAC, the National Contest Acceptance Corporation. Sounds great, but the phone number the guys handed out to people who wanted to check was just another phone in their boiler room. Naturally they gave themselves a good report for being legitimate. And if people said they'd never heard of the NCAC, the guys acted all surprised and tried to embarrass the callers by telling them how famous the group is. Headquarters in New York and all."

"That is so evil. And cruel."

"We're still working with Justice to freeze bank accounts all over creation."

"Wow."

Amy's father was silent. His story had been told. Amy then talked to her mother. She said that Amy sounded tired. "You're not staying up too late are you?" Mrs. Herbert asked. "Are you getting your rest?" This and other questions reminded Amy of how difficult it is to be a mother at a distance. Amy reassured her that her daughter was doing the laundry regularly, eating sensibly, and taking care of her skin.

Chapter 20

Monday mornings at the university are often much easier on the classroom furniture than other days, especially during the early class hours. Students who have gotten little sleep during their weekend revels use Monday morning to re-charge their systems, making it necessary to interrupt for awhile the ongoing pursuit of truth and beauty. Because Professor Miller's critical thinking class met, by student standards, at an early hour, Monday sessions were often less fully populated than Wednesdays or even Fridays. This particular Monday the seating was even thinner than usual because a paper was due. This reflected a universal principle of student behavior. On due days, many of the students who do not have the paper finished stay away from class also. Some hope to claim illness, some are still working on the paper, some may fear the frown of the professor. In any event, professors worldwide often look with wonder over the decimated ranks of their classes on the days that papers or other assignments are due.

The students in Professor Miller's class who did come gathered themselves into small groups to feel less abandoned. Before they sat down, some put their papers on the table at the front of the classroom, one or two proud that they had finished, but most simply eager to get it out of their hands to symbolize their being finished with it. A few students held on to their papers and perhaps traded with other students to see what else could be said about one's personal use of reason. Two or three kept their papers hidden in their notebooks, just in case the class attitude became negative toward those who completed the assignment on time.

After these varied little dramas, almost all struggled to wake each other up by engaging in sleepily animated conversations about any topic that came to mind. The topic of the class meeting, logical fallacies, did not come to mind. One of the great principles of the unwritten Constitution of Academia, student version, is that requiring reading or any other work for the same day a paper is due represents cruel and unusual punishment and is therefore unconstitutional. Only the truly scholarly will do the reading, and they, for fear of becoming social outcasts among their friends, rarely admit to it.

While Amy and Markayla had quietly exchanged papers with two other students and sat reading their peer's work, a small group awakened each other by engaging in philosophical analysis.

"The world belongs to those who tell the best stories, not to those who reason the best. Advertising is not an argument. It's a story."

"But advertising is all about appearance and emotion. It's anti-thinking."

"Yeah, well appearance always beats thinking. Girls know that guys can see better than they can think. That's why they spend more time putting on make-up than they do reading philosophy."

"But it's gone way beyond make-up. People use fake hair, fake eye color, implants, you name it. They suck the fat from their stomachs and squirt it into their lips. Women pull the hair off their legs and men stick hair into their heads."

"Don't forget nose jobs. They get fake noses, too."

"They do not."

"No? Well they no longer have the nose they were born with. They have a fake nose."

"Oh, so I suppose braces give you fake teeth."

"The point is, people are pretending to be what they are not, just to be attractive or get something."

"So? Not everybody's born with perfect looks. Some people like to help level the playing field."

"It's being false."

"Is it false to put a squeaker in a dog toy to inflame their instincts? When a dog hears the squeak, he thinks he's hurting a little squirrel. It makes him enjoy it."

"So now men are dogs, and women are squeaker toys. I can't believe you."

"No, all I'm saying is that men have instincts to protect women."

"Men have instincts, all right, but I don't think I'd describe them as protective."

"But why should we have to pretend to be vulnerable or weak? Can't guys handle confident, independent women? Why do we have to act? Be fake?"

"So then we're gonna stop using makeup because that's fake?"

"Yeah, and we're going to open our own doors and pay for our own meals."

"I already do that."

"Yeah, and we're all going to stop trying to be cool."

"Yeah, right."

❖ ❖ ❖

At five minutes after the hour, someone was overheard to say, rather loudly, "Where's Dr. Miller?" For the case was that Professor Miller, always reliable and normally very punctual, had not yet arrived in the classroom. No one had the answer, so the conversations continued as they had.

When the classroom clock displayed ten minutes after the hour, many students began to wonder aloud whether Professor Miller would make an appearance at all. There was hope in many voices as they said, "Maybe class is cancelled today." Amy and Markayla, papers ready, hoped their efforts had not been in vain. They talked about what to do with their papers if Miller did not come.

By eleven minutes after the hour, the suspense had gotten too much.

"Why don't we just call him?" someone finally suggested. Another student pulled out a phone.

"What's his number?"

"How would I know?"

"Where's Gina? I'll bet she has his number."

"Gina's not here this morning."

"So what should I do?"

"Call the switchboard and ask for the philosophy department."

"Wait, his office number is on the syllabus."

A call to Professor Miller's office was answered, after several rings, by the department secretary. No, she had not seen Dr. Miller that morning. Sometimes he went directly to class. No, he had not called in sick. No, she did not know where he was. That was enough information gathering for the class. Some students had already begun to leave, and the others waiting for the outcome of the phone call now decided that there would be no class. No one wanted to ask for Miller's home phone number, since that would represent an unreasonable effort. And he might just have been home and asked the class to wait for him.

"What about our papers?" someone asked.

"The secretary says to bring them to the office," said the person with the phone.

Therefore, with joyful hearts at the cancellation, the remaining students left. Those with papers headed for the department office. Some decided afterwards to return to their rooms to get some extra sleep, while a few of the faithful decided to go on to the Cave and have their usual after-class coffee. Amy and Markayla decided to join the group. Markayla had, however, cleverly brought an insulated mug of her own coffee with her.

As the students sat down at their usual large booth, a visiting professor with a heavy accent came up to them. He was holding out his plate with a sandwich on it.

"Look at this sandwich," he said. "Only two sheets of ham for six dollars ninety five. That is outrageous." He clearly felt wronged, but did not know how to protest, other than to make public the swindle. The students shook their heads in sympathy, and he moved to another table, glancing back at the service counter to see if the employees were watching. He hoped they were being shamed.

"He should be glad they didn't give him more," Jennica said. "The ham here isn't all that great."

"Yeah, if life is a sandwich, university life is indigestible."

"Not much to chew on."

"A lot of it is predigested."

"Gotta eat what the professors like."

"Trouble is, it's always academic liver and Brussels sprouts."

"'Here, eat this. It's good for you.' They always say that."

"Got to swallow what they feed us and then spit it back out on the tests and papers," David said, repeating one of his favorite ideas.

"Okay," said Julie, "that metaphor has gone far enough. No more talk about spitting up, please. I've done enough baby sitting to have an all-too-real image of that."

"Always give them what they want. The first rule of making other people happy." David almost added, "And dogs like vomit," but restrained himself because he liked Julie.

"They say we're supposed to think for ourselves, and then they tell us what to think."

"Yeah, aren't we here to, like, find ourselves? I mean, I don't want to be defined by somebody else. I want to become my own person."

"So what you're saying is that you don't know who you are?"

"Of course I know who I am. I have a driver's license and I can look at it anytime I want."

"Oh, ha ha."

"That was tremendously funny," said Jennica, with a deadpan and expressionless delivery.

"I'm trying to figure out who I might be, who I should be."

"Why can't you just be yourself?"

"Oh, that's the most original advice since the snake said, 'Why not just try an apple?'"

"I want to do something significant with my life," said Amy, "and not just sit around and consume products."

"You want a life with some purpose, when most people in the world want a life of regular meals."

"Yeah, I mean, we're like, 'Oh, disaster, I broke a nail!' and in some places it's like, 'Gosh, another one of my kids starved to death today.'"

To the group's surprise, the usually quiet Markayla spoke up. "Yes, this is true," she said. "There is a need for many people to help."

"So are you going to dedicate your life to feed the starving in far-off countries?"

"Do you know," Markayla said, "that the world is now a small place? There are no longer very many far-off countries. You think Kenya is far away? Kenya is stepping on and stepping off an airplane. Meanwhile, all you must do is sit."

"But there are needs here in the U.S., too." Julie was not keen on living where she might not be able to shower every day.

"Yes, you can help the needy in the morning and still shop at the mall at night. It's a tough life, but I can see you're up to it," Jennica said.

"Oh, shut up."

"The problem is, how to choose. And it's just that what seems important to so many people seems to me to be thin and selfish. Like we're all just trying to look good while we do nothing and are nothing."

"We're just all actors."

"See? We aren't anything. We're just acting. Pretending to be something."

"And some are much better actors than others."

"Hah! Imagine someone who can't even act their own life well!"

❖ ❖ ❖

While this conversation continued, Amy noted that the time for her appointment was approaching, so she got up and politely excused herself, an act of decorum that scarcely anyone noticed. She crossed the courtyard outside the Cave and walked toward the path informally known as Stonewalk by most students, running among some eucalyptus trees along the edge of a large landscaped hill separating some of the classroom and office buildings from the student services complex.

On the other side of the trees was a moderate patch of lawn, where Amy could see two boys playing Frisbee. Sitting in the shade and leaning up against a nearby tree, two girls talked. They had books and papers all around them, and some in their hands, as if their intention had been to study together, but as Amy walked by, she heard one of them relating a conversation. "And then he goes, 'Don't worry. We'll get it in plenty of time.' And the other guy goes, 'But you just said she froze you out.'"

Then, near the edge of the trees, Amy saw a dancer. He was dressed in ballet tights and doing leaps and pirouettes, half hidden in the small forest. It was as if he did not want to be seen. He was half singing a wordless melody to accompany his movements.

Seeing the dancer put Amy in mind of Tina the Ballerina and her father's proverb. "The ballerina lives not for herself, but for her dance." The saying seemed to be taking on new meaning as a result of her recent experiences. Now she began to think that living for the dance must mean living for the opportunity to give to others. That's why she was on the way to see the counselor now, in hopes of doing something for Tina Nicole. The ballerina was there to be a helper. Maybe that is why Amy had enjoyed helping Matt fix his car. The dance was her service to those who need her. Matt might have been able to fix his car by himself, but Tina Nicole did not seem to be able to help herself. She was too confused. She needed someone to do what she could not do. Amy hoped that this conference with the counselor would be just the action that Tina would have taken if she had been able.

Dr. Miller had once said, "Those who can think well should think for those who can't." Amy had thought at the time that such an idea was somewhat egotistical and perhaps even dangerous. "That's probably what dictators think," she had concluded. But now, she had a different view, and thought that Tina was truly someone who could not think well. It was a hard question. "How do you help someone who doesn't want to be helped?" she wondered. "Someone who is so certain of a false idea that the truth does not appeal to them, does not even seem real?"

"Counselor Blakely will see you now."

Mrs. Blakely sat behind a large, ornate desk strewn with papers and knick knacks. It was not the neat desk Amy had somehow expected. Nor did Mrs. Blakely's face reveal the expression Amy had expected. She looked cold, perhaps hostile.

"You are Amy Herbert," Mrs. Blakely said looking at papers in a manila file folder rather than at Amy.

"Yes. I'm here about my roommate, Tina."

Mrs. Blakely looked up at Amy.

"Your email about Tina Davidson, saying that she needs help because she has, what do you call them, 'strange ideas and thoughts that aren't real,' seems to me to be offensively intrusive and judgmental. Just who are you to criticize her ideas?"

"I'm not criticizing, I—."

"Your letter certainly implies that. Are you saying that I do not understand English?"

"No. It's—."

"You say she 'doesn't know what is real and what isn't.' And what makes you think you can judge her reality for her?"

"It's hard to explain. It's just the way she acts, and—."

"You mustn't expect others to be just like you. There are large differences in behavior. Just because someone is different is not a reason to condemn or criticize them or think there is something wrong with them. Maybe there is something wrong with you, instead. We live in a diverse, multicultural society. And it is our right to live as we want as long as we don't try to impose our ideas on others." Mrs. Blakely looked down into the folder again, reading. Then she stood up and walked around to the front of the desk, near Amy.

"These things in your email." Amy could already tell by the dismissive tone that Mrs. Blakely was not persuaded. "She lights candles. She buys a radio or two. She cannot read Spanish so she is confused by the word *Abierto*. These are all normal behaviors." There was a pause. "In fact, Ms. Herbert, tell me. Have you ever taken the MMPI?"

"I don't even know what that is."

"The way you single out ordinary events as if they had special meaning makes me think that you may be suffering from abnormal thinking yourself. Tell me. Do you hear voices?"

"No. Mrs. Blakely, please listen. Tina thinks people are watching her. Isn't that some kind of symptom?"

"Young men are always watching attractive young women," Mrs. Blakely replied, with particular stress on *attractive*. The counselor made yet another trip to the manila folder.

"Ms. Herbert."

"Yes?"

"Are you sexually active?"

Amy closed her eyes for a moment. She thought to herself, "This can't be real. I must be dreaming. This has got to be a nightmare." When she opened her eyes, Mrs. Blakely was still there, stern expression and all.

"I've asked you a question," she said, almost snottily.

"I'm sorry. No."

"No, what? No, you didn't hear the question or No, you are not sexually active?"

"No, I'm not sexually active."

Mrs. Blakely had an expression of triumph (which to Amy looked like an ugly smirk) on her face, as if to say, "I thought so." She began to circle around behind Amy. "And I assume that Tina is a normal, healthy girl with regular dates."

"I don't think so. I've never seen any guys around her. No one calls."

"But you certainly don't monitor her every moment, I hope, do you?"

"No. But she's never mentioned a guy or a date or dressed to go out or anything."

"Well, some people are more discreet than the Miss Noseybodies of the world." The counselor was now behind Amy, talking to the back of her head. "You can be honest with me. You disapprove of Tina, don't you? You are envious and frustrated that the girl has a satisfying expression of her natural sexuality while you are too tight and rigid to find your own. You seem to be very uptight and obsessive. I think you want

Tina to be ill because you reject her lifestyle. Perhaps you are projecting your own insecurities onto her."

"No, please believe me. That's not it at all. There is something wrong with Tina."

"Why must you be so oppressively moralistic? Tina is not hurting anyone, is she?"

"No."

"Then why do you insist on butting into her life in an effort to force your values on her? And worse, how dare you come to us to ask us to help you force your narrow views on the poor girl? I resent that. I deeply resent that."

Amy wondered if the next words would be, "Get out of my sight!" or something similar. Instead Mrs. Blakely sat down and made a few scribbled notes in the manila folder. Amy wondered whether mention of Tina's book would make a difference. She decided that copying barcodes could easily be interpreted as normal also. So she said nothing about it.

"Do you think her parents should be called?" Amy asked a little more faintly than she intended.

The counselor stopped writing for a moment and looked up. "Tina's life is no business of her parents. She's an adult, protected by privacy laws. You have heard of the right to privacy, haven't you?"

"I guess so."

"She guesses so," the woman said contemptuously, resuming her energetic scribbling.

After a minute or two, Mrs. Blakely closed the folder with a clearly symbolic slap, her hand slamming down on the top of it, indicating that the case was closed and the discussion now over. She looked at Amy.

"If Tina is really having problems, there is the free clinic available for substance users who would like to take a break for awhile."

"I don't think she takes drugs or anything."

"You don't think. That's the truth. The truth is, you don't know." She stood up. Amy stood also.

"So, then, I shouldn't do anything about Tina?" Amy asked as they walked toward the door.

"Ms. Herbert, the question is not what should be done about Tina, but what should be done about you. Tina is an adult. In fact, she is more an adult than you, because she hasn't come to me complaining of your intrusive, busybody behavior. Get your own life and stop being so up tight about others. Live and let live. And leave the girl alone."

"I was just trying to help." Amy felt that wave of emotion that signals the near onset of tears.

"That's the motto of oppressors all over the world."

Amy walked out the door. When she was outside the building, she began to run.

There was a knock. Amy opened the door to find Melanie, the resident assistant, standing there. As usual, Melanie looked tired, and now a little sad, as if the burden of the world had become unusually heavy. Her head was upright because of a wide, studded leather collar, but her eyelids hung heavily and her frame seemed to slump under the weight of life. Even the tattoo on her cheek seemed faded. Maybe it was a temporary tattoo that was washing off, Amy thought. In a bizarre moment, Amy felt a kinship with Melanie, the pierced, dyed, tattooed, shop-worn girl. It was a kinship of the tired and depressed. Amy thought that if she had insight into Melanie's life, there would be much to sympathize with. "Hi, gang," Melanie said to the three roommates. There was no lilt in her voice, just enough breath behind the words to get them out. "I just dropped by to see how Tina is doing."

"Tina? She's fine. She's right here." Amy pointed to Tina, who was, as usual, lying on her bed listening to one of her many radios through the headphones. When Melanie saw that Tina could not hear what was being said, she motioned for Markayla to come to the door, too. Then, speaking softly, she said, "I saw Tina earlier today sitting in the stair well up at the top, above the second floor. You know, where the stairs go up to the hatch in the roof. It's dark up there."

"What was she doing?"

"Just sitting, I think. I thought I heard her say something, but I couldn't make it out."

"Was she with someone?"

"Not that I could see."

"I am very worried about that girl," Markayla said. "There must be some help we can get her." Then, remembering the story Amy had told her about the visit with Mrs. Blakely, she added, "Some help from her parents or from the authorities off campus."

"Well," Melanie said, "I can't give out her parents phone number. You'll have to ask her for it yourselves."

"Okay. We'll see what we can do," Amy said.

"Thanks," Melanie said, and turned to go. Amy's sensibilities were still close to the surface from her own emotional wrenching earlier that day, so that watching Melanie's sad walk brought moisture to Amy's eyes. "There's someone else who needs a helping hand and a loving heart," she thought.

"Whatever she's doing to find happiness, she sure seems to be looking in the wrong places. Then again, maybe she's just tired. Maybe I'm the problem, as Mrs. Blakely says." She sat down at her desk and looked at her ballerina.

An hour or two had passed after Melanie's visit. Amy and Markayla were once again deep into their studies. Amy sat peering at the screen of her notebook computer and taking notes, while Markayla had just stopped reading long enough to remove her glasses and rub her eyes. She was thinking about making a late cup of coffee.

The quiet was ended by rapidly pounding footsteps on the landing. They came closer and closer and then suddenly stopped. The door burst open to reveal Shelley, eyes wild and hair flying.

"Amy! Amy!" she said breathlessly, "Satan! Satan worshippers!" She was breathing so hard, she could speak only with difficulty.

"What?" asked Amy.

"Who are Satan worshippers?" Markayla asked, putting her glasses back on and focusing on Shelley.

"Room 230," said Shelley, still panting, "right here. Across the courtyard. They're drawing pentagrams and all kinds of evil diagrams and, and—" there was just a little pause, "—they are sacrificing chickens!"

A look of alarm flashed across Amy's face, but it quickly faded as she still sat there, looking at Shelley, standing in the doorway still breathing hard and waiting for a reply. Markayla looked from Shelley to Amy. Amy's body still faced her desk against the wall; only her head was turned in the direction of the doorway. Then, without saying anything, Amy looked down at the corner of her desk, then turned her head back to the computer screen and continued to read. Seeing Amy's lack of response, Markayla stood up, agitated and concerned.

"Satan worshippers are sacrificing chickens?" she said, a trace of fear in her voice.

"No, Markayla," said Amy, still looking at the screen. "The geometry study group ordered take-out chicken. Go back to your work."

"You're no fun," said Shelley, with a frown. She looked over to see if she had gotten a rise out of Tina, but the girl appeared to be asleep.

"Doesn't she ever study?" Shelley asked, gesturing toward Tina.

"I think she studies in the library," Amy said. "She's gone a lot. But I've never really asked her."

"So why are we so jolly tonight? Contemplating death again? Rich uncle die and leave his money to a cat instead of you? Found lipstick on Matt's collar?"

"No, Shelley," Amy said.

"Bathroom scale slandering you again? Maybe it's only water bloating."

"That's not it."

"Oops. I know. You're doing the calendar X's, and you're always cranky then. Sorry. I should have known."

"Amy had a bad experience with someone today," Markayla said, trying to be vague enough so that Tina would not understand, just in case she was not asleep. "And she does not want to talk about it," she added, seeing a look of intense curiosity rush across Shelley's face.

Shelley frowned. "Okay be that way," she said with mock petulance. "But maybe I know some things you don't know, too."

"Shelley," Amy said, "I'll tell you all about it later."

"Ooh, promise?"

"I promise."

"Zits and all?"

"Yes, zits and all."

Chapter 21

Wednesday morning Professor Miller's classroom was almost full. Those students who had been absent Monday had completed their assignments and brought them, together with a range of plausible excuses, to class to hand in late. A few hoped that Miller might be absent this day, also, but there was no sign on the door canceling class.

At three minutes after the hour, the hopes of those few were dashed as Professor Miller stomped into the classroom and slammed down his briefcase. He appeared frazzled and tired. As he looked around the room, he did not seem to be looking at anyone. There was an anxious, distracted look on his face. Murmuring ran through the classroom as students quietly mentioned this strange behavior.

"All right," he said, half angrily, "let's start."

Now he searched the room intently, as if looking for someone. Several students smiled brightly, as if to say, "Hello, I'm here, in case you're looking for me." He was not.

"Can we turn in our papers now?" a lanky student named Tom asked. "You weren't here last time and we didn't know what to do with them," he lied.

Miller was about to answer when the door opened. He snapped his head over to look and one hand grasped the table in front of him. Julie Carmichael entered. Miller looked surprised. Julie looked surprised that he was surprised, but then Miller relaxed and turned back to the class. Julie gave a little shrug and found a seat. One student whispered to another, "Guess who's dating Miller. Did you see those looks?"

Professor Miller pulled out his notes and some overhead transparencies and began to set up his discussion of logical fallacies. He interrupted himself briefly to say, "Oh, I'm sorry I missed last time. I got back from my, uh, my conference late and couldn't make class." As he spoke, he seemed to be watching the door almost like a hunted man. Several times during the early part of his remarks, he glanced over at the door. But no one else came in, not even the regular stragglers that Miller often greeted with, "I didn't know you had a class starting at 8:10 today. What time does your class start next time?" There was no humor, no sarcasm in Miller today. He appeared to be flushed and upset. But he made an effort to play his role of critical thinking professor.

Of all the fallacies of reasoning Professor Miller taught, and there were more than three dozen, by far his favorite was the *argumentum ad populum*, the appeal to the masses. He enjoyed teaching how persuaders like advertisers, politicians, and salesmen used this emotional sway to hawk their products. "Those who analyzed propaganda during the Second World War called this the bandwagon appeal," he was telling the class. "Jump on the bandwagon, do what everyone else does, follow the crowd, be a sheep." There was a particularly loud *p* sound as he pronounced *sheep*.

He felt more individual, singular, even unique by feeling that he knew enough about this appeal to expose it from several angles. "Think of all the actions you engage in that are influenced merely by popularity, from the food you eat to the clothes you wear to the way you behave in your relationships. The desire to jump on the bandwagon is sometimes over-powering, especially for young people like yourselves."

"He'll never jump on the fashion bandwagon," a girl in the back muttered.

Miller was confident that he would never fall for such a transparent ploy. He sneered at advertisements with appeals like *best selling* or *number one.* He was less certain that his students could do their own choosing.

"It's time to drop the adolescent flock urge and learn to think for yourselves," he continued. "If all of your friends stuck their heads into a cement mixer or swallowed a handful of squirming cockroaches, would you do that, too? Just because everybody's doing it?"

There was a resonant sound of "Eeeww" in the room as a number of the girls expressed their repugnance at the thought of swallowing live bugs.

"It's time you learn to drop the phony decision-making criterion of popularity and base your judgments on the standard of reason. Reason is the only standard of the thinking, sane person. No other so-called standard is worth dung.

"I'm toast," Amy whispered to Markayla.

"Why?"

"In my paper I argued that reason wasn't a standard."

"Uh oh."

The conversation would have continued, with further explanations, but Miller looked over where the girls sat, and they were forced to pay attention.

Contrary to his usual activity, Professor Miller wrote very little on the board during the hour. A few students had already come to suspect his intent in writing complex terms on the board and then not erasing it after class, and one or two of them thought, "The next class won't be impressed by today's board." There was only an isolated *tu quoque* and an *argumentum ad hominem* that Miller had written up there almost absentmindedly. By the end of the hour, Miller was looking decidedly stressed and fatigued.

"We will continue with fallacies next time," he said. The class began to bustle in preparation for leaving. "Oh," he added, looking at Amy, "Amy Herbert, I want to see you after class."

"Now I know I'm dead," Amy told Markayla, as they lurched into their backpacks. "If I'm still alive, I'll see you back at the dorm."

"Okay," Markayla said. "I am going to the library first."

Professor Miller did indeed want to talk to Amy about her paper. He asked her if now was a good time to return with him to his office, so they went back together. Neither one said anything during the walk.

Miller took his seat behind his desk while Amy swung her backpack off and sat in a wooden chair across from his desk.

"Do you have any idea why I wanted to see you?" Miller said, already with an edge in his voce. Amy wondered whether the anger he seemed to have in class was entirely caused by his response to her paper.

"Is it about my paper?" she asked.

"Yes, it is."

Miller had the paper on his desk. He showed it to her. She did not see any marks on the first page.

"Amy, about this paper, 'The Values of Reason.' This is your paper, is it?"

"Uh huh." Amy debated with herself about explaining her position in the paper.

"Is there anything you want to tell me about it?"

"I'm not sure what you mean. Do you mean about why I said reason was a process rather than a standard? I didn't know that was wrong. I was just arguing that we need values to make reason work. That values are the standard and that reason is only a process for thinking with values."

"Well, that's all a bunch of silly claptrap, but that's not what I'm interested in."

Can you, dear reader, imagine being in Amy's position, being told first that her paper was "silly claptrap," and then that such a fact was not even the point of the meeting with the professor? Amy wished that fear and surprise did not always squirt so much adrenaline into her system. She felt her heart begin to pound and her mouth dry from the shot. The room seemed too warm.

"What I want to know is where did these ideas come from?"

Amy wondered whether Miller wanted to blame someone for her "silly" ideas. Would he write an angry letter to her source? What was going on in his mind?

"Well, they are my ideas, based on my reading. And talking with my dad, mostly. And experience."

"Your ideas." There seemed an undertone of skepticism in the way Miller pronounced those two words. "Did you do any research for this paper?"

"No, you said to write a paper about the value of reason in our own lives."

"So you didn't search the Web for any help?"

"No. Was I supposed to?" A new fear hit Amy. Had she misunderstood the assignment? Miller noticed that the girl was growing pale.

There was a very uncomfortable pause. Amy was about to apologize for not doing research and for misunderstanding the assignment when Miller dropped the paper on the desk. Amy wondered whether she was imagining what seemed to be hostility or contempt in the way he dropped it. Miller leaned forward just slightly and looked into Amy's eyes. Speaking evenly and not loudly, but with a controlled anger, he said, "What would you say if I told you that I have indisputable evidence that you plagiarized this entire paper from the Internet?"

In his novel *Joseph Andrews*, Henry Fielding describes the reaction of his hero to the false charge of wrongdoing with a housemaid as follows: "As a person who is struck through the heart with a thunderbolt looks extremely surprised, nay, and perhaps is so too—thus the poor Joseph received the false accusation. . . ." In a similar way, Amy looked as if she had just been hit in the face by a board and called an unprintable name. Her look of astonishment greatly surprised Professor Miller, who had expected the blushing of guilt accompanied by immediate tears, sobbing, and confession.

Up to this point, Amy had thought she had a pretty good grip on reality. But when Professor Miller made the accusation, using the phrase *indisputable evidence*, her mind seemed to blank. She could not think for a moment.

"No," she said, through the cotton in her mouth, "that's not true." She was shaking her head. "That's impossible. I wrote the paper myself. I didn't copy it."

Instead of lightening somewhat, Miller's expression grew even darker. He opened his desk drawer and pulled out another paper. It was a Web printout. He tossed it on the desk, on top of Amy's paper, as if to trump it. There was her title, "The Values of Reason." Miller picked up both papers, turned them around, and put them side-by-side for Amy to compare. Both had the same paragraphing. The words of the printout were the same as her words. Amy became light headed and confused. Her usually analytic mind could not even find the starting place to reason about what had happened. All she could think of was, "This can't be. This can't be."

"I don't think that denying reality is going to help your case," said Miller bluntly.

Amy's brain was still staggering. "I don't know. I wrote this paper. I don't know how it got here," she said, pointing to the Web printout.

"You realize that the grade for cheating of this magnitude—an entire paper—is failure in the course, an academic dishonesty notation on your transcript, and possible expulsion from the university? We don't tolerate cheaters here."

"But I didn't plagiarize. I wrote this paper." Amy was having trouble breathing.

"But you cannot explain its presence on the Web."

"No, but. . . ." She did not know what else to say.

"Then how can you say you didn't copy it? The facts show that you did."

"I know it appears that way," Amy said, still bewildered, "but the appearance is not true."

"Don't talk to me about appearances," said Miller bitterly. "Tell me about facts. What reason do I have to believe that what I see here is anything other than proof that you have cheated? Copied? Plagiarized?" He was almost vicious in his tone, something Amy had not seen before. Other students had always described him as friendly and considerate. But something had changed since his trip to the conference. "You can't get away with this," he continued. "Denying your guilt is not going to help you. It will only make it worse. We can see to it that you are banned from any university in the state system."

Amy felt herself less and less able to sustain her self-control. The emotions were welling up against her will, against her ability to remain businesslike. Already her vision had begun to blur from the water collecting in her eyes, though no streams had yet run down her cheeks. Her nose was getting ready for a needed sniffle.

Miller recognized the symptoms, of course, but instead of backing off or offering a sympathetic word to calm her, he snarled, "And don't think your feminine wiles will help you. I can see right through them."

For the second time in a few minutes, Amy felt almost as if she had been struck, and once again the blow was accompanied by surprise. To be accused of using "feminine wiles," not just to escape the consequences of a supposed crime, but at any time and for any reason, was almost beyond Amy's imagination. She had never thought of herself as *having* any "feminine wiles" to use. Until this moment, she would have thought the accusation about as likely as an emergency room doctor telling a crash victim, "And don't pretend you're in pain, either. I can see right through that."

Had the circumstances been different, Amy most likely would have laughed at the dissonance between the accusation and her knowledge of her own character.

But Miller was a changed man. The odd thing about a change forged from the metal of a self-inflicted personal disaster is that there is no guarantee that the change will be positive. The "disambiguation" resulting from the realization of personal folly does not necessarily result in enlightenment or wisdom. It sometimes produces an even deeper darkness. The way to redeem a bad experience is to become a better person from it. But Miller had convinced himself that the flaw lay not in his reason, not in his values, but in his humanity. He had been too soft and allowed that softness to cloud his thinking. Had he been thinking clearly, he never would have trusted Gina to make the stock transaction for him. He would have done it himself, and done it right. And if Gina had not manipulated his feelings and deceived him about her age, he would never have taken her to Las Vegas in the first place.

This thinking, of course, involved substantial historical revisionism on the part of Professor Miller, because at no time during his dance with Gina had he ever thought that feelings or even the counterfeiting of feelings were needed or that he was ever paying particular attention to her feelings. One of the great benefits of the contemporary world, he had thought, was that a man no longer needed to lie to a girl about affection or mention the word *love* in order to prosecute his interests with her. What a great victory that the phony exhibition of emotions, those clever manipulators, could now be ignored. Only now he thought that he must have been deceived by his feelings, and he resolved never to allow that to happen again. He was on the alert. Reason and reason only would be his guide from now on. No girl would ever be able to use tears or pleading to dethrone his sovereign reason. The one sitting before him was an easy conquest. He did not even want to feel sorry for her.

"If you're going to fall apart and blubber all over the place," he said roughly, "perhaps you had better go do that somewhere else. At any rate, I want to see you again on Monday. Meanwhile I'm going to talk to the Academic Dean and consider what sanctions we should impose on you."

Amy could not speak. She rose quickly and left Miller's office almost shaking, thoroughly distraught. As she walked quickly back toward the dorm, she was crying in the most controlled way she could manage, crying against her will, tears and mascara and nose all running. Compared to what she was feeling, her crying was remarkably stifled.

Amy rushed back into her room and threw herself on the bed. She finally could not contain herself any longer, and the lesser tears that had begun in spite of her efforts to suppress them gave way now to open sobbing.

Amy cried for some time, her face buried in her pillow, grinding what little makeup she wore into the increasingly wet pillow case.

As her emotions began to calm down somewhat, she sat up on the bed and dropped the pillow. Her face was still contorted with grief, but her loud sobbing had given way to a quieter cry. As she looked forward, she saw through her blurry tears that Tina Nicole was watching her. Amy had no idea when the girl had come into the room, or whether she had been there all along. Seeing Amy look up, Tina got up from her bed and went over to her.

Tina put her arm on Amy's back and began to caress it. "I'm sorry, Amy," Tina said with evident compassion. She sat on the bed next to Amy and comforted her for a minute or two. Amy wondered what Markayla would think to know that Tina had such feelings.

In another minute, Tina asked, "Did they kill your kids, too?"

The question brought Amy to another reality, the reality of Tina's distress. It was tragic and a solution seemed impossible, rather like her own new disaster.

"No, Tina," Amy said. "I don't have any children." She wondered what or whether to tell Tina about her situation. "I just have a problem that has upset me."

Instead of asking about the problem, Tina said, "Tell me a story." It seemed an odd request. Tina had never seemed to be particularly attentive when Amy told her father's latest story to Markayla. But perhaps a story would be helpful in some way to Tina. Amy was surprised that one of her father's stories came right to mind, but as she began to tell it, she realized why it had come.

"Okay," she said. "Let me blow my nose first." She did. "This is not a story from my dad's detective work, but one he told me when I was growing up." Amy's father was a firm believer in teaching stories, parables, fables of all kinds, as a means of getting his daughter to think, as well as teaching her good values. Amy had heard this one more than once.

"Some people were in a rowboat crossing a lake. The lake was smooth and glassy. As the people looked into the water to see the fish, one of them said, 'Look, our oars are broken.' And right at the waterline, each oar looked as if it had been broken, but then continued in the water. But another person said, 'No, that's an illusion. The oars look broken in the water, but we know they are not, because we can pull them out and see.'"

Tina made no response, but kept looking at Amy as if waiting to hear more.

"The meaning of the story is that appearances can be deceptive. Usually, we discover what is real by looking around at what we can see. But sometimes we have to test what we see by what we know is real. Like the way the moon looks really large when it's first rising, but then looks smaller as it gets higher in the sky."

"Why does it do that?" Tina asked.

"It doesn't do anything. It's an optical illusion. It just looks like it's changing size. We use our knowledge of what's really true to reveal deceptive appearances." Amy was thoughtful for a minute.

"Sometimes appearances are against us," she said, "even though we know that the reality is on our side."

Thinking of Tina, as well as of herself, Amy added, "It's important to know what's real and what isn't, in spite of how things look."

"Yes," Tina said.

"And I know my oar is not broken," said Amy sadly and gently, "though I don't know how to prove it."

"I liked your story," Tina said. "I've been in a boat. We rowed across a lake. When we hit a rock, I thought we would sink. But no water came in."

"I'm glad you didn't sink," Amy said. Then, picking up her tone and forcing herself to be stronger, she added, "Come on, Tina. Let's get ready for lunch." Amy went into the bathroom to wash her face and put her hair back together. Tina put on her shoes.

Just in time to go with them, Markayla returned from the library, carrying more books than she probably should have in one load.

"Research," she said. Then, noticing that Amy's face looked red and puffy, she asked, "Are you doing all right? You do not look quite yourself."

"Oh, it's nothing. Just that I'm probably going to be kicked out of the university. And that's after they flunk me out of critical thinking and put a note on my transcript that I'm a cheater."

"This is not even funny," Markayla said, arranging the books on her desk.

"No, I'm serious. Miller says I plagiarized my critical thinking paper, and he's going for the throat. I *am* dead meat after all." Amy was by now so emotionally exhausted that she felt more depressed than tearful, so that her blunt remarks did not make her want to cry.

"How could he say you plagiarized your paper?" Markayla was becoming indignant.

"He had a copy of it he got from the Web."

"What? No!"

"I'm serious."

"Did you put it there?"

"Of course not."

"Then how could that be?"

"That's the question. But I didn't copy my paper. You saw me writing some of it."

"Yes. Even if I had not seen you, I know you would never copy another paper like that. Where is the learning in copying? Plagiarism is the short cut of fools."

Amy could not help but smile weakly.

"Well," Markayla continued. "I am with you. I stand by you. I will help you."

"I want her for my attorney when we grow up," Amy thought to herself, "as well as my forever friend."

"Waswahili wa pemba hujuana kwa vilemba," said Markayla. Amy had never heard that one.

"What does that mean?" she asked.

"It means, 'The Swahili people know each other by their turbans.' We are alike. And I will stand by you."

"Thanks, Markayla." Amy was touched.

"Are you a Swahili?" Tina asked.

"It means, 'Birds of a feather flock together,'" Amy said.

"Birds? Why birds?"

"Let's go to lunch. You ready for lunch, Markayla?"

Markayla looked resigned. "I think so."

Chapter 22

By early evening, Amy felt composed enough to think more clearly, so she spent some time trying to imagine how her paper could have gotten on the Web. Could she have accidentally uploaded it somehow? Could Tina have done it? Amy remembered noticing that her notebook computer was often in a different position from when she had left it—she usually left it open, but since Tina had arrived, the cover was often closed when she got back from class or the dining commons. Then again, the computer could have moved innocently when Markayla or even Tina used it for some ordinary purpose.

At a creative loss, Amy decided to call her parents. First, she gave them a long narrative of the events, interspersed by constant assertions of complete innocence. Then she said, "I have no idea how this could have happened. What do you think, Daddy?"

Her father had a career full of experience creating several different explanations for each set of facts in a case, for this was the common method of solving crimes. Take the evidence and create some different stories that might explain it. Then choose the story that fits best. His first thought was that Amy's paper had been compromised when it left her custody (these are the terms with which he thought of the situation).

"Did you lend your disk to anyone to look at your paper or even to use the disk for some other purpose?" he asked.

"No. I copied my paper to a disk only to take it to the lab to print. I printed right from the floppy and never copied it onto the hard drive of the lab's computer. The disk is in my disk case, where it always has been.

"Did you make more than one printout of your paper, or did you lend a copy of the printed paper to anyone?"

"No. No one has seen my paper. I didn't even take it to the Writing Center because it was just two pages and I didn't need any help with bibliography style."

"Could you have copied the paper from the Web to use for research and then confused your notes?" her mother suggested.

"No, I didn't use the Web at all."

"We would understand if you made a mistake, honey. It could have been an accident or you might have forgotten what you did." Amy's mother thought the paper had probably been copied, as the evidence suggested, but that her daughter somehow did not intend to cheat.

"No, Mom. I didn't make a mistake." No one spoke for a moment. "But I know what it looks like. That's just the problem."

Amy's father had too good an opinion of his own training of his daughter and of her integrity to believe immediately that she was guilty. And he had seen many cases where the truth was much more bizarre than the obvious explanation. His next thought was that Amy may have had a falling out with her boyfriend. He knew from experience that in many crimes, the victim knew or was related to the criminal. One of his favorite sayings was, "Most people are killed by their friends." He had repeated it often to Amy. She was not surprised, then, to hear his next question.

"How's your boyfriend?" he asked. "Mark, isn't it?"

"His name is Matt and he's not my boyfriend," Amy said. "He's fine."

"You still on good terms with him?"

"Yes, daddy, I like him. He likes me, I think. He acts like it. He wouldn't do this, if that's what you're thinking."

Detective Herbert did not argue the point. "Who else has access to your computer?"

"Just my roommates. But I'm sure Markayla didn't do it and I don't think my other roommate could—would—do it. She's not really the kind of person who would."

"How do you know?"

"Trust me on this one, daddy." Amy didn't want to say anything that Tina might overhear, even though the girl was once again lying on her bed and wearing her headphones.

"Who else has a key to your room? The janitor, your resident assistant, maids?"

"Daddy, we don't have maids," Amy said. "I only see the janitor when the plumbing breaks, which is not very often. And the RA seems pretty honest."

"Isn't she the one with all the tattoos?"

"Yes, Daddy, but half the people here have tattoos. It's a fad now."

"Well, keep an eye out the next time you see her and see if you can detect any signs that might provide information."

"Yes, Daddy."

"Do you leave your door unlocked when you are not in your room? Someone could have taken your floppy and copied it and then returned it without your knowledge."

"No. We always lock the door when no one is here. Otherwise TV sets and notebook computers disappear."

"Is anyone mad at you?"

"I don't think so."

"Has anyone threatened you or does anyone have a reason to want to hurt your university career?"

"No. Nobody that I can think of."

"Anyone jealous of you?"

"Oh, like that's realistic." Then, repenting of her sarcasm, she added, "Sorry, Daddy. But no, nobody is jealous of me."

"What about the professor? Does he have anything against you?" her father continued.

"No, he doesn't even know me. I've never spoken to him until today when he told me to see him after class."

"Is he married?"

"How would I know? Oh, wait. He does wear a ring, I think. What are you getting at?"

"Do you think he might try to use this situation to take advantage of you?"

"Oh, Daddy. Handsome, curly haired professors, married or single, don't try to seduce girls like me." Besides, Amy was thinking, Professor Miller seemed to have his eye on someone else in the class. Someone else who was much more attractive.

"Well, just be careful as things develop," he said.

"Yes Daddy," Amy said in a tone that let her father know she was rolling her eyes. "If he offers to take me to Paris, I'll be sure to check to see if the tickets are real."

In the middle of this conversation, Tina suddenly opened her eyes and said, staring at the ceiling, "Okay." She took off her headphones and got up off the bed. "I'm going out for a snack," she told Amy. Then she walked out the door.

Amy turned back to the phone conversation. Her father noticed that she had not spoken for a few moments.

"How about you, Seepy? Are you feeling okay about school?" Detective Herbert knew well that some students sabotaged their own academic careers as a way of escaping a hateful situation. And Amy knew the implications of his question. But the use of his nickname for her meant that he asked the question with love, and she realized this, also.

"Yes, Daddy. Until today, I was enjoying school. In spite of the work."

"Are you getting enough rest?" Amy's mother asked.

"Yes, Mom. And I walk to class, so I'm getting exercise, too."

The call ended after Amy's father promised to think over her situation and consult with some friends in the department. Amy did not feel like asking her father the usual question about catching criminals.

Amy's next thought was to call Matt. Maybe he could help her understand what had happened. He knew something about the Web and computers.

The phone was answered with a high-pitched French accent. "Prager residence. Fifi the French maid speaking."

"Matt, I'm in big trouble."

"Amy? What's going on?"

"Dr. Miller found a copy of my philosophy paper on the Web and he thinks I plagiarized it from there."

"Uh oh," was all Matt could think to say.

"I'm probably going to be kicked out of school. The least they'll do is flunk me in critical thinking." Amy stopped for a minute, thinking her voice had a whine to it. She swallowed and lowered her tone a little. "The thing is, though, I can't understand how my paper could have gotten on the Web. I didn't copy it from there."

"Did you give a copy of your paper to anybody?"

"No. The only copy is right here on my computer."

"You do have a backup on a floppy disk, don't you?"

"I copied it to a floppy to print, but I've got that disk right here."

"And it hasn't gone anywhere?"

"No. I'm pretty sure. And no one suspicious has used the computer as far as I can tell," she added, preempting the next obvious question. "You know we always keep the room locked when no one is here."

"Okay. Well—." Matt thought for a minute. "Have you opened any suspicious email attachments, like from people you don't know? Any free games? Funny pictures?"

"No, I never open those. You told me they were dangerous. I delete them."

"Have you let any suspicious programs through your firewall?"

"What's a firewall?"

"Amy, you're kidding. You do have a firewall, don't you?"

"How would I know? What's a firewall?"

"Is your computer on right now?"

"Yeah. Why?"

"Turn it off. I'll be over in a couple of minutes."

Matt was not the type of person to blame himself for every misadventure, but he felt guilty and angry that he had not noticed before the lack of a firewall on Amy's computer. As he walked hurriedly over toward her dorm, he banged his palm against his forehead several times, uttering an accompanying, "Stupid, stupid, stupid." He felt that he had somehow let Amy down, left her unprotected. The knight had been sleeping while the dragon singed his lady's dress.

Amy needed a long hug from Matt before she would allow him to look at her computer. Matt had never felt Amy squeeze so tightly. He instinctively matched the strength of her embrace with his own, pressing her to him until he felt her begin to relax. He could smell the scent of her hair as their heads took part in the hug. She smelled good.

"Oh, Matt." Amy's eyes were glistening.

"Don't worry, Amy," Matt said softly. "I'll help you." It would be years before Matt learned not to say, "Don't worry," to a woman.

"What if I get kicked out of school? What if I fail critical thinking?" She wondered whether she had a future, or rather, what kind of future she would face. And what of the example of her life? Who would want to imitate a flunked-out, supposed plagiarizer, a hypocrite who claims to believe in truth and integrity but whose hand was allegedly caught in the chocolate chip cookie jar? Bringing dishonor on herself was one thing. Dishonoring her faith was quite another.

"We'll work on that later. Let's look at your computer first and see what's up."

Matt turned the computer on and watched it boot up. While he waited, he grabbed an apple from Markayla's fruit bowl and chomped into it. Because he was watching the screen, he did not see Amy shake her head, smiling fondly. When the computer was ready, he began to click and choose various items. Soon he had a look of doubt, of curiosity, then concern. He opened several windows as he hunted around the various parts of the computer, parts Amy had never seen. Amy saw him shake his head.

"What did you find out?"

"I'm afraid you're one dead kitty," Matt said.

"What do you mean?"

"No firewall."

"Huh?"

"On a network. In a university dorm. You've probably had every word you've ever written copied from your computer by now."

"Nuh uh." Amy thought he was kidding.

"Children in Brazil are probably reading your works and profiting from them even as we speak."

"Matt, this is serious. And what's a firewall?"

"You don't have any lurid diary entries about me on this thing, do you?"

"Matthew."

"It's a program that keeps hackers from getting into your computer by the back door."

"What back door?"

"Over the network." Matt lifted the cable from Amy's notebook to the wall.

"You mean people can get into my computer over that cable?" Matt nodded. "So someone could have copied my paper from another room in the dorm?"

"They could have copied it from the Ukraine," Matt said. "The network is connected to the Internet. In fact, I'd be surprised if they don't have a kiddie porn server running off this thing by now."

"Matt, you're joking."

"Let's hope so," he said in a tone that did not encourage Amy.

Matt downloaded some free firewall software and rebooted the computer. He watched as the various services asked for permission to connect to the network.

"I don't see any rogue servers trying to run," he said at last.

"So does that mean my stuff is safe now?"

"Well, the barn door is closed. But who knows where your chickens have been?"

The thought reminded Amy of the plagiarism problem again. She slumped down on the bed, exhausted.

"Why is this happening to me?" she asked of no one in particular.

"Sometimes, all we can do is trust the Lord," Matt said.

"I know God is not an insurance policy or a vending machine. I don't believe in him so that when I drop the soap, it won't hit my foot. But this is so out of the blue. I feel like a train fell on me."

Matt considered her train metaphor for a minute, but said nothing.

There was a knock on the door. It was Shelley, breathless again.

"Oh, Matt!" she said, excitedly, seeing him first, "I've got the perfect quote for you." Then she recited in a deep tone of voice, "'There is, indeed, nothing that so much seduces reason from vigilance as the thought of passing life with an amiable woman.' That's from Samuel Johnson. Get it? Amiable, Amy?"

"Maybe you should still be an English major," Matt said.

"No, I think I like literature too much."

"Shelley, I'm in big trouble," Amy said. She was too spent to break down again, but her face showed that she was very unhappy.

Shelley looked at Matt with alarm. "Oh, no! Not—."

"Plagiarism," Amy interrupted. "I mean, I've been accused of plagiarism, but I didn't do it."

A lengthy and highly repetitive explanation followed, together with a handful of new tears and the need for a few tissues. Amy blew her runny nose energetically, half angry that she was upset and tearful and sniffling in front of Matt. She had never allowed herself to blow her nose so vigorously in front of him before because she thought it was unladylike. But on this occasion, she was distracted and cranky with herself. Matt thought, "Wow, she can really honk."

"I sure wish I knew what was going on in my life," Amy said. "First I get blamed when I try to help Tina, and now my reputation is ruined and I'm going to be kicked out of the university for something I didn't do. And until now, everything was going so well."

"Maybe this is just a hole in the plot of your life," Shelley said. She sat down on the bed next to Amy.

"A hole?" Amy asked, only mildly curious.

"You know, like those books where, for chapters one through fifty the two characters hate each other and then in Chapter Fifty One they both eat a tomato and fall in love and all their problems disappear? Or like this one character will be a heartless bad guy who kicks dogs and slaps women, except that when it's convenient for the plot, he marries an ex-nun or something? Or the detective hero takes ten cars full of cops with him to the first three drug busts, but then he decides to go to the next bust at an isolated warehouse all by himself, and to our amazement, it's a trap?"

"So, my problem is the contrivance of a bad plot? My life is a bad plot?"

"Don't get me wrong," Shelley continued. "My own life is full of plot holes, too. But plot holes don't necessarily mean anything. They just happen."

"I'd prefer to think that everything happens for a purpose, and that my life is not just a badly plotted play."

Shelley thought for a moment. "That would be nice. And sometimes, it would explain so much. Especially in hindsight. Other times, I'm not so sure."

"The more practical thing is, What am I going to do? How can I defend myself? It seems hopeless."

"Nothing is hopeless," Matt said.

"Maybe I should just drop out." Amy was looking down at her fingertips and rubbing them.

"No, Amy," Shelley said. "That's like killing yourself to spite a zit."

Amy looked at Shelley. "Yeah, but was your life ever destroyed by a zit?"

"Well, there was this time in junior high—."

"Shelley, this is serious, and you're not helping."

"I know. I'm sorry, but you handed me the line. I had to run with it."

"Uh, I'll leave you and Shelley to talk," Matt said, edging toward the door. "Meanwhile, I'll be praying for you and for the best outcome of all this."

Amy got up off the bed and gave Matt a little hug. "Thank you, Matt. You're special."

"And the best thing to do is turn your computer off when you're not using it."

"Okay."

"Hey," Shelley said, after Matt left and closed the door. "I prayed the other day, too."

"Really?" Amy was a little surprised.

"Yeah. Ron and I were on his bike and we hit a gravel spot on the edge of the pavement and started to skid. I prayed, 'Dear God, don't let us get killed.' And the rear tire got back on the pavement. It was like a miracle or something."

"How neat," Amy said, trying to smile a smile she found it difficult to feel. "I need a miracle like that, too. But I don't expect a miracle to solve all my problems."

The two friends continued to talk for a long while, stream-of-consciousness style, ranging over topics that included Ron and Matt, junior high and high school, life at the university, professors, food, and a number of others. Shelley was her usual funny and outrageous self. They chatted along, Amy almost merrily too, until first Tina and then, shortly afterwards, Markayla, returned to the room. Amy had deeply appreciated the welcome distraction from her cares.

Chapter 23

Amy had been so relieved that Dr. Miller had allowed her write another paper to replace the plagiarized "silly claptrap" of the first one. She had worked on this one so hard to please him, worked on it up to the last minute. But now, as she clutched the essay in her hand, she was worried about getting it to Dr. Miller on time. He had given her just so much extra time. She had used it all, staying up almost all night finishing it before falling asleep for just a few minutes. Amy could not believe that she had overslept. She was always up on time, even when her alarm did not work. But now she was almost late with her paper. It could not be late, or it would get a zero. She ran upstairs in the academic building and then down the long hallway toward the classroom.

Something was wrong. She could not find Room 266 where her critical thinking class met. The hallway was quiet. The building looked strange and unfamiliar and yet familiar, too. She ran from door to door, and even though the room numbers were wrong, she looked inside each one to see if she could see Dr. Miller or recognize her classmates or find anyone who might know where they were. The rooms were all empty.

The clock in the hall read 8:47, only three minutes until her essay would be late and she would fail. Her heart pounded. She felt flushed. Her mouth was dry.

"Maybe everyone finished early and Dr. Miller is back in his office," she thought. Quickly she ran down the hallway.

As she was about to take the stairwell, she noticed the door to the last classroom on the left was open. Inside she could see Dr. Miller sitting at a desk in the front. She sighed, releasing some of the tension. She was at least a minute early. She breathed deeply once or twice to slow her panting and her pounding heart, then walked inside with deliberate slowness. She tried to appear calm.

Dr. Miller looked up. He was not smiling. He looked hostile.

"Here's my paper," Amy said, holding it out to him.

Dr. Miller did not even glance at it. He did not take it. He did not even look Amy in the eyes. He looked back down at the work on his desk.

"It's not late," she said, as another jolt of fear-induced adrenalin shot through her body and made her heart pound again.

Dr. Miller looked at the paper she held out and then knocked it away with the back of his hand.

"Plagiarized," he said with a snarl.

"No!" said Amy, her eyes shooting wide open.

"Plagiarized, like all the others," Dr. Miller said. He pulled a printout of an article from his desk drawer and tossed it contemptuously on his desk. "Plagiarized claptrap."

"No!" she screamed. "I wrote them. I wrote them all. Please believe me."

"Why should I believe a cheater? And don't think you can make me change my mind by working your feminine wiles on me," Miller continued, looking at Amy's body rather than into her eyes. "It won't work."

Amy looked down at herself to see what Miller was looking at. She was wearing only her black underwear.

Alarmed, confused, frightened, ashamed, feeling exposed, Amy dropped her paper on the floor and ran blushing from the room without another word. As she ran down the hall, her bare feet slapping on the shiny floor, students leaned out of the doorways watching her.

"Isn't that the girl who plagiarized all her papers?" someone asked.

"Looks like she tried to use her feminine wiles on Dr. Miller."

"The campus police are on the way to get her."

Her fear increasing, Amy ran down the stairs, nearly falling, staggering awkwardly in her hurry to skip steps. The voices of laughter and criticism rang in her ears. Tears were welling in her eyes. Her face was flushed both from exertion and from shame. She was just pushing the door open, horrified at the thought of running across campus undressed, when Tina came up behind her and put her arms around her.

"Amy! Amy! Are you all right?" Tina asked.

The room grew dark. She felt her body falling and then rising. Tina was there holding her. Amy was sitting on her bed. Tina was next to her. Amy gulped. Her heart was still pounding. She was panting.

"Were they hurting you?" Tina asked.

"No, no," said Amy, trying to recover her breathing. The disorientation took a few minutes to dispel as her brain shifted back to a wakeful reality. Amy and Tina sat on the edge of the bed for several minutes while Amy slowly resumed a normal breathing pattern. Amy checked the landmarks of reality in the room, visible in the dimness of the bathroom nightlight. Markayla was sleeping peacefully; the faint green glow from the back of her notebook computer shone on her desk; a lone candle flickered near Tina's bed.

Amy felt of her T-shirt and even pulled up the bottom edge slightly to check on the color of her underwear. White. Even in the semidarkness, she could tell it was white. She exhaled.

"I'm all right," she said at last. "Thanks, Tina. Thank you for caring, for helping." Amy wondered how her nightmare had appeared from the outside. "What was I doing?"

"It sounded like they were hurting you," Tina said, not adding any specifics.

"It was just a bad dream," Amy said, attempting to smile in order to reassure Tina. "Though that's by far the worst one I've ever had." Then she added, mostly for Tina's sake, but perhaps a little for her own, "It wasn't real. Thank God it wasn't real."

In high school Amy had experienced occasional anxiety dreams, usually involving an inability to remember her locker combination. Sometimes she could not find her locker or perhaps not remember which one was hers. But the most common dream was a failure to remember her combination, almost always right before class. She was familiar with the experience of awaking in the night with a pounding heart.

In real life, she had never even hesitated over her combination. She remembered it even now in her second year of college: 16, 43, 0. It was not difficult.

Then, last year, as a university freshman, her anxiety dreams changed. Instead of forgetting a combination, she now forgot to hand in an assignment, or perhaps even to do it. She never found funny those jokes students like to make when they pretend an assignment is due: "Did you get the paper done for today?" In spite of her careful system for noting assignments and due dates, she was still momentarily unsure that a paper was not really due that day. It always started her heart pounding. She hated that.

In the past, she had found herself in her dreams in an empty classroom, wondering where to turn in a paper. But this dream was the first one where Professor Miller and other students were present. It was the first one where she had been ridiculed and accused of plagiarizing all of her papers. And it was only the second time in her life, waking or sleeping, that anyone had ever suggested the possibility of Amy even having, much less using, "feminine wiles." Amy smiled a wry smile in spite of herself. That part of the dream, along with the plagiarism part, clearly came from her waking experience with Dr. Miller. "Too bad that wasn't just a dream, too," she thought.

That morning, Amy kept quiet about her dream until she and Markayla were sitting together at breakfast in the dining commons. They had found a private enough corner where low conversation would not be overheard. At that hour of the morning, many students were still asleep or just getting ready. The breakfast crowd had not yet arrived.

Amy had no trouble remembering the details of her dream. Unlike many dreams that fade quickly when we awake, Amy's dream had been quite clearly etched in her memory. She told the story quietly but emphatically, pausing to repeat certain parts where she had felt particularly fearful or embarrassed. Markayla listened quietly, nodding regularly as if she understood. At the end of the narrative, Amy looked down at the breakfast she had scarcely begun and drifted into a meditative gaze.

"You know, Amy," Markayla said, "I have had that very same dream." Markayla took a sip of coffee, and then winced and looked at the cup. She put the cup down.

"You've had the same dream?" Amy asked.

"Oh, yes," said Markayla. "Only in my dream, I am carrying a tray of apples, brought from America, to the poor in a local village back home. As I walk toward the town elders to present the tray, children and dogs surround me, trying to get at the apples. The children pull on my arms and the dogs pull on my clothes. The apples begin to spill. The tray has no lip. It is flat, so the apples roll off easily. I try to balance the tray to keep the apples from rolling off, but soon they are all gone. The children grab them and run away, laughing and biting into the apples."

"And the dogs?"

"The dogs just bark at me. But when I get to the elders and have only an empty tray in my hands, they frown at me and tell me to leave their presence. They call me a useless girl. They tell me I am too ambitious, that I am trying to do too much. One of them says that I could have brought one apple in each hand safely. Then he quotes the proverb, 'Haraka haraka haina baraka,' which is like the English proverb, 'Haste makes waste.' It means there is no blessing in too much hurry to do something."

"What do you think it means?" asked Amy.

"I do not know what this dream means. Perhaps it means something, and perhaps it means nothing. I wondered for awhile, after dreaming this two times, if the dream means that I am too ambitious to want to become an American lawyer. Perhaps I should be more humble in what I attempt."

"Do you still think that?"

"No. I want to listen to God, not to dreams. God can speak to me in dreams, but I do not know that this dream is from God. I think it is from worry, like your dream. I do not think we should allow ourselves to become prisoners of dreams we do not understand. We know they are only dreams. They seem real when we are asleep, but when we wake we know they are only dreams."

"It's odd that sometimes we wish our dreams could be true and our reality could be a dream. But in this case, I'm glad my dreams aren't true."

"Perhaps Tina's problem is that she thinks her dreams are true."

"I wish I knew. The way I think of it is that when people experience a dream or imagine something, the thought has a little tag that labels the idea as not real. When people go crazy, their brains wash away the tags and they can't tell the difference between what's real and what isn't."

"So they lose the label that says 'this is real cloth' as it is ripped out of the clothing of their thoughts."

"Well, sort of, but not exactly. Tina thinks that unreal things are real, so it's more like she's lost the tags that say, 'this is a synthetic fabric.' Real things still seem real, but imaginary things seem real, too."

"Well, you must not be crazy yet, because you still know when you have a dream."

"Yet?" Amy said.

"I am only kidding."

"I remember when I was little, my dad would pretend that my stuffed animals were alive and that I had hurt them or hurt their feelings. For awhile I wasn't always sure whether he was kidding. I'd ask, 'This is just betend, isn't it daddy?'"

"We all like to pretend."

"Yeah. The scary thing is, we all sometimes wish that what we imagine could be real. People who get their wishes are called visionaries, and people who only believe that their wishes are real are called crazy. Telling the real from the imaginary is one of the big things in life. Trouble is, we all like self deception. It's so much kinder. We talk about true and false, but we should be talking about reality and imagination."

"Everyone who falls in love knows what you are talking about. What girl or boy has not wondered whether the signs of returned interest are real or are imaginary? We fear that we are imagining or making a wrong interpretation. But we wish so hard."

Amy wondered if this comment was an admission that Markayla had been in love. She decided not to pursue it. "Yeah. We want our love to be returned so much that we start to think it really is, when maybe it isn't. We believe what we want to, and reason gets bounced out of the way."

"We must not let reason get bounced out of the way. It is necessary for a happy life. It is how we understand reality, after all."

"But how do we know what's real? We might all be dreaming now. You can't prove we aren't. And besides, we live in a world where people talk about an infinite number of truths, all equal, all true, even though contradictory."

"Now you are being clever like the professors and other students. Clever but foolish. You know that there are not an infinite number of truths that conflict. You know there is God's truth."

"Right now, that's the only thing that keeps me sane," Amy said, still wondering what in the world was going on in her life.

"And you cannot reason about whether or not we are all dreaming. We simply know when we are not dreaming. It is knowledge apart from reason and apart from proof and apart from demonstration. Just like the existence of our families or trees or even—." Markayla stopped and looked around the room. "—Or even coffee. We cannot prove they are there, we just have to know they are."

"Don't let Dr. Miller hear you talking like that. He doesn't believe anything you can't prove by reason."

"Dr. Miller is a smart man who says many true things," Markayla said, "but I do not think he is always right."

"Markayla!" Amy said, pretending to be astonished. "How can you disagree with the great Dr. Miller?"

Markayla deliberated for a few moments.

"Markayla," Amy said. "I'm only teasing."

"Nevertheless," she said finally, "he is not always right. Reason is important. It is necessary. But it does not lead us to every true thing."

The girls returned to the dorm and Markayla headed off to a business class. Her professors liked the Tuesday-Thursday class schedule because they could run a company on the side while coming to campus only twice a week. Amy noticed that while she and Markayla had been at breakfast, Tina had dramatically neatened up her area. Her desk was almost completely cleared off, her clothes were all put away somewhere, and her books were all lined up along the wall.

"Wow," Amy said, "great clean up job, Tina."

"Can I talk to you, Amy?" Tina asked.

"Sure. What's up?"

"I know you're sad and all and that things are bad for you right now."

"I'll survive. Somehow."

"I just wanted you to know that I've been given permission to go upstairs."

"Upstairs?" Amy wondered whether Tina was moving to a new room. That would explain the packing. However, the dorm had only two floors. There was no upstairs from this room in this building.

"So I'll be leaving you soon."

"I'll miss you, Tina. But where are you going?"

"I'm sorry I won't be able to protect you anymore."

"Protect me?"

"You'll have to go out to eat without me. Be careful."

"I'll try."

"I wanted to thank you for helping me. For being my friend."

"But where are you going?"

"I'm returning to my orb."

"Your orb? What's that?"

"I was here to use my special powers to earn my rule. My time here is accomplished. But I want you to know I appreciate your friendship. When I get to my orb, I will send you 800 million dollars. It's available for thank you gifts to those who have helped me."

"I don't understand."

"You see my name isn't really Tina. That was just a name for this realm. My granted name is Astrea."

"Astrea?"

"I'm the goddess of star fire."

Amy was silent. She did not know what to say.

"I wanted to return earlier but there has been a war going on among all the planets and the higher beings. I had to wait. Now it's almost ready. When everything is ready, I'll be going."

"How are you going to get where you are going?"

"I'll walk into the next dimension."

"Tina, are you sure you didn't just dream this?" Tina was silent. "Or imagine it? I mean, maybe it isn't real?"

"No, no, I'm not crazy."

"But remember that dream I had last night? It was just a dream, even though it seemed real. So maybe you have dreamed this and it isn't real?"

There was another pause. Amy felt overwhelmed. She had no idea how to handle a situation like this. She thought about shouting, "Tina, you have to be reasonable!" but she knew that Tina already thought she was being reasonable. Finally, she asked, "You're not leaving right away are you?"

"I'm not sure. I'm waiting for the final sign."

"What is the final sign?"

"There will be a message on the radio."

Amy thought she would make one last attempt.

"How will you recognize the message as one for you and not for someone else?"

"They use a special name on a secret channel."

"And how do you know you can trust the message?"

"There is a special code word. It's all been worked out."

Amy felt like crying. But this time it was not for herself.

Chapter 24

When Amy arrived at the Math Department office to go to work, she noticed that Professor Elderberry, the department chair and the person who had hired her in the fall of her freshman year, was looking much more somber than usual. Usually, his lively eyes and gentle nature made her feel happy and welcome. He had always entertained her with his great sense of humor. Amy could not recall ever seeing him angry or unhappy. Now he was not exactly unhappy, but Amy could sense that he was concerned about something. Thinking that it was not her place to ask him about his somber mood, she started her work as usual, picking up some filing.

As she walked past his office, Elderberry said, "Amy, have you got a moment?"

"Sure." She walked in, still hugging a pile of stuffed manila folders.

"Come in and close the door. We need to have a personal conversation." Amy put the file folders down on the top of the filing cabinet just inside the office and closed the door. "Sit down," he continued. "Now, I want you to promise me that you will keep this conversation strictly confidential."

"Okay, I promise," Amy said, simply. She looked around at the familiar objects on his desk and credenza and at the too many books crammed into the shelves of his bookcases.

"You've been working for me for about a year now. Isn't that right? Most of your freshman year and now beginning your sophomore year."

"Yes, that's right," Amy said, still not knowing where the conversation was going to go.

Then, in a more serious tone, Professor Elderberry asked, "Amy, do you respect me?"

"I've always thought well of you. Everyone likes you."

"Have I treated you with kindness?"

"Of course. And I appreciate that. You don't lose your temper."

"Would you say, then, that we are friends in a way?"

Even though Amy still did not know where Professor Elderberry intended to go with this conversation, she felt somewhat alarmed. Perhaps her suspicions about Gina and Professor Miller were coloring her perceptions. Or perhaps just the promise of secrecy combined with the idea of being friends was unsettling. She answered carefully, "Yes, we are friends, I guess." She wanted to add "in a professor-student sort of way," but that seemed too cold and formal. She did not want to hurt Elderberry's feelings, and so far, he had not stepped out of bounds.

Amy struggled to find a way to make things go the way she wanted. She noticed the photograph on his desk and turned it more directly toward him. "How's your wife?" she tried to ask convincingly. Elderberry picked up the photograph and put it on the credenza behind him.

"Fine," he said, in what she thought an odd tone.

Amy was now thinking to herself, "If he says, 'Call me Nick,' I'll scream." In spite of herself, a fantasy image ran through her mind, where she and Professor Elderberry were running along a beach holding hands. She almost shuddered visibly.

"So, then, we should be completely honest with each other." Elderberry's words snapped her out of her reverie.

"Completely honest." How Amy hated this enormous, wide open generalization. "What will I do," she thought, "if he makes an 'inappropriate suggestion' as Jennica calls it?" She said a quick prayer. "Lord, please don't let Professor Elderberry tell me he loves me or ask for a date or worse." Then she got the idea of answering in a way that might help derail any coming embarrassment. She told him, "I try to be completely honest with everyone, including my boyfriend," she said. Telling him she had a boyfriend might help.

As a child, Amy had expected every prayer to be answered by the requested results. Prayers that were not answered according to her wishes were upsetting and cause for being out of sorts with God. Over the years, though, a few prayers that had been rejected had turned out to be real blessings. She had learned that sometimes *No* is an excellent answer. She had even prayed a few times, "Thank you God for answering *No* to that prayer."

Now as an adult, Amy had concluded that *Yes* and *No* were only two of the possible answers. She now believed there were four. There is, "Yes, here you are," the answer people usually want. There is, "No, that's not in your best interest," the answer that the humble understand best. There is, "Wait on that one," the answer that both builds and requires patience. And then there is the fourth answer, which was to be the answer to Amy's prayer today.

"I believe you are an honest person," Professor Elderberry continued. "But I know how we all sometimes make mistakes. Is there something you want to tell me about a mistake you may have made regarding something in my office?" Amy had not the slightest clue what he was talking about. But at least her previous fears seemed unfounded.

"Something in your office?"

"Something that may have been taken from my office."

"I assure you, Professor Elderberry, I would never take anything from your office." Color began to appear in her cheeks. The fourth answer is the most amazing. It is, "Here is something altogether different." It had happened to Amy before. An answer that she did not expect, did not imagine. Sometimes it was the answer to the prayer she should have prayed had she known what to ask for. And sometimes it was an answer that passes understanding.

"I know you wouldn't do such a thing on your own. The question is, did you perhaps help anyone else take something from my office?"

In matters of personal integrity, Amy was not easy to fluster. She found strength in the arms of honesty, so the bit of color in her cheeks never turned into a blush of embarrassment. She did reveal how deeply she felt the accusation by lowering her voice. She looked into Professor Elderberry's eyes and said softly but clearly, "Absolutely not." Her eyes glistened from some would-be tears she refused to release. She continued, "I hope I've shown that I'm a very ethical and trustworthy person. I would never knowingly help anyone steal something from you—or from anyone else."

Professor Elderberry's experience over the years had taught him that the guilty will often deflect an accusation by referring to the absence of proof. Instead of saying, "I did not steal that," a guilty person may say instead, "There is no evidence that I stole that." Amy had "failed" that guilty test by clearly denying the theft. Elderberry had this in mind as he continued.

"The fact remains," he said, "that it appears that someone has stolen copies of exams from my office. During the day, the department door and sometimes my office door are open. But the filing cabinet is always locked. There are two keys: mine and yours. The exams are kept locked in the filing cabinet."

"I always try to keep the cabinet locked and I've never lent my keys to anyone," Amy said, with just enough emphasis on *never* to sound quite confident of the assertion.

Another thing Elderberry knew was that the guilty will often become elaborately creative in suggesting alternative explanations of how the wrongdoing might have occurred. Amy could have suggested that Professor Elderberry had forgotten to lock the filing cabinet, that a copy center worker had colluded to make an extra copy of the exams, or that Elderberry had inadvertently left the exams on his desk at some point. The girl sitting before him looking hurt and troubled had suggested none of these red herrings.

Elderberry thought to himself, "She's just cut off an out for herself. She could have said she lent her keys to a few people for various reasons." The man began to think he might be torturing an innocent girl, so he decided to see how she would react to the one piece of evidence he did have.

"Amy, I'd like you to read this note and tell me what you think," he said, handing her a small piece of paper with a few handwritten lines on it.

> Dear Dr. Elderberry:
>   Last night in the Cave I overheard two guys talking about getting advance copies of an exam from your of-

fice. They mentioned getting help from Amy Herbert. I
do not know the guys.

A Friend

A third truth that experience with cheating issues had
taught Professor Elderberry is that the hardened guilty
sometimes become too quiet or too vocal, saying nothing or
protesting too much, while the soft guilty, especially the
women students led astray by temptation or love, often break
down and sob out their confession once enough evidence
shows that their deed is known. Amy was clearly not hardened. Elderberry knew enough about her to be certain of
that. She did not protest with a lengthy, dramatic, and phony, "No, no, no, no, no." But so far, she had not broken down,
either. The careful, analytic, and humane professor waited to
see what she would say.

Oddly enough, Amy's first thought as Professor Elderberry reached the note across the desk and let her read it was,
"I'm going to have another nightmare. I just know I'm going
to have another nightmare."

Amy shook her head and let the note fall on the desk. She
slumped a little and looked weary, as if she thought protest
was futile.

"Professor Elderberry," she said, sounding as tired as she
looked, "I did not and would not ever help anyone get advance copies of an exam. I know that is cheating and that is
wrong."

Elderberry's expression was much kinder than she expected. He looked almost as if he believed her, or wanted to.

"I have no clue how to explain this note," she continued.
"You probably know I've been accused of plagiarism, too,

and I can't explain that either, even though I didn't do it. I don't know what is going on. My life is in the pits right now."

Elderberry was struck by the fact that Amy mentioned the plagiarism charge, which he had not heard about. No cheater in his experience had ever used an additional accusation as part of a defense. He suddenly found her comment almost amusing. Such a naïve innocence, he thought.

"It almost sounds as if someone is out to get you," he said, with a slight smile.

"I know," Amy replied, seriously.

Professor Elderberry knitted his brow a little. "Amy," he said softly, "I think I want to believe you. I will accept your word, for now, that you are innocent." Amy moved back in her chair slightly and relaxed her shoulders a little. "Tell me. Do you live in the dorms?"

"Yes, Pelletier Hall. Room 204. It's on the card I filled out for you."

"And where do you keep your keys when you are in your room?"

"In my purse, usually."

"Do you ever leave them on your desk or toss them on the bed while you go down the hall or to the bathroom?"

"Not usually. Maybe once in awhile," she said, being strictly honest. As everyone knows, keys have a way of relaxing in the oddest of places and are often found where their owners would swear they never put them. It would be impossible, then, for Amy to swear that her keys were always obediently in her purse.

"So maybe once out of a hundred times, you left your keys on your desk while you were in the shower, and a roommate or a friend might have come in and borrowed them without your knowing it?"

"When I take a shower," Amy said with more emphasis than before, "the outside door is locked."

"What about your roommates?"

"Markayla is my best friend from high school. I've known her for five years. She's one of the most honest people I know. And she wants to be a lawyer, so I'm sure she would never jeopardize her chances of getting into law school. And besides," Amy added as an afterthought, "I doubt she knows two guys on campus. She studies a lot and isn't interested in guys right now."

"Any other roommates?"

"Well, Tina—." Amy stopped. How could Amy explain Tina? "And Tina is very shy," she said, "and doesn't interact much. I don't think she could do anything like what you are suggesting."

Amy was feeling a weird sense of déjà vu by talking about Markayla and Tina as possible suspects. This was the same discussion she had had about the plagiarism issue. Could there be a connection? It was crazy to think so. But why was the world insisting on accusing her of cheating all of a sudden?

"You said something about a boyfriend," Professor Elderberry said, interrupting Amy's brief reflection.

She had already forgotten that she had used that term. "Um, yes, Matt," she said, almost sheepishly.

"Is he in 318?"

"No, he's an Ag major."

"Tell me, then, have you finished recording all the grades for the last exam?"

"For calculus?"

"Yeah."

"Uh huh. They're in your gradebook."

Professor Elderberry took the gradebook out of his desk. He still used a paper gradebook instead of a spreadsheet to make it easier for his student workers to carry around and record grades. Or perhaps it was in part because he was just a little old fashioned, and he liked the tangible character of a grade record that could be paged through. He even liked the smell of the paper.

He flipped to the tab with the grades for Math 318 and went over to the column for the latest test. He ran his finger down the column.

"Did you notice anything unusual about these grades?" he asked.

"It seemed to be pretty much the usual spread for a first exam," Amy said. "I think the bottom was lower than usual."

"Did Don grade these tests?" asked Elderberry, referring to the graduate student who graded most of Elderberry's tests for him.

"Yes, he handed me the stack himself."

"Ninety two looks like the highest. Valerie Wang has lived up to her quiz scores. And there's Becky with a not unexpected seventy." Becky had been batting her eyelashes at Elderberry during almost every class so far this term. Now he knew why. She wanted some extra credit to push her over the C minus and into something stronger. Too bad she did not know she was wasting calories. "Four percent," Elderberry continued, aloud. "Ouch."

Elderberry was quickly becoming convinced that something was not adding up. There were no obviously high scores from students who had been weak on the quizzes. The scores on the test seemed to be quite consistent with the quiz scores, except for two students who had been mediocre on the quizzes but earned single digit scores on the test. That was not the sign of taking advantage of stolen exams.

"I'll tell you what, Amy," Professor Elderberry said at last. "I need to do some more investigating and thinking about this. I want to look over the test papers and see if I can resolve some issues. Meanwhile, let's just continue as we were."

"You mean you're not going to fire me?" Amy asked, a little surprised.

"Oh, no, Amy. In fact, I'm sorry if I've upset you. There's something about you that tells me you are a good girl. That you haven't done anything wrong. It just shows." Then he added, silently to himself, "I hope I'm right." He had been deceived before by putting too much confidence in apparently honest and open students. They were always hard to read. But he was still willing to take another chance on what seemed a reasonable trust.

"Thank you." Amy wondered whether she was going to lose it right then. That choking, tingly feeling that says, "One big load of tears, coming right up," gripped her body. She rose, said, "Thank you," again and walked quickly out of his office. Out the department door.

Elderberry leaned back in his chair. It squeaked. He put his hand to his face and gazed unseeingly at a knick knack on one of his shelves. "Four percent," he thought. "How could anyone get four percent on the first test of the term, when so much of it is simple review?"

Chapter 25

Critical thinking this morning had been very awkward. Sitting in the classroom of a professor who had angrily accused her of plagiarism was almost too much for Amy to bear. She had taken a seat in back, among the inattentive students. She tried to concentrate, but her scant notes revealed that she was getting little out of the hour. Being accused of copying her paper one day and then the next day being accused of helping others cheat had fractured her concentration. And the last conversation with Tina Nicole hung over her like impending doom. She was depressed. The sarcastic comments about Professor Miller, the notes passing to and fro, and the other antics of the back row scarcely bothered her now.

"Why did I even come to class?" she asked herself.

But she survived the hour. She did not cry, though she felt like it once or twice. A pat on the hand from Markayla, who had joined her in the back as a friend and supporter, helped give her a little extra strength. She was careful not to make eye contact with Miller. She felt like someone who had been suddenly buried in the collapse of a building or mountainside. "What is happening? Is this real? This can't be true," she was thinking. She felt stunned, disoriented, even a day after Elderberry's accusation and two days after Miller's. Life seemed out of control.

Neither roommate went to the Cave after class. Markayla went off to the library. There was no coffee in the library, but it was an environment Markayla found attractive and help-ful. Books were handy, of course, but more than that, the at-mosphere encouraged a studious state of mind. Amy headed back to the dorm to rest. Stress had exhausted her. Walking back across campus, she half expected the grass and trees to have a sinister appearance, but they looked as beautiful as they had before these events. Now, the beauty seemed some-how incongruous, but it was there, still.

Back at the room, Amy dumped her book bag heavily on-to her bed. Tina was in the shower. Amy picked up Tina's wadded-up T-shirt and underwear by the door and tossed them on the girl's bed. Then she sat down on her own bed and stared across the room blankly. She felt like a zombie.

A short yell from the bathroom caught Amy's attention. Then there was a longer scream followed by a clatter that sounded like something hitting the bathtub and sliding around. The door opened quickly and Tina stood there drip-ping wet, the towel she was holding also soaked.

"They saw me naked in the shower!" she said excitedly. Her face was contorted with fear and disgust. "They put it on the Internet!"

By now Tina was standing on the carpet outside the bath-room, still dripping. Her eyes were wild. A small stream of water drained from the towel onto the carpet.

"Tina, you're still wet. Dry yourself off." Amy passed Tina and went into the bathroom to get a dry towel, which she handed to Tina in trade for the soaked one. "Stand here," she said, pointing to the tile just inside the door. No one can see you from here."

The shower was still running, so Amy walked over, all the while looking around for a camera, and turned off the water. Her shower radio lay in the tub, the hanger handle broken and the case cracked. Amy picked it up and watched the water drain out of it.

"What happened to my radio?"

"They put a camera in it. They saw me in the shower."

Amy picked up the radio. "Who put a camera in it?"

"The Abiertos, group number two."

Amy looked over the radio. Her father had given it to her as a back-to-school present. She could see no camera lenses. This seemed to be another example of Tina's imagination.

"Where's the camera?" Amy asked.

"In the box. I saw it. It flashed at me."

Amy turned the radio on. To her surprise, it still worked. She showed it to Tina.

"I don't see any camera."

"There," Tina said, pointing to the red LED that lit when the radio was turned on.

"That just means it's on," Amy said.

"The camera is on. They saw me naked." Tina clutched the towel more closely to her body, as if to hide better from the camera's leer.

Amy remembered going to a theme park once with some friends from high school. One girl refused to use the park's bathrooms because the toilets had automatic flush mechanisms that included a red LED, apparently to show that they were turned on. The girl seemed to think that there was, or might be, a camera behind the dark plastic sensor plate. Amy had seen the news reports about cameras being placed in restrooms and about people bringing cameras into theme parks, so she could understand that girl's decision, even though it seemed pretty far out, even a little paranoid, to Amy. In Tina's case, the conclusion seemed completely irrational. Who would put a camera into a radio to take pictures of Tina?

Amy remembered the comment Matt had made about cameras being everywhere and about everyone ending up being "naked on the Internet." She wondered if Tina had somehow turned that comment into a belief about herself. It was silly, but Tina seemed to be utterly convinced. She did not seem able to understand the difference between a joke and a serious comment. Amy looked over at the girl. She was now dry and getting dressed. She was turned away, so Amy could not see her face. But Amy thought she still seemed shaken. Poor Tina.

Then Amy remembered two more things. She remembered the video catalog she had seen in Matt's room, with cameras the size of a rubber eraser and lenses the size of—of LED's. And Shelly believed that Jeremy had somehow connected to Kristen's PC camera to watch her and her roommate. Could her shower radio actually have a camera in it? No, the idea was stupid. There were no wires, no antenna, except maybe inside. It couldn't be. She shook her head as if to shake out the thought. Still, she could not get the idea out of her mind. She stuck her fingers in her hair and gritted her teeth. What if the radio had been rigged? There were rumors that some students had master keys to every room on campus, and who knows whether Melanie might not be persuaded to aid in a prank? Now Amy was not thinking about Tina but about herself. She always turned on the radio when she showered. She always turned it off when she was finished, to save batteries. But maybe this once she had left it on, causing Tina to see the glowing LED. But if a hidden camera were somehow in the radio, turned on when it was turned on. . . .

Amy was beginning to frighten herself, more because she recognized that she was beginning to think like Tina than out of a real belief that she was being spied on in the shower. "I'm not going to wig out," she thought. "This is all too weird. It's just a radio."

Still, it wouldn't hurt to check. If Jeremy had been spying on Kristen and Becky in their room, then he might be doing the same thing here. The thought of a wireless camera, and of spying over the Internet gave Amy a chill: What if pictures of her *were* posted somewhere on the Net? Her heart started to pound, as it always did when she frightened herself.

She stopped debating and picked up the radio again. Was this the same radio her father had given her, or was it a different one? She tried hard to remember exactly what it had looked like when she opened the box. She couldn't quite remember. This radio looked like the right one, but the exact design had faded as the original radio's details had been mentally tuned out and taken for granted. She recalled Sherlock Holmes' mild chastisement of Watson for not knowing how many steps there were in a frequently-used staircase. "You observe, but you do not see." Amy gave a shrug of frustration. "Why didn't I pay more attention?" she asked herself.

"You should throw that away," Tina said.

Amy turned. Tina was standing there, scowling at the radio. She had finished dressing, but was still agitated.

"I'm going to have Matt look at it. He can tell if there's a camera in it."

"They put me naked on the Internet," Tina said. She was looking at the radio with near hatred. "I'm going out," she concluded and walked out the door without saying anything more.

On her desk under her study lamp, the radio looked normal to Amy. It still looked new, but that was probably because it was new. Not enough time had passed for it to get a coating of soap scum and mineralization. She could see no obvious parts that could be identified as a lens. The clear plastic window that revealed the dial did not reveal any obvious peephole for even the tiniest camera to leer through. But what was inside? She turned the unit over and over, looking for screws. None were visible. Was it glued shut? It had not opened when Tina knocked or threw it to the floor of the tub.

Amy tried to open the battery compartment. It seemed stuck shut. Had someone glued it closed after doctoring the insides, to prevent anyone from finding out the truth? No, that was silly. Still, the tab did not seem to work. Amy grabbed a metal nail file and attacked the tab. After a few attempts, it yielded and the compartment popped open. Almost to her disappointment, there were no suspicious wires or other parts. Only the batteries were inside.

Amy put down the radio and looked at the clock on her desk. Matt would be out of class in half an hour, and he could help her.

It was a very long half hour. Amy tried to study, but couldn't concentrate. Every five minutes, she picked up the radio and looked for screws or shook it or put her eye close to the grille to see if she could make out anything suspicious. She turned the radio on several times and peered at it closely to see if anything looked suspicious. Each time she turned it on, the little red LED came on, just as it always had. Now, however, it seemed to have a sinister appearance.

Amy began calling Matt's room well before the time she knew he would be back. After the fourth or fifth call, he answered.

"Hi, Matt, I need your help," she said, without any preliminary chit chat.

Matt immediately recognized Amy's voice, so he said, "I'll be glad to help. Is this Lisa or Julie?"

"Not now, Matt. It's Amy. Can you come over and help me take something apart?"

Matt knew that Amy had a serious agenda by the way she had cancelled his repartee. So instead of joking about how he could guarantee taking something apart but not putting it back together, he said, "Sure. What are we talking about?"

"A radio."

"Okay. I'll be right over with my take-apart-a-radio tools." Matt had three levels of tools. The first level was a compact kit of small tools, including screwdrivers, pliers, a file, and other assorted items useful for working on small appliances or household repairs such as door locks or electrical outlets. This kit was kept in a drawer of his desk. The second level was his main toolkit, about twenty pounds of somewhat larger tools such as adjustable wrenches, socket wrenches, larger screwdrivers, a small hammer, a hacksaw, and so forth. These tools he kept in the trunk of his car. With them he could replace a water heater or change out a radiator (either the room-heating or the car-cooling kind) or install a sprinkler valve. Baby Blue Eyes, his small air compressor, was technically a second-level tool that should have been kept in the trunk or even in the garage, but she had found favor in Matt's eyes and was privileged to live in his apartment, as has been noted. His third level of tools he called his "dismantle a nuclear power plant" level. Some of these tools also lived in the trunk of his car and some in the garage of his apartment complex. They included large pipe wrenches, an automobile hydraulic jack, a sledge hammer, a torque wrench, and so on.

Knowing that the repair was minor, then, Matt just grabbed his small toolkit and hopped on his bike to ride over to Amy's dorm. No need to take the car if the big guns were not needed.

On his ride over, Matt happened to meet Jennica. They talked for a few moments, engaging in the usual, "How's it going?" kind of conversation between casual friends. Actually, Matt usually greeted her with, "How's my favorite blonde?" because of Jennica's pretended obsession with the stereotype her natural hair color had forced her into. Today, Matt thought about asking her for a strand of her hair, so that he could plant it on his shirt to tweak Amy, but recalling the nature of the phone call, he sensed that now was not the time to do that. So he offered her some of the popcorn from the half empty bag he was carrying and told her he had to be on his way. Jennica gently declined the popcorn but paid Matt with a smile anyway.

Matt's view of Amy's serious mood was confirmed when Amy handed him the radio at the door. His last girlfriend would have talked for at least half an hour before getting around to the radio. She seemed to have an unlimited supply of words. Her habit was to ask one question, such as "How was the game?" and after a three-word reply from Matt ("It was okay"), she would begin to talk rapidly and somewhat loudly until Matt's ears finally came to rest on his collar.

Today, his quiet girlfriend, Amy, just said, "Hi, Matt. Would you open this up for me?"

"Sure. Doesn't it work?" He took a large mouthful of popcorn and then traded her the bag for the radio. He kept the toolkit in the other hand so he could put it down near the repair.

"Yeah, it works. But I want to see inside." She didn't want to lie and say it didn't work.

"Okay." Then he added, "The handle's broken."

"Can you fix that, too?"

"I don't know. We'll see."

Matt looked over the radio, much as Amy had done, hunting for screws.

"I couldn't find any screws," Amy offered. "Think it's glued shut?"

"Maybe. More likely the screws are cleverly hidden." Matt opened the battery compartment. He took out the batteries, and in the cradle underneath two screws were visible.

"Duh," Amy said, mentally slapping her forehead. "I should have taken out the batteries."

"You haven't taken apart as many radios as I have," Matt said, in a gesture of consolation. "These do look promising, though we can't be sure." He knew from the experience of taking apart many appliances and home electronics never to assume that any visible screws were *the* screws holding an object together. More than once he had removed some screws that by all rights should have been the right ones, the ones holding the casing together, only to hear something fall apart inside the thing he was working on, while the casing remained as tightly held together as ever. The tinkle of little parts falling down inside a stereo or television was always a sickening sound.

"If those are the screws for the bottom end, where are the ones for the top?"

"Let's hope there aren't any. There may be a plastic tab holding that end together, and when we remove these screws, the casing will swing open. Otherwise, the screws may be hidden behind the speaker grille on the front or under the label."

The hope was fulfilled. The screws in the battery well were the right ones. The plastic tab theory proved correct, also. The radio swung open, awkwardly because the battery wires prevented the bottom piece from coming off freely, but the halves separated enough to grant a look inside.

The view was undramatic. All they could see was the back of a circuit board with many little soldered points and the magnet part of the speaker.

Amy was beginning to feel foolish when nothing out of the ordinary was found. Matt was pointing out parts to her that she did not care about. She pretended to be interested. She thought about saying, "Thanks," and asking Matt to put the radio back together, but she decided to take the investigation to its limit: She was, after all, her father's daughter. So she said, "What's under the circuit board?"

After a few minutes removing the battery wires to free the back completely, Matt removed five more screws and carefully lifted the circuit board. The board balked because the radio control knobs jutted through the front casing. Matt had taken apart more than one item that at the last minute had produced the snap of breaking plastic, or worse, the sproing of spring-loaded parts flying invisibly in every direction, never again to be found where they secretly landed in the carpet or behind a box.

Amy interpreted Matt's carefulness to his fear of what he might find. In truth, he had no suspicion of evil at all. He acted as if he were taking apart a bomb because the springs of experience had taught him to be careful.

At last he freed the circuit board from its final catch and lifted it up and away, turning it over as he did so. Amy's eyes eagerly searched the board and there she saw it—a small black cube with a tiny round hole in the top. It was just about in the right place to be peering through the grille. "What's that?" she asked, almost breathlessly.

"That's an adjustable potentiometer," Matt said.

"Is that like a camera?"

"A camera?" Matt asked, wondering where in the world this girl had gotten that idea. "No, it's a variable resistor. When they set up the radio at the factory, they tweak the circuit with these little guys."

"What is the hole in the top for?" Amy asked, still not completely satisfied.

"That's for a little screwdriver, to dial in the right setting."

Other than the grille, which, Amy admitted at last, could not be seen through, there were no holes in the front of the casing. Still, Amy asked Matt to identify several other components. He knew most of them, but they all had non-camera sounding names like *capacitor* or *transistor*. There was no doctored circuitry, no camera. There was only the guts of a shower radio and nothing more.

"Do you think you can get it back together?" Amy asked tentatively.

"Put it back together?" Matt began, with amplified incredulity. Then, recovering himself, thinking that it still might not be a good time for some teasing, added, "I think so."

Matt had learned a lot as a kid by taking things apart to see how they worked, or at least how they were put together.

In fact, one of the earliest lessons he was taught by his parents was, "Don't take anything apart that we are still using."

Later, he learned a second lesson that joined his own experience with parental wisdom: "Don't take anything apart while it is still plugged in."

As he became stronger and could begin to use wrenches in addition to screwdrivers and pliers, he was given the third lesson of childhood disassembly: "Don't take anything apart unless Dad is helping you."

Many old small appliances gave up their secrets to Matt in his young days, and in exchange for converting them into pieces, he learned much about how consumer products are manufactured. He had even developed a theory that the assemblers of small appliances had special, secret tools to reach impossibly positioned fasteners. His idea was that women named Irma did most of the assembling. A film in high school had shown small appliance assembly lines of mostly women, and he had given them all the name Irma. When he encountered a particularly problematic screw which no ordinary screwdriver could reach, he always said, "Looks like I need an Irma tool for this one." He always imagined some sort of tool with multiple bends or movable articulations that fit exactly. Perhaps it entered one side, turned a corner or two and then engaged the fastener, just so. Without the exact, secret, special tool, it was always more difficult to remove and re-install those screws and nuts.

This radio had no unexpectedly difficult angles, and Matt managed to replace all the parts and snap the case back together in just a few minutes.

"Before you put the screws back in," Amy said, touching his arm, "tell me there is no camera anywhere inside." Matt turned his attention from the radio to Amy and looked searchingly into her eyes.

"Are you all right, Amy?" Amy blushed. She felt like a fool.

"Yes. But there's no camera is there? Tina thought there was."

"Oh," Matt said, in a tone of sudden understanding. "No, no, there is no camera anywhere inside. We've both looked all through the radio and there are only radio parts. No cameras."

"Okay."

"Now we can put the screws to this puppy."

The screws went back in easily as well. Matt turned the radio on and dialed in a clear station. The music played normally.

"Wow, it still works." Matt was happy and just a little relieved. Not every repair went so well. "We'll need some airplane glue to fix the handle," he said. "I don't suppose you have any in stock?"

"We're just out." Amy was feeling enough relief to recover her wit. But she was also still embarrassed at her own obsession with the radio.

"Super glue?"

"Sold the last tube this morning."

"Epoxy?"

"Sorry, we're stuck."

"That was almost funny. But what kind of store is this?"

"So, Matt, tell me. Is it possible to put a TV camera in a radio like that?"

"Sure. Remember that video catalog I showed you with all the tiny cameras?"

"All too well."

"You could use something like that with battery power. You'd have to keep changing the batteries, though. And without a cable from the camera to your monitor, you'd have to use a wireless broadcast with a little transmitter. But all that's possible. Why? You think someone is spying on you? Or Tina?"

"I don't think so. But, and I know this sounds silly, but would you mind looking at the shower to see if there is anything in there? Like a hole for a camera or something?"

"Be glad to." Matt was feeling somewhat amused, but he knew the possibilities and had heard enough stories not to laugh at Amy's concerns. However slight, there was a possibility of finding something.

There was nothing in the shower. No spots, holes, lenses, mirrors, plates. Matt even looked closely at the shower head. He looked down the drain, using the small flashlight from his toolkit. Then he moved to the rest of the bathroom itself.

"My guess is that Tina's imagination has run away with her," Matt said as he looked carefully along the walls. "It's possible, even logical, to think there is a camera with a little LED blinking at you, but ultimately perhaps it's not rational."

"But how do you know whether you're being rational or just paranoid?"

"That's a good question."

"I mean, Tina seems so reasonable, or at least logical, in the way she talks, and yet what she says is just, for lack of a better word, crazy."

"Yeah, Tina's disconnected, I think."

"But isn't that scary? How do we know we aren't going to have the same thing happen to us? I mean, okay, I admit it. I was really kind of scared that there might be a camera in the radio. I got all worked up over it and everything."

"But now you know there isn't one, right? I showed you and you believed it?" Matt was examining the medicine cabinet as he spoke.

"Well, yes. But Dr. Miller has shown me what really looks like proof that I copied my paper from the Internet, but I didn't. How do you explain that? Am I going crazy?"

Matt stopped his inspection and walked over to Amy. He put his arms around her and held her close. She wondered how he knew just the right time to do that. She felt herself starting to cry. Matt remembered the words of a high school buddy, "When a girl starts to cry, stop talking." So he refrained from telling her not to feel sad or that everything would be okay.

Not many minutes later, Amy was wiping her eyes as she looked in the mirror. "I hate crying. I always smear my mascara and look like I've been punched. And I seem to have taken up crying as a hobby recently. I'm sorry."

"Anyone ever tell you you're cute?"

"Only you. Oh, and Ron said I was kind of cute once."

"Only once? I'll have to talk to him."

"I wish I looked like the girl in your picture."

"Amy—."

"Did I tell you Tina says she's going to her orb soon?"

"Her orb? No you didn't. What's an orb?"

"I don't know. What do you think it means?"

"I don't have any idea. Think she'll run away?"

"I hope some opportunist doesn't take advantage of her. Who knows what she might believe, or do. She just can't think straight."

"Has she talked that way before?"

"No. This is the first time. She seems to be getting worse."

"Maybe you should call her parents."

"I've been thinking about that. I'd need to get their phone number, and that seems hard without getting Tina suspicious. I can't just ask her."

"Does she have an address book?"

"I've never seen one."

"Well, keep your eyes open. And in the meantime, pray."

"For a miracle. And while you're at it," Amy said, looking away from Matt so she would not get teary-eyed again, "pray for a miracle for me, too. Otherwise, it looks like my college career is in the dumpster."

Chapter 26

Amy spent much of the night tossing and turning, thinking, crying, worrying, praying, and then starting the cycle over. In the midst of her stroll down the path of life, a mountain had begun to fall on her, and the rocks continued to pound her into the dust. The plagiarism charge, the threat of failure and expulsion from the university, the seemingly incontrovertible evidence, the stupid comment about feminine wiles, the note tying her to exam cheating. And then there was Tina Nicole. Poor Tina. And that horrible counselor. What was going on? And here she had thought herself stressed last year as a freshman by what now seemed an easy workload and a carefree existence.

She looked at the clock so often that the numbers seemed almost frozen. Twice she wondered if digital clocks could start to run slowly as the batteries went down. Then she noticed that the time had ever so slowly advanced into the early hours, causing her to get upset that she had not yet fallen asleep.

At one point, she thought she heard people talking. Alarmed that she might be hearing voices that were not there, voices that would mean for certain that she was losing her grip on reality, Amy bolted upright in bed and listened carefully. She could hear Markayla's quiet breathing in her peaceful sleep across the room. It was strangely a source of irritation for the exhausted and now cranky girl. Then she thought she heard the voices again. Turning her head back and forth in order to locate the direction of the sound, she zeroed in on Tina's bed. The nightlight shining through the door from the bathroom cast just enough light for Amy to see that Tina was wearing headphones. Tina must have been listening to the radio when she fell asleep, and now the voices talked to an inattentive audience. Amy felt herself relax a little, feeling more than ever the heavy tiredness on her body. She flopped back on the bed, pulled the covers back over her, and put her pillow over her head to shut out the sounds.

Insomniacs can seldom say when exactly they fall asleep. They can often remember counting the rotations of the blades in the ceiling fan, or hearing the romantic noises of cats outside, or how they tried futilely to find the right position to lie comfortably. But what time it was when they finally fell asleep for any length of time, they do not know. In Amy's case, however, it was just before dawn when her body and brain collapsed into neutral and sleep took her off for the troubled journeys of another dimension. Amy was usually a moderately light sleeper, but she did not stir at all when Tina's bed squeaked slightly or when the well-oiled door made a single click.

As hard won as it was, Amy's sleep was not without difficulty. She dreamed that she was in jail, locked away in a dark and dripping cell after being convicted of plagiarism.

"She'll never get out," a voice said. Then she heard screaming and shouting, and in her dream she saw people storming the prison.

"Someone get her!" yelled a deep voice. They were coming for her, to kill her. Imprisonment was not punishment enough.

More voices seemed to be talking loudly, and one said, "Call the fire department." Her cell seemed to be on fire. Did she smell smoke? She heard footsteps, pounding along the floor, approaching her cell. They were coming for her. It was a mob with torches and pitchforks. She felt like a hated ogre. Were they going to burn her out?

Now someone was hammering. Strong men hit the door to her cell with sledge hammers. It would not be long until the door flew open and she was murdered in her bed. The hammering was loud and fast. Then it slowed and got louder. Now the men with hammers had firearms and the hammering was gunshots. They were firing into the lock to break it. Amy ducked to the floor to keep from being hit. She awoke from the worsening nightmare just as the door to her dorm room flew open. The door swung all the way open and slammed against the wall.

"Amy! Hurry! It's Tina! Come. Get up!" The voice was Melanie's. Amy struggled to shake off the last vestiges of sleep and stand up. The lights in the room came on. Amy squinted painfully, the lights nearly blinding her. Melanie rushed over and grasped Amy's had, pulling her out of bed.

By this time, Markayla was awake, too. "Tina? Where is Tina?" She began hunting for her glasses.

"Come on," Melanie said.

"Okay, I'm coming," Amy said and moved toward the door, grabbing her robe from the floor, where it had been dumped during the restlessness of the night. The cold of the night air helped her fight the sleepiness.

"Hurry, Amy. She's on the roof. I think she's going to jump." There was genuine concern, if not fear, in Melanie's eyes. They ran.

When Amy and Melanie got downstairs and around to the front of the building, they saw five or six other students standing on the lawn and looking up. Tina stood on the edge of the roof near the street. She was wrapped in a bed sheet and wore a garland like a crown, made from the local trees. Instead of looking back down at the others or responding to their appeals, she was standing silently looking into the sky.

"Come down, Tina," someone said. "Everything will be okay."

"Why is she up there, anyway?"

"Don't know," someone else said. "Bad trip, I guess."

"Nah. It's more like too much party and too little girl."

"But she's not stumbling like she's blasted."

"It's more like she's been popping."

"My sister got drunk one time and climbed on the roof."

"Did she jump?"

"Nah. She hurled all over the people trying to rescue her. Don't stand too close."

"Hey, Tina, jump! I dare you!"

Amy looked furiously over to see who had said that. It was Jeremy.

"Shut up, Jeremy," Amy said harshly but quietly. The girl clinging to Jeremy to keep warm made half an effort to scold him as well.

Looking back up, Amy said loudly, "Tina, it's Amy. Please come down. I want to help you. Please."

"Yes, Tina," said Markayla, who had come up behind Amy, "we are here to help you. We will see that everything is all right."

Tina looked down in her roommates' direction. Amy was not sure whether Tina recognized her or Markayla. Tina's face showed no acknowledgment. She turned her head and looked back into the sky. Then, holding the sheet up like a cape, or like wings, Tina said, loudly and out into space, "I am the goddess Astrea. I am ready to return."

"Told you she was drunk," someone said.

"Are those teddy bears on her pajamas?" someone else asked. "Why is a goddess wearing PJ's with teddy bears on them?" The questioner was obviously amused.

Tina inched her toes over the edge of the roof.

"Tina, no! Come down. You'll get hurt!"

"No!" someone else said.

"Tina!"

A siren could be heard in the distance, approaching. Then a second siren joined in.

"I hear you," she said softly, so that Amy could barely make out her words. "I am coming."

Tina closed her eyes and wrapped the sheet around her in an embrace. She did not jump. She simply let herself fall off the roof. Two girls screamed.

"Whoa!" Jeremy said.

The landscaping around Pelletier was fully mature, having been planted when the dormitory was built twenty years ago. As a result, Tina fell only about six feet before she hit the top branches of a tree. Her body fell snapping and crunching through the slender branches, then rolling and bouncing onto thicker ones until the tree had no more to offer. After another short free fall, she hit a thick hedge next to the building. Finally, she landed on the over watered soil under the bushes with a gentle thud.

The bystanders rushed up toward her. Her body was still mostly wrapped in the bed sheet, but spots of blood began to soak into it. Leaves and debris and mud stuck to her arms and face and in her hair.

"Tina! Tina!" Amy was yelling, as she came up to the girl. She wanted to take Tina's head in her hands, but knew she should not move her. So she wiped the hair and mud from Tina's forehead. "Oh, Tina."

Tina opened her eyes slowly. "Amy," Tina said. Then she closed her eyes.

By this time the paramedics had screeched into the parking lot near the dormitory, an ambulance was pulling into the entrance just a hundred yards away, and the campus police were scorching the road just outside.

Soon Tina had been immobilized on a spine board and loaded into the ambulance.

"Is she dead?" someone asked.

"Looks like it."

"Did you see the trees and the blood? Probably broke every bone and ruptured every organ in her body."

As Amy wiped enough water from her eyes to begin to see clearly, she saw Jeremy standing there.

She gave him a look of disdain. "Jeremy, how could you? You don't even live around here. You are such a jerk."

"Hey, Amy, I didn't think she would jump," Jeremy said gamely. "That's too bad. And you should be careful who you call a jerk. It's not like I pretend to be so holy and then plagiarize my papers or anything."

The gossip mill had already spread the news, Amy realized. Now her reputation was ruined. No one would ever trust or respect her again. She knew now she would have to drop out. But that was for later. The siren of the departing ambulance refocused her attention on Tina. She ran over to Melanie. "Melanie, I'm going to the hospital," she said. "Markayla, you should go back to bed. There's nothing you can do at the hospital. I'll go with you later on during the day." Before Markayla could answer, Amy ran back to the room and called Matt.

A sleepy "Hello?" was answered with, "Tina jumped off the roof! I don't even know if she's alive. She's bleeding. She didn't look good. Can you take me to the hospital?" Amy was already pulling jeans on while she cradled the phone against her shoulder. Since she was already wearing the usual T-shirt for her sleepwear, she was nearly dressed. She stuffed the bunches of extra shirt into her jeans and zipped them up.

"Hello?" Matt said again, not sure what he had just heard. Amy was speaking quickly and excitedly while Matt's brain was still strolling into consciousness.

"Matt, it's Amy. Tina has jumped off the roof. We need to go to the hospital." Amy was now looking for socks.

"Hospital? Okay," Matt said. "What time is it?"

"I don't even know. It doesn't matter. I'll meet you at your car in five minutes. Where are you parked?"

Chapter 27

Matt and Amy arrived at the hospital and learned that Tina was still alive, but in critical condition. None of the doctors or nurses would say whether they thought the girl would live. No one was willing to make any comment. All assured Matt and Amy that everything possible was being done. No one would give any details because Matt and Amy were not relatives.

The two spent the night in the emergency room, waiting for news that never seemed to come. They could have collected the repetitions of "They're still working on her," and printed them up in a small book. Amy's imagination wandered through scenes of a dead girl that no one wanted to admit having lost. The delay was to concoct a plausible story or to blame someone else. Or perhaps the staff was still looking for the doctor. The middle of the night must be a difficult time to find someone who knows something.

Matt's imagination was different. He imagined Tina opened up from head to toe, most of her organs under repair or removed, all her limbs in casts. In his mind, he saw a half-dozen monitors, pumps, and machines all attached to the frail girl's body. Six or seven people stood around examining X-rays, EKG tapes, lab reports, charts, holding test tubes of blood up to the light and shaking their heads with regret.

The reality was that Tina had been treated throughout the night. Spaced out at half-hour or hour intervals, she had been medicated, cleaned, bandaged, and X-rayed. Now she was lying by herself in a curtained off section of the emergency room, while an occasional person, usually an orderly, looked in to check on her IV drip. A single monitor measured her heartbeat, blood oxygen, and blood pressure. It was set to sound an alarm if any vital sign went outside the prescribed boundary. She was alive but asleep.

Matt and Amy were resting, possibly dozing, heads together, holding hands in the waiting room, while a television talked to itself. The night had been a quiet one for the hospital, and the two students had only the company of a little old lady, who waited, sad and alone, for news about her husband, who had suffered an apparent heart attack in his sleep.

Someone in light blue hospital clothes came into the room. A label on his shirt said "Carlson."

"Are you the friends of the Jane Doe attempted suicide?" he asked Matt and Amy. They stirred, no longer lingering between waking and sleeping.

Amy did not recognize the description as referring to Tina, and was about to say, "No," when Matt spoke up.

"I guess so. We're friends of the girl who jumped off the roof at Pelletier Hall on the campus."

"She's my roommate."

"I see. I'm Dr. Carlson. Well, the good news, if that's what it is, is that she didn't succeed in taking her life. The bad news is that she managed to bang herself up pretty well. However, I'm upgrading her from critical to serious." He sounded tired, even bored. Matt was struck by the irony of being upgraded to serious condition. "We thought she was really hurt, but it turns out she's only seriously injured." He wondered if these thoughts came from not enough sleep.

"You think she was trying to kill herself?" Amy asked, with evident surprise. The doctor looked at her with one raised eyebrow.

"Well, I doubt that she jumped off the roof for amusement. The toxicology for drugs and alcohol have so far come back negative. Was she drinking or taking drugs last night?"

"No, she never drank or did drugs, ever, as far I know."

"Was she depressed over school or romance or anything? Boyfriend dump her recently?" The doctor's tone seemed to imply that being dumped by a boyfriend would be an obvious reason for jumping off the roof.

"No. She said she was going to return to her orb."

"Her orb?" The doctor sounded displeased.

"Yeah. I think she was having mental problems."

"Are you a psychiatrist?" It was a rhetorical question, with an edge on it.

"No. I'm just a college student." Amy said, sheepishly. She still remembered her time with the school counselor, so she backed away from the information.

"Does the girl have any ID? A driver's license or school ID?"

"I could look."

"That would be helpful. We need some ID to get the records going. Do you know how to get in touch with her parents?"

"No. She hasn't ever mentioned them."

"Well, once we get her ID, we can get the other information through the school."

"Her name is Tina Davidson."

"All right. But bring in her ID as soon as you can. We've got to get the insurance billing going."

"Can we see her?"

"Not now. Give her some time to recover. She needs to give verbal permission for a non-relative to see her. She can't do that right now. Come back Monday and see. And bring her ID."

The doctor left without ceremony. Matt and Amy looked at each other. "That guy was real nice," Matt said. "Imagine him working on a patient. 'Does this hurt?' 'No.' 'Darn.'"

"Matt. Don't say that. He's taking care of Tina."

"Still. Tina may have too much imagination, but that guy seems not to have any. He can't imagine that Tina might be nuts, and he can't imagine that other people might be human beings with feelings. Makes you wonder what it really means to be sane."

"It's not what you do, but why you do it that tells whether you're sane or not."

"Like what?"

"Like talking to yourself, Mr. Mechanic."

"Huh?"

"You were talking to yourself that day when I helped you with your car."

"Maybe I was just singing along with the radio."

"You were arguing with your tools or something."

"And you know I'm sane, huh?"

"I usually think so."

"See?"

"But I'm biased, too."

"Biased? How?"

"Well, I told Elderberry you were my boyfriend." Amy blushed a little as she said it. She did not know why she chose this time to reveal the fact. It was an impulse.

"Oh, really?" Matt was surprised and touched. He had

been the King of Patience over the last year. He had often felt that Amy was either the Queen of Indecision or the Princess of Gradualism. Now she seemed willing to come closer. He tightened his arm around her a little more. She rested her head on his shoulder a little more fully.

"Would you want a girlfriend who's going to be kicked out of college and probably disowned by her parents?"

"Amy, I'd want you no matter what. You're a treasure."

"Aw, that's sweet." Then, feeling awkward about the moment, she added, "In fact, that's so sweet, I think I need a drink of water to wash it down."

"You are one of a kind, young lady."

"Yep, they broke the mold after me."

"You're just different. Witty. A little crazy, in a good sort of way. I think I like you."

"You think so, but you're not sure?"

"Hey, I'm a modern guy. Don't want to go overboard with the commitment stuff."

"Would you climb the highest mountain for me?"

"Maybe a medium hill with a snack bar at the top."

Amy gave Matt an elbow in the side.

"Ow. That didn't hurt."

"Darn."

"Hey, you ought to be a doctor."

"Just one thing, Matt."

"Yeah?"

"If I'm going to be your girlfriend, does that mean we have to be all mushy and syrupy all the time?"

"You ask this after you have just fractured my rib with your elbow?"

"No, it's just that you know I'm too shy to be all touchy feely and kissy wissy, especially in public. I just want to take things slowly."

"So we should slow down this passionate rush into heavy romance that we've been engaged in the past year or so?"

"Matt, you're losing points."

"Just my luck. Boyfriend for two minutes and I'm already losing points."

"And from now on, when we're walking across the quad and you want to check out the cheerleaders, try not to gawk and stare and drool so openly. It just looks bad."

"I don't know what you're talking about."

"You almost choked the last time. Just remember the girl in the photo in your room. She's sensitive."

"Okay. Whatever." There may have been a slight sigh.

They sat in silence for a few minutes. Then Amy said, "You know, I can see why people like the world of their own imagination. We can do anything in our fantasies. We can own an eighty-gallon air compressor when in real life we only have a little tiny one."

Matt gave Amy an odd look. "Amy, you sometimes amaze me. What's this about an eighty-gallon air compressor?"

"I was speaking in terms you could relate to. We can always imagine something better."

"That's what motivates us. We see in our minds something better and then work for it."

"Or if we are unwilling to work for it, we just fantasize about it."

"Yeah, there's always something better to wish for because the real world isn't always what it's cracked up to be."

"It's pretty cracked up, though."

"You're getting awfully witty in your old age."

"It's the disasters of life that have made me wise."

"'Pain is the chalk; laughter is the eraser.'"

"My chalkboard has quite enough on it for now, thank you," Amy said, raising her voice a little and looking up and waving at the ceiling. "Still," she added, thinking of Tina, "I really have no complaints."

"Yeah, you've got a great boyfriend."

"And he's so modest, too."

"And he has a great car."

"Well, let's not push it."

"Poor Bertha," Matt said. "She can't get any respect."

Amy started thinking about Tina again, hoping that she was doing all right. She felt angry with herself and with the counselor and with the doctor for not doing more, for not better understanding Tina's problem.

"Why do we have to wait until someone does something obviously crazy before we help them?" she asked.

"A lot of perfectly sane people act like they are crazy. That's considered normal now. You know how a lot of people say, 'I know this is stupid, but I want to do it anyway'? That's considered being sane. As long as you know you're rejecting reason and values and standards, you can do anything you want and still think of yourself as an even furrow."

"It's only when you do something dumb and think it's really great that people know you're going over the edge."

"Like walking off the roof of a building."

"Yeah." The vision of Tina walking off the roof made Amy shudder as she remembered it.

"But people are always doing stupid things and later on saying, 'It seemed like a good idea at the time.'"

"Well, that's true. In fact, we're doing something dumb right now."

"We are?" Matt looked around to see what was so dumb.

"Yeah. We're sitting here in this horrible hospital waiting

room for no reason. Why don't we go back to campus?"

"Why don't we?" They stood up.

Amy looked around the room and saw again the little old lady, sitting so alone and quietly weeping. Amy felt a wave of compassion rush over her. She walked over a few steps toward the woman. "Ma'am?" The woman looked up. "I hope everything will turn out well for you. I'll be praying for you."

"Thank you, young lady," the woman said. She looked drained and weak. Amy touched her hand and tried to smile.

When she walked back over to Matt, he offered Amy his arm and they left the waiting room. Just as they were about to turn the corner in the hallway, a nurse spoke to them.

"Excuse me, honey," she said, looking at Amy. "Are you the friends of Tina, the girl brought in from the school last night?"

"Yes, we are."

"You can bring her ID in on Monday. We can Jane Doe her until then with no problem. The insurance department doesn't work on weekends, so there's no need to make a special trip back here just to bring her wallet. Bring it when you come for a visit Monday." Matt noticed that the nurse cleverly avoided saying something like, "Forget what that jerk doctor told you."

"Should we bring anything else? Like clothes or a hairbrush?"

"Sure. You can bring her a change of clothes and her personal items."

"How long do you think she'll be here?"

"I have no idea, honey. But we'll take good care of her. I hope she will be able to go home soon."

"Me, too. Thanks."

As Matt and Amy drove back toward campus, the early morning sun was already up.

"I can't believe how stiff I am," Amy said. "My shoulders and my joints ache."

"My back hurts. Those chairs were terrible."

A thought occurred to Amy. "Just think, Matt. Tina's parents won't even know about what happened to her until at least Monday."

"And that's probably only if Tina wants them told. Privacy laws, you know."

"Don't remind me." The phrase brought to mind her interview with the counselor.

Soon they turned off from the highway and headed down the street leading to the campus. In a few blocks they saw some activity ahead, outside one of the apartment buildings just down the street from campus. Yellow police tape had marked off an area around one of the units. Three blue vans were parked nearby, one of them backed up onto the sidewalk right outside the front door of the unit.

"Hey, look. Something's going on." Matt slowed the car. A dozen students were standing around watching, some still on their bicycles, stopped mid trip by curiosity. "Let's see what's going on," Matt said, stopping the car.

"Matt, let's not."

"Okay, just a minute. You can stay here."

Matt got out and walked over to the group of bystanders.

"I wonder if someone got robbed or something," he overheard someone say as he arrived.

"I don't know," someone else said. "Did you hear about the girl who killed herself last night?"

Matt walked a little farther to find someone else to ask. He approached two students watching from the doorstep of the apartment next door.

"What happened?" Matt asked.

"It's the FBI," one of them said. "They've busted Jeremy, the lady killer."

"Jeremy Schneider? He lives here?"

"He did. But now that they're cleaning the place out, I guess he doesn't anymore."

"What did they bust him for? Drugs?"

"Don't know. I never saw him high. Although he may have kept a stash for the facilitation of romance, if you know what I mean. Maybe some parent is upset about what happened to his daughter."

A man wearing a jacket with huge *FBI* letters on the back came out of the apartment with a boxful of books. Then two more agents came out and another went in. Judging by what they now carried—table lamps, stereo equipment, clothing, books—they were taking everything out of the apartment. They loaded the items into the vans.

"What do they want with his clothes?" asked one of the apartment neighbors of his friend. "Think they're stolen?"

"They already took all his computer stuff," his roommate said. "I guess now they're just cleaning him out."

"Where's Jeremy? Did they arrest him?" Matt asked.

"Don't know. This was already going on when we got out here. They didn't make a lot of noise. I always thought they used a battering ram and a loudspeaker and all that. We didn't hear anything."

❖ ❖ ❖

When Matt got back to the car, Amy was asleep. She did not wake up when the engine started or when the car began to move. Only at the first speed bump in the parking lot did she open her eyes.

Chapter 28

That Monday, the critical thinking class had an air of the surreal. Amy felt like an alien, like an unwelcome visitor. She wondered why she continued to attend a class she was about to be kicked out of anyway, the class that, through no fault of her own, had ruined her university career. And she was anxious to get this particular session over with so that she could get to and through the second and probably final meeting with Professor Miller in his office. She expected to hear that she was not only being given an F in the course but expelled from the university. Or perhaps he would tell her she was being turned over to the Academic Dean for further torture before expulsion. At any rate, she tried to tell herself to be calm and not worry because her doom was predetermined.

After her death at Miller's hands, she wanted to go with Matt to the hospital to see about Tina. Amy hoped the doctors would let them visit their friend. She thought it odd that concern for Tina had somewhat lessened her horror at her academic fate. Being emotionally torn in two directions had somehow strengthened her. She had expected to be a blubbering idiot by this time and felt strange that she was not. Sitting there in class, she felt quite sober.

Professor Miller made the class seem even more bizarre by his changed behavior. He had ceased to prepare for class. There were no more films, no special anecdotes, no overhead transparencies, not even any pompous expressions or fancy terms for the board. Instead, he appeared to be merely a talking textbook, simply repeating the material directly from the reading. One of the students in the back even asked, "Since when did Miller become Professor Tape Recorder?"

The class was still covering logical fallacies, so Miller dutifully talked about *argumentum ad hominem* and *petitio principii*, but he said nothing that was not in the text itself. There was barely a "This is important," or "Pay attention to this." The man who began the term as a rather interesting teacher was now decidedly a bore. Those students who had read the assignment soon put their brains on autopilot and began to attend to other, more important tasks, like passing notes or playing games on their notebook computers or using instant messaging on their cell phones. Those students who had not read the assignment (more than half the class) paid some attention and made a few more notes than did the readers. But even they were forced to stifle yawns and look at their watches.

Professor Miller still showed signs of being irritated and edgy, only to a slightly smaller extent than he had earlier. His voice was gravelly, perhaps even a bit shaky at times. At what seemed to be a peculiar time about halfway through the class, he stopped discussing the *tu quoque* fallacy, and asked, "Has anyone seen Gina Roper? She's not been in class recently."

No one had. One student said, "I haven't seen her since the day before you left for that conference." For some reason, Miller began to blush. He felt his face reddening, so he turned to the board and wrote *tu quoque* on it, and then underlined and outlined the letters until he thought the blush had gone.

When the hour had ended, Professor Miller began to pack up his notes more rapidly than usual. Just as he was about to hurry out the door, Amy had come down to the front of the room and was at the door.

"Dr. Miller?"

"Yes, what is it?" He acted as if he did not want to be bothered.

"Did you still want to see me today?"

"See you? Uh, oh, yes, yes, I do. But come by in about fifteen minutes." Her annihilation seemed so unimportant to him that he had evidently forgotten about it. She wondered if reminding him had been a mistake. No, she thought, he would have remembered eventually.

"Okay." Amy's stomach turned into a painful knot. Fifteen more minutes. All of a sudden that seemed like a long time. There was no class discussion to distract her. She wondered why people told her that at the moment of crisis, they always felt calm. She felt nauseated now that her hour was upon her. She began to wonder whether she would throw up on Miller's desk. She tried to find a drinking fountain.

Professor Miller stepped quickly back to his office and closed the door behind him. He plopped himself into his chair so forcefully that it slid back and hit the wall. He scooted it back and grabbed the phone. He punched the buttons hard.

"Records," said the voice on the other end.

"Hi, Sylvia?" Miller was trying to sound calm and relaxed.

"Yes, this is Sylvia."

"This is Mark Miller in Philosophy."

"Oh, hello, Dr. Miller. What can I do for you?"

"I'm trying to locate a student who has been missing class recently."

"Do you have his ID number?"

"No, she was having trouble registering for my class because of financial aid."

"What's her name?"

"Roper. Gina Roper. She's a freshman, if that helps."

A few moments passed while Sylvia entered the information into her terminal. Miller could hear the clicking of the keyboard over the phone.

"If you have a phone number, that would be helpful," Miller said, partly to fill up the silence.

"Let's see. No, I don't have any Gina Roper registered this semester."

"Not at all?"

"Let me see. No, there's no Gina Roper of any class level registered this semester. The only Ropers I have are two males."

"Are you sure?"

"Let me check something else." Miller could hear more keyboarding. "No, she's not listed as having been admitted, either."

"What?"

"I'm looking at the Admissions screen right now, and we have not admitted a Gina Roper this year. Could she have gotten married recently and changed her name?"

"I don't think so."

"Well, if you'll give me awhile, I can have Admissions go back and search the applicant lists and see if she applied but was never admitted."

"Uh, yes, that would be good. Can you send me an email when you find out?"

"Sure thing."

"Thanks, Sylvia."

"You're welcome, Dr. Miller."

Professor Miller hung up the phone and sat back in his chair. Apparently Gina had never enrolled in his class, after all. Maybe she was just one of those freeloaders who sit in as long as possible, trying to get a free education. Large lecture classes sometimes had clandestine auditors all the way through the term. Maybe she was a high school student just looking for some kicks. Seventeen was young even for a freshman.

Miller's phone rang, putting an end to his line of thought.

"Hello, Dr. Miller. It's Christine." The department secretary was always careful to call him Dr. Miller.

"Yes, Christine."

"Amy Herbert was here to see you, but I had to tell her to reschedule for later."

"What? Why?"

"There are two gentlemen here from the FBI who want to talk to you. They say they've been looking for you. Shall I send them down to your office?"

Professor Miller thought he was about to have a heart attack.

At the Cave, the students had gathered as usual to talk about the class. There was little to say. Many were thinking they would want refills to their coffee this morning because the class had failed to shake off their sleepiness.

"Well, that was a crashing bore," said Jennica.

"And what's with Miller, anyway? He's getting all weird on us."

"Tell me. Did you see the way he acted when Jeff said, 'So, even if you use a *tu quoque* excuse, the police will still come for you'?"

"Yeah. Miller looked really shocked and said, 'What police'? as if they were right outside the door. What's with him, anyway? Has he been selling drugs or something?"

"I hope he isn't going to wig out on us and not be able finish teaching the class. Then we'd have to take it over again next term."

"That would be a royal bummer."

Just then Julie Carmichael joined the group. She looked at Jennica and said, "Did you tell them your big news?" She plopped her book bag in a chair.

"What big news?" Jennica asked.

"About you and Elderberry." Julie walked over to the counter to order a coffee.

"What?" Jennica asked.

"Ooh, tell us," several voices said in unison.

"There's nothing to tell," said Jennica. "I don't know what Julie's talking about."

Like a pack of whimpering and drooling dogs watching a rabbit through the cracks in a fence, the students sitting at the booth watched Julie eagerly, growing ever more expectant about what she would tell them on her return. Julie seemed to take a little extra time pouring powdered creamer into her coffee. She came back to the booth with a broad smile.

"Tell us, tell us," everyone said.

"Well," Julie began, making sure she had eye contact with

everyone, "last night about six o'clock I was walking through the math courtyard on the way here to get a bite to eat." Jennica's look of confusion had disappeared as she now knew what Julie was going to relate. She shook her head.

"So anyway, Jennica is standing there talking to Sandy Kline when Professor Elderberry walks out of his office. He sees Jennica and it's like there's this sudden glow on his face, big smile, totally 'There's-my-woman' look. Then he drops his briefcase, rushes up to her and gives her this full-on embrace and kisses her.

"He didn't kiss me."

"Then he holds her by the shoulders at arm's length and says, 'Jennica, I love you!'"

"Wow." The audience was awestruck at being in on such a juicy piece of news.

"Oh, Jennica, is that true?" It was too good to be true, but everyone hoped it was.

"Does Elderberry really have the hots for you?"

"So, Jennica, did you slap him into next Tuesday?"

"No! She thanked him!" Julie was proud to be an eyewitness, the possessor of the facts.

"Oh, wow!"

"This is too much!"

"Does this mean you're going to get an A in Crypto?"

"Wait a minute you guys," Jennica said. "It's not what you think. In fact, it's actually sad, because I think Professor Elderberry is losing his marbles."

"Oh no! Just imagine! The whole faculty is fruitcaking on us! First Miller, now Elderberry. Who's next?"

"Shelley thinks it's the English Department. She says they've been on the edge for years."

"But wait. Tell us what happened."

"Well, as Julie says, Sandy and I were standing in the courtyard talking when Professor Elderberry comes out of the department office. I don't think he came out to see me. He was just on the way home. He had his briefcase and jacket and everything. And the first thing he says is just a normal 'Hi, Jennica,' and he nods at Sandy because he doesn't know her. Then he gets this really thoughtful look on his face, then this wild look, then a smile, and then he hugs me."

"I'll bet I can guess what he was thinking."

"Ooh, so he did hug you! Did he tell you he loves you, too?"

"So then he pushes me back and he has this goofy, happy look, and then he tells me he loves me. But then, he grabs his briefcase and coat, turns around, and runs back into the department office."

"He does sound like he's lost it."

"I don't know. Scientists are kinda strange that way. Probably forgot his calculator or something."

"So are you going to file a harassment charge?"

"What did you say when he hugged you?"

"Why didn't you slap him?"

"Did you give him a dirty look?"

"It wasn't that kind of a hug. It was more like a "Thank-you" hug or a "I'm-so-happy-I'd-hug-a-tree-but-you're-closer" hug. Besides, I was so surprised, I didn't know what to do. He was acting so weird. I just said, 'Thank you.'"

"You like him, don't you? Gonna be a little item? Gonna get that A?"

"Just shut up. I'm going to get an A in Cryptography through the efforts of my own pencil," Jennica said, smelling a dumb-blonde-stereotype behind the comment. "That is, if Elderberry can keep it together."

"Isn't he married?"

"I feel sorry for him," Jennica concluded. "I've never seen him this way. He's been worried lately."

"Isn't Amy his student worker?"

"Yeah, I think so."

"Maybe she could tell us something."

"Wonder if he gives her hugs."

"Think she'd say, 'Thank you'?"

"Oh, come off it, you guys."

"Where is Amy, anyway? She's usually here after class. And where's Markayla? And Gina? And David? Seems like everybody has disappeared."

In partial answer to the previous question, Amy and Markayla were riding with Matt on the way to the hospital. Amy had Tina's student ID card. She could find no information about Tina's parents or her home town. That would have to be furnished by the school or Tina herself. Amy was almost surprised how little she actually knew about Tina. There had been so little communication during these few weeks. Amy felt all the more sympathy for that tortured girl, who had borne her sufferings completely by herself.

At the emergency room, they asked about Tina and were told that she had been taken to Intensive Care. They rode the elevator upstairs and walked into Intensive Care.

"We don't have any Tina Davidson here, nor any Jane Doe, either," the staff nurse said, checking a list on a clipboard. Amy's heart sank. Her first thought was that Tina had died and her body had been moved out of the room. She looked at the beds she could see in the ICU. Only three were visible, the rest being curtained off. Tina was not in any of them.

"Did you ask at the information desk in the lobby?" the nurse asked.

"No, we came in through the emergency room."

"Go to the main entrance and ask there."

Too many skipped heartbeats later, the three stood at the information desk in the lobby asking about Tina.

"Room 204." Amy was relieved. Very relieved. She sat down for a minute before they went upstairs. Tina had been moved out of ICU into a regular ward. That had to be a good sign.

"How interesting that Tina's hospital room is the same number as our dorm room," Amy thought. But she did not mention it to Matt or Markayla. Maybe it was not that interesting. Even though her father was always saying, "Coincidences usually aren't," in this case it really was just a coincidence.

Tina greeted them almost brightly. "Hi, Amy. Hi, Matt, Markayla. How are you?" She was sitting up in bed. She even raised her right arm a few inches in half an attempt to wave a greeting.

"More to the point, how are you?" Amy asked.

Tina's right arm was heavily bandaged from the elbow to the hand. Only her fingers poked out at the end. Her left arm, lightly scratched, was hooked to an IV next to the bed.

Her right ankle, sticking out from under the bedsheet, was wrapped in elastic bandages. There was a small bandage on her neck. Her forehead and face were scratched up, but unbandaged. There was a slight discoloration of her skin, whether from bruising or an antiseptic was not clear.

"I'm fine," Tina said, and then winced with pain as she attempted to shift her position in bed. "I feel okay. Look." Tina reached her bandaged arm over the covers and pulled them back. Her thigh was heavily wrapped with gauze and tape. Markayla put her hand over her mouth and backed up. She felt unwell and sat down in a chair. There was no gaping, gory wound, only a bandage. But the thought of the injury and the faint but distinct odor of the bandage were too much for Markayla. She was wise not to consider a career in medicine.

Tina lifted her hospital gown enough to reveal a heavily taped chest.

"Broken ribs," she said simply. "And my butt hurts, too, but I won't show you that. They say I'm lucky."

Matt felt sorry for Tina, but he found himself suppressing a smile.

"I've been sleeping a lot."

"How's the food?"

"Okay, I guess." Tina searched her mind a moment. "I don't remember. I guess it's fine."

"Do you have much pain?" Amy asked.

"They give me pills. It just sort of aches and pounds a little. It's hard to get to sleep. But once I go to sleep, I sleep a long time. I have strange dreams."

"We hope you will soon be able to rejoin us in our dormitory room," Markayla said from her chair, hoping that the comment would make Tina feel still loved and welcome. She thought that Tina would probably not return to school, but did not want to make the poor girl feel unwanted.

None of the trio of friends was willing to say anything about what the news media would have called "the incident," had it been covered. Tina was writing a different chapter now, it seemed. And all three were somewhat encouraged by how alert she appeared. She seemed rational and calm now, even cheerful. Her unintentionally deadpan, matter-of-fact manner was actually amusing.

A nurse entered the room, carrying a tray with little pill cups on it. "Time for her medicine," she said to Amy and Matt, who stepped out of the way for a minute. The nurse approached Tina and said, raising her voice a little as if she thought Tina was hard of hearing, "I've brought your medicine."

"My chest hurts, right here," Tina said, holding her fingers on her sternum and thrusting forward first one shoulder and then the other as if in an attempt to reduce the pain.

"I'm sorry, dear," the nurse said in a kindly tone. "That's because the tape on your chest has to be tight to hold those ribs in place. Be careful not to move around too much. The pain won't last forever."

"I didn't try to kill myself," Tina said to her.

"Yes, we realize that. You just rest. You have some very serious injuries. How are you feeling?" As she spoke, she put the tray down, selected a pill cup and poured some water into a glass.

"Did I tell you my parents are coming tomorrow?" Tina asked. "I called them, I think."

"Yes, they are on the way," the nurse said, bringing the pills closer for Tina. "But you didn't say how you feel."

"I feel okay. I just ache. What's that?"

The nurse held Tina's hand and poured the pills from the cup into Tina's palm. "This one is for your pain, this one is to prevent infection from your wounds, and this one is to make sure your thinking is clear."

The last words caught Amy's attention. As a result of her "accident," Tina was taking medicine that she might otherwise have refused. It was the fourth answer again. Amy's prayers had been answered not at all in the way she had thought they might be. "I guess some miracles include blood," she thought.

As the three students walked out to Matt's car, Amy said, "Thanks, Matt, for driving us over."

"Hey, no problem," he said.

"And thanks, Markayla, for coming with us. I'm sorry we took longer than I expected and kept you from your studying."

Markayla stood still, so Amy and Matt stopped, too.

"Amy, this was no problem. I am honored to come with you and visit Tina. I would have come with you and Matt early Saturday morning. I may seem to be too studious and I might become ill at the sight of bandaged wounds, but I realize very well that life is not about me. It is like your father's saying, 'The ballerina lives not for herself, but for her dance.' There is something beyond us that we must live for. A higher meaning, a higher goal. I study to give my life to others. If I study only for myself, I am a fool."

Amy felt a sudden shift in her understanding, as she realized now that she had spent so much time thinking about the second half of her father's saying that she had neglected to understand fully the first part. "The ballerina lives not for herself." Her own life and the events in it, good or bad, were less important than how she used them to serve others. "Maybe there's even some good reason for all these personal disasters," she thought. She imagined herself a grandmother, with her grandchildren sitting around her feet. "Yes, children," she told them, "I remember being kicked out of the university in my day, after being unfairly charged with cheating." The thought almost helped. No, it did sort of help. If only a little.

She remembered one of Matt's farm sayings, "When the plow horse steers, the row is crooked; when the farmer steers, the row is straight. Let the Farmer steer." These thoughts, while they did not result in complete inner peace and the end to her worries, did help Amy feel less anxious about her situation and more hopeful that eventually everything would somehow work for the best.

The trio returned to campus just in time for Amy to head off to class. After class, Amy debated about joining Markayla in the library, but decided instead to return to her room. She walked in, tossed her book bag down and sat on the edge of the bed to take off her shoes. She happened to notice her notebook computer on her desk. It was still in the same position she had left it.

Just as she pulled off one of her shoes, there was an authoritative knock on the door.

"No one knocks like that except Shelley," Amy thought. "Although with my luck, it's either the police coming to take me away or the Academic Dean, telling me to leave the campus immediately and never return." Then she thought that there was the real possibility of a visit from Student Affairs officials, telling her that she had been expelled. "Here comes another unpredictable event. I hope it's not a nasty one." Then again, she thought, it could be Melanie or even a neighbor. Amy got up and went to the door, still holding the shoe. When she opened it, instead of Shelley's smiling face, she saw two men with serious expressions. They wore suits. They were holding badges in front of them.

"FBI," the first man said. "My name is Special Agent Wilkins, and this is Special Agent Daws. We're looking for an Amy Herbert." They seemed unusually tall. They looked down into her eyes, scrutinizing her face. She would have smiled, even gamely, but she could not.

Amy was yet once again the unwilling recipient of too much adrenaline. "We're looking for an Amy Herbert," rang in her ears. She could not believe how sinister the little word *an* could sound. The two men could have been looking for just plain old Amy Herbert, but no, they were looking for *an* Amy Herbert. What did that signify? She stood still, heart pounding, face flushing, throat drying. The FBI was hunting her. Had found her. Why? What did they want? Were they here to arrest her for plagiarism? Was plagiarism a federal crime?

"I'm Amy Herbert," she heard herself say. She noticed that she still had her shoe in one hand and felt stupid. She debated tossing the shoe on the bed. The she wondered about how she looked with one shoe on and one off.

"May we come in?"

The agents entered the room and glanced quickly around, as agents always do.

"This is not about plagiarism," Amy thought. "No, this is

about something worse. First it was plagiarism, then it was cheating, now it's some other crime I cannot imagine. They are out to get me, and I don't even know who *they* are. I wonder if someone told them I pushed Tina off the roof or something."

"Feel free to finish dressing," Agent Daws said, nodding toward the shoe in Amy's hand. Amy sat at her desk and put the shoe back on.

"Do you have a personal computer?" Agent Wilkins asked without emotion.

"Yes, it's right here."

Noticing that Amy's face was drained, Agent Daws said in a somewhat soft tone, "You're not under any suspicion of wrongdoing, miss."

Agent Wilkins took over before Daws could continue. "We're investigating the activities of another person who is under suspicion of having committed several computer crimes. In the process of our investigation, we have developed information that indicates a computer you use may have been compromised by the suspect. May we look at your computer?" Amy got up from the desk and walked over to her bed, where she let herself plop down.

Agent Wilkins sat down with the notebook and ran tests from a CD-ROM for about ten or fifteen minutes. Amy was beginning to calm down after the reassurance, but she was still worried. Her hands rubbed idly back and forth on her bedspread. She looked at the floor, mostly.

"Did you write a paper called 'The Values of Reason'?" asked Wilkins.

"It is about plagiarism," Amy thought. "They've called the FBI over this?" Perhaps they had told her she was not a suspect just to put her off her guard. Her mind raced in several directions at once, and as a result, got nowhere. She looked up at Agent Wilkins.

"Yes," was all she said, at last.

"How long have you had this firewall installed?"

"Just the last week or so. My, um, boyfriend, put it on for me." The expression, *my boyfriend*, still felt strange in Amy's mouth. "It's supposed to protect my computer from people trying to read or erase my files."

"Or copy them," said Daws.

"Well, Miss Herbert," Wilkins said, "it seems that the firewall was a little too late to protect your paper. It was copied from your computer around October 3 and immediately thereafter posted to, um, let's see, Essay Xpress, a free-paper site, a term paper mill."

"But who would do that? And why?"

"Are you acquainted with Jeremy Schneider?"

Amy blinked. "Yes, I know who he is, but—."

"Well, his computer files show that he copied and uploaded your paper. What we are unsure about is why. Essay Xpress does not require a paper to be traded for another paper, and there is no record that he downloaded anything from that site either before or afterwards. And yours is the only paper he uploaded. So both self interest and philanthropy seem to be ruled out. Can you think of any reason he would do this deliberately to cause you to be accused of plagiarism?"

"No, that makes no sense. I can't believe he would do something like that."

"Your professor, Miller, received a tip-off email on October 4 from a free email account. We are investigating to determine who sent that. As far as we can tell, only one person knew at that point that your paper had been uploaded to the paper mill.

"But why would Jeremy do that?"

"That's what we were hoping you could tell us."

"I've hardly spoken a dozen words to him this year." She remembered the unpleasant phone call when he asked her for a date and the incident with Tina. She had called him a jerk. But that was only a couple of days ago. That was almost their entire interaction this year. Was she being punished for saying no to a date? The idea was stupid. It was a stretch. But it was all there was.

"This sounds really dumb, but he did ask me out."

"Before October 3?"

"Uh, yeah, maybe the first or second."

"And did you go out with him?"

"No, I told him no thanks. Other than that we haven't spoken more than two words this year."

The two agents looked at each other. They were both chewing over this information mentally, trying to assess the likelihood of cause and effect. "Would this Schneider boy get *that* upset over being rejected by *her*?" they seemed to be thinking. Daws lowered his brows a bit as if he discounted the possibility. Wilkins tilted his head from side to side a couple of times, as if his head had to lean in the appropriate direction when thinking about a pro or a con. Finally, he gave a little shrug. His face told Amy that he was undecided.

"Well, that helps," Wilkins said.

"By the way, Miss Herbert," Daws added, almost as an afterthought, "we've had a talk with your professor, Dr. Miller, and he understands the situation. I think he realizes now that you wrote the paper."

Chapter 29

The next morning, Amy returned to her room after break-fast. Markayla had skipped breakfast that day and was sitting at her desk eating a banana and drinking a cup of *real* coffee, one that she had brewed herself, as usual. She was just about finished with the *Wall Street Journal.* Amy listened to the distinctive crinkle of the newsprint as Markayla turned the page.

"Ah, Amy, you have returned," Markayla said, barely looking up. "How was your meal?" She took an obvious sip from her mug.

Amy knew that Markayla was feeling above the dining commons' breakfast.

"It was okay. Apple and berry crepes dusted with pow-dered sugar, hot croissants with melted butter and raspberry jelly—."

"Stand away from me so that when the lightning strikes, I will not be burned, too," Markayla interrupted. Then she added, "Oh, Professor Elderberry called. He wants to talk to you."

Lightning did strike Amy. Or at least, her heart gave one of those unpleasant little leaps that hearts do when they are startled by unexpected and ominous news. She coughed as her heart skipped a beat.

"Professor Elderberry? What does he want?"

"He did not say. But he said you do not need to return his call. He said he would talk to you when you come in to work this afternoon."

"I hate adrenaline," Amy said.

The shock of the news wore off, but the little stomach butterflies kept Amy company off and on throughout the day. Uncertainty was always a torture. At least with Dr. Miller, she had known he detested her and thought her guilty and said her paper was claptrap. But with Dr. Elderberry, she did not know what to expect. Was the news going to be good or bad? And why did she have to suffer two episodes of cheating accusations in close succession, in the same term, in the same lifetime?

To make things worse, Professor Elderberry was not in the office when Amy arrived for work. No one was. The secretary was gone off somewhere. All the office doors were closed except that of Professor Czesidek, the visiting professor that year. He seemed to be talking to himself, in a tone of complaint, about "two sheets of ham." Amy decided not to say hello to him right away.

Amy checked her work list and then sat down to record some grades, all the while feeling almost too stimulated to concentrate. But recording scores was largely mindless copying, so she managed.

It was not long until she heard a familiar laugh. It was Professor Elderberry, outside, saying something about what a great day it was.

"Amy!" he said when he came through the door and saw her. "I'm glad you're here." He had an almost boyish grin on his face. He looked younger than his handful of years before retirement. Amy felt encouraged. He would not be triumphant in her destruction.

"The riddle is solved," he said, almost gleefully. "Come into my office and close the door."

Amy wondered just who would be shut out from hearing this news by closing the door. "It must be a habit of secrecy," she thought. As Amy sat down across from his desk, Professor Elderberry remained standing for a few moments, actually rubbing his hands together. "He must be pretty happy," she thought. She knew that one of Elderberry's reasons for becoming a mathematics professor was his love of problem solving. He liked all kinds of problems, not just those involving numbers. In fact, Cryptography was his favorite course to teach.

Elderberry gave Amy what seemed to be a warm look. She thought for a moment that he wanted to hug her. Then he sat down. His eyes were amazingly alive.

"It all came together when one of my cryptography students wrote the first short paper," he said. "No, no, wait. Have to back up." He paused a moment to think. "A year or so ago, the people in IS said they were experiencing attempts to breach the faculty network, so even though they said they were taking extra precautions to lock it down, I got my own personal hardware firewall and added a software firewall." Elderberry looked into Amy's eyes, and asked abruptly, "You know what a firewall is, don't you?"

"I do now." Amy did not elaborate.

"So I thought I had taken care of the worry about hackers getting in from the network, and there was no way anyone could get at the material on my PC."

"But I thought the tests were taken from the filing cabinet."

Elderberry waved his hand back and forth. "Don't get ahead of me." He wanted to tell his story. I thought my PC was safe from any back-door attack, but they seem to have gotten in quite literally through the front door."

"I don't understand."

"They walked into my office, sat down at my computer, and got in directly."

"How would they get into your office?" The slightest fear came into Amy's mind. Would he say that she had let someone in?

"Colleagues have told me that master keys are as common as grass on this campus."

"Really?" Amy thought of her dorm room. The idea of freely available master keys was cause for a whole new wave of paranoia. But she squelched the thought. She'd had enough of that kind of thinking for this year.

Elderberry was continuing. "In fact, there's a joke going around the faculty. If you really want your students to read something, just label it *confidential* and leave it on your desk overnight."

Amy waited to hear about the computer break-in. She knew she did not need to ask any more questions.

"So, back to the cryptography paper. One of my cryptography students wrote a paper about password hacking. You know, breaking into computer systems by guessing or developing passwords. In it she said hackers always start with available personal information like middle names, kid's names, birthdates, and so on. She also said that many people use the same password for everything. Her sentence was,

368 ❖ THE MILLION DOLLAR GIRL

'Using a single password, if guessed, is like someone finding the master key to a building.'"

Amy nodded to express continued interest and uttered a little, "Hmm."

"Well, I was just leaving the office on Friday, thinking about my daughter's birthday coming up, when I saw Jennica in the courtyard. She's the cryptography student I mentioned. All of a sudden it came to me. The password to my computer, the network, and my file encryption were all the same. And it was my daughter's name. And her name had been published as part of a photo in a university brochure. I felt completely exposed."

"Oh, no!" was all Amy could say.

"Yeah. Oh, no. It was forehead slapping time, big time." Amy was secretly amused that Professor Elderberry would use a slang expression like *big time*. "But I also realized then how easily someone could break into my PC from the front door, so to speak. One master key gets you in the building, in the department office, and into my office. One password gets you all the way through to the test."

Amy was going to say something, so used was she to prompting her father during his narratives over the phone, when Elderberry continued merrily along.

"Then the light really came on." This statement required both hands to make a large gesture. Seeing how animated he was telling his story almost made Amy feel happy, too. Elderberry was almost bouncing in his chair. "You'll recall we glanced at the grades of the students for the 318 test to see if we could tell which ones had profited by the stolen exams, and there seemed to be no indication."

"Yes, I remember. The grades seemed pretty normal."

Elderberry's eyes narrowed. His voice changed into an almost TV-detective tone. "Except that there were two very low F's. A four percent and a nine percent." Amy knew that this was somehow significant, but she had no idea why.

"Uh huh. Those guys must not have studied at all."

"No. That's just it. They did study. They studied very hard."

"I don't understand."

"They studied the wrong test." Elderberry was gleefully triumphant.

"The wrong test?"

"The actual test, the test I gave them, was locked up in the filing cabinet, as you noted, all copied and ready to hand out. I wrote that one at home. But there was another test, from last year, on the computer in my office."

The light was coming on for Amy, too.

"So instead of getting a filing cabinet key from you or anyone else," Elderberry continued, "they broke into my computer and printed off a copy of what they did not know was the old test, which they then studied. They studied hard. They memorized all the wrong answers." Elderberry was enjoying himself. He almost laughed.

"That is so bizarre," Amy said.

"It's amazing how we sometimes get trapped by our own assumptions. I assumed that no one could get into my computer. Mine was a poor example of problem solving."

Amy felt her respect for Professor Elderberry increase by his willingness to criticize himself.

"Once I realized how easily someone could get access to the wrong test, everything else fell into place," he concluded. "Made perfect sense. And the culprits are obvious. Mr. Four

Percent and Mr. Nine Percent virtually signed their names. Jeremy Schneider and David Simmons."

Professor Elderberry leaned back in this chair and relaxed. His tale was told. He put his hands behind his head and looked at Amy. Then a quizzical expression came over his face. He dropped his arms and let them rest on the arms of the chair. He continued to look at Amy, studying her face intently. He was still thinking.

"The only loose end in all this is you, Amy. I'm still a little confused about why they would drag your name into their discussion. It does seem reasonable that they were the two overheard by our little correspondent, doesn't it?"

Amy almost said, "Let's hope so," thinking that she did not want a third accusation of cheating arising in her life. But she settled for, "Yes, it does."

"Did either of them ever ask you for a key of any kind, perhaps?"

"No. I hardly know either one. David is in my critical thinking class, but I don't really know him very well. And I know Jeremy only to say hello."

Elderberry shook his head. "Well, there are always anomalous bits of data that don't quite fit into any explanation," he said, "even the correct one. But, no matter."

After a moment he went on. "Tell you what, Amy. As a token of my affection for you, I'd like to take you out to dinner. Have you ever eaten at the Shooting Star? It's supposed to be the best restaurant in the county."

"The Shooting Star?"

"Yes, Amy. I'd like to take you to dinner at the Shooting Star."

"But Professor Elderberry—."

"I want to make up for making you feel bad about this whole cheating thing."

"Well, that's very generous, but you don't have to—."

"And besides, my wife is anxious to meet you. I've told her all about you, and what a good worker you have been in the department."

"Really?" Amy was embarrassed at herself for this weak reply.

"And I hope you'll bring a friend. Do you have a friend who could come along, too? What about this boyfriend you mentioned earlier?"

Amy was a bit flustered, but she managed to say, "I'll ask him. His name is Matt."

"Good."

Amy called her parents as soon as she got off work, rather than waiting until after her dinner. She could not wait to tell them she was once again without a shadow over her.

"You've really had it piled on thick," her mother said. "But I'm glad it's over now. Amy, we always believed in you."

"It's been a month I'd rather not relive," Amy admitted. "But I guess now I can say I've grown up, gotten a clue, all those clichés. And, oh, if suffering builds character, I now have more character than I'll need for awhile."

"So, then, everything has worked out?"

"Yeah. Except that everybody probably thinks I'm a total crybaby by now. I've cried more the past couple weeks than I can ever remember. And we won't even get into the adrenaline part. I must have a strong heart."

"We were always behind you," her mother said. "How are you feeling now? Have you been sleeping okay?"

"I guess so," Amy hedged, not wanting to complain of her insomnia from worry and stress. "But how are you two doing?" She wanted to move away from the subject of herself, now that the good news had been delivered. After all, she thought, life is not about her.

"We're doing fine, Seepy," her father said. Then he surprised her. He continued to talk. "By the way, we had an interesting case at work that ended in arrests just today. We caught a ring of con artists."

"Oh, I love the con stories best," Amy said.

"I was there to help put on the cuffs. They were about to fleece a guy who had just inherited a pile of money from his father."

"How did they do it?"

"The ringleader's girlfriend pretended to be a student at the university where the guy taught—he's a professor. She sat in his class and kept going to his office and asking for help until she got him interested in her and they flew down here for some fun. The ringleader and his helper had a fake stock brokerage set up. The guy was in the process of transferring almost a million dollars when his bank got suspicious and contacted us. We set up a stake out and interrupted their little plan."

"Wasn't the professor suspicious?"

"No. He swears even now that it was he who got the girl interested in him. And get this. She just showed up in his class a week ago Monday. Talk about a fast operator. She must have really dazzled him. And you should see her. Like a fashion model. She's 24, but the prof didn't know that. She looks young for her age and could pass for 17 or 18. Really a perfect set up. No wonder the guy couldn't resist. He never had a chance. You know these girls and their feminine wiles."

"Oh, Daddy, don't say that."

"What?"

"Never mind. Go on."

"And, get this, her boyfriend is a slightly pudgy, middle-aged guy. No one would ever suspect they were working together. And the guy who ran the fake office has the countenance of someone's most trusted friend. He's probably in his sixties and very smooth. They're all smooth."

"So he had no idea he might be cheated?"

"Nope. In fact, even now, he's still dumbstruck, I think. When we first confronted him, he denied that he even knew any of the cons, including the girl. He acted like he didn't know what the deal was."

"So he didn't thank you for saving his money?"

"Not exactly. First of all, he's married, so he didn't want his wife to find out that he was in another city with a beautiful girl. He could lose a chunk of his inheritance in a divorce following an infidelity scandal. And second, the scheme he thought he was in on is illegal, and he knew that. And his university probably has a regulation against dating students currently in a professor's class, so for all he knew, he might get in trouble there. So if they had taken him, he probably never would have reported it. These folks did their homework and planned a great scheme, making it hard for their sucker to complain. Besides, this guy is sort of a pompous type, who wouldn't want anyone to know he got fleeced. That's why he still thinks he's the one who got the girl interested. Ego thing, you know. He would have kissed his money and the girl goodbye and kept quiet about it, I'll bet."

"Even for a million dollars?"

"Looks like it. We had a heck of a time getting the truth out of him."

"Well, I know it's not unheard of for professors to get involved with students," Amy said, thinking of Miller and Gina. She wondered what Gina would say when Amy told her about the con scheme her father had exposed.

Amy's next call was to Matt. She quickly summarized the news. Then she asked, "Have you had dinner yet?"

"No," Matt said, putting down the sandwich he was halfway through. "Why?"

"I'd like to take you out to dinner tonight. And get this, Professor Elderberry wants to take us to the Shooting Star on Saturday."

"The Shooting Star? I think I like him." Anyone who was willing to pay for an expensive meal predisposed Matt in his favor.

"So, anyway, would you like to go out? I know it's short notice."

"Can you remember a time when I have ever refused food?"

"See you in a few, then."

"And, I have a present for you, so I'll come get you."

"A present? In that case, hurry." Matt could perceive that Amy was feeling much better. The recent heaviness of her life was lifting.

When she opened the door, Matt was standing there, actually dressed a little better than usual. His shirt had a collar. His pants were not jeans. His shoes were atrocious.

"Hey, Aim-o," he said. "I brought you a little token of my affection." He handed her a box about the size of a desk dictionary.

"Ooh, what is it?"

"Might be chocolate."

"Nope, too light weight," she said. "Unless you've already eaten most of the pieces."

"Might be jewelry."

"And with equal probability, it might be matching cans of spray oil. His and hers." Then, finding that explanation almost convincing to herself, Amy added, "Oh, Matt, please say it isn't oil."

"It's not oil."

Amy shook the box. It made no sound. She peeled the wrapping paper off and read the label on the box: "Fast Ethernet Personal Network Router with 4-Port Switch."

"Is this just an old box you used or is this what's in the box, too?"

"It's what's in the box."

"And that is what?"

"A router."

"A router. Gee, thanks, Matt. I've always wanted one of these. What does it do?"

"It adds an extra layer of firewall protection to your computer. A hardware firewall to add to the software one we put on your notebook."

"So I'm extra safe."

"Yep. Extra, extra safe. And it has four ports so that if Markayla gets her own computer, she can use it, too."

"Hey, that's neat." The gift was about as romantic as a frying pan, but Amy realized that this was Matt's way of saying he really cared for her. Maybe she would survive this term after all. Amy put her head on Matt's shoulder and relaxed a little. "Thanks," was all she felt safe in saying, lest more words lead to an obvious and embarrassing choke. She tried to keep her sigh quiet so Matt would not notice. She was still too stressed from the recent events to feel completely safe and relaxed, but the embrace helped a lot. However, she would not allow herself to let that tear out, no matter how hard it tried to escape. Soon she lifted her head and looked at Matt.

"I really appreciate your help. And you." She snuggled her head back on his shoulder. Matt was touched.

"Hey, Babe," he said, acting nonchalant. "That's what hairy chests are for."

Matt's flippancy began to influence her. She lifted her head again and smiled. She was about to make a teasing comment about the lack of hair on his chest, when she noticed that one of her hairs had been left behind on his sweater. Picking it off, she held it up in front of his eyes and demanded with a mock accusation, "Whose hair is this?"

Matt knew that he could take one of two directions. The politically correct direction would be to say, "Why, Amy, my dear, it's yours, of course. It couldn't belong to any other woman on earth." The other direction was much more entertaining, though, so he naturally took that one.

"I don't know," he said. "What color is it?"

Amy gave a little cry of disbelief. Then, pretending to examine it closely, concluded, "Blonde!"

"Hmm," Matt deliberated. "Dark blonde or light blonde?"

Another little cry of surprise and disbelief, this one even more forceful. Amy narrowed her eyes, "It's light blonde," she said between her teeth.

"Well," Matt said, "that narrows it down to four."

For this news, Matt received a punch in the arm.

"Ow," he said. "What's that for?"

"You wicked man," Amy said.

"Maybe so," Matt said, "but I'm your wicked man."

"Well, maybe so, maybe not," Amy said, pretending to become suddenly aloof and uncaring.

"Okay, Amy, you win. After knowing you, how could I possibly ever want another girl?"

"Oh, so you're saying that knowing me has been such a bad experience that it's soured you on all women, huh?"

Matt smiled at her. Then he brushed the hair off her forehead affectionately and said, "Amy, you're one of a kind. I probably wouldn't trade you for a million dollars."

"Probably? Oh, thanks."

"You know I care. Tell you what. Come close and I'll whisper those little words you want so much to hear."

She let herself be drawn back into Matt's embrace. He bent down, put his mouth close to her ear, and whispered, "Cookie dough."

Bonus Materials

It seems that all the films that come out on DVD now include extra bonus features, often including "The Making Of" material. So, if print is going to have any chance at all of competing with video, why shouldn't novels have bonus features, too? Therefore, here is my contribution.

The Making of *The Million Dollar Girl*

The Million Dollar Girl was written in 2002. I had always wanted to be a writer and I had written a few abruptly-short short stories as well as a couple of non-fiction books. So, when the opportunity presented itself, I decided to try a novel. I once wrote a satire about college life, so this is not my first work of extended fiction, but it is my first novel, with a plot or two and some characters.

There were 150,000 different books published in 2002 by 10,000 publishers. *The Million Dollar Girl* was not one of them. Sales by famous novelists were under pressure because of so many new novels. Makes a great excuse to say, "That's why no literary agent would touch this book." Whatever. So it slept on the shelf and on the hard drive until 2005, when I decided to have a few copies printed for friends. You must be one of them, or know one of them.

Look at this book as just a fun read. I wanted it to be more successful thematically, but just couldn't quite pull it off on a first try.

Sources

The plot involving Professor Miller was suggested by the book, *The Big Con*, by David W. Maurer, which describes the operation of this particular type of scheme, from the nineteenth century forward (the book was written in 1940). Those who have seen the movie *The Sting* will recognize the outlines of the big con. When I read the Maurer book, I thought how fun it would be to use this con scheme as a plot to show the limits of reason accompanied by pride instead of by good values. I also probably drew upon Jay Robert Nash's *Hustlers and Con Men* (1976). At any rate, astute readers will recognize that some of the characters' names are appropriate to their roles (Professor Miller's first name, Gina's last name, and of course Larson E. Trimmer).

The opening film scenario shown by Professor Miller comes from the famous crash of Turkish Airlines Flight 96, near Detroit on June 11, 1972. The main source was the NTSB report, though I am also indebted to the book *Air Disasters*, by Leo Marriott, Stanley Stewart, and Michael Sharpe.

The restaurant fire was suggested and informed by *Blaze: The Forensics of Fire*, by Nicholas Faith.

The plot involving Tina was suggested by my own experience over many years with a mentally ill friend and my reading about mental illness. The details (buying several radios, the value of green, the strange questions about killing one's children) all are real examples from a paranoid schizophrenic man. Fortunately, he has never jumped off a roof.

Many of the details of student behavior and comments are taken from life examples, also. Since I have taught at the college level for many years, picking up student attitudes, comments, and actions has supplied me with plenty of material. Amy's diving under the dashboard of Matt's car to help him install a brake booster is a real event, for example. Markayla is based on a composite of three students from Kenya who graced my classroom in the past. The Swahili comes from another student. The incident about students studying the wrong test in an effort to cheat is also historical. (In the actual case, a chemistry professor left a fake test on his desk where the students found it.)

There are also a few allusions to (or, if you're cruel, jokes stolen from) sources, particularly films. For example, the comment about "waking up dead" alludes to the film *Charade*, while the comment about there being many sugar free drinks on the market (to prevent hyperactivity) is an altered reference to the film *Real Genius* (where the comment refers to decaffeinated coffee). Quotation or allusion is common in films, where a famous scene or comment is repeated in many subsequent films. So I did a little of that here, too.

Deleted Scenes

Another feature of DVD films is the offering of outtakes or deleted scenes. These clips help give us insight into the creative process. Much of the time, we concur with the filmmakers that omitting a given scene was a good idea because the scene is not quite up to the quality of the rest of the film or it alters the plot or character in an undesirable way.

I thought the same kind of offering would be helpful for a work of written fiction, so that readers could see some examples of what was cut out or altered from the drafts. It is often said that the true secret of good writing is knowing what to leave out. Here is a selection of deleted scenes that should reinforce that point. And for further reinforcement, know that I left out from this sample some even worse scenes.

Deleted from Chapter 3

Amy was not ready to tell her new friend the full story about Tina the Ballerina, or how Tina listened patiently to all of Amy's problems. Shelley might not understand. If there is one, all-powerful object of fear in the modern world, it is fear of being laughed at. Those who do not fear rejection, hatred, even violence, still fear ridicule. The most hardened criminal cowers in the face of ironic laughter. Pascal says that the motive of every action of life is the pursuit of happiness, even among those who hang themselves. However, there is yet a more powerful regulator of human behavior, and that is the desire for validation. "I love you," may win some hearts, but "What you're doing is good," wins many more. We all want to believe or at least to feel that we matter, that our lives are being lived to some purpose. Some people join gangs and destroy property to feel validated, while others may run for office, seek riches, or write books. Whatever devalidates us makes us feel wretched and worthless. And much more than logical criticism, it is ridicule that is devalidating. Ridicule tells us that our actions (perhaps our lives, too) are not just wrong but laughable. To fail well is a great and positive learning experience, so being merely wrong is not necessarily devalidating. But to suffer critical laughter is to suffer the sweep of dismissal. Many great inventions have never come to the aid of mankind simply because their inventors could not bear to be laughed at. Condemn us for our weak and hungry egos if you will, but the desire for—the need for—validation is the true hunger of the heart.

All this to say that Amy, like many another person who harbors unusual ideas, was unwilling to share them with Shelley until she felt more secure in their relationship.

Deleted from Chapter 12

"Wanna see my bellybutton?" Shelley asked, lifting her T-shirt and exposing her tummy. "Her name is Barbie. Can you say hello, Barbie?" Shelley took the thumb and forefinger of each hand and squeezed her navel open and closed to match the words she spoke in a cartoon voice.

"Hi there, Amy. I'm Barbie the Bellybutton. I'm always at the center of attention when we're at the beach. Can your bellybutton come out and play?"

"No!" said Amy directly to Shelley's navel. She had been watching Shelly's navel "talk" and had neglected to look up at Shelley before answering. This realization made Amy feel foolish. Just then, however, Tina returned to the room, holding onto Matt's hand. Amy was Tina's security net, and since Matt's was Amy's, um, friend, then Matt was a legal surrogate.

"What are you guys doing?" she asked, with an almost troubled look on her face. Who knows what her mind was doing with this subject matter.

"What are you guys doing?" asked Amy, not altogether comfortable seeing Tina holding Matt's hand.

"The performance is over," Shelley said. "The curtain falls." She dropped her T-shirt. "Oh, oh, curtain calls," she said excitedly, flapping her shirt up and down a few times.

"What?" Tina asked with a little confusion and somewhat urgently.

"We were just having a bellybutton contest, and I won," Shelley said to Tina. "Mine talks and Amy's doesn't."

"Theater majors," said Matt.

"Are such stereotypes?" asked Shelley.

"Well, I gotta run. Barbie and I need to go find Ron and go for a ride on his bike.

Deleted from Chapter 14

"If I were playing a role, you wouldn't notice."

At this comment, Amy's eyebrows went up, as if to say, "Huh?"

"Look, aren't the actors in high school and college plays usually really lame?"

Amy remembered being in some plays in high school. "I guess," she said.

"That's because they are acting rather than being a character. They try to form themselves into a character and act the way they think another person would behave and it comes out fake and obvious. The good actors form the character to themselves and then act like themselves, except for the differences the character has, like speech or something. They don't think of themselves as acting. That's my opinion."

"I can't believe you actually said something serious."

"The great actors can change themselves into another personality, but those are the types who get academy awards."

"But why don't actors follow the obvious step of being themselves when they act?" asked Amy.

"Fear," answered Shelley. "Only by deliberately and badly pretending to be someone else can they escape the fear of changing themselves or of exposing themselves. What if the audience thought they were really like the character they portray? Or worse, what if they really are? Killers, lechers, cheaters, or worse, boring, uncool rejects?"

"Are you sure you weren't a psych major before rather than an English major?"

"Then there's the fear that the actor will be believed by the other actors or the audience."

"What do you mean by *believed*?"

Deleted from Chapter 16

Matt needed to make a phone call. Calls from pay phone. There are more pens in student pockets than pieces of paper. Matt pulled out a pen and was visually casting about for a piece of paper, contemplating ripping out a page from the phone book, when Amy caught on and flipped her hand over, palm up, to be written on. Matt cradled the phone between his head and shoulder to free both hands to write. He held Amy's hand in his the way he would a scratch pad and began to jot down the address. He had not acknowledged Amy's gesture of helpfulness and appeared nonchalant outwardly, as if her action was the obvious thing. Writing on her warm, soft hand was quite enjoyable, he thought. And Amy rested her arm against him so it would not get too tired to hold up. Inside his mind he seemed to hear a voice that said, "You've got to marry this girl." But that began a debate, when another voice seemed to say, "Why? What reason? Because she gives you her hand to write a note on? That's crazy. Sober up, Prager." He turned awkwardly around a bit (the cradled phone making it difficult to move his head) and looked at Amy. She smiled sweetly. He turned away. Soon he realized he had botched the address. "Was that 3121 or 2131?" he asked. "Green Street? Oh, Janeen Street. With a J? Okay. Got it." The conversation over, he hung up. "Thanks for the use of your hand," he said.

"You've left your mark on me," she said. "Including a scratch out."

"You offered."

"Oh, that's the right reply," she said sarcastically.

Deleted from Chapter 16

Amy took Tina with her to find Matt.

They arrived at Matt's room but he was not there.

"My dad says you can tell a lot about a guy from his check book register and credit card receipts. They always collect those during an investigation. Since Matt has no money to create very many receipts, I guess we'll have to learn about him from some other clues."

Amy looked around the room. "What can you tell about Matt from what you see?" she asked Tina.

"He's definitely a guy," Tina said, surveying the storm-damage appearance of the room. Clothes, books, empty food containers, a bicycle, some sports equipment, even a hammer, were all strewn semi-randomly around the room.

"He must be rich," Tina continued, "because everything has money on it."

"Ah," said Amy, but look more closely. Put your detective's thinking cap on and look at the detail, not just the overall scene. What kind of money do you see?"

"Change. Lots and lots of change."

"What kind of change?"

"Nickels and pennies, mostly. And an occasional dime. The dimes look lonely."

"Bills?"

"None."

"Quarters?"

"No. Don't see any," Tina said, looking around from the table next to the sofa, to the coffee table, to the kitchen counter, to the bookshelves, to the desk. "Oh, here's one."

"Then what about your conclusion relating to riches?"

"Maybe he isn't so rich."

"And have you ever ridden in his car?"

"Yes. Remember, we rode in it last week."

"And was it a new, fancy sports car?"

"I think it was rather old and creaky."

"Do wealthy people usually drive old and creaky cars?"

"I doubt it."

"Good, Tina. You are catching on."

Tina smiled, as if Amy's comment actually gave her some happiness.

"Okay, now let's look at something else. What else do you see?"

"Lots of junk," said Tina, confidently.

"That's exactly right. It's good to have a general view of the situation. But we also need to look at the specifics. Look, for example, at what makes up the junk. What specific pieces of junk do you see?"

"Clothes."

"That's right. What can you tell me about some specific clothes?"

"They've mostly already been worn and need washing. Eww, this one stinks. And there are more T-shirts than anything else."

"Great, Tina."

"This is fun," said Tina. "What else?"

"Well, we can tell a lot about a person by looking at the information they read. What kind of information do you see around here?"

"Books," said Tina, picking up one and examining it as if she were a detective. "This is a textbook. A history textbook," she added, making a face that few history professors would appreciate. "But we kind of already know that he's a college student."

"That's right. So what else can we learn about him?"

"Well, here's a pile of old newspapers. They're several days old. So maybe he sometimes keeps up on the news."

"What section is on top?"

"Sports."

"Um hm."

"And here," Tina continued, moving over to the coffee table, "are some advertisements. 'The Tool Warehouse.' Here's other stuff for hardware stores. And here's one for a computer store."

"Which tells us?"

"He likes tools and computers?"

"You get an A."

Deleted from Chapter 16

Friday afternoon was Amy's favorite time of the week. The entire weekend was in front of her, and she felt as if there was time enough for both work and rest. The campus always seemed unusually deserted at this time, giving it a peaceful mood that made relaxing all the more easy. After picking up a few books in the library, Amy went to the student union to check her mail and then sit in one of the comfortable chairs that during the week seemed always occupied. After what seemed like a long time stretched out with her feet up on a handy coffee table, Amy began to feel sleepy. Instead of napping where she was, she decided to head back to her room. She got up, tossed the junk mail into the trash, put the letter from a friend into a book, and began the walk across the nearly empty green spaces. It was almost like being on a sightseeing trip through some grassy, wooded meadows.

Deleted from Chapter 18

"What's made you so biased toward your frontal lobes?" asked Shelley. "You analyze everything."

"My dad's a detective."

"Ooh, a private eye, who chases wayward husbands and reports back to the wronged wives?" Shelley asked, very dramatically, putting her hands over her heart at the "wronged wives."

"No, he's a police detective."

"So he studies clues. Let's see if I can be a detective." Shelley's curiosity was once more put in suspense while her need for drama took over. "They say you can tell a lot about a person by examining the detritus of their lives," she continued, picking up the wastebasket next to Amy's desk. "Ah ha! Crumpled paper. Smashed together with anger after reading the unwelcome contents? Are you a jilted lover, perhaps." Then, opening the crumpled paper, "Oh, this looks like a woman's handwriting. Your own, I presume? Don't attempt to deny it, if it's true. We have experts who can compare handwriting."

"That's scratch paper. . . ."

"Okay, let's look for clues on your desk." Shelley looked at Amy's desk. On it, lined up with modest neatness were the figurine of a ballerina, a box of tissues, a mug with pens and pencils, a set of books between ceramic sleeping cat bookmarks (a dictionary, a Bible, several textbooks, a few magazines), a photograph of a middle-aged couple with Amy between them, and a clock. On the wall was a class schedule, a calendar, and a photograph of a young man.

"You're a dance major?"

"No."

"Art major?"

"No."

Shelley paused and stuck her index finger under her nose in dramatic detective style, as if contemplating the case.

"Let's see what we can discover about your roommate," Shelley said. She looked at Markayla's desk. On it were a bowl of fruit (apples, bananas, oranges)

Deleted from Chapter 19

"Some seem to have a lot more lives than others."

"But think—."

"We're young. When we get older, we can worry about all that meaning stuff. Right now, we're still mostly empty blackboards."

"The questions is, What do we write?"

"I hate writing."

"Why do we have to write anything?"

"I want pictures."

"If we don't do our own writing, someone else will do the writing for us."

"Maybe they write better, so that's okay."

"Hey, I know. Maybe we can copy. I want to copy a beautiful, wealthy person's words."

"Yeah, you want to live a plagiarized life, like lots of people. If you're going to copy, why not copy advertising? Everyone there is deliriously happy and successful."

"At least after they use the right product."

"Didn't we already talk about advertising? We're going in circles."

Deleted from Chapter 21

"Amy, I've got Greg Jordan on the phone with me. He's a computer guy down here. He wants to ask you some questions about your computer setup."

"Okay," said Amy.

In the background, she could hear her father whisper, "And remember, she's only nineteen."

"Hello," said the voice on the other end.

"Hello, Mr. Jordan," said Amy.

"You have a notebook computer, is that right?"

"Yes," said Amy confidently.

"Are you on a dialup or a LAN?"

"I don't know," Amy said. Jordan could almost hear the frown.

"Okay," said Jordan, with just a little testiness coming into his voice. "How many wires do you see coming out the back of your PC?"

Amy looked. "Two."

"Okay, and one of them eventually goes into the electrical outlet, is that right?"

"Let's see. One of them goes into a black brick and then a bigger wire comes out of the brick and plugs into the wall. I think that's the power supply."

"Yeah. So look at the other wire. Where does it go?"

"Into the wall."

"And where it goes into the wall, is it flat or round?"

"Sort of halfway."

"Does the wire say anything on it?" Jordan asked with a slightly irritated tone.

"Let me look." Amy picked up the wire. "Yes," she said, "it's got a million letters on it, all along it."

"Start reading," Jordan said.

Amy read. "CAT 5 UTP 24 AWG 4 pairs E13892 and a little symbol and then AWM 2835 60 degrees C CSA LL81295 FT4 ETL verified EIA slash TIA dash 568A."

As soon as she had read "CAT 5" Jordan had turned to Amy's father and said, "She's on a network." Amy continued reading, not knowing that no one was paying attention.

When she stopped, Jordan said, "You're on a network."

"I knew that," Amy said.

"Then why didn't you say so?" Jordan asked, irritated.

"You didn't ask. You asked about something else."

"I asked if you were on a network."

"You said dialup or LAN."

"A LAN is a network."

"I didn't know," Amy said with a bit of apology in her voice. She didn't like Jordan very much.

"Now tell me, what kind of a firewall do you have on your computer?"

"What's a firewall?" Amy asked.

Jordan thought briefly about asking Detective Herbert, "Is your daughter a blonde?"

How odd it is that we so often devalue others just because they do not know what we know, and what we therefore think everyone else should know. And regarding the blonde reference in the unspoken comment, had Jennica heard that, she would have said, "See, I told you." We are stereotypers, however much we deny it.

For the next few minutes, Greg Jordan not very patiently took Amy through her computer's operating system and checked on the running processes and available software, only to conclude that her computer had no firewall at all.

"Okay," he said.

Jordan took another fifteen minutes of his valuable time to talk Amy through the downloading and installation of a free software firewall. A look at the firewall's alerts revealed that there were no evil servers running on the girl's machine.

Amy's computer was now protected from attack from the outside. In fact, the computer itself was now invisible on the network, because the firewall was set to cloak the computer's presence. The gate had swung closed. But the horse was already out of the corral.

Deleted from Chapter 27

"Did you hear what Shelley McConnell did? She waited outside her boyfriend's classroom and just before he came out, she put a long-stemmed red carnation between her teeth."

"Who's her boyfriend?"

"Ron Gorshak."

"Don't know him."

"Anyway, when he looks at her, she bats her eyelashes at him."

"In front of everyone else? I could never do that."

"You don't know Shelley."

"So then what?"

"So then Ron takes the flower from her mouth and puts it behind her ear. She closes her eyes and stands on her tip-toes."

"Yes? Come on."

"So he kisses her."

"Aw."

"On the forehead."

"Huh?"

"Yeah, so then Shelley goes, 'You missed.'"

"So what did Ron say?"

"He gave her a little peck on the lips."

"Just a little peck?"

"Yeah, he was embarrassed, I think."

"How do you know all this, anyway?"

"Brandy Wang was Shelley's front man, watching to signal her when Ron was about to come out. She told me the whole thing."

Colophon
Body text set in Georgia 12 point
On 16-point leading
Headings set in CG Omega

www.ingramcontent.com/pod-product-compliance
Lightning Source LLC
Chambersburg PA
CBHW071153250626
47159CB00001B/70